ALSO BY MARGARET LEROY

**Trust**

**Alysson's Shoes**

**Postcards from Berlin**

**The River House**

# Yes,
# My Darling
# Daughter

# Yes, My Darling Daughter

Margaret Leroy

**Doubleday Large Print
Home Library Edition**

SARAH CRICHTON BOOKS
Farrar, Straus and Giroux
New York

This Large Print Edition, prepared especially for Double-day Large Print Home Library, contains the complete, unabridged text of the original Publisher's Edition.

SARAH CRICHTON BOOKS
**Farrar, Straus and Giroux**
**18 West 18th Street, New York 10011**

ISBN-13: 978-1-60751-852-5

**This Large Print Book carries the
Seal of Approval of N.A.V.H.**

Mother, may I go out to swim?
Yes, my darling daughter:
Hang your clothes on a hickory limb
And don't go near the water.

# Yes,
# My Darling
# Daughter

# 1

It's pleasant here in Karen's kitchen, talking about our children, sipping chardonnay, with before us on the wide oak table the wreck of the children's tea. I glance around the circle. You can tell that everyone's dressed up in honor of the party—Fiona has glittery earrings, Michaela is wearing a clingy wrap top that frames her lavish cleavage. But only Karen has a proper costume: she always feels that as hostess she has license, and today she's a rather glamorous witch, in a black chiffon frock with a raggedy hem and with lots of Rouge Noir on her nails. Behind her on the windowsill there are lighted pumpkin faces, and the candle flames shiver and falter in the draft that sneaks in around the frame.

The children yell. We turn toward the open door of the living room, watching as the magician pulls some spiders out of his sleeve. Leo, Karen's husband, who's in there keeping order, applauds with great enthusiasm. The magician is exceptional, everyone keeps saying so—Karen was brilliant to find him. He looked quite ordinary, arriving in his grimy van, prosaically dressed in jeans and a Coldplay T-shirt. But now, in his cloak of indigo silk with a silver pattern of planets, he has a presence, a mystery.

"I do like clever hands," says Michaela. "Can I take him home with me?"

He flings two scarves up into the air that come down tied together. The children watch wide-eyed. All their own outfits look a little random now—masks hanging off, cloaks slipping from shoulders. Josh, Karen's son, is at the front, with stick-on scars from Sainsbury's on his arms, and Lennie, her little girl, is sitting next to Sylvie, dressed as a witch's black cat. Sylvie has bunched up the skirts of her snowflake dress and is absently sucking the white ribbon hem. She really wanted to be a cat like Lennie, but the black cat costume in Clinton Cards was one of the most expensive, and I took the cheaper snowflake outfit from its peg and held it against her, hoping to persuade her without her getting upset. She looked at herself in the mirror. The dress was white and frothy, of some muslinlike material, with trailing ribbons. She has hair like lint, no color, the slightest smudge of freckles on her nose. Pale things suit her. For myself, I like color, I'd love to dress her in the rainbow, but too much brightness seems to overwhelm her. She smiled at her reflection. She was pale and perfect against the whiteness of the dress, and to my relief she was easily persuaded. Though I hate these moments, always—the everyday abrasions, the things I so long to buy for her that I'm sure would make her happy, at least for a little while. None of the other mothers around the table, I suspect, would understand this; nor would they know the panic I feel when Sylvie grows out of her shoes, or at the arrival of a birthday invitation requiring a present I haven't budgeted for.

The women are exchanging the numbers of party entertainers. I let their voices float past me. Through the window behind Michaela I can see into Karen's garden, where the brown light of evening is draining down into the wet, heavy earth. The shape of the tree house where Lennie and Sylvie play in summer is sharp as though cut with a blade against the luminous sky. It's so still today—not a breath of wind, not a sigh. When we came here, Sylvie and I, when we parked and got out of the car, the stillness fell over us, a stillness like a garment, unbroken and entire. Even the wind chimes hanging from someone's apple tree were silent, no sound at all in the wide, parked-up street but the clear, sweet pipe of a bird. There was a rich smell of October, of earth and rot and wet leaves. Sylvie ran on ahead of me. I'd put her in her white summer sandals to match the snowflake outfit, and they have hard soles that made a clear *click click* in the stillness. I called after her, "Be careful, Sylvie, don't get too far ahead." She turned to face me, standing on tiptoe, reaching her arms out to either side, her face intent with concentration, as though she were balancing in a tricky, difficult place. As though she could fall off.

"I can hear my feet, Grace. I can hear them."

"Yes," I said.

"I've got noisy noisy feet. I could be a dancer. Listen, Grace. I'm a dancer, aren't I, Grace?"

"Yes, you're a dancer," I said.

She did a neat pirouette, pleased, self-aware in her elaborate dress, then ran on again, white as a wisp of smoke or mist against the gray of the pavement, at once so pale and so vivid, like she was the only living thing in the whole still, darkening street.

A few doors up from Karen's house, someone came out with a pumpkin and put it on their windowsill and lit the candle inside. We stopped to admire the pumpkin. The face was carved with panache: it had a toothy, rakish grin.

"He's smiling, Grace, isn't he? He's smiling at us."

"Yes, he's smiling," I said.

She was happy for a moment, trusting, feeling the world to be benign. I wrapped my hand around hers. Her skin was cold, but she nestled her hand quite firmly into mine. I love it when she's happy like that.

The magician is building to his grand finale. He wants a volunteer. All the children have raised their hands, urgent and eager, frantic to be chosen. Sylvie too has put up her hand, though not so keenly as the other children. There's often a little reserve about her, something held back. I will him: Please don't choose her, please please don't choose Sylvie. But he does, of course, drawn perhaps by her reticence. He beckons to her, and we watch, all the mothers, as she walks out to the front and he seats her on his chair.

Karen glances toward me with a quick, reassuring smile. "She's doing great," she murmurs.

And she's right: for the moment Sylvie seems quite poised and controlled, clasping her hands together neatly in her lap. Her lips are pursed with concentration. The expression is precisely Dominic's.

The magician kneels beside her. "No worries, okay, sweetheart? I promise not to turn you into a tadpole or anything."

She gives him a slight smile that says

this is naive of him, that of course she knows how the world works.

He scribbles in the air with his wand, mutters something in Latin. A flourish of his cloak entirely covers her for an instant. When he flings back the silk with a slight air of triumph, a real live rabbit is sitting in Sylvie's lap. The children applaud. Sylvie hugs the rabbit.

Fiona turns toward me. "That's your little girl, isn't it?" she says. "That's Sylvie?"

"Yes," I tell her.

Sylvie is stroking the rabbit with cautious, gentle gestures. She seems oblivious of the other children. She looks entirely happy.

"I'm not surprised he chose her," she says. "That white-blond hair, and those eyes."

"She was sitting right at the front, I guess," I say.

"She's just so cute," says Fiona. "And I'm always fascinated by the way she calls you by your Christian name . . . Of course, in our family we're rather more traditional."

"That didn't come from me," I say.

But she isn't really listening.

"Was it something you felt very strongly about?" she says.

Her crystal earrings send out spiky shards of light.

"Not at all," I say. "It was Sylvie's choice. It came from her. She never called me Mum."

The woman's eyes are on me, taking in my short denim skirt, my jacket patterned with sequins, my strappy scarlet shoes. She's older than me, and so much more solid and certain. Her expression is opaque.

"Just never said Mama? What, even when she was just beginning to talk?"

"No. Never." I feel accused. I swallow the urge to apologize.

"Goodness." She has a troubled look. "So what about her dad? What does she call him?"

"She doesn't see him," I tell her. "I'm a single parent. It's just us—just me and Sylvie."

"Oh I'm so sorry," she says. As though embarrassed that she has called out this admission from me. "That must be quite a struggle for you," she goes on. "I honestly just don't know how I'd cope without Dan."

There's a surge of noise from the living room, where the children are tidying up under the watchful eye of the magician. The rabbit is in a basket now.

"He's doing the games as well," says Karen. "Isn't that fabulous?"

Leo comes to refill his glass. He's wearing a polo shirt that doesn't really suit him; he's one of those substantial men who look best in formal clothes. He greets us with the exaggerated bonhomie that men always seem to adopt on joining a group of mothers. He comes from Scotland and has a mellifluous Gaelic accent. He puts his arm round Karen, caressing her shoulder through the chiffony fabric of her frock. I can tell he likes the witch outfit. Much later, perhaps, when the party is over and the clearing up is all done, he will ask her to put it on again.

Michaela leans across the table toward me. She wants to talk about nurseries. Am I happy with Little Acorns, where Sylvie goes? She's heard that Mrs. Pace-Barden, who runs it, is really very dynamic. She has her doubts about nannies. Well, you never get to see what they're actually up to, do you? She heard about this nanny who fed the kids on a different flavor of Jell-O every lunchtime because the mother said to be sure to give them plenty of fruit. I turn with relief from Fiona. In the living room, the magician is setting up a game of apple bobbing. The girls make an orderly queue, though Josh and some of the other boys are racing around at the edges of the room.

The wine eases into my veins. I have my back to the living room now. I let my vigilance relax, enjoying this conversation. I love to talk about Sylvie's nursery school—it's my one big luxury. I was thrilled when they gave her a place. The candles glimmer and tremble on the windowsill, and behind them, in Karen's garden, darkness clots and thickens in the hollows under the hedge.

Out of nowhere, some instinct makes me turn. It's Sylvie's go at apple bobbing, she's kneeling by the bowl. I don't see exactly what happens. A commotion, a scrabble of boys near the bowl, and then water everywhere, all over the stripped pine floor, and on Sylvie's hair and her clothes. I see her face, but I can't get there in time, can't undo it. I'm too late, I'm always too late. She's kneeling there, taut as a wire, the other children already backing away from her: tense, white, the held breath, then the scream.

The children part to let me through. I kneel beside her and hold her. Her body is rigid, she's fighting against me. Her screams are thin, high, edged with fear. When I put my arms around her, she pushes against my chest with her fists, as though I am her enemy. Everyone's eyes are on us: the other children, fascinated, a little superior; the women, at once sympathetic and disapproving. I glimpse the magician's look of startled concern as he gathers the other children together for the next game. I try to sweep her up in my arms, but she's fighting me, I can't do it. I half carry, half drag her into the hall. Karen comes after us, closes the living-room door.

"Grace, I'm so sorry," she mouths at me through Sylvie's screams. "I forgot Sylvie's thing about water. It's my fault, Grace, I should have told him . . . Look, don't forget her party bag, there are pumpkin biscuits—" She thrusts a colored plastic bag in my direction, but I can't take it, my hands are full with Sylvie. "Don't worry, I'll keep it for her. Hell, Grace . . ."

I kneel there clasping Sylvie on the pale, expensive carpet in Karen's immaculate hall. Sometimes when Sylvie works herself up like this, she's sick. I know I have to get her out.

"It was a lovely party," I tell her. "I'll ring you." Sylvie's screams drown out my words.

Karen holds open the door for us.

I maneuver Sylvie down the path and along the darkening pavement. Her crying is shockingly loud, ripping apart the stillness of the street.

When I get to the car, I hold her tight against me and scrabble in my bag for the keys and manage to open the door. I sit in the driver's seat, holding her close on my lap. We sit there for a long time. Gradually she quiets, the tension leaving her. She sinks into me, crying more gently. Her face and the front of her dress are wet from the water that splashed on her and from her tears. Her eyelashes are clumped together, as though with cheap mascara.

I dry her face and smooth her hair.

"Shall we go home now?"

She nods. She climbs into the back and fastens her belt.

My hands on the steering wheel are shaking, and I'm cautious at intersections. I know that I'm not driving well. My car smells as always of pollen from the flowers I deliver; I flick a broken frond of fern from the dashboard onto the floor. I glance at Sylvie in the rearview mirror. Her face is absolutely white, like someone coming around from shock. There's a dull weight of dread in my stomach, the feeling I always try to overlook or push away: the sense I have that there's something about Sylvie that is utterly beyond me. There's too much sadness in her crying, too much fear.

My flat is in Highfields, in a street of Victorian terraces. Long ago, this was an imposing address; now it's the red-light district. In the street near my door, there are smells of petrol and urine, and the thick, unwholesome perfume of rotting melons from the market. The sky is the color of ink and absolutely cloudless. Later, once it's fully dark, there will be lots of stars. A couple of prostitutes are huddled on the corner next to Kwik Save, bare-legged and quietly talking, a blue vague haze of cigarette smoke around them.

There's a nervousness I feel always, coming back to our home. The flat is on the ground floor, with an alleyway beside it, and I worry about intruders—about the rootless, drifting people I often see in the street. Sometimes I think I should have chosen somewhere different, more rational. And it's drafty, high-ceilinged, hard to heat, with a temperamental boiler in the bathroom. My elderly landlady, who smells of eucalyptus and wears a moth-eaten leopard-skin coat, explained about the boiler when we moved here, but I've never got the hang of it. And it all has a rather empty feel; the flimsy wicker furniture that was all I could afford is really too insubstantial for these high-ceilinged rooms. But it has French windows and a scrap of garden—a patchy lawn, a wall of yellow London brick, a mulberry tree that's trained against the wall. To be honest, I probably chose it because of the mulberry. It was fruiting when we first came here, and urged on by the landlady, I picked a mulberry each for Sylvie and for me. Sylvie held her hand out. I put the mulberry onto her palm.

"Hold it lightly," I told her. "Careful you don't crush it."

Her eyes were round and very bright. She kept her hand flat, lowering her mouth to her hand—with a kind of reverence, almost, as though the fruit were some precious thing. I thought she might not like it—that the taste would be too complex, too subtle, the winey sharp-sweetness of it—but she loved it, ate it slowly, ceremoniously. Her hand and her mouth were stained with vivid juice.

I open up, turn the light on. Everything is as it should be. My living room greets me, orderly and tranquil, the calico curtains, the apples in a bowl. Some sunflowers I brought back from the shop—not fit to sell, but still with a day or two's life in them—are glowing on my table.

Sylvie is exhausted now. When I sit on the sofa and pull her down beside me, her body is heavy, her head droops into my chest. I breathe in the scent of her hair. As I watch, her eyelids flicker wildly. Between one breath and the next, she sinks deeply into sleep. Scarcely breathing, I lay her down on the sofa, carefully, as though she could easily break. I cover her with the duvet from her bedroom, tuck in Big Ted beside her. When she wakes she'll be fine, as though none of this had happened.

I sit there for a while, relishing the silence and the sound of her peaceful breath. I think of the women at the party, sitting around Karen's table, their orderly lives and platinum wedding rings and confident opinions. I wonder what they have said about me, about Sylvie. I imagine their conversations. *Poor Grace, what a pain for her . . . Of course kids have tantrums, but not like that, not when she's nearly four . . . It's so important to let them know where you stand. You have to be consistent . . . Well, of course, Grace is on her own. That can't help when it comes to discipline . . .*

And Karen—what will she be thinking? Will she be joining in? Solicitous, concerned, perhaps a little disapproving? Karen matters so much to me. I'm grateful for her friendship, yet always uneasy because it feels so unequal. I could never ask her and Lennie to visit us here; I know just what she'd think about the syringes in the street. We always meet at her place, where there's a family room that's full of books and toys and sunlight, and the whole wide garden to play in with its tree house and velvet lawns.

I met Karen on the maternity ward, after giving birth to Sylvie. It was a strange time. You're opened up, your body breached, all your defenses down. I scarcely slept at all, the ward was so noisy at night. Instead I'd lie and stare at Sylvie through the transparent walls of her cot, just stare and stare. I couldn't believe that such a perfect creature existed. Or in the day I'd hold her for hours, feeding her or just rocking her in my arms. Thinking, She is *mine*. *My daughter*. And when she startled when a door banged and I felt the fear go through her, I thought, She only has me. She only has me to keep her safe. I knew that I would do anything to protect her, that I'd die for her if I had to, I wouldn't have to choose, I'd just do it. There's a kind of exultant freedom in that knowledge—to love someone more than you love yourself. Not by any effort of will, but just because you do.

Sometimes I thought of Dominic, imagined that maybe he'd come. It was just a little bright flicker of hope that wouldn't be extinguished—like those novelty birthday candles that keep relighting however often you blow on them, that simply won't be put out. In my half-hallucinatory state after the nights of insomnia, I'd think I could hear his voice, which is rather loud and authoritative when he isn't being intimate, or his firm step coming down the ward. I'd picture it all, too vividly: how he'd come to my bedside and scoop Sylvie up in his arms and hold her against him, staring at her like I did, loving her like I did. I couldn't stop thinking these things. Though the rational part of me knew it was just a crazy fantasy. It was spring half-term, he was probably skiing at Val d'Isère with his family.

I was aware of a woman watching me from the opposite side of the ward: dark hair trimly pulled back, a serious, sensible look. She had an older boy and a constant stream of visitors. I knew that her baby was called Lennie, that she'd been born a little early and had lots of bright black hair that would fall out in a day or two. This woman noticed things, I could tell that. I knew she'd have seen I hardly had any visitors. Just Lavinia, my boss, who came dripping beads and bracelets, with a worn, exquisite silk scarf that she'd found in a Delhi market looped around her head, and bearing greetings and gifts. Some woolly things she'd knitted, and some Greenham Common wire that she'd kept since the 1970s, when she'd gone on an Embrace the Base demonstration with thousands of other women and had cut off a bit of the boundary fence with wire cutters, and a tape of whale sounds that she promised would help Sylvie sleep. Flowers too, of course, a lavish bunch of them, the yellow daylilies I love. My life was far from perfect, but at least I knew my flowers were the loveliest on the ward.

Lavinia peered down at Sylvie.

"She's so beautiful," she said. "Little bud." Touching her with one finger, on her brow, like a blessing. "Little perfect thing." And then, hugging me close, "You're so *clever*, Gracie!"

I was happy with Lavinia there: it was almost like having my mother back. But after she'd gone, I cried, I couldn't stop crying, holding Sylvie to me, pushing the tears away so they wouldn't fall on her face.

Karen came over then, Lennie in one hand, box of Milk Tray in the other. She sat beside me and put the chocolates down on my bed.

"It can all feel a bit much, can't it?" she said. "Last night I had to sit in the bath for hours before I could pee. And that bloody woman who came round this morning to talk about contraception. I told her that intercourse wasn't exactly top of my to-do list at the moment . . ." She pushed the chocolates toward me. "Come on, get scoffing. You need to keep your strength up."

Watching me, her clear, steady gaze. She knew it wasn't the pains of birth that made me cry. But we bonded over these things, the scars and injuries of labor. She lent me a rubber ring to sit on, which helped with the pain from the stitches; she was a great advocate of salt baths; she fed me on her chocolates. And I told her about Dominic, and she listened quietly. Knowing her as I do now, I can see how generous she was to me. Karen is a

traditional wife—there's a deep conser-
vatism in her. She reads newspapers that
are full of adultery stories and photos of
once-glamorous women who dress too
tartily for their age. She buys whole books
about how to bake cakes. She might well
have judged me—that would have been
her instinct. Yet she was so accepting:
she welcomed me into her life. And I've
always been grateful for that, the way she
reached out to me then.

"Look at our two," she'd say. "Astrologi-
cal twins. We must meet up when we're
home. They could grow up together . . ."

I go to the kitchen to ring.

"Karen. I'm so sorry. It was such a great
party. Your Halloween parties are always
so brilliant," I say. "She loved it. Really.
The magician and everything . . ."

I can hear Mozart playing in her living
room.

"I shouldn't have forgotten about the
water thing." Her voice has an anxious
edge. "It's not like you hadn't told me. I
was stupid, I should have warned him."

"No, it's my fault," I tell her. "I should
have kept an eye on her. I hope we didn't
spoil anything."

"For God's sake," says Karen. "It's just a shame you had to leave."

"Yes," I say.

There's a little silence between us. The music spools out, the balanced phrases, perfect, poised. I don't want to hear what I know she is going to say.

"Grace, I hope you don't mind me mentioning this." There's caution in her voice. She's choosing her words with care. "But we think you really need to get help."

I feel a kind of shame.

"All kids have tantrums, don't they?" I say. "I just try not to get too worked up about it."

"Of course all kids freak out sometimes," she says. "But not like this, Grace. Not like Sylvie. She just sounds so—well—*desperate*." And, when I don't say anything, "Basically, Grace, we think you need to see someone. A psychologist. Someone professional."

I hate the "we." I hate to think of them sitting there in Karen's opulent kitchen discussing me and Sylvie.

## 2

When I get to Jonah and the Whale on Monday morning, Lavinia is already busy. She's taken down the pumpkins from the Halloween display, and she's potting up autumn gentians on a table of curled wrought iron. The table is rusting but elegant, one of her flea-market finds. She has lots of bracelets on her wrists, and she's fixed back her hair with a sweep of magenta muslin, a tie-dyed scarf from Gujarat, which has a long, silky fringe and a gold thread woven through. The thick, sweet smells of the flower shop wrap themselves around me—wet earth and mingled pollens.

Lavinia is a widow. Her husband was an orthopedic surgeon, and I always feel he was a difficult man, though she only ever speaks of him with affection. He died ten years ago, of cirrhosis of the liver. She'd been a physiotherapist: she opened the flower shop after his death with the insurance money, wanting to make a fresh start. "Why Jonah and the Whale?" I asked once, expecting something deep about loss and new beginnings, but she smiled in that way she has—enigmatic, a little self-mocking—and said that she just liked the way it sounds. She lives alone, but she never seems lonely. She knows so many people—Buddhists, artists, performance poets, from her hippie days. On Sunday, she tells me, she had three rather decrepit musicians around for a paella, and they played Cole Porter in her living room.

I tell her about the party, about what happened with Sylvie. She turns to me and listens till I've finished, her quiet eyes taking me in.

"Poor kid," she says then. "Poor you."

Her eyes linger on me. There's a little

crease penciled between her brows. She never gives me advice, and I'm grateful for that.

I put flowers out on the pavement at the front of the shop—buckets of lilies with reddish pollen that stains your skin like turmeric; hydrangeas of the richest, densest blue. I've planted the hydrangeas in azure metal pots, choosing the containers with care. I love the way the clashing colors seem to shimmer and sing. There's a winter rawness in the air, the cold scrapes at my skin. My hands are always chapped, working here. I own numerous pairs of fingerless gloves that I dry out on the hot-water pipes in the back room near the boiler, and I change them during the day, yet whatever I do, in winter I'm never quite warm.

It's a slow morning, as Mondays usually are, and Lavinia sends me off in my car to do the deliveries. First a big traditional bouquet, roses and carnations, for a silver wedding. The woman who answers the doorbell has stiff curled hair and a ready smile, and behind her an orderly house that smells of lavender polish and detergent. This fascinates me always, the glimpses of people's houses, these slivers of other lives. Next, there's a planted arrangement, some winter cyclamens, for a nervous young woman whose hair falls over her face. The cyclamens seem so right for her—these fragile, pale, self-deprecating flowers. She stands on her doorstep and looks at me with an uncertain, surprised air—as though this is all a mistake, as though she feels she's not the kind of woman people would buy flowers for. As she talks, she keeps touching the side of her face in a little self-comforting gesture. I drive away, feeling a loneliness that might be hers or mine.

The last call is to one of those modern estates where the numbering doesn't make sense. I need number 43, but 37 seems to lead straight to 51. I stop the car and get out, walk down the road and peer into all the alleyways, trying to find the right house.

It's how I met Dominic, delivering flowers. I was eighteen. I'd only just begun working for Lavinia. I was thrilled with the job, after temping in tedious offices ever since I'd left school.

It was a planted arrangement—the most

expensive we do—in a wicker basket. I'd written out the card myself. I'd been the one to take the call. An older woman, a privileged voice, with cool, immaculate vowels: "Happy Birthday, dearest Claudia, with all my love, Mama." A spiky bit of wicker from the basket had worked loose, and as I took the flowers out of the car, I snagged my finger. The cut was surprisingly deep. I wrapped a tissue around it. The blood soaked rapidly through, but I noticed only after I'd rung the bell.

He was a big man, forty-something, and wearing a linen shirt with rolled-up sleeves. He looked at me as though I amused him. I was wearing my usual kind of outfit—a little cord skirt and stripy tights and boots with high, spindly heels, too high to drive in, really. I was suddenly very aware how short my skirt was.

"Flowers for Claudia Runcie," I said.

He was looking at me, he didn't look at the flowers. He still had that pleased, amused air.

"Well," he said.

He took the basket from me and noticed my hand.

"Whatever happened?" he said.

"I cut it," I said.

"Okay. Stupid question," he said. "You'd better come in. You're dripping on my doorstep."

He thrust a huge handkerchief at me. I wrapped it around my hand.

It was a large, airy kitchen, with that pale, distressed kitchen furniture that looks as though it's been sourced from some Provençal street market. I thought, If I had a proper kitchen, this is exactly how I'd like it to look. There were photos on the mantelpiece, of a boy and a girl, black-and-white, in silver frames. The photos were rather beautiful, soft focus, cleverly lit. There were masses of birthday cards and a silver helium balloon, for Claudia presumably.

"I'm Dominic," he said.

I told him my name.

He hunted in the drawers of the cabinets for a Band-Aid.

"Where the hell does she keep them?" he said.

I had an immediate sense of his wife, of Claudia, as the center of things, the heart of the home, the one who held it together, who knew the best photographers and where to find exquisite kitchen units, and whose Band-Aids had their allotted place in her drawer. I sensed his absolute dependency on her. What I didn't know then, but was soon to learn, was that they never made love. It was a comfortable, prosperous marriage but with no sex or closeness. At least, that's how he told it.

He found the packet. I put out my hand for the Band-Aid, but he'd taken one out and was peeling off the backing.

"Give me your finger," he told me.

Right from the beginning I did just what he said.

He stuck the plaster in place with rather excessive thoroughness, but I wasn't going to move away. He had a faint scent of leather and cigars, a very male scent. His closeness felt extraordinary, thrilling with a shiver of sex, yet somehow safe too, as though he were familiar to me, as though I knew him already. I felt how much bigger he was than me. I liked that.

"Better now?" he said.

"Yes. Thank you."

He stood back a pace and smiled at me. A sudden smile of startling candor, with a little crease on one side of his mouth. It's weird thinking about this now. It's Sylvie's smile exactly. Where his hair was starting to recede, the skin had a vulnerable look. I wanted to reach up and touch it. The thought sent a clear, bright line of sensation through me.

"So. Grace. I think you should have a coffee. After losing all that blood."

"Thanks," I said.

"You do drink coffee, don't you?"

I nodded.

"That's a relief. Claudia's into this foul herbal stuff. Chamomile. It's like hay. Why would anyone drink hay?"

I felt he was telling me too much, giving too much away—that he shouldn't be criticizing her like this to me, a stranger, even about such a very trivial thing.

While the kettle was boiling, he found a place for the flowers on the mantelpiece.

"Good flowers. Did you do them?"

"Yes."

"They're rather lovely," he said. "Well, you look the arty type. I can tell from the stripes." He gave my legs an appraising look.

We drank our coffee. Somehow he learned a lot about me.

When I left, he asked would I be okay to drive, and I said I was fine, I didn't feel faint in the least—though that wasn't true exactly. Two days later he rang the shop and asked me out to the Alouette for a meal; where he effortlessly seduced me.

Eventually I find number 43, down an alleyway. The man who opens the door is unshaven and in his pajamas. Hot air from a sickroom brushes against me, with a smell of camphor and stale sheets. He's embarrassed, seeing me there. It must all have been going on for a while; the house is rearranged to accommodate his illness. I can see the living room behind him, with the sofa made up as a bed. There's opera on the stereo, a vigorous soprano, her voice pulsating with passion. The contrast is saddening—the music with its fabulous energy and emotion, and his wasted, restricted life.

For lunch I buy baguettes from Just A Crust. On the way back, as always, I linger outside the patisserie on the corner. They sell the most wonderful cakes there, all decorated with jeweled marzipan fruit, and with names that sound like the names of beautiful women. We eat our baguettes in turn in the back room.

The afternoon passes slowly. At three Lavinia goes out for a walk and a smoke.

Just after she's gone, I see a woman approaching the shop. She's in her seventies perhaps. She's wearing a crisply cut jacket, her hair is a lacquered gray helmet, her eyebrows are plucked and thinly penciled in. Everything about her is polished and exact. Seeing her, it enters my mind that this grooming has a defensive purpose for her, as though this slick, varnished surface will somehow keep her safe. I watch as she draws nearer, tapping along the pavement on her pointy, shiny shoes. At the door she hesitates just for a heartbeat, then clears her throat, walks determinedly in. I know what she's come for. I feel a brief apprehension. I wish Lavinia were here.

The flowers are for her husband, she says.

"The funeral director said he'd take care of it all, but I wanted to choose them myself. It seemed important somehow."

Her hands are clasped tight in front of

her. I can feel the tension in her, her fear that she might come undone.

I bring her a chair and show her our catalog. But she can't choose. The decision has too much importance. It's as though she believes that if only she can choose with absolute precision, everything will be mended and she'll somehow bring him back. I understand. I've felt that.

I turn a page of the catalog. A photo catches her eye.

"Maybe something with cornflowers," she says. "They were his favorites. He always loved that blue."

She looks away then, her eyes fill up, the tears spill down her face. The massive grief washes through her, there's nothing she can do. She's embarrassed but can't stop it happening. Tears make glossy streaks in her thick cake makeup. I'm relieved for her that the shop is empty. She's a private person, I know how she hates this extravagant public display.

"I'm going to bring you a drink," I tell her. "You just sit there till you're ready. We've got all the time in the world."

I go to the back room and make her a

coffee. Her grief has got inside me. My hand shakes holding the spoonful of coffee; the soft brown powder sifts down.

She's grateful. She wraps both her hands around the mug, as though needing something to cling to, as though the world seems insubstantial to her. She tells me about her husband. He was diabetic, he'd been taken into this nursing home—it was just for a week, she'd felt she needed a rest. How could she have been so selfish? They didn't do his blood sugars properly, not as she'd have done. It's all her fault he died . . .

I listen, feeling helpless. Not saying much, not comforting her or telling her that everything's okay. I know that wouldn't help her. And when we've chosen the wreath, I take her to the back room so she can tidy her face, because I can feel that matters to her.

"Bless you," she says when she goes.

Her grief hangs around in the shop for a while, pressing down, a heaviness. I think of my mother's death, of sitting in the crematorium chapel feeling that empty swing of sickness through me, thinking about her life and all its limitations—the bitterness that had never left her after my father walked out—and that now it would never get better, now she was out of time. The bleakness of that.

We close at five-thirty. We mop and tidy up, and I peel off my soggy gloves and hang them by the boiler.

"You get yourself an early night," says Lavinia as we leave.

"I'm all right," I tell her.

Her eyes rest on me a moment, but she doesn't say anything more.

# 3

There are several different routes to Sylvie's nursery. I take the one that goes down Newgate Road. I know I shouldn't do this. The decision is made somewhere deep inside me, almost without conscious thought.

I park a few yards from the house. The darkness is thickening, no one will see. I'm invisible here, a faceless person, a shadow in the street. I wind my window down an inch. There's a cold scent of autumn, a tang of smoke and rotten leaves, and the high, sharp bark of a fox. I tell myself I'll only stay a moment.

The blinds are still up in the drawing room that faces onto the street, and tawny lamplight spills across the paving in the garden. Tonight I'm lucky. Dominic's car is here, so he must be at home. In the room, you can see all the things that Claudia has chosen—the subtle gray shades of the walls, the sketches in thin metal frames, on the mantelpiece a single orchid of a cool, watery green. The room seems so enticing in the mellowness of the light. I suddenly feel how cold I am sitting here, still chilled from the day. I wrap my arms tight around myself to try to stop myself shivering. I feel a deep, dangerous loneliness.

As I watch the drawing room, Charlie, their son, saunters in. He's still in his school uniform, but it's rumpled, his shirt hanging out. He's tall now, visibly taller every time I see him, coltish, his hands and feet too big for him, a pale thatch of hair on his head. He looks around vaguely for something, then ambles out of the room.

I feel the quick fever of excitement that always comes over me here. I wonder if I will see Dominic.

But it's Claudia who comes in. She walks right up to the window, which is a little open, and leans out, her arms on the sill. If she looked really hard, she might see me now, but I'm sitting quite still in the shadow, and anyway, would she even know who I am? Does she know about me and Sylvie? Dominic never told me. There's so much he never said. She lingers there for a moment. Maybe like me she's just breathing in the scent of rot and bonfires, the smell of approaching cold that paradoxically seems so full of promise. Then she closes the window and reaches up to pull on the cord of the blind. Her head is back, and briefly the lamplight catches on the arch of her throat and the bright blond fall of her hair. She's thin, she has a figure that speaks of Pilates classes and always being a little hungry. Her arm looks angular, stretching up, the amber brightness gleaming on the bony curve of her wrist. Then the blind slides down.

I watch for a moment longer. There's another shape in the room now, a shadow choreography behind the blinds. But the shapes are vague, indeterminate—it's Charlie again, perhaps, or Maud, their daughter. I can't tell whether Dominic is there. I think of this life of his that I am excluded from—that I was always excluded from, even when we were closest. The everydayness of him that I know nothing about. What he's like at family mealtimes or at dinner parties with friends or kicking a football around with Charlie in the garden. I never knew him doing any of these things. I knew him only as a lover—tender, passionate, curious, in those lavish afternoons we'd spend together in my bed, when I'd feel a complete, exact pleasure in his insistent fingers, his easy, deep slide into me, the sweet, assiduous movement of his mouth. Or cool, closed-off, rejecting, in that terrible moment at the Alouette, the moment we couldn't get back from. I'd been taking antibiotics for cystitis, but I hadn't known that they could interfere with the pill. I told him I was pregnant, saw the instant retreat in his eyes. Cold crept through me. His look told me everything: his narrowed eyes, the way he stared at me as though I were his enemy. I knew the whole thing was fractured before he started to speak—explaining in his measured voice that of course I'd want to get it done privately, that he knew a good gynecologist, that naturally he'd pay.

A familiar nausea rises in me. I sicken myself. I cannot live like this—parking near his house, ringing him just to hear him on his voice mail. Looking in on another life that isn't mine, that can never be mine. This is wrong, I know that. I'm bitterly ashamed of it. I'd never admit to anyone—Karen, Lavinia—that I do this. I try to move on, but nothing seems to work for me—the introduction bureau, the speed-dating evening at Crystals nightclub—none of it gets me anywhere. No other man seems quite real. They're too young, too insubstantial; they don't overwhelm me as he did. I have to *make* myself like them, check off their good points. Like with a man I met at Crystals, who seemed to have an interest in me: I spelled it all out in my head—his perfectly ironed white shirt, his floppy Hugh Grant hair, his smell of soap and cologne. Trying to convince myself.

I resolve that this is the last time. I promise myself I will never do this again—never, never. I drive off rapidly, but the nausea doesn't leave me.

At the nursery it's Beth who lets me in. She's arranging the children's artwork on a table ready for going home. She's Sylvie's favorite assistant. She has curly hair haphazardly pinned up, and warm brown eyes.

She smiles at me.

"Sylvie's in the story corner," she says. "Oh—and I think Mrs. PB wanted a word— she told me to tell you."

There's a scurry of anxiety at the edges of my mind. "Has Sylvie been okay?"

Beth makes a little rocking movement with her hand.

"So-so," she says. "You know—most of the time."

I know she's trying to smooth something over.

I go into the garden room. There are alphabet posters and trays of toys in gorgeous fruit-gum colors, and the warmth is welcome after the chill of the streets. I always love to come to Little Acorns. Our life may not be perfect, but in sending Sylvie here, I know I have done my best for her.

The children who haven't yet been picked up are on cushions in the story corner: one of the assistants is reading them *Where the Wild Things Are*. It's a favorite book of Sylvie's, with its fabulous monsters at once predatory and amiable, but she isn't paying attention. She's hoping for me, she keeps looking toward the door. As I go in, she comes running across the floor toward me. But she doesn't fling herself on me the way another child might. She stops just in front of me and I kneel and she reaches her hands to my face. She gives a theatrical shiver.

"You're *cold*, Grace."

I wrap her in my arms. She smells so good, of lemon, gingersnaps, warm wool. I breathe her in: for a moment I am completely happy. I tell myself, This is where I should be living—in the present, with Sylvie, not always looking behind me and longing for what I can't have.

"Ah. Ms. Reynolds. Just who I wanted to see."

Mrs. Pace-Barden is at her office door. She has cropped, graying hair and dark, conservative clothes. There's something wholesome and vigorous about her. I always imagine her as a hockey coach, urging recalcitrant young women to keep their minds on the game.

She bends to Sylvie.

"Now, Sylvie, I need to have a word with your mum. Would you go and get your coat, please?"

Sylvie's fingers are wrapped like bandages around my hand. I sense her reluctance to let go after a whole day without me. I don't know what will happen—whether she'll do as she's told or instead just stand here, mute and clinging, with her opaque, closed face and her fingers clenched around mine. Karen once said to me, explaining why she likes to stay at home with her children, "The thing is, you know your own children inside out, like nobody else does—you know just what their triggers are. I mean, Lennie hates having her food mixed up and is *horrible* after chocolate, and Josh used to have this thing about heads apart from bodies . . . You always know how they're going to react . . ." Saying it with the certainty that I'd nod and say I agreed. And I thought, But I *don't*, I *don't* know, not with Sylvie.

But this time it's okay. She holds on just for a moment, then heads off to the cloakroom. She must have been using pastels:

her fingers have left a staining like ash on my hands.

"Now, why I wanted to see you," says Mrs. Pace-Barden. "I'm afraid we had a bit of a scene with Sylvie again today." She's lowered her voice, as though anxious to save me from embarrassment. "It was when the water play came out. Unfortunately, Sylvie can be rather aggressive when she gets upset—"

I feel a hot little surge of anger. I've told them over and over.

"You know she's scared of water play," I say.

"Of course we do," says Mrs. Pace-Barden. "And we took that into account. We were careful to see she was on the other side of the room. But as I'm sure you'll appreciate, we can't stop the other children from enjoying a full range of activities—not just for one child. I'm sure you can see that, Ms. Reynolds."

"Yes, of course." Shame moves through me.

"To be honest, I just can't figure her out. I'm not often defeated by children, but this . . ." Some unreadable emotion flickers across her face. "We need to talk about it. Wouldn't you agree?"

It isn't a question.

"Yes, of course," I tell her.

"I'd like to make an appointment for you to come in," she says.

"But I'm not in a hurry. We could talk about it now."

"I'd really rather have a proper discussion," she says. "I think we owe that to Sylvie."

Her seriousness unnerves me.

"Perhaps a fortnight today?" she says.

I know this isn't negotiable.

We fix the time. She goes off to her room.

Sylvie comes back with her coat and slips her hand into mine, and we go out into the foyer.

"Now don't go forgetting your picture, Sylvie," says Beth. She turns toward us, holding out the drawing. "It's one of her houses," she tells me.

I glance at it—a house in pastel crayons, precisely placed in the middle of the page. Just the same as every day. She's been drawing houses for several months, and she draws them over and over. They're neat, exactly symmetrical—four windows, a chimney, a door—and they're always bare and unadorned. Never any people—though she knows how to draw stick people now, with triangle skirts for the women and clumpy big boots for the men—and never any flowers in the garden. Sometimes she draws blue around the house, not just for the sky, but all around, a whole bright border of blue, so the house looks like it's floating. I said to her once, "It's such a nice house in your picture. Does anybody live there?" But she had her closed look, she didn't tell me anything.

I hold the picture by its corner; pastel smudges so easily. We say goodbye to Beth and go out into the evening.

In the middle of the night I wake, hearing the click of my bedroom door. I'm afraid. Just for an instant, a heartbeat, taking in the shadow in my doorway, dark against the crack of yellow light from the hall, I think that someone has broken in, that someone is looking in at me—a stranger. I can't make out her face, she's just a sil-

houette against the hall light, but I can
see the shaking of her shoulders as she
sobs.

I'm drenched with sleep. I can't get up
for a moment.

"Oh sweetheart—come here."

She doesn't come.

I put on my bedside light and drag
myself out of bed. My body feels heavy,
lumbering. I go to her, put my arms all
around her. Her skin is chilly. She doesn't
feel like a child who's just tumbled out of a
warm bed. Sometimes in the night she'll
kick off all her covers, however securely I
tuck her duvet in around her, as though
her dreams are a struggle.

She lets me hold her, but she doesn't
move in to me. She's clutching Big Ted to
her. Her face is desolate. She has a look
like grief.

"What did you dream about, sweetheart?"

She won't tell me.

She moves away from me, makes to
get into my bed. I slip in beside her, wrap
her in my arms.

"It's all over," I tell her. "The nightmare's

over. You're here with me now. Every-thing's okay."

But she's still shuddering.

"It's not real, Sylvie," I tell her. "What-ever you saw, whatever happened in your dream. It didn't really happen, it was only a dream."

Her eyes are on me, the pupils hugely dilated by the dark. In the dim light of my bedside lamp they're a deeper color than usual, the elusive blue-gray of shaded water. The terror is still on her. When she looks at me, it's as though she isn't seeing me. Nothing I say makes sense to her.

I try again, needing to say something, anything, hoping my voice will soothe her.

"That's what a dream is," I tell her. "It's something your mind makes up—like a picture show in your head. Sometimes a horrible one. But it's gone now, it's over. It doesn't mean anything."

The front of her pajama top is damp from all the crying. I feel I ought to change it, but she's starting to quiet. I don't want to rouse her again. I stroke her hair.

"This is the real world, sweetheart. You and me and Big Ted and our home and everything . . ."

Quite suddenly the tension leaves her. Her hand that's clasping the teddy bear eases open, her fingers are lax and fluid, her eyelids flutter and close. I want to say, Why do you do this, Sylvie? Why are you so unhappy? But she's asleep already.

# 4

On Saturday something cheering happens. Even the timing is perfect—because Sylvie and I are about to set off for Karen's. If he'd rung a moment later, we'd have been gone. This timing is a good omen.

"Now, am I speaking to Grace Reynolds?"

A man's voice, light, pleasant, with a smile in it.

"Yes," I tell him, a fragile hopefulness flaring up in me.

"Grace, it's Matt. We met at that weird evening at Crystals, remember?"

"Of course I remember."

"Grace, to get to the point, I'd love to take you out to dinner. If you'd like that."

"I'd like it a lot," I tell him.

"Great." He sounds relieved, as though it matters.

We fix the time, the place—next Thursday, and we will go to Welford Place. It's a restaurant by the river I've sometimes driven past. It used to be a gentlemen's club. Quite different from the Alouette, I guess—no red-checked cloths or accordion music or menus scrawled on a board. I imagine silkily ingratiating waiters and a silver trolley that's heaped with indulgent desserts.

I can't recall if I told him about Sylvie. It's probably best to make sure.

"I'll have to fix a babysitter. For my little girl," I tell him.

"Of course, Grace. Look, just ring if there's a problem."

I put down the phone and stand there for a moment. I remind myself of his white linen shirt and the hair falling into his eyes: I remind myself I liked him. I have a distinct, thrilled sense of newness. This is all so easy, so straightforward—both of us unattached—and I told him about Sylvie and he didn't seem to mind.

It's a gorgeous afternoon, honeyed sunlight mellowing everything. I decide we will walk to Karen's. It isn't that far. Sylvie brings her Shaun the Sheep rucksack with some of her Barbies inside. We talk about the things we pass: a glove that someone has dropped in the road, which looks from a distance like a small dead animal; a caterpillar that Sylvie spots on the pavement, no longer than her thumbnail and the fresh, bright green of limes.

"We must be very careful when we come back," says Sylvie. "We mustn't tread on the caterpillar."

In the tree-lined road where Karen lives, there's a cat that sits in a circle of sun.

"The cat has yellow eyes," says Sylvie. "Look, Grace."

She strokes the cat with a gentle, scrupulous touch, and it rubs against her, purring hugely.

"He likes me, Grace," she says.

I watch her as she pets the cat: just like a normal child.

At Karen's, the girls go up to Lennie's room. They'll probably play their favorite hospital game with Lennie's Barbies. This always seems to involve a lot of amputation and bandaging. We sit in the kitchen, where there's a scent of baking and citrus, and Karen's Aga gives out a welcome warmth. Leo and Josh have gone sailing today, as they usually do on Saturdays. You can hear the liquid sound of chatter and laughter from Lennie's room— Karen has left the kitchen door open. I notice this, and briefly wonder whether she leaves the door ajar when other, more predictable children come to play.

Karen complains about homework. Josh has been given an alarming math project to finish by Monday morning.

"It's the poor old parents who have to do it, as usual," she says. "Why can't they just give us a break for once?"

She puts the coffeepot to perk on the stove.

During the half-term holiday, she tells me, Josh's homework project was to make a model castle. Karen found cereal boxes and paint, and he put together something with a vaguely medieval look, though the turrets kept collapsing. But when she dropped him off at school at the end of the holiday, there were far more fathers than usual accompanying their children, all of them carrying the most complicated constructions, one complete with a miniature canon that fired.

"All Josh's mates laughed at him and said his castle was crap," she says. "What's the point? It's nothing to do with kids actually learning stuff, it's just competitive parenting . . ."

Karen's coffee has a kick to it. I drink gratefully. She takes muffins out of the Aga and puts them to cool on a rack.

"Let's have one now," she says, "before the little vultures get at them."

The cakes are still hot to the touch, and taste of butter and orange, with a glittery crust of vanilla sugar on top.

I tell her about my phone call, and her eyes are bright and excited. I'm touched she's so pleased for me.

"And you've been out with exactly how many guys since being ditched by the Rat?" It's her usual name for Dominic.

"Nobody else. Not properly," I tell her.

She has a satisfied smile. "You're ready, you see. It's like I always said. You're ready to move on now. Guys can pick up on that."

Karen is one of those people who live in an ordered universe. Her world is like a tidy house where everything matches and fits—where you meet the right man once you've achieved some special state of preparedness. Which I always feel leaves out that whole scary, unnerving randomness of who you meet when: of what happens. But just for now, I like the theory. It makes me feel it's all meant.

"I'll babysit," she tells me.

I hug her.

"You're an angel. Thank you."

"Well—it's important," she says. "A fresh start, someone completely new. Just what the doctor ordered. And he's taking you where?"

"To Welford Place."

"Oh." She fixes me with a rather analytical gaze. "It's classy, Grace. You need to look the part."

"Karen, what are you trying to tell me exactly?"

Her eyes move across me. Today I'm

wearing jade fishnets, a little black skirt, cowboy boots from a thrift shop, and a cardigan I knitted from some wool I found in the corner shop, which I loved because it's the exact sooty blue of ripe bilberries.

"You always look lovely," she says placatingly. "It's just that it's all a bit *kooky*. He does what, your Matt?"

"I can't remember exactly. Something financial."

"Well, then. I think you ought to come with me."

I follow her upstairs. As we pass Lennie's room, we glance in through the door. It all seems happy. They're busy with Lennie's toy stove. They seem to be cooking a naked Barbie in a saucepan, and Lennie has a plastic knife in her hand. Both girls are smiling gleefully.

Karen's bedroom has a scent of rose geranium, and a sleigh bed covered in white with crocheted flowers. On the dressing table are silver hairbrushes, handed down from her mother, and family photographs in leather frames. It all speaks of continuity, of her sense of where she belongs. I envy her this sense of connection: it looks so solid, so comforting.

She opens her wardrobe and riffles through her clothes. Karen likes classic things, trench coats, silk shirts, cashmere. She pulls out something pale blue, with a sheen—a satiny blouse with long, full sleeves and buttons made of pearl. She holds it against my face to see if the color will suit me. I feel it's all wrong for me—too cool, too grown up—but the feel of it is wonderful, the fabric smooth and fluid against my skin.

"Well, go on," she says. "Try it."

I pull off my cardigan and put it on. It's low in front, in spite of the demureness of the sleeves, and cut to pull your breasts together. I'm surprised to see I have a proper cleavage. Karen puts her hands on my shoulders and turns me toward the mirror. We look at my reflection.

"Mmm," she says. "I like it. And you could put your hair up."

"I always wear it down."

"Why?"

"Oh, I don't know—because I always have done, probably."

She gives me a skeptical look. I feel my face go hot.

"Okay. I confess. It's because it's how Dominic likes it."

"*Liked* it. He's in the past, Grace." She wags her finger with mock severity. "Remember, no more father figures," she says.

I told Karen once about my father. Just the outline—well, there isn't much to tell. I told her how I remembered him, how big he seemed, and his warm smell, and the thrill I'd felt when he'd carry me around the streets on his shoulders, and I couldn't imagine what it was like always to view the world from such a height. And my mother just saying, one day when I was three, *Your father's gone*, and not knowing what she meant by that—thinking she meant he'd gone but would come back again, so for years, when I heard a taxi stopping in the street, I'd rush to the window, a little bud of hopefulness opening up inside me. Karen was fascinated. "Well, there you are, then," she'd said, convinced that my passion for Dominic is all tied up with this loss, that it's all about recovering my lost father. She's probably right, but knowing doesn't help much. I can't untie it.

She sweeps up my hair in a twist at the back of my neck, fixes it with a sparkly clip from her dressing table. I look somehow more definite, as though I'm more clearly drawn in.

"Fab," says Karen. "Kind of *Breakfast at Tiffany's*. And maybe some earrings— just little ones . . ."

I grin at my reflection, the cleavage, the new hair. It's fun, this dressing up. I half notice and then dismiss the sudden silence from Lennie's room. I feel a light, fizzy excitement.

She opens up her jewel box. A ruby glows with a dull, rich light. I watch her careful fingers move the jewels aside.

"I've got some sweet pearl earrings somewhere—"

There's a sudden scream from the play-room, a rush of steps on the landing, a bang as the door is thrown back. Lennie erupts into the room, flings herself on her mother. Her face is blotched with furious red. She's sobbing, outraged. She's crying too passionately to speak. I think, Oh God, what's happened? What did Sylvie do?

I can see across the landing through the open door. Sylvie is still in Lennie's room, wrapping a Barbie in a blanket. She has her back to us. She seems quite unconcerned.

Karen kneels by Lennie, holds her. "Was it something that happened, sweetheart? Did you hurt yourself?"

Lennie's breath comes in shaky gasps. "She says I'm not Lennie." The words tumble out through her tears. "But I *am*, Mum, I *am*."

Karen strokes Lennie's hair away from her wet, bright face. She's frowning.

"Of course you're Lennie," she says.

"She says I'm not," says Lennie again.

"Sylvie said that?"

Lennie nods.

"Sylvie does say funny things sometimes," says Karen. "You know that . . ."

I go across to the playroom.

"Sylvie, what happened? What did you say?"

She isn't looking at me. She's preoccupied with the doll, extravagantly solicitous, wrapping the blanket close around it with fastidious care. Her face is a mask. She's humming very quietly.

"You've got to tell me," I say.

I reach out, hold her face between my hands, so she can't escape me, so she has to look at me. Her skin is surprisingly cool for a child who's been playing indoors.

"What did you say to Lennie? Did you tell her that isn't her name?"

She shrugs.

"She's not," she says. "Not really. She's not *my* Lennie."

She jerks her head, slips from my hands.

"Lennie's really upset, can't you see that?" I say. "I want you to tell her you're sorry."

Sylvie says nothing. Her back is turned to me now. She's busy with the Barbie, running her finger around its face in a detailed little enactment of maternal tenderness.

"Sylvie, will you say sorry?"

"She's not my Lennie," she says again.

I feel a pulse of anger. Just for an instant I could hit her—for her detachment, her coolness, the way she eludes me, the way she slides from my grasp.

"All right. We're going home, then," I say.

She puts down the doll that she was tending with such deliberate care, just dumps it on the floor at her feet, as though she has no interest in it. This was meant to be her punishment, to show my disapproval, but it's like she's glad to leave. Without being asked, she heads downstairs to find her coat and shoes.

I go back to Karen's bedroom.

"Karen, I'm so so sorry. I think we'd better go now."

Karen's face is tightly closed, holding everything in.

"Really, you don't have to," she says.

"I think we should," I say.

I'm still wearing the blue silk blouse. I can't take it off with Lennie there.

"We'll be downstairs," says Karen. "Remember to take the clip too."

I catch sight of myself in the mirror. I'm not so sure now that Karen's clothes suit me: the paleness of the fabric makes my face look hard and tired. The gloss has gone from the day.

When I go downstairs, Sylvie is ready and waiting to leave. She has her shoes and coat on. She has her back to Karen and Lennie, her face quite still, no feeling in it, her eyes fixed on the door. Lennie has stopped crying now, but she's pressed into her mother, frowning at Sylvie's back, with Karen's skirt clenched fiercely in her fist. It's happening again: I'm leaving Karen's house embarrassed and ashamed.

## 5

Outside it's dark and cold now. We can see the smoke of our breath as we pass beneath the streetlamps. Sylvie slips her hand into mine. I feel her small, cool touch; my anger seeps away.

She walks slowly, as though her shoes weigh her down.

"I'm tired, Grace. I don't want to walk. My feet hurt."

We could catch the bus, but I'd rather save the fare.

"Will you walk if we go past Tiger Tiger?" I ask her.

"And see my house?"

"Yes. The shop will be closed now, but we can look in the window."

She nods.

"I want to see my house," she says.

It's only a slight detour. Tiger Tiger is in a row of expensive shops two streets down from Karen's, next to the organic deli. It specializes in dollhouses and hand-made wooden toys. The shops are all shut up now, but at Tiger Tiger the window is lit. We stop there, looking in.

Some of their most impressive things are in the window display—a rocking horse with mane and tail made from real horse-hair, some jointed German teddy bears, all the dollhouses. There's a castle with exuberant crenellations; a Gothic mansion with ivy painted all over the walls; a splendid Georgian town house that has the front pulled back so you can see the family of beribboned mice that live there, the wallpaper with cabbage roses, the tiny button-back chairs. As a child I'd have adored it, this enclosed, enchanted world. But Sylvie gives it only the briefest of glances.

Behind the lit part, the rest of the shop is in shadow. The marionettes that hang from the ceiling catch briefly in the headlights

from the road. There's a vampire with clotted, bloody fangs; a pale, anorexic princess
in a wisp of silk; a witch. The witch has hair
like cobwebs and gappy teeth and white
and vacant eyes. The marionettes look a
little sinister hanging there in the quick, thin
shafts of light that pass across them, their
hair and the fringes on their outfits shivering very slightly in the movement of air from
some secret vent or opening. The air in the
shop must never be quite still. When I was
a child, they'd have frightened me, but
Sylvie isn't frightened. She often seems
so afraid, yet the things that usually terrify
children—gaping mouths with teeth, or
zombies, or heads apart from bodies—
never seem to worry her.

"There's my house," she says, with a
slight sigh of satisfaction. "There it is,
Grace."

The one that she loves is the smallest
one, really only a cottage, with slate gray
tiles and roughcast whitewashed walls.
This always surprises me. I'd have thought
she'd have gone for the mansion or the
Georgian town house. I feel again how
I don't know her, can't predict her. The
house is squat, symmetrical, like the

houses she draws. Maybe that's why she likes it. It has shutters at the windows, and moss is painted on the tiles.

Lights from the shopwindow shine in Sylvie's eyes. Her whole face is luminous, looking at it. She presses up to the glass, her face flattened against it, her hands on either side of her face, the fingers splayed.

"That's my house, isn't it, Grace?" she says again.

I bend to her.

"Yes. That's the one you like the best."

She's pushing against the glass as though she could push through. I worry that she'll set off an alarm, that perhaps the window is wired.

"Who lives there?" I ask her.

When she turns her head toward me, you can see the perfect oval, blurring at the edges, where the glass has misted with the warmth of her breath. She has a puzzled look, a little frown stitched to her forehead, as though there's something obvious I haven't understood.

"Me, Grace," she says. "That's my house. I told you."

"It's like the ones you draw," I say.

She doesn't say anything for a moment, just stands there looking in.

"I want it, Grace."

"Sweetheart, I know you do."

When I crouch beside her, I see the marionettes reflecting in her eyes in tiny, immaculate images.

"I really really want it. Will you buy it for me, Grace?"

"Perhaps one day," I tell her.

I'm always vague when she asks, in case my plan goes wrong. I never know when something will happen to throw out my calculations—a rise in fees at the nursery or Sylvie growing out of her dungarees or her shoes. I have a special account, and each week I save just a bit, just as much as I can manage. By February—when it's her birthday—if nothing goes wrong, I hope I'll have enough. This gives me a warm, full feeling, that I can buy this dollhouse for her. I see her in my mind's eye, playing with it, intent, with a quiet, composed face, the look she has when she's concentrating, singing to herself in a breathy, tuneless hum. I brush my lips against her cool cheek, feeling a rush of love for her.

Because we are happy together for the

moment, I try to talk to her about the afternoon.

"Sylvie, what happened at Karen's?"

She doesn't say anything.

"Why did you say that to Lennie?" I ask.

Her face is blank, giving nothing away. She shrugs. It's almost as though she's forgotten.

"She's Lennie, and she's your friend," I tell her. "She got upset when you said that. Friends are precious. You don't want to upset your friend."

She turns from me. I wish I hadn't said it.

"I want to go home now, Grace," she says in a flat, expressionless voice.

We walk home mostly in silence. She says her feet hurt.

## 6

Welford Place has an old-fashioned country-house glamour, all burgundy and gold, with chandeliers. Matt greets the headwaiter, and we are led to our table. I feel so different from usual, my hair heaped up, and wearing these pale, grown-up clothes. I'm aware of men's glances brushing against me.

Our table is by the window, looking out over the river, and the curtains are looped back to frame the view. The night outside is festive: in the trees on the opposite bank, there are strings of lights like colored beads, their jewel colors reflecting in the dark river water.

"It's beautiful," I say.

We sit and smile at each other, sharing a slight sense of triumph in achieving this, in coming here.

"You look fantastic with your hair like that," he tells me.

I make a mental note to thank Karen.

It's good to be here—not being a mother for once, just being me. I'm always so pre-occupied with Sylvie, alert to every nuance of her mood. Perhaps it isn't good for us. The room smells of roasting meat and the perfume some woman is wearing, sultry like gardenia, and there are starched linen cloths on the tables, and ornate silver cutlery weighing heavy in your hand. The wine is a Bordeaux, like velvet. I think of my usual evening routine—scrubbing down the kitchen, slobbing around in a baggy T-shirt, eating Sylvie's leftovers. It's somehow a surprise that this other world still exists—a world of glamour and very expensive claret, and feeling men's gaze on you, warm as a breath on your skin. I feel a light, expectant happiness. Maybe, as Karen said, it's a new beginning, the opening of a door.

We order guinea fowl with polenta, and talk about ourselves—inconsequential things to start with, music we like, places we've been. Matt seems to have traveled everywhere—India, Peru, Namibia, where he hiked down the Fish River Canyon. I have to confess that I've only been to Paris, on a school trip. But maybe he enjoys this discrepancy, the way it makes him seem a man of the world.

I note the things I like about him, ticking off the boxes—his clean smell of cologne and ironed linen, the fringe that falls over his face. I briefly remember when Dominic first took me to the Alouette: how he held my gaze and I knew he could see it all in my face, so nakedly, and I knew we were there already. I push the thought away. I tell myself it doesn't have to be an instant thing.

Matt refills my glass. I feel drunk already, high on the shiny hopefulness of the evening. The guinea fowl is delicious, with a rich, dark, subtle gravy. We eat appreciatively. A little silence falls.

"Your daughter," he says then, tentatively. "Is the guy—I mean, is he still on the scene?"

"I had an affair with someone," I tell him. Trying to sound casual. "A much older man. He was married."

"And now?" he says delicately.

"He's in the past," I tell him. Very deliberate, definite. Tonight I mean it, I'm certain. "I was terribly young when I met him."

"Yes," he says. Perhaps a little too readily for my liking, as though he can easily imagine me being terribly young. "And anyone since then?"

I don't know if I should pretend. Is four years a very long time to go without a man? Will he think me strange?

"No, nobody since," I tell him.

"You must be very strong," he says. "Bringing up your daughter on your own."

"I don't feel strong," I tell him.

"I guess it's lonely sometimes," he says.

"We manage—but yes, it can be lonely," I tell him.

And I see in that moment that, yes, I'm lonely, but maybe I don't have to be alone. That it isn't forever, this sense of restriction I have, of walls that press in whichever way I turn. That it could all be different.

"I can feel that in you, that you've been hurt," he says.

He puts his hand on mine. It feels pleasant, reassuring.

"And you?" I say. Deliberately vague.

"I lived with a woman for a while," he tells me.

He takes his hand away from me. He moves things around on the table—the saltcellar, the bottle of wine—like he's playing a game on an invisible board.

"What happened?" I ask him.

He slides one finger around the rim of his glass.

"I travel a lot on business," he says. "And there was this weird thing. That when I was away from her, I used to long to be with her—just yearn to be back home with her. I'd get obsessed, I couldn't think of anything else."

"I can understand that," I tell him warmly. Knowing about obsession.

"But when I got back, I used to find she wasn't how I'd thought. It would happen so quickly. We'd row again, and every-thing would annoy me. There were things she did that would get right under my skin. Stupid things. Like, she used to eat lots of apples and leave the cores on the floor . . ."

I make empathic noises. Resolving that from now on I will always bin my apple cores immediately.

He looks down for a moment, flicking some lint from his sleeve.

"It's strange, isn't it?" he says. "Like you can only love the person when you're miles away from them. Like it's just a dream you have . . ."

We move on to easier things—our families, where we come from. He leans across the table toward me, his gaze caressing my face. Over the white chocolate panna cotta, I feel a little shimmer of arousal.

We go out to his car. It's a frosty evening, with spiky bright stars in an indigo sky. Our breath is white. He's parked by the river, where swans move pale and silent against the crinkled dark of the water, and there are dinghies tied up. You can hear the gentle jostling of the water against their hulls.

"Thank you. That was a wonderful evening," I tell him.

"Yes, it was," he says.

At his car he doesn't immediately take out his key. He turns toward me, putting one hand quite lightly on my shoulder.

"Grace. I'd like to kiss you."

"Yes," I say.

He presses his hands to the sides of my face and moves my face toward him. He kisses my forehead, my eyelids, moving his lips on me very slowly, smoothing his fingers over my hair. I love his slowness. I feel a surge of excitement, the thin flame moving over my skin. I have my eyes closed. I can hear the sound of the water and his hungry, rapid breath. When his lips meet mine, I am so ready for him. He tastes of claret, he has a searching tongue. We kiss for a long time. He pulls me close: I feel his erection pressing against me.

Eventually we move apart and get into the car. He turns on a CD—Nina Simone. The music is perfect, her voice smoky, confiding. He drives back toward my flat, and neither of us says anything. Most of the time he rests one hand on my thigh. I feel fluid, open.

He turns into my road in Highfields and pulls in at the curb.

"You could come in," I tell him.

"I'd like that very much," he says.

He wraps his arm around my waist as we walk toward my doorway, then slips his hand up under the blouse, sliding his fingers between the silk and my skin. I think of him moving his hands all over me, easing his fingers inside me.

I unlock the outer door. And then the sound assaults us the moment the door swings open—a thin, shrill wailing. Matt moves a little away from me. I curse myself for inviting him in, but now it's too late to turn back.

"I'm so sorry," I tell him.

I push at the door to the living room. The crying slams into us, suddenly louder as the door swings wide. I sense Matt flinching. Well, of course he would.

Sylvie is on Karen's lap, shuddering, gasping for breath, her face stricken. She turns her head as I go in, but she doesn't stop sobbing. Karen has a tight, harassed look. The glittery glamour of Welford Place seems a world away now.

"This is Matt—this is Karen. And Sylvie," I say above the wailing.

Matt and Karen nod at each other. They

have an uneasy complicity, like strangers thrown together at a crime scene. Nobody smiles.

"She had a nightmare," says Karen. "I couldn't settle her."

Sylvie stretches her arms toward me. I kneel on the carpet and hold her on my lap. Her body feels brittle. She's still crying, but quietly now. Karen stands and smooths down her clothes with an evident air of relief.

"Can I make anyone a coffee?" she says.

"Please," I say for both of us.

Matt says nothing. He sits on the arm of the sofa in a noncommittal way, so it's not quite taking his weight.

Karen goes to the kitchen. Sylvie's crying stops, as though it's abruptly switched off. She clutches me, her body convulses. She vomits soundlessly all over the blue silk blouse.

"Shit," says Matt quietly.

He moves rapidly to the window, keeping his back to us. Karen comes, takes Sylvie's shoulders, steers her to the bathroom.

"I'll clean her up." She's definite, brisk. "You change."

I feel a profound gratitude toward her.

I rush to the bedroom, unbutton the blouse, grab the first T-shirt I find.

Matt is standing in the hallway. He has his car keys ready in his hand.

"I guess I'd better go, let you get on with it," he says.

"You don't have to leave," I tell him. "Really, you don't have to."

I glance down at the T-shirt I put on without thinking. It has a picture of a baby bird and says CHICKS RULE.

"No, really, I think I should," he tells me. "Don't worry, I'll see myself out."

His face is a shut door.

"Thanks for the evening, it was lovely," I say lamely.

He reaches out and touches my upper arm through the cloth of my T-shirt—tentatively, as though he's afraid of what might come off on his hand.

"It was great," he says heartily. "It was lovely to meet you, Grace. Look, I'll be in touch."

But we both know he won't be.

I stand there, hearing him leave—the percussive sound of his feet on the pavement, the car door slamming, the hum of the engine as his car moves away. There's such finality to all this, each sound like the end of a sentence. He drives off, out of my life. I guess that for him I am just another illusion: like so much else in his life, I am not what he hoped for, not what he thought. Disappointment is a charred taste in my mouth. In the hallway I can still smell his cologne. It fills me with nostalgia already.

Karen has cleaned Sylvie up and found her a new pajama top.

"I'm so sorry," I tell her. It's what I so often say to her. "I'll get the blouse back to you just as soon as I've washed it."

"It's hand wash only." There's a hard edge to her voice. "You might want to put some bicarb with it to get rid of the smell."

"Yes. It'll be good as new, I promise."

I catch sight of myself in the mirror. I look all wrong in this jokey T-shirt with my hair up—as though I'm a teenager pretending to be a grown woman. I wrench the clip out of my hair.

# 7

"Ms. Reynolds. Please come in."

Her window looks over the garden. There was frost in the night. Today there's a thin yellow sunlight and the dazzle and shimmer of melting ice, and the grass is striped with the sharp, straight shadows of trees. Children bundled in scarves and hats are playing on the jungle gym. You can hear their shouting and laughter.

I sit in front of her desk. There's a pain in my jaw that I woke up with this morning, some kind of neuralgia probably. It nags at me, I wish I'd taken some Nurofen. The secretary brings the coffee tray.

Mrs. Pace-Barden pours coffee into a little gold-rimmed cup and slides it across the desk toward me. My hands feel big and clumsy clasped around the tiny cup. She pours some for herself but doesn't drink it.

"I've brought you in today," she says, "to have a little talk about Sylvie."

She's solemn, unsmiling, her forehead creased in a frown, but I tell myself this is good, that she's taking Sylvie so seriously.

"Yes," I say.

"I have to tell you, we do find Sylvie's behavior very worrying."

She has rather pale eyes, which are fixed on my face.

"Yes, I know," I tell her.

I sip my coffee. It's weak and bland, but scalding hot because the milk was heated. It hurts my throat as I swallow it.

"These tantrums she has—well, lots of children have tantrums, of course, we're used to that . . . But not like Sylvie," she says.

She leaves a pause that's weighted with significance. I don't say anything.

"My staff do find it very difficult," she

says then. There's a note of reproach in her voice. "When Sylvie has one of her tantrums, it takes the assistant's total attention to settle her. Sometimes it takes an hour. And this is happening several times a week, Ms. Reynolds."

"Yes. I'm sorry," I tell her.

"And this phobia of water. D'you have any idea what started it?"

"She's always had it, really," I tell her. "It's a fear of water touching her face. I mean, children are just frightened of things, aren't they, sometimes? For no apparent reason?"

"Of course. But Sylvie's reaction is really very extreme. You see, Ms. Reynolds, water play is very much part of the environment here. Most children love it. They find it relaxing."

"But couldn't she be in another room or something?"

Her face hardens. Perhaps I sounded accusing.

"We're always careful that Sylvie is as far away as possible. But even that isn't enough for her. And obviously we can't ban it entirely—not just for one child."

"No, of course not," I tell her.

Her eyes are on me, her pale, unreadable gaze.

"And if anything, it all seems to be getting worse now. Wouldn't you say so?"

"It certainly isn't getting any better," I say in a small voice.

"I was wondering—have there been any changes in your circumstances? You know, anyone new on the scene?"

I think of Matt with a tug of regret.

"Nothing like that," I tell her. "We have quite an uneventful life."

She picks up her cup, takes a pensive sip.

"And this house she draws over and over. The house with the blue border and the doors and windows always just the same . . . We do encourage her to draw other things. Beth tried to get her to draw some people—you know, just very gently. 'Can you draw a little girl for me?' But she wouldn't. She's a good little artist, I'll grant her that, but I worry that there's something rather obsessive about it . . ."

I remember girls at school who'd mastered horses or brides, who always did the same doodle in the margins of their books.

"I think she was just so pleased she'd learned to draw houses," I say.

She ignores this. She leans toward me, her fingertips steepled together.

"Ms. Reynolds." Her voice is low, intimate. "I hope you don't mind me raising this, but you're quite sure that this isn't a place where something happened to her?"

There are patches of burgundy in her cheeks. I hate this. I know she's asking if Sylvie might have been abused.

"I'm absolutely sure," I tell her.

"You see, it can be a way that children cope with trauma—this kind of obsession. Reliving the trauma over and over, trying to make sense of it. Beth did try to find out. She asked her who lived in the house. But Sylvie wouldn't say."

"Maybe she doesn't think about who lives there."

"Well, maybe not," says Mrs. Pace-Barden, not persuaded. "Let's hope I'm wrong. I can see that this is all rather painful for you. But for Sylvie's sake these things have got to be addressed."

"If there *was* anything, I would know," I tell her. "She's always with me, or here at nursery, or playing with Lennie, her friend. There's nothing I don't know about."

"As parents, we like to think that," she says. "We think we know all there is to know about our children. I understand that—I've got children of my own. But sometimes we can delude ourselves. Sometimes we don't know everything . . ."

She takes the coffeepot, refills my cup, although it's still half full. It's a moment of punctuation. I feel a flicker of hopefulness—that she will come up with some help for Sylvie, some kind of program or plan.

I see her throat move as she swallows. She isn't quite looking at me.

"I hope you don't mind me raising these things. But we need to get this sorted out. Because, to be frank, Ms. Reynolds, unless the situation improves, I'm really not sure that we can keep your daughter here."

I put my cup down. Slowly, concentrating hard so the coffee won't slop in the saucer. Suddenly everything has to be done with such elaborate care.

"I'm sorry," she says. "I can see this is a shock for you. But the truth is, we just don't have the resources to cope with a child with problems on this scale. She's a one-to-one a lot of the time, and that's not what we're about here—not with the three- and four-year-olds. It's intended to be a preschool class. They're learning independence. We really can't cater to children as needy as Sylvie seems to be . . ."

I fix my gaze on the garden through her window. Everything seems to recede from me—the fretted shadows across the bright grass, the wet black branches of trees—and the children's voices sound hollow, remote, like voices heard over water.

"But surely there must be someone who could help us?" I hear how shrill my voice is.

"Well," she says slowly, "there *is* a child psychiatrist I know. We've used him before, with children here. Dr. Strickland. He works at the Arbours Clinic. It's possible he could take Sylvie on for some play therapy."

"All right. We'll see him," I say.

"Good," she says. Her smile is switched back on again, her hockey-coach buoyancy restored. "I think that's an excellent decision. I'll write to him, then," she tells me.

Outside, there's the drip and seep of the thaw, and the sky is blue and luminous. I walk rapidly along the road, through the moist, chill air and the dazzling yellow sunlight. I feel fragile, cardboard-cutout thin, my vision blurred with tears.

# 8

I hunt around in my kitchen. I'm out
of chicken nuggets, which are Sylvie's
favorite dinner, but there's cheese, and
plenty of vegetables. Tonight I will make
something different and healthy, a vege-
tarian crumble. I fry tomatoes and onions,
stir in chickpeas, make a crunchy topping
of bread crumbs and grated cheese.

Sylvie is in the living room, playing with
her Noah's ark. She has lots of plastic
animals, and she's putting them in long,
straight lines, so they radiate out from the
ark like the beams from a picture-book
sun. She sings a whispery, shapeless

song. She's wearing her favorite dungarees, which have a pattern of daisies. When she bends low over her animals, her silk hair swings over her face.

While the crumble cooks, I clean and tidy everywhere, so the flat is gleaming and orderly. There's a rich smell from the oven, a luxurious scent of tomatoes and herbs, like a Mediterranean bistro. My jaw still aches with a blunt, heavy pain. Perhaps this is something more serious than neuralgia. I work out the date of my last dental checkup. Four years ago, when I was pregnant, when you get treated free.

I bring the crumble to the table, serve up Sylvie's portion.

"We're having something a little bit different today," I tell her.

I start to eat. I'm pleased. It tastes good.

Sylvie moves a chickpea around on her plate with her fork.

"I don't like it," she says.

"Just try it, please, sweetheart. It's all there is to eat today. We're out of chicken nuggets."

"I don't want it," she says. "It's yucky. It tastes of turnips."

"You don't know that. You can't know what it tastes of. You haven't even tried it. Anyway, when have you had turnips to eat exactly?"

"I *do* know, Grace." She pokes a chickpea with her fork and raises it to her face and smells it with a noisy, melodramatic sniff. "Turnips," she says.

I hear Karen's voice in my head, brisk and assured and sensible—knowing just what she'd say: *You can't let her have her own way just because she doesn't like vegetables. Children need boundaries, Grace. You can't always let her get away with everything. She'll run rings around you . . .*

"Sylvie, look, I want you to eat it. Just some of it, just a bit. If you don't at least try it, there won't be any pudding."

She puts her fork on the table, precisely aligned with her plate, with a sharp little sound like the breaking of a bone.

"I don't want it." Her face is hard, set.

"Sylvie, just eat it, okay?"

My chest tightens. I feel something edging nearer, feel its cool breath on my skin. But I try to tell myself this is just an everyday argument—a child refusing to eat, a parent getting annoyed. I tell myself this is nothing.

Her eyes are on me. Her gaze is narrow, constricted, the pinpricks of her pupils like the tiniest black beads. She looks at me as though she doesn't recognize me, or doesn't like what she sees.

"I don't like it here," she tells me. Her voice is small and clear. "I don't like it here with you, Grace."

The look in her eyes chills me.

I don't say anything. I don't know what to say.

"I don't like it here," she says again.

I stare at her, sitting there at our table in her daisy dungarees, with her wispy pale hair, her heart-shaped face, this coldness in her gaze.

Rage grabs me by the throat. I want to shake her, to slap her, anything to make that cold look go away.

She pushes the plate to the other side of the table, moving it carefully, not in a rush of anger, but very controlled and deliberate. She turns her back to me.

"Stop it. Just stop it." I'm shouting at her. I can't help myself. My voice is too loud for the room, loud enough to shatter something. "Jesus, Sylvie. I've had enough. Just stop it, for God's sake, will you?"

She sits quite still at the table, with her back to me. She presses her hands to her ears.

If I stay, I'll hit her.

I go to the bathroom, slam and lock the door. I sit on the edge of the bath, rigid, my fists clenched, my nails driving into my palms. I can feel the pounding of every pulse in my body. I sit there for a long time, making myself take great big breaths, sucking the air deep into my lungs like somebody pulled from the sea. Gradually my heart slows and the anger seeps away.

I'm aware of the pain again. It's worse now, drilling into my jaw. I find two Nurofen at the back of the bathroom cabinet. But my throat is tight, they're hard to swallow. I've sucked off all the coating before I get them down. They leave a bitter taste.

In the living room, Sylvie is on the floor again, busy with her Noah's ark, humming softly to herself, as though none of this had happened.

"I'll make you some toast," I tell her.

She doesn't look up.

"With Marmite?" she says.

"Of course. If that's what you'd like."

I make her the toast, put milk in her cup. I eat a few mouthfuls of crumble, though my appetite has gone. I clear the table.

"Shall we watch television?"

She nods. We sit together on the sofa, and she curls in close to me, taking neat bites of her toast. If she drops a crumb, she licks her finger and dabs at the crumb and sucks it from her fingertip. It's a wildlife program, about otters in a stream in the Scottish Highlands. She loves the otters, laughs at their quick, lithe bodies, the way they slide across the rocks as sleek and easy as water. As we sit there close together, it feels happy again between us, the bad scene just a memory, faint as the slight bitter taste in my mouth.

"Sweetheart, I'm sorry I shouted at you," I tell her. "I don't feel well. My tooth hurts."

She's nestled in the crook of my arm. She looks up at me. "Which one, Grace?" she says.

"It's here." I point to the sore place. "I'll have to go to the dentist. He'll probably take it out."

She reaches across and rests her hand against the side of my face.

"There," she says.

The tenderness in the gesture melts me. I hug her to me, bury my face in her hair, in her smell of lemons and warm wool. She lets herself be held.

# 9

The receptionist greets me. She's married to one of the dentists who work here. She has a faded prettiness and bleached, disheveled hair.

"Toothache?" she says.

"I'm afraid so."

"Oh dear." She shakes her head, a little disapproving. "You shouldn't have left it so long."

The waiting room has a fish tank and comfortable chairs. I sit and watch the fish. They have a transparent, unnatural look, like embryos, and their slow, threaded

dance is hypnotic. There's the faintest antiseptic smell, like that green, astringent liquid the dentist gives you to rinse with. It's
very warm, and quiet with double glazing
at the windows, so all you hear is the softest hum of traffic from the street. It's pleasant sitting doing nothing, the warmth
easing into my limbs.

There are papers and magazines on the
table beside me. I look casually through the
magazines, hoping for something glamorous, for opulent taffeta frocks and fetishy
shoes, but they're all just real estate jour-
nals.

A woman comes in and speaks to the
receptionist. She's dressed discreetly, in
business black with sensible pumps, but
I can't help staring at her. Her face is a
mess, the skin around one eye all bruised
and broken. Someone must have attacked
her. Perhaps she lives with a violent man.
She sits beside the fish tank, very straight
and still, as though moving too much could
hurt her.

The dentist's wife puts down her pen.

"So how's your little one doing, Ms.
Reynolds?"

She knows Sylvie well. I may put off my own visits, but I never miss Sylvie's checkups.

"Sylvie's fine," I tell her.

"She's how old now?"

"She's three."

"They're so lovely at three." Briefly, her face softens. She has a hazy, nostalgic look. "They grow up so quickly," she says.

"Yes, I guess so."

"My two are at university now. It seems to happen so suddenly. But I'll tell you one thing—you never, ever stop worrying. Whatever you do, you always feel you might have got it wrong."

"Yes. I can imagine that."

Her husband calls her in to help with the patient before me. She doubles as his dental nurse.

I glance across at the woman with the bruising. I wonder about her life and the little steps, each seeming perhaps so innocuous, that have brought her to what looks like a very bad place. How easily this can happen—sleepwalking into trou- ble. Maybe she senses my gaze on her: she glances up, catches my eye. I feel myself flush; I turn back to the magazines, pull out a local paper, the *Twicken-ham Post*.

I keep my eyes down, looking at the paper, pretending to be interested. There are pictures of school award ceremonies. I read my horoscope. There's a recipe for grapefruit-and-poppy-seed cake, which sounds delicious and which I attempt to memorize. I wonder if poppy seeds are expensive and whether they stock them at Kwik Save.

Something catches my eye then, a double-page spread in the center of the paper: "The Real Ghost Busters: Cynthia Johnson reports." Intrigued, I start to read. It's all written in that bland, gossipy style you find in small local newspapers.

Things that go bump in the night are all in a day's work for Dr. Adam Winters, of the Psychic Institute at Hampton University. Dr. Winters talked to me in the disappointingly prosaic setting of his office in the Department of Psychology. A soft-spoken man, whose gentle voice belies his evident energy and fascination with his subject, he has investigated ghosts, poltergeists and cases of telepathy. Sounds like an exciting job? "Mostly it's quite routine," says Dr. Winters. "For instance, if someone claims to have telepathic powers, we might set up an experiment where they have to make predictions, and we analyze the results to see if their guesses are better than chance. Basically we're applying scientific methods of inquiry to the things that happen to people that they can't explain . . ."

There's a photo of Adam Winters with the article. It's a grainy photo, you can't really see him clearly. He's lean and dark, and his chin is shadowed with stubble, and he has a startled air, like someone has just called his name. I contemplate the photo for a moment. I decide he's the kind of man who'd corner you at a party and stand too close and talk at length about some obsession of his—someone who'd undoubtedly think that I was rather frivolous. Then I smile at myself for conjuring up this entire persona for him.

I can hear the edgy, mosquito whine of a drill from one of the surgeries. I don't want to think about it. I focus on the article, which has lots of stories of local ghosts.

There's a gallery at Hampton Court that's
haunted by the ghost of Catherine
Howard, whom Henry VIII beheaded: dogs
won't go over the threshold. Adam Winters and his colleagues visit the sites of
the hauntings and measure fluctuations in
electromagnetic fields.

> I ask him if he believes in ghosts, but he's
> guarded and noncommittal. He tells me,
> "A scientist should never say that any-
> thing is impossible . . ."

I look up as the woman in the black business suit is called in. I notice how stiffly she
moves, her body as fragile as eggshell.
Then the door bangs shut behind her and
I'm alone in the room.

I turn back to the paper, skim through
the rest of the article. I'm about to turn the
page when the last few lines spring out at
me as though they are illuminated.

> But Dr. Winters doesn't confine his
> researches to ghostly apparitions. One of
> the cases he's currently investigating is
> that of four-year-old Kevin Smith (not his

real name). Kevin wakes sobbing every night and says he wants to go home, and sometimes he talks about a place where he says he used to live. His mother wonders if Kevin is remembering a previous life . . .

The room tilts. I can feel my heart, its rapid, jittery beat.

I put it to Dr. Winters that many children live in a fantasy world. "Of course," he says. "And that's why we have to look at these cases very carefully. In fact, accounts of children apparently remembering past lives are actually quite common, though most of them come from cultures which have a belief in reincarnation, like the Druze of Lebanon." And he tells me there are psychiatrists who claim to use past life regression to heal physical symptoms and phobias.

I ask him what he thinks of all this. "I've never investigated a past life case that I found completely convincing," he tells me. "But there's a U.S. psychiatrist, Dr. Ian Stevenson, who devoted his life to exploring this phenomenon—and some of his cases are really very persuasive . . ."

I jump as my dentist's door swings back. An elderly man in a drab gray coat comes out. He's touching his face with his fingers, as though to check that it's still there. The dentist's wife takes his credit card. I read hungrily on, my heart juddering.

So what does Dr. Winters make of Kevin? He's diplomatic: he gives me a guarded smile. "As a scientist, I never say never," he tells me.

Have you had an experience that you can't explain? Dr. Winters would love to hear from you. You can contact him at this e-mail address . . .

I grab my bag and scrabble around for a pen.

"Ms. Reynolds, could you come in now?"

The dentist is standing at the door of his surgery. I fold up the paper and tuck it under the magazines.

I get in the chair, and the dentist pokes around in my mouth. He's a bony, lugubrious, kindly man. He allows himself a melodramatic sigh.

"And when did you last come to see me?" he says.

"I can't remember exactly. I'm afraid it's quite a while."

He shakes his head, as though wearily resigned to human weakness.

"I'll see what I can do," he says mournfully. "But in the end we'll probably have to extract it."

He drills my tooth, puts in a filling, prescribes some antibiotics.

"To be honest, I really don't know if this is going to work," he says. "You should make an appointment for eight weeks' time. But any trouble, you come back sooner, okay? Any twinges."

I promise that I will.

I go back into the waiting room. The dentist's wife follows. If she wasn't here, I might steal the *Twickenham Post*. The work will cost a lot. I arrange to pay in installments. She fixes my next appointment.

Outside, I'm amazed that everything is just the same as it always was—the lumbering buses, the crowd of pedestrians jostling at the traffic lights—all solid, vivid, predictable, just as they were before.

# 10

It's a cold, dreary December—dark days, with a raw, searching wind that often has flakes of snow in it, and sometimes a rain that looks like water but feels like ice on your skin. In our garden, the mulberry branches are bare, and the lawn is muddy and sodden, and leaves from the trees in the Kwik Save car park drift up against the wall, their extravagant russets and yellows darkened and dulled by the wet. It's a struggle to keep the flat warm, with the ceilings so high and the heating so elderly and erratic. The wind sneaks in through every little crack. At night I pile my coats on top of Sylvie's duvet.

At the flower shop we're stocking up for Christmas, with poinsettias and amaryllis bulbs and mistletoe, which I love for the remote, pearly glow of its berries, like something seen through clear water. And Lavinia brings in willow wands and patch-work scraps of fabric, and when the shop is quiet we sit in the room at the back and make up Christmas garlands—some of them very simple, woven from twisted twigs, and more formal, traditional ones with ribbon and berries and greenery— and sometimes I like to use colors and fabrics that nobody else would think of, bows of brown paper or shimmery Indian ribbon. When I get home, my hands still smell of juniper.

A letter comes, with the Arbours Clinic slogan on the envelope—HELPING FAMILIES HELP THEMSELVES—and a rainbow drawn by a child. I feel a rush of hopefulness. Now someone will come to our rescue, someone will understand. I rip the enve-lope open. We have an appointment with Dr. Strickland at the start of January. I'm pleased. It doesn't seem too long to wait. I worry that Sylvie's sneakers are scruffy—I don't want them to think that I am a neglectful parent—and I take her to buy some new shoes for the appointment, pink suede boots with laces, which I can't really afford.

I yearn for Dominic. I ring the house in Newgate Road, hoping to hear him on the voice mail, so hungry for something of him, just for a moment to have his voice vibrating inside me. I choose a time when Claudia should be meeting their children from school, but to my horror it's Claudia who answers. I put the phone down rapidly, ashamed.

And all the time I wonder about the article I read. Sometimes—most of the time— I tell myself it was nonsense, a deluded, New Agey fantasy. I remind myself that people need something to cling to— anything to protect ourselves from knowing, really knowing, that we are mortal beings. Sometimes the mind won't let that knowledge in.

I remember the night my mother died. I'd spent several hours that afternoon at her bedside in the hospital. She'd been doing so well with all her rehabilitation, she was starting to walk again, two months after her stroke. She'd been sitting up in bed, alert and vivid, wearing the bright new bed jacket I'd brought her, and with some lipstick on, and talking about what she'd do when they discharged her—the pelargoniums she was longing to plant. She was worried she'd missed the start of the growing season. The ward sister rang at eleven that night to say she'd died. I just said, "No, she hasn't," my voice quite calm and unconcerned. "Really. Don't worry, she's fine, I was with her this afternoon . . ." I simply didn't believe it. When the nurse persisted, I thought it was a practical joke. I actually said that. "This is a joke, isn't it? You're having me on . . ." She wasn't thrown. It can't have been the first time this had happened to her. She kept on talking, her manner gently insistent. "Miss Reynolds, I'm really sorry, but you need to listen to me. I'm ringing from Stanton Ward. Your mother had another stroke. This time it was a massive one. It was very sudden. She wouldn't have felt any pain . . ." But I couldn't take it in. Just *couldn't*. Like there was a door in my mind, shut fast, that couldn't be prized open, wouldn't let this knowledge through. And mostly I think

that's what all these beliefs are, really—
doors in the mind, keeping the dark out.

Yet sometimes I find myself thinking,
Perhaps it's true. Perhaps the soul goes
on. Perhaps some of us have a memory
trace—some imprint of a previous life—or
a psychic link with the past. And always,
just wondering that—just touching on it so
lightly, even for a second or two—there's
a sense of something shifting, the present, certain, obvious world dissolving all
around me, as everything I thought I knew
begins to fall away.

Sometimes I wonder about Adam Winters and kick myself that I didn't manage to
note down his e-mail address. At least I'd
have a choice then. But I can't imagine
how it would be if I met him or what on
earth he'd make of Sylvie and me. I simply
can't envisage it. I think of him in his university department—his glamorous career, his
adulatory students, and me in my flat in
Highfields, cooking chicken nuggets, reading old copies of celebrity magazines. And
what might it do to Sylvie to give so much
weight and attention to all the strange
things that she says? Everything might get
worse then. There are lots of good reasons

to forget all about him. I tell myself it's as well that I don't know how to reach him. At least it stops me from doing anything rash.

"Lavinia," I say one morning. We're working at the back of the shop. It's a bitter day, with a light sleet thrown on the wind. "Lavinia, there was this thing I read. About the paranormal—ghosts and so on. This guy who researches into it. D'you believe in all that?"

She's wearing a fisherman's sweater. Long cuffs of heavy oiled wool hang over her hands. She pushes her sleeves up, folding them over and over; her gestures are so graceful. She has many silver rings, and a cinnamon staining of nicotine on the insides of her fingers.

Her thoughtful gray eyes rest on me. There's a question in them.

"It depends which bit you mean," she says then. "I do believe in the spirit world—that there's a spiritual dimension." She gives a little self-deprecating shrug. "For God's sake, Gracie, you know me."

I smile, and think of the house where she lives—the tarot cards, the crystals in her windows, and in her hall a low black table with beeswax candles—and when she throws one of her parties, she sticks a notice to it: "Buddhist altar: please do *not* put your glasses here."

"Sometimes . . ." she says slowly. "Sometimes I think, What if we just don't get it? What if our dying isn't at all as we've always believed it to be?"

She comes across to me, rests her hand for a moment on my shoulder. I'm making tree decorations, diminutive pipe-cleaner angels with frocks of blackberry silk.

"Hey, those are yummy. You clever girl . . ." She turns from me, spoons coffee into our cups, pours water from the kettle. "Why are you asking, anyway?"

"It's just this thing I read."

She waits for a while, but I don't say anything more.

"Mind you," she says then, "you have to be a bit careful. People are gullible. It's easy to start believing all kinds of crazy stuff . . ."

Outside, the sleet is starting to thicken; big, feathery flakes of snow sift gently down. I can tell she's musing on something. I wait for her.

She stirs sugar into her coffee. As her hand moves around, her intricate rings give off glints and sparkles of light.

"When I was a physio student," she says, "I had a skeleton to study. I kept it under my bed. And I had no end of bad luck. My boyfriend had dumped me, and everything seemed to go wrong . . ."

The warmth of the coffee spreads through me. I drink gratefully. Snow stitches its pattern on the window.

"And Teresa, my friend—she's Irish and superstitious as hell, and she said it was the skeleton that was making all this happen. And she marched me off to Brompton Oratory to get the skeleton blessed. We took it in a Topshop bag." She shakes her head slowly. "I mean, can you imagine? And we met this priest—he was absolutely ancient, he had this kind of pleased air. I guess he couldn't believe his luck. Two girls in very short skirts with a shopping bag full of bones."

She's staring out the window, where the snowflakes turn and turn as they fall and fur the sills with white. Her expression is gentle with nostalgia.

But I'm impatient. "And what did he

say? Did he give it a blessing? Did better things start happening?"

There are cut-off fronds of juniper on the table. She trails her finger through them, so they release their aromatic resins. Her bracelets make a faint metallic sound.

"He stood there looking at us," she says. "He had these very blue eyes, startlingly blue, like a child's eyes. And he said—I've never forgotten—'It's not the dead we should be afraid of, but the living.'" Her appalling Irish accent makes me smile. "'My daughters, always remember, it's the living we should fear . . .'"

# 11

The Arbours was once a private house. It's a solid, whitewashed building, imposing amid its cedar trees and lawns.

The receptionist has nail extensions—navy blue, with stick-on gems. We sit in the waiting room, which smells of damp and beeswax. Thank-you cards from children have been pinned up on the walls, and there's a heap of ancient children's books. I read *Frog and Toad* to Sylvie, self-conscious about my mothering, wondering if we're already being analyzed, if the receptionist with the long, jeweled nails is marking my parenting out of ten.

Dr. Strickland comes to greet us. He's a scented, immaculate man, white-haired, with a neat goatee. He shakes my hand. His skin is cool and soft, like some smooth fabric.

"I ask everyone who comes here to spend some time in the playroom," he tells us. "It helps me to understand you. I'll be watching you through a one-way screen, but you'll soon forget I'm there. So just enjoy yourselves . . ."

The playroom is all in primary colors, with lots of inviting toys—a stove, blocks and LEGO bricks, a heap of dress-up clothes. Sylvie goes straight to the stove and makes me a Play-Doh meal, which she cooks in the red plastic saucepans. I watch her as she plays—her decorous gestures, her silky, colorless hair. She's so poised, so self-possessed today. It's the only time I've ever wished that she would be really difficult.

We're joined by a woman with parrot earrings and a wide white smile. She says she is Katy, the play therapist, and she will play with Sylvie while I talk to Dr. Strickland. She directs me to his office, which looks out over the lawns. It's a blowy day, wind wrenches at the branches of the cedars, but his room is hushed and silent. He gestures me to a chair. To the side of us there's one-way glass looking into the playroom.

"Right, Ms. Reynolds." He picks up a fat silver pen, pulls a notepad toward him. His cologne is too sweet for a man. "So when did you first begin to believe that Sylvie has problems?" he says.

I don't like the way he says "believe." But I talk about her tantrums and her waking in the night, and he writes it all down with the fat silver pen.

"And she has a phobia of water," I tell him. "Especially water touching her face."

"Yes, Mrs. Pace-Barden told me. Was there any traumatic event that might have triggered her fear?"

"No, there was nothing," I say. "I've thought about that a lot."

"So when did you first begin to notice the problem?" he says.

"She always hated bath time, right from a tiny baby," I tell him. "We manage. I put in two inches of water, and she just does a quick in and out with absolutely no splashing. When I wash her hair, I use one of those face shield things from Mothercare."

"You need to help her play with water in a relaxed situation," he says. "Help her learn to feel safe with water."

"Yes. I've tried that," I tell him.

I think of all the things I've tried to make her less afraid—playing at hair salons with her Barbies, buying a special watering can for watering the flowers. I think of her shuttered face when I've suggested these things. *No, Grace. I don't want to.*

He frowns at the notes in front of him.

"Now, the other things—the screaming and the waking in the night. Do they go back a long way too?"

"Yes. But they seem to be getting worse. It's almost every night now."

"Is there anything else that concerns you?"

"Mrs. Pace-Barden was worried because she always draws the same picture," I tell him.

"What's in this picture?" he asks me.

"It's just a house," I tell him.

I think he will ask, like Mrs. Pace-Barden, Did something happen to her there? But instead he smiles a brief, ironic smile.

"I have the greatest respect for Mrs. Pace-Barden," he tells me, "but if we took on every child who repeatedly draws a house, the NHS would be in an even more perilous state than it is . . . Now, let's go back a bit," he says.

He asks about Sylvie's birth, how well she fed, her developmental milestones. This all seems quite straightforward.

Then he leans a little toward me.

"Now, I think you're in the unfortunate position of being a single parent?" he says.

I nod. It's the part of the consultation I've been dreading.

"So what about her father? Does she see him?" he says.

"No," I say. Afraid he will think that this is an explanation for everything.

"When relationships break down, it's natural to feel a certain amount of anger." He has a sibilant, unctuous voice. "Absolutely natural. And I'm wondering if you felt that?"

I tell him yes. I've planned what I will say.

"I'd have liked him to be there for her—to be a father to her."

"Of course," he says. "That's absolutely normal. And Sylvie herself of course will yearn for a father figure, and for those things you can't provide, that only a father can give."

I hate him putting it like that. I don't say anything.

"Now, when you look at Sylvie," he says, "do you perhaps sometimes see her father in her?"

I shake my head. "I can see they're alike, of course, but Sylvie's very much herself," I say.

"All right. Thank you, Ms. Reynolds."

He moves his notepad between his palms, aligning it precisely with the edge of his desk. "Now, I'll take you through the possible diagnoses," he says.

I feel a quick, warm surge of hope. I tell myself that he is the expert, this scented, immaculate man, and that now he is going to help us, to diagnose Sylvie and heal her.

"As you know, I've been watching Sylvie play, and it's really been very instructive.

Given the history, one possible diagnosis would be autistic spectrum disorder. And Sylvie does have some rigidity of behavior and thought. But, against that, she has good eye contact and good communicative intent, which autistic children never have, and her fantasy play is excellent. Autistic children don't play like Sylvie, they can't create these rich symbolic worlds. Post-traumatic stress disorder would also be a possibility, but there's no evidence in what you told me of any traumatic event. Though obviously something may have happened that you're not aware of. Sometimes we don't know our children quite as well as we think we do . . ."

"I'm sure nothing happened," I say.

He ignores this.

"Now, I've also been looking for signs of ADHD, but Sylvie's attentional skills are really very good. She has absolutely no difficulty concentrating. Rather the reverse, in fact. I'd say her ability to focus is perhaps a little exceptional."

Perhaps I should be pleased that he sees these good qualities in her. But I feel my heart sink. I glance into the playroom, where she's showing Katy her new pink boots and smiling. She's being a perfect little girl—in that way she sometimes has that seems *too* perfect, as though she's acting the part. I'm willing her to get upset, so that he will see.

"So my diagnosis would be a phobic disorder, possibly caused by a constitutional vulnerability in Sylvie and triggered by some unknown environmental event. And though she quite clearly doesn't fulfill the diagnostic criteria for autistic spectrum disorder, she does have a mild impairment of social and interpersonal functioning. Perhaps made worse by the fact that there are certain issues around your parenting of her . . ."

I wonder what he is going to say about me. I feel a dull, heavy ache in my chest.

He leans toward me, his fingertips pressed together in mock prayer.

"There *was* something that concerned me when I saw the two of you play." His voice is intimate, confiding. "I noticed that she doesn't call you Mum or Mummy. And I wondered why you'd objected to that?"

"It was Sylvie's decision," I tell him.

A picture slides into my mind. Sylvie is two, and we're in the garden by the mulberry tree. I kneel in front of her, cradling her face in my hands. *Sweetheart, I want you to call me Mum. That's what children do, that's what Lennie calls her mother* . . . She turns away from me, her silk hair shading her face. *No, Grace.*

"She's never called me Mum," I say.

Doubt flickers over his face. I know he doesn't believe this.

"You see, what concerns me here is your rather weak boundary setting. That there isn't a clear enough boundary between yourself and your child. That's so important for successful parenting. Sylvie needs to know you're the adult, that you're the one in charge. It's not so healthy for children to feel their parent is their best friend."

"I don't think she sees me like that," I say.

But I know he isn't listening: I know he's sure he has found the key to decoding our relationship.

"Over-involvement can be a danger for single mothers," he says. "Perhaps especially with a daughter, and when you have only one child. Sometimes the mother will see the child almost as part of herself, and that's terribly unhealthy for the child. You need to maintain that boundary. It's crucial for Sylvie's mental health. I'd really like to see her calling you Mum."

I don't say anything.

His glance flicks down to his wristwatch. I know the consultation is coming to an end. Despair drags at me. If he can't help me, who will?

"Now, unless there's anything else you need to ask . . ." he says.

In the playroom, Sylvie is trying on dress-up hats and laughing. I feel a stupid anger with her for behaving so perfectly. I'm willing her to scream, to do something unnerving or strange, but she pulls on a hat with a feather and grins at her reflection in the mirror. Two minutes and it'll be over, and my chance to get help will be gone.

I clear my throat, but I'm not looking at him.

"I read something in a newspaper— about children with problems like Sylvie's." My mouth feels thick and dry. I hadn't planned to say this, but I don't know what else I can do. "It said that some psychiatrists will do regression to try and help the child—you know, hypnotize them . . . Take them back . . ." My voice fades.

His face tenses, sharpens a little. I feel it's the first time I've really got his attention. I don't know if this is a good thing.

"Correct me if I'm wrong," he says, "but I think you must be referring to the past life lobby."

"Well. Kind of."

My voice is thin and high.

He screws up his mouth, as though he has a bitter taste.

"I'm afraid it's true, there *are* such people," he says. "Sadly, even the medical profession does have its lunatic fringe."

"I thought I'd just mention it . . ."

I look out into the gardens, at the lawns, at the great, swaying cedars. I would like to be out there, to feel the cool air on my skin.

"Ms. Reynolds." He picks up his silver pen, leans forward. He's brisker suddenly, more formal, an edge of concern in his voice. "Do you have a particular interest in these kinds of things, would you say?"

"Not really. It was just that the little boy in the article sounded so like Sylvie . . ."

He coughs slightly. "What I'm trying to get at, Ms. Reynolds—could you tell me, have you ever experienced anything that would incline you to believe in the paranormal?" His words are measured, careful.

I don't see why he's asking this.

"What kind of thing?" I ask him.

"Sometimes people can hear things, voices in their head that sound like other people. Is that something you've ever experienced?"

**Shit.**

"No. Nothing like that," I tell him.

"Any hallucinations at all? Seeing things that aren't there?"

"No. Never."

"And in your family? Mother, father, grandparents—any problems with mental illness or anything like that?"

"No. My mother wasn't a very happy person, but no, nothing like that."

"And her father's family? What about them?"

"I don't really know," I tell him. "It wasn't that kind of relationship. To be honest, I don't know anything about them . . ."

My voice fades. I feel a brief, hot shame.
He nods, as though this is what he expected.

"I also have to ask you this—for Sylvie's sake, you understand. Are you—or have you ever been—a user of illicit substances? Cannabis? Amphetamines?"

I shake my head. Though I did once eat some hash brownies at a party at Lavinia's—she grows cannabis plants in her window boxes; we had a riotous evening, but afterward I was sick.

"Right, then." He permits himself a little quiet sigh. "Look, I really don't think we need to invoke the paranormal to understand your daughter. The truth is, sometimes it's easier to embrace some extravagant theory than to examine our own behavior," he says.

"I just thought I'd mention it," I tell him. I can't believe how stupid I've been.

He leans back in his chair again.

"So there you have it, Ms. Reynolds. Sylvie has a phobic disorder and some slight impairment of social functioning, probably exacerbated by rather weak boundary setting. I can see, of course, that you find her behaviors difficult. But I really don't feel she fits the criteria for our service."

I swallow hard.

"So you can't help us," I say.

He frowns. Perhaps I put it too baldly.

"I didn't say that exactly, Ms. Reynolds. But sometimes the best way in isn't via the presenting problem. Sometimes we need to intervene in a different part of the family system. And I do feel that there are issues here about boundaries and over-involvement, and also some unresolved anger about Sylvie's father and how he treated you. And what I think we should do here is to focus on you rather than Sylvie. To assist you with boundary setting and to help you handle Sylvie's behaviors," he says.

There's a weight like lead in my stomach.

"I have an excellent colleague, Dr. Jenny Martin," he says, "who I'm sure would be able to help. She's really very approachable. If you're happy with that, then I'll fax her my notes and you can ring for an appointment."

He gives me Dr. Martin's number and takes me through to find Sylvie. She says goodbye to Katy and slips her hand in mine. She looks up at me with a little pleased smile, perhaps expecting praise for her immaculate behavior.

We walk slowly out through the grounds of the clinic. The boughs of the cedars creak as they move, with a strange, high sound like a human voice.

"It was nice there," says Sylvie. "I liked the stove, Grace. The stove was nice, wasn't it?"

I feel despair. All that effort—the time off, the planning what to say, Sylvie's boots I could barely afford—and all for nothing.

"I knew you'd like the stove. It's just the same as the one in Lennie's bedroom," I say.

"She isn't Lennie," says Sylvie.

I don't say anything.

# 12

One Saturday, when Leo and Josh have gone sailing, we take the girls to the zoo. It's a beautiful afternoon—pellucid sunlight, razor-sharp shadows, a keen chill out of the sun. We buy ice creams, though really it's too cold for them. The girls run on ahead of us.

"Sylvie seems great today," says Karen.

"Yes. I hope so."

I tell her about Dr. Strickland, about being referred for counseling myself. Karen listens intently.

"Don't just dismiss it, Grace," she tells me when I've finished. "Maybe it would be good for you to see someone on your own. You've been under such a lot of stress. You never know, it might be useful."

"But it isn't *my* problem, it's *Sylvie's*."

"I know that's how it must seem. But problems aren't always all that clear-cut in families," she tells me.

The girls have finished their ices and come to drop their cones in the bin. Sylvie gives me a quick, light hug. I bend to her, and she kisses me with sticky, scented lips. I bury my face in her hair. The sun has brought out its musk.

"You smell of the sun," I tell her.

"Really, Grace. How can I smell of the sun?" she says. *"Really."*

It's her sensible voice, showing she knows how the world works. She rushes off, laughing, with Lennie.

We pass the gibbon enclosure, where the fence throws a crisp black patterning over the grass, an immaculate shadowy stenciling. The girls make monkey faces and pretend to hunt for fleas in each other's clothes. We're walking straight into the sun, which is sinking already, red as flame and dazzling. It hurts your eyes to look at it. We pass the tigers, two great animals sprawled in a pool of florid light, their bright coats rippling with their lazy, sleepy breath. We come to the llamas and camels.

"I really love camels," says Karen. "They're funny. I love their snooty expressions. You look at all these animals and you've got to think God really had some very odd ideas."

On impulse, I turn to her.

"Karen, d'you believe in reincarnation?"

She grins. "Coming back as a monkey and all that?"

There's a red glaze on my vision, the afterimage of the sun.

"Well, yes. Or as another person . . ."

"Tell you what," she says. "I've always thought I'd like to come back as a cat. Ideally an indolent pedigree cat with a truly besotted owner. Lots of smoked salmon and lying around by the fire." She turns to smile at me; then stares, eyes widening, suddenly appalled. "Grace, my God, you're *serious*, aren't you? You *mean* it."

"I read this article," I tell her, "about kids with problems like Sylvie's. And someone

had this theory that they were remembering a past life . . ."

There's a moment of heavy quiet
between us. Her lipsticked mouth is a thin,
red gash in her face. She shakes her head
a little.

"Grace. This life is the one we've got,
the only one we'll get." She makes an
expansive gesture, her arms opening out-
ward as though to take everything in—the
animals and grass and trees, our laughing children, the wide, bright arch of the
sky. "This is it, Grace. This is it, this is all
we'll get, and we just have to make the
best of it."

Sylvie has a bad day. When I pick her up
from the nursery, her face is blank and
stretched.

"We had trouble again today," Mrs.
Pace-Barden tells me. She's stern, a little
distant. "This time it wasn't the water play,
just one of the boys who was being rather
boisterous. He'd made something with
the LEGO that he was pretending to use
as a gun. We scolded him, of course, but
Sylvie couldn't cope at all. I'm really very
worried, Ms. Reynolds."

"We had our appointment with Dr. Strickland," I tell her.

"That's excellent," she says. "I just hope he'll be able to produce some kind of miracle."

It shocks me, the way she thinks that Sylvie needs a miracle. I murmur something noncommittal. I don't want to tell her what happened at the clinic.

In the night Sylvie wakes and comes to my room. I'm sunk in sleep, in some yearning dream of Dominic, and the sound of her sobbing tugs at me, hauling me up to the surface of my dream. As I hold her tight against me, I can feel her heart pound.

"It was just a nightmare," I tell her, as I always do.

I lead her into my bed, leaving the bedside lamp on so the dark won't frighten her if she wakes again. She presses into me. Her breathing slows.

It's a very still night, very cold. When I'm certain she's completely asleep, I go to fetch the duvet and coats from her bed. At the window in the hallway, which doesn't have a curtain, I can see where frost has scribbled on the pane. I heap the extra bedding on top of her—gently, so I won't disturb her—and ease myself in beside her. She doesn't stir. Though she's so close, I can't hear the sound of her breathing, but where her arm rests against mine, I feel the tentative pulsing in her wrist, the vibration of it passing into my body.

I lie awake for a long time. I think about the frost out in my garden—about its attention to detail, its white grip on everything, its silver calligraphy on the branches of my mulberry, and how it will crisp the fallen leaves that have gathered in the gutters, and how each blade of grass will be held in a separate steely sheath. I imagine I can hear it—like the faintest metallic whisper in the stillness.

I'm almost asleep again when I'm jolted awake by footsteps in the alley by my window. My pulse quickens. I worry as I always do that someone will break in, but then hear their voices and know it's just one of the prostitutes and her client. You'd think they'd want to find somewhere more sheltered on a night this cold. There's a bit of low conversation: a male voice, suddenly loud, distorted, a rushed volley of Catholic expletives, then the quiet talk again and footsteps going away. She'll be glad it was over so quickly. I hear the high, lonely bark of a fox, rapidly receding as it runs through the wasteland along the backs of the houses, the untended gardens and empty lots. Then that too fades into silence.

Sylvie shifts in her sleep, moving into me so I feel her warmth against me. When she's sleeping, her face softens; she loses that strained look she has. I stare at her in the light of the lamp, and her scent of musk and lemon wraps around me. I lie there gazing at her, my little stranger. Physically, I have her by heart—all the detail of her face, the sweet, precise curve of her cheekbones—yet in some other, deeper sense, I scarcely know her at all.

We have an important commission at Jonah and the Whale—a funeral, a big one, a flamboyant send-off for a local patriarch who ran a chain of pharmacies and gave a lot to charity. He has died at eighty-five with all his family around.

"That's a good death," says Lavinia. "To have spent your life doing something respected and useful and to have lots of children and die in your bed when you're old. That's pretty bloody enviable."

The dead man's wife is exacting about the detail of everything. Her flowers will be all white, a heap of marguerites.

On the afternoon of the service, Lavinia shuts the shop and we go to watch the cortege. The hearse is a Victorian carriage, jet black and lovingly polished, and there are two black horses with elegant, feathery plumes, and on the coffin in the carriage the marguerites we've done. It's the loveliest contrast—the formality of the horses and carriage, a picture from another time, like something in sepia from a Victorian album, and the flowers, casual, almost wildflowers, like an armful of daisies just picked and flung down there, creamy white like buttermilk. There's a cold, rough wind that catches at the manes and tails of the horses; their black plumes shake and shiver. The horses are restive, pawing at the pavement. As they move, you can see the ripple of their muscles, the wiry sinews gliding under the skin. Everyone stops. There's a knot of people gathered on the pavement, mostly mothers and children, and the children love the horses. Everyone is smiling. You feel so blessed, so grateful in that moment on the pavement, everything blown and swirling, the tossing of the horses' manes, the aliveness of the wind.

# 13

It's Sunday. It's cold, far too cold to go out for a walk, with a bitter, gritty rain. I make popcorn, and we sit on the floor by the gas fire in the living room, the bowl of popcorn between us. We have cards and glue and scissors and heaps of old Sunday papers I've kept, and copies of *Heat* and *OK!* Today we will make a collage. I have the television on. It's a black-and-white film from the thirties, starring Betty Grable with high suede pumps and complicated hair. Neither of us is watching it. This makes me guilty, always—they say it's bad for children's language, this constant background chatter—but it makes me feel less lonely, having other voices here.

I flick through a weekend supplement, distracted by the fashion pages, which have dresses made from recycled parachute silk. Lavinia would love them. Sylvie works steadily, nibbling her lip. She has to cut slowly, concentrating and squeezing hard with each cut, because the scissors are rather too big for her hands, and as she cuts, she holds her breath. When I find a picture I think she'd like, I add it to her pile.

An advertisement catches my eye. It shows a man on a wide, rocky shore, and he has the same body type as Dominic, that rather heavy, solid look, and he's wearing a long green riding raincoat that swirls around him as he walks, exactly the coat that Dominic used to wear. I always instantly notice things that are like Dominic's—his signet ring, club tie, the smell of his cigars. Sometimes I'll turn in the street, reeled in by sudden longing because some passerby is wearing Dominic's cologne. Now, looking at the photograph, I can smell him, feel his touch. The advertisement is for a firm that sells clothes for outdoor pursuits and sportswear. In the background, there's an open, empty seascape—white sand, dark rocks, bright sky.

Sylvie notices me staring at the picture. She's sitting opposite me, and she has to twist her head so she can see the picture properly. Her gaze flicks from the photo to my face and back again to the photo, her eyes widening, brightening; then she flings herself against me. The side of her face and body are hot from the gas fire. She gives me a brief, hot hug. I can feel her heart pound.

"You found it, Grace," she says. Her smile is like a light switched on.

I don't understand what I've done. I wonder briefly, crazily, if she has some secret knowledge of her father, if somehow, unknown to me, she has found out about him, if she knows this looks like him. She reaches out and touches the page with one finger, in the gentlest stroking movement, like a caress.

"There it is," she says. "That's my seaside, isn't it, Grace?"

"Of course," I say. "You can put it in your collage."

"It's beautiful, isn't it?"

She has a luminous, confident smile, as though something has happened that she has been expecting. She startles me. She's so sure, so vivid.

I look at the picture more carefully. It's a clever photograph. The light on the water is clear but somehow tentative. You can tell the weather keeps shifting here, blowing in from the sea. The white beach glimmers in the uncertain sunlight; the sand is flat and silky wet and just recently smoothed by the tide, and the black rocks have a crust of chalky barnacles. It's shallow a long way out, the tide must sweep in rapidly, and the shadows of clouds are moving across the water, deepening its color to the most lavish cobalt blue. Right at the edge of the picture, there's a little harbor with fishing boats.

"Yes. It's beautiful," I say.

I start to tear out the page.

She reaches over and grabs my arm.

"Be careful, Grace," she says sharply. Her fingers are fierce on my wrist. "Don't tear it."

"Okay. I'll cut it," I tell her.

I take the scissors and start to cut. She watches me, holding her breath.

"Be very very careful," she says.

I hand it to her.

"There. You can stick it down now."

She shakes her head.

"I want it to go by my bed. Can we stick it by my bed, Grace?"

"Of course," I say, surprised. "If you want to."

I find the Blu-Tack, and we stick the picture to the side of her wardrobe so she'll be able to see it when she's lying in bed.

Her collage no longer interests her. She sits on the bed with her legs folded under her, gazing at the picture. Her face is flushed and thrilled. She sits there for a long time. All evening she seems happy.

That night, when I've tucked her in, I sit by her bed for a while. With only her bedside lamp on, her room seems larger, emptier. Dark thickens in the corners, and under her clothes that are hanging on pegs on the back of the door. Sitting here quietly, I start to see things in these patches and clots of impenetrable shadow—the shapes of spiders or distorted faces. I wish I could manage more furniture, perhaps a desk for Sylvie and a chest of drawers for her clothes. We look as though we're just squatting, like we haven't really moved in. If we had a bit more furniture, it might not feel so lonely here.

Sylvie is nearly asleep, her eyelids flickering extravagantly. She yawns, turns over; she has her back to me. My heart is racing, but I try to make my voice quite calm.

"Sylvie, tell me about your picture. Why's it so special, sweetheart?"

For an instant I think I've missed the moment, that she's asleep already.

But then she turns back to face me.

"That's my seaside, Grace." Very matter-of-fact, as though this should be obvious.

"It's a beautiful place," I say again.

"Yes," she says. "I lived there, Grace."

I sit very still for a long, slow moment. Cold moves over my skin.

"I don't know about it," I say.

"Don't you, Grace?" She seems surprised.

"No. I've never been there. You'll have

to tell me. Can you tell me anything? Can you tell me about it?"

"It's my seaside," she says again. "I lived there."

"Tell me where you lived," I say.

"I lived in a little house," she says. "A white house." She turns away from me again, gives a vast yawn. "That's where I lived. And I had a cave and a dragon."

It's the ordinary, the everyday, rushing in again, the world righting itself. I feel a wash of mingled disappointment and relief. It's something she's seen in a story-book at nursery school, or a fantasy she's invented, part of an imagined world.

"Wow. A dragon's cave," I say, keeping my voice quite level. "A dragon is *fabulous*."

She opens her eyes then. There's a little vertical crease between her brows. Something in my voice doesn't please her.

"Grace, I'm not being silly." She frowns at me. She's slightly annoyed at not being taken seriously. "I did. I had a dragon."

"It's certainly a lovely place," I say again.

"Yes, Grace," she says. "That's where I lived. Before."

Later, I ring Karen.

"This thing happened with Sylvie," I say. "And I don't know what to make of it."

"Okay. Tell." Wariness creeps into her voice.

"There was this picture in a magazine. Just a photo, in an advertisement. A scene beside the sea. And it was like she recognized it. Like it was somewhere she knew."

"Grace, just slow down a bit, okay? What did she say exactly?"

"She said she used to live there."

"That was it? She said she used to live there?"

"She said, 'I lived in a little house.'"

She pauses, taking this in. I can hear Mozart playing on her stereo, the poised, elegant music she loves.

"Grace, kids do come out with all sorts of weird stuff, you know that. What else did she say?"

"She said, 'I lived in a little house.' And I said, 'Tell me about it,' and she said, 'I had a cave and a dragon' . . ."

"She said she had a dragon?"

I can hear the smile in her voice.

"I know how it sounds," I say. "And half the time I think that too, that it was all just fantasy. But she really seemed to know the place."

"It's your filter, Grace. It's since you read that article. Sometimes we hear what we're looking to hear," she tells me.

"Yes, I guess so . . . But perhaps I could find out where it is. You know—the place in the picture. Maybe if somebody knew where it was . . ."

"For God's sake, Grace," she says. "It doesn't mean anything, what she's saying. Kids say the oddest things. Well, don't they? Lennie used to go on about this new mummy she had. Over and over. 'I've got a new mummy . . .' Then we realized she meant her babysitter . . ."

"It was strange, though," I tell her. "Sylvie just seemed so *happy*."

There's a pause, as though this unnerves her.

"You need to get some perspective, Grace," she says then. There's a shred of anxiety in her voice. "You don't want to feed her obsessions. I'm sure that isn't the way."

## 14

But the next Saturday, when we go to Karen's, I have the picture in my bag.

Leo hasn't gone sailing today. He has some work to do. He joins us in the kitchen for a slice of Karen's apple cake. I'm so happy to see him. It's a gift, it's what I hoped for.

Leo comes from the west of Scotland. He has an uncle who lives there still, in a low, rambling house on the coast. It's miles from anywhere. The mail comes once a week. They visit him there sometimes, and Karen says it's extraordinary, a place of mists, and seals, and moisture that seeps into everything, and silence that presses down on you so it's hard to stay awake. It's magical, but afterward, she's always so glad to get home again to the clatter and vigor of London.

I take Sylvie's picture out of my bag. Karen is suddenly still, transfixed, a slice of apple cake poised between her plate and her mouth. I can feel her eyes on me.

"Leo—I wondered—could you look at something for me?" I hold the picture out to him. "D'you know where this place is?"

He takes the picture from me in his ample freckled hand. I feel an urge to say, like Sylvie, Be careful, don't crumple it.

"I thought it might be in Scotland," I tell him. "I thought you might know where it was."

He's looking at it, mechanically smoothing out the corners with one finger. Karen has put her apple cake down. Her gaze narrows.

"That's the picture you told me about, isn't it?" she says.

"Yes."

Her face is stern.

"Grace, just don't. Let it go. You're just

making everything worse. For God's sake, surely you see."

Leo looks from one to the other of us, curious, amused, aware that something is happening that he doesn't understand.

"I just wondered if you knew it," I say. "I mean, d'you think it's in Scotland?"

He shrugs. "Could be."

"But it's not near where you come from? You don't recognize it?"

"No. But it's not a lot to go on. It could be Brittany maybe. You could try Brittany. Round Mont-Saint-Michel, perhaps. There's some fabulous coastline there."

"Where else do you think?"

"Ireland, obviously—the west coast. The Atlantic coast of France, perhaps. Parts of Cornwall, even. Grace, there are an awful lot of places it could be . . . What's this all about, anyway?"

I take the picture back and put it away.

"It's just a place that Sylvie likes," I tell him.

The minute he's gone to his study, Karen puts her hand on my wrist. Her fingers are urgent, insistent. "Grace. Why are you doing this?"

"I thought I'd try and find out whatever I could about the place. You never know, it just might help." I know I sound placating.

Her mouth thins. "Grace, you're just encouraging her. She needs to let go of all that stuff, not just get deeper in."

"But I've tried that. I've tried to ignore it . . ."

She's quiet for a moment. She isn't looking at me.

"Look, I've been thinking," she says then. Her voice is delicate, cautious, placing the words like little stones between us. "You don't think it's some kind of wish fulfillment, do you?"

"I don't know what you mean."

"Grace, to be honest, I'm not sure quite how to put this. But you *are* on your own, and maybe that isn't so easy for Sylvie. Perhaps she's inventing a childhood where she has a father around."

"But it's not a big issue," I tell her. "I think she just accepts it—her father not being part of her life. It's how we've always lived . . ."

"Grace, I know you do your best for Sylvie. I mean, God knows, I wouldn't manage at all. I'd be an absolute *disaster* without Leo. And Fiona said that to me after the Halloween party: 'How on earth does Grace manage so well on her own?'"

I remember the woman with spiky crystal earrings, who seemed so worried because Sylvie wouldn't call me Mum. I hate to think of people talking about me. It gives me a hot, shamed feeling.

"But, I mean, let's face it, Grace," she goes on, "there *is* something missing from her life. I mean, it isn't perfect. It isn't what you'd choose . . ."

There's a bookshop around the corner from Jonah and the Whale. On Monday, in my lunch hour, after I've bought our baguettes from Just A Crust, I go there with the picture in my bag. It's a hushed, rather solemn place. The owner sits at the desk reading a fat biography. He has long gray hair in a ponytail, and he gives me a ponderous smile.

"I want to look at travel books," I tell him.

He points me toward the back of the shop. "About anywhere in particular?"

"Not really. I'm just browsing."

I pull out books on Scotland, Ireland, Brittany—anything with color illustrations.

I flick through all the photographs. There are lots of places a bit like Sylvie's picture, but nothing that's exact: one stretch of photogenic coastline looks much like another. I flick through a French travel guide, briefly distracted, remembering my one trip abroad, the school trip to Paris my mother scrimped and saved for. Remembering how I loved it—the glamorous dark of the churches with their shimmer of votive candles, the smells in the markets of nectarines and rank goat cheese and wine. How it filled me with a longing to live a different life, to be one of the women who sipped their coffee in cafés on the pavement, their hair sleeked back and thin gold chains at their throats, to be elegant and entitled.

I put the guidebook back on the shelf. There's nothing here to help me. I thank the owner and go out into the street.

Next to the patisserie there's a travel agent. I look in at the window. It's empty—just one woman at a desk. She's dressed in a trim blue uniform, like a flight attendant, and her hair is expensively dyed in different shades of blond. She's adjusting her lipstick in a mirror in her compact.

I go in, pull the picture from my bag. She snaps her compact shut. Her smile is glossy and poised.

"I know this sounds kind of silly," I say, "but I wondered whether you possibly knew this place?"

She takes the picture from me.

"I can't say I do," she says. "Well, obviously, it's a coastal location . . . Hey, you're from the flower shop, aren't you?"

"Yes," I tell her.

"I like that shop," she says. "Though I never get why you sell all those things with rust on . . ." She looks back at the picture. "To be honest, most of our clients tend to head for the sun. This looks more kind of northern."

"Yes, I guess it could be."

"Somewhere in Scotland maybe?" she says. "Not that I've ever been there. Cute guy, though. I like the raincoat . . . Well, I don't know who could help you, really. I could have a word with one of the others when they come back from their lunch. But it's not a lot to go on. Would you like me to keep the picture and give you a ring?"

"No, it's okay." I'm too emphatic. I'm terrified of losing it.

"It's somewhere you'd like to travel to?" she says.

I nod. It seems easiest.

"I'll see what I can find you," she tells me. "Something that might fit the bill."

She finds me a brochure for a holiday in Scotland. You stay at Inverlochy Castle and visit a whiskey distillery. I put the brochure politely away in my bag.

The afternoon passes slowly. It's a dark, heavy day with a little cold rain and a smell of smoke and petrol fumes—the sort of day when London seems gray and dirty and you notice all the litter in the streets. I don't know what else I could try. Perhaps I could ring the manufacturer of the raincoat, but it seems unlikely they'd help. There's nothing in it for them.

We don't have many customers. I watch the intricate webs of wet where the rain runs down the window. Disappointment seeps through me like a stain. I've been so naive, so gullible, getting so excited about the things that Sylvie says. Karen was right—it's all just Sylvie's wish fulfillment. She's inventing a childhood where her family is complete. I hated Karen saying

that, it made me feel a failure, but I know
there's something in it. I decide I will put
all this behind me, forget about the article and this whole strange past life thing.
Resolving this, I have a flat, dulled feeling—but also a sense of ground beneath
me, the everyday world restored.

At half past three I go to have a coffee
in the back room. I take the picture out
and spread it on the table as I drink.

Lavinia comes in search of a cigarette.
She taps one out of her packet, she'll
smoke it in the street. She glances at me
where I sit, my head in my hands, the
photograph opened in front of me.

"Hey, what's up, Gracie? You look a bit
dejected. Is everything okay?"

She comes across and puts her arm
around me. Her touch is comforting: you
feel so cared for. She's wearing her scarf
from Gujarat with the gold thread woven
through, and the silk fringe brushes my
face. I rest my head lightly against her.
She glances down at the cutting.

"Oh," she says. "Coldharbour."

I stare up at her.

"You *know* it? You *know* this place?"

She nods.

"Sure."

"I've been asking everybody," I say. "I couldn't find where it was. Nobody seemed to know it."

"It's in Ireland—Connemara. A fishing village."

The room seems to lurch around me. My heart thuds. I don't feel the way I expected to feel. I have a sense of shock—that this is an actual place, that it has a solid existence, just like Lavinia and me, the shop, the London traffic. That it's *real*.

"You've been there?" I say again, stupidly. "You recognize it?"

She smiles at my insistence.

"I lived in a commune there for a while—well, a little way up the coast from there. It's near where Teresa's family come from. I mean, this is years ago, Gracie. When people did those things . . ."

"A commune? Sleeping with everybody?"

She grins.

"Well, yes, there was a bit of that, but mostly it was lentils and meditation. I didn't stay long. It was all fantastically worthy, but I got so fed up with having to clean the loos. Plus I yearned for a choice of lipsticks and a proper cappuccino . . . Yes, that's definitely Coldharbour. You can see the lobster boats. Why the interest?"

"I found this picture in a magazine. And Sylvie got so excited. As though she recognized it."

She's looking at me thoughtfully, but she doesn't seem alarmed.

"You do hear these stories," she says slowly. "Kids who seem to remember things that they couldn't possibly know. You're never sure what to make of them. I'd been wondering what was going on, to be honest. These hints you've been dropping—some of the things you've said . . ."

So I tell her all the things that Sylvie has said, and she sits and listens quietly, her clear gray eyes taking me in.

I'm excited when I pick Sylvie up from Little Acorns.

We drive through the slow rush-hour traffic. When we stop in a queue at a rotary, I look back at her surreptiously. In the amber glow of the streetlamps, her skin has a translucent look. She seems drained, worn out by the day.

My heart is pounding.

"That place in your picture, sweetheart— the place you like so much . . ."

She doesn't respond.

"You know, the picture we stuck on your wardrobe."

"Yes, Grace."

The traffic edges forward. The heavy, smoky smell of the streets comes in through my half-open window. I glance at her again in the rearview mirror. She's holding her Shaun the Sheep rucksack; she has it clutched to her chest as though for warmth or comfort. The rucksack seems too big for her, as though the day has shrunk her. The pale beams from the passing headlights move across her body.

"Can you tell me what it's called—the place in your picture?" I say.

She doesn't seem to be listening. She's staring out the window, where a man and a big German shepherd are walking along the pavement, and the dog has all her attention. I should have chosen a better time to do this, a time when I could properly see her face.

"Does the place in your picture have a name?" I ask again.

Perhaps she doesn't hear me. Her face is still and has no color.

"Sylvie. Your village, your seaside. Can you remember the name?"

I hear the edge of insistence in my voice. Perhaps I should just leave this, but I feel a kind of compulsion. As though so much depends on what she says. As though I'm just a few seconds away from understanding this mystery.

But Sylvie says nothing.

I don't know what to do now. Frustration surges through me. I'm desperate for some response.

"Lavinia told me she knew the place. She says it's called Coldharbour. Is that right?" I ask her.

Immediately I know I shouldn't have phrased it like that.

The traffic slows. My pulse skitters off. I'm watching her in the mirror.

She smiles a small, quiet smile. She hugs her rucksack to her. She has a satisfied look, as though the name pleases her.

"Yes, Grace. Coldharbour." She says it precisely, carefully, with gaps between the syllables, as though it's something quite new to her, as though it's a word she's just learned. "It's a nice name, isn't it?" she says.

"Yes, sweetheart."

But I kick myself. I posed the question wrongly, I shouldn't have suggested it. I see now that I should have waited for her to tell me the name.

"I lived there, Grace," she says. "And I had a cave and a dragon."

I feel how she eludes me, like water leaking through my hands. There's nothing to hold on to, it seeps and trickles away.

# 15

I dream about Claudia, though neither she nor Dominic is with me in the dream. I'm wandering around an antique shop, and I have to buy her a vase. This is very important, very significant. But I can't find one that's right for her. They're decorated with frills and bows and sprigs of ceramic flowers, and I know they're not her kind of thing—she'd want something quiet and elegant. In the dream I have such certainty about what Claudia needs. I hunt through all the shelves in the shop, but the vases all just get more vulgarly elaborate, the ornaments sprouting with the vigor of shoots in spring as I watch. I'm in a panic, paralyzed, unable to choose her gift.

I wake and see that it's morning, and Sylvie has slept right through. My mind feels clean, like a washed sheet. I push back the living-room curtains. There's a sky of the tenderest blue, and a fresh, clean, new-beginnings kind of sunlight. Things are starting to happen in my garden, buds fattening and opening out, and some snowdrops that I planted in the autumn are glimmering under the mulberry. In the clear spring light, the everyday world feels so solid and complete: the table laid for breakfast, the roar of traffic in the street, the weather forecast on television. All these things just so, just as they should be; and Sylvie, sipping her milk so her mouth is rimmed with white, and caught in a beam of sun that glistens her hair. This is the real world, I tell myself, and all those other things—the things I'd half begun to believe—they're just some crazy fantasy. Like Karen said, all children say weird things. I shall listen to Karen and put all my strange speculations behind me.

I get Sylvie ready for nursery. She's just learned to tie the laces on her sneakers. It takes a while, she chews her lip, her forehead creased in a frown, but she's pink with pleasure when she's done it. She seems much more at peace today. I think how next week I shall finally have the money for the dollhouse, just in time for her birthday. I love to think of the light in her face when she learns that at last it's hers. I tell myself that things will all go better now, that this is a new beginning—the undisturbed night, the gift of a shiny new day.

We go out to the car. The sun is low in the sky, and our shadows are as tall as trees, with tiny heads and great big clumpy feet.

"Look at my shadow," says Sylvie. "I'm a *giant*, Grace."

In the cloakroom at the nursery, Beth is pinning up a springtime display, which has lots of animals and blossoming trees. The room is full of light. I hug Sylvie.

"Have a great time, sweetheart," I tell her.

She gives me a quick, cool kiss, her lips just grazing my skin. I watch her walking away from me into the garden room, confident, unhesitating. I know she will have a good day.

"So. Ms. Reynolds."

Mrs. Pace-Barden's shadow falls across me. I turn. She's wearing one of her crisply cut suits. She smiles, but not with her eyes. There's a mouse-scurry of fear at the edges of my mind.

"I'd like a word," she says.

I follow her into her office. There's a tic beneath my eye, a little random pulse.

She leans toward me across the desk. Her hands are clasped tight together—you can see the lilac mapping of veins beneath the skin—but her voice is calm, emollient.

"Why I wanted to see you, Ms. Reynolds—we had a staff meeting yesterday evening. We were talking about Sylvie."

"Yes."

The tic by my eye is stronger now. I'm very aware of its rapid, jittery pulsing. It obsesses me. I worry that Mrs. Pace-Barden can see that there's this odd twitch in my face.

"We had a good, long discussion, and I'm afraid we were all agreed."

I don't say anything.

"I'm so sorry to have to tell you this, but

we're asking you to remove Sylvie from the nursery. We agreed we would keep her just till the end of the month."

"*No*. Please don't. Don't say that."

"Now, please don't go getting upset, Ms. Reynolds." She's looking at me warily. Scarlet flares in her face.

"But—why so soon? Why can't you keep her till Easter?"

"To be frank, Ms. Reynolds, it's a health-and-safety issue. I have my staff and my other children to think of."

"But we went to see Dr. Strickland . . ." My voice is edgy with protest. "I'm really trying. I mean, I'm doing everything I can."

"I know, Ms. Reynolds," she says in her soothing Vaseline voice. "And believe me, I really hope you get there. That you find out the source of Sylvie's troubles."

"But where will she be happy if she isn't happy here?"

"I'm sorry, Ms. Reynolds, but that really isn't my problem. We just don't have the resources here for children as needy as Sylvie."

I can't quite speak. There's a weight pressing into my chest.

She takes me out through the cloakroom, where Beth is sticking some paper rabbits onto her springtime display. I glance at Beth, but she doesn't meet my eye. She has a furtive, embarrassed look.

"Believe me," says Mrs. Pace-Barden on the doorstep, "we do sincerely wish you both well. I'm only sorry things haven't worked out for her here."

I turn, head off toward my car, walking with great concentration, each foot placed in front of the other, as though the pavement is glazed and my feet could start slipping away.

## 16

Sleep is a door I can't get through. I lie in my bed with open eyes, staring into the sepia dark of my room, at the clotted black that gathers in the corners and the delicate stippling of apricot light where the glow from the streetlamps seeps in. Questions jostle in my mind. Can I find another nursery to take her at such short notice? And even if I manage it, will the same thing happen again? Will it just go on happening? What kind of life is now unfolding before us? I go through these questions again and again. I can't find any answers.

Around two, the traffic noise dies down

and there's a provisional quiet—the wary, uncertain silence of London nights, the silence occasionally split open by some abrupt noise from the streets, the scream of a siren, a burst of drunken singing. My body is exhausted, but my mind is utterly clear. I think of all the practical things that have now become so difficult. Like the dollhouse I was hoping to buy for Sylvie's birthday. I was so excited about it, but now I will need to save my money for groceries and shoes. In case I can't find her another place, in case our life caves in on us.

A distant church clock strikes three, its hollow sound clear in the quiet. I lie on my back, stare up at the ceiling. Shadows move across it as a little air tugs at my curtains, and the intricate plaster moldings are drawn in with lines of dark. I scroll through all the people I know, trying to think of someone who could tell me what to do. But there's no one.

And then as I lie there—not knowing, despairing—a thought sidles into my mind. That there's someone else I could go to, someone who *should* be helping me. I think of Dr. Strickland saying, *Her father's family? What about them?* and remember the shame I felt when I said I didn't know. I realize I am going to do the thing I vowed I'd never do. There is knowledge he has that might point me in the right direction. I have to try this, for Sylvie's sake.

I ring him from my cell phone just after I've dropped Sylvie off at Little Acorns, before I drive to the flower shop. A nervousness like nausea surges through me.

It's a woman's voice I don't recognize. He must have a different assistant.

"I want to speak to Dominic Runcie," I tell her.

"And you are?"

"My name's Grace Reynolds," I tell her. "He'll know who I am."

"I'll see if he's available."

There's silence for a moment. I hear the thud of my heart.

"Just putting you through," says the woman brightly.

I have a sense of shock. That this is so easy—that he is there, at the other end of the line.

"Grace. What a surprise." His voice moves through me.

"Yes, isn't it?" I say stupidly.

"You're well and everything, are you?" he says.

"Yes, thank you. And you?" I'm very polite and careful.

"Absolutely flourishing," he says. "Yes, really very well indeed. So, what can I do for you, Grace?"

I hear the wariness underneath his words. I know I have to reassure him.

"I wondered if we could maybe meet up. For half an hour or so. There's something I need to talk about with you. It won't take long, I promise."

Dominic says nothing.

I think how when we loved each other, when we would speak on the phone, sometimes we wouldn't talk for a while and I'd hear his breathing down the line. I always loved that, the way his breathing quickened when he wanted me. But now there's just silence between us, like an absence.

I try again.

"Would that be possible, do you think? I'd be so grateful."

He clears his throat. "I don't see why not," he tells me. "As long as we can keep it brief . . ."

"Thank you."

Happiness floods me. That I am going to see him—be close enough to reach out my hand and touch. For a moment that cancels out everything else.

"There's a café near the flower shop," I tell him. "Or maybe you'd like to suggest a place."

"No, that should do nicely," he says. "I've got a space tomorrow. Half eleven tomorrow morning."

I tell him this is perfect—that it's really completely ideal.

All day the world seems bright to me. The shop is full of spring flowers, and their colors thrill and dazzle me—tulips of bright toy-soldier red, a basket of planted-up bluebells like a little scrap of sky. An elderly man as thin as a crane fly chooses some roses for his wife. The blooms all have to be perfect, and I think how loving this is. There's a little thought that dances in the margins of my mind, twirling and waving and luring me on, a thought I try not to respond to. I push it away, but it goes on smiling, smelling of sherbet and waving its veils. That maybe this is all meant—that all this has happened to bring us back together again. Part of me knows this is nonsense, that I'm being overexcited, manic, and yet I can't stop thinking it.

At the end of the day I pick up Sylvie. She has five pictures she's drawn, all houses and all identical—a roof, a door, four windows—and each with a border of blue. She gives them to me to carry.

"She had a good day," Beth tells me.

Of course she did, I say to myself. I tell myself it will all work out now. Dominic will solve this for me. Dominic has the key, the explanation. Everything will be different now. He always gave me the sense that he could sort everything out. At least until it all went wrong—but now I'm not thinking of that.

"You're singing, Grace," says Sylvie as we walk toward the car through the thickening dark that tonight has a scent of pollen and changing weather.

"Was I? I didn't realize."

I'd been planning all the things I have to do this evening—whether my prettiest clothes are clean, and I'll need to straighten my hair . . .

"Why are you singing?" she asks me.

"I guess I just feel happy today," I tell her. "People sing when they're happy, don't they? Like you when you hum to yourself. And sometimes you don't know you're doing it . . ."

"You don't often sing, Grace," she says.

## 17

I get there far too early and choose a table by the window. I took ages getting ready: I put on lots of mascara, and I'm wearing my bilberry cardigan and a very short velvet skirt, but now I worry I'm too dressed up, that I look like I'm trying too hard. The day has clouded over, and a little rain is falling. You can hear the rush of raindrops on the pavement by the window, like many hurrying footsteps.

I see him coming through the door. My heart pounds. I try to smile, but my mouth feels stuck. He comes straight up to the table and smiles and kisses the top of my

head. The scent of him fills me with longing.

"Grace. How are you? You're looking
well."

"I'm okay," I tell him. "Well, sort of."

He sits, leans a little toward me. It's a
long time since I've seen him this close.
I can see how the years have marked
him—his hair rather paler and growing
more thinly, the skin around his eyes
more creased.

"Thanks for agreeing to meet," I say.

He nods. His eyes are scanning my
face, and I wonder what he sees.

The waitress comes. She has a beguil-
ing French accent and pointy leopard-skin
boots. He gives her the exact same smile
he gave to me—easy, lightly flirtatious. He
orders for me without asking me first—a
cappuccino and a *pain au chocolat*. I can
see how he still likes knowing about me,
knowing what I would choose.

"You had something you wanted to talk
about," he says then.

"I wanted to talk about Sylvie. My daughter." I clear my throat. "*Our* daughter. She's
called Sylvie . . ." I have a moment of con-
fusion, not knowing if it's written on the

form he fills in from Child Support, not knowing if he even knows her name. The smell of his cologne makes it hard to think clearly.

He nods carefully.

"Look, I'll show you," I say.

I take her picture out of my bag. It's a photo I love—a little half smile, her fringe falling into her eyes.

I see his throat move as he swallows. I can tell how wary he is. I see that he is frightened of this moment.

He reaches out his hand and takes the picture. I watch him as he looks at it, this image of our child. A flicker of something unreadable crosses his face. He looks at the picture for quite a long time.

He clears his throat.

"She must be—what—three, now?" he says, his voice a little muffled.

"She's almost four," I say.

"The years fly by," he says.

He passes the picture back to me. I put it in my bag. The waitress brings our coffee and cakes.

"So tell me about it," he says.

I take a sip of coffee. It's hot, it hurts my tongue.

I've fantasized so often about this moment—the moment when we meet again, after all this time. I've worked out all the details: how he comes upon me and Sylvie in some green and elegant place—in my very favorite version it's some exquisite park in Paris—and Sylvie is at her sweetest and I'm wearing my spindliest heels and our hair is bright and blowing in the sunlight; and he's smitten by what he's missing, and thinks how lovely we are. That's how I've imagined it. Yet here I am, exposing all my weakness, showing that both as mother and daughter we have such imperfections. I hate this.

"She's a wonderful child, and I love her so much," I tell him.

"Well, of course, Grace," he says.

"But—she's not exactly *easy*. She has her troubles," I say.

I tell him about her phobias and the tantrums and the nightmares. I don't mention the strange things she says—not yet.

He listens with a concerned look. Then, when I've finished, he reaches out and puts his hand on mine. I feel all the familiar arousal at his touch, everything opening up to him, but with an underlay of weariness—sadness even. As though I live the before and the after at the same time, the yearning to make love with him and the bleakness I'd feel if I did.

"Darling," he says, and I like him calling me that. As he knows I will. "Darling. You *were* very young when you had her."

As though it had nothing to do with him. I don't say anything.

"You mustn't take it all so to heart," he tells me. "I mean, to be frank, you've always been a worrier . . . Children have their ups and downs. It's probably just a phase."

"No, really," I say. "It's worse than that."

"Well, maybe that's how it seems, Grace. But mothers do sometimes get a bit—*over-involved*. You know, get things out of proportion, when really everything's fine. Claudia—well, I can't tell you . . ." He smiles. The thought amuses him. "She's another worrier. She does *obsess* about things."

I haven't come here to talk about Claudia.

"Her nursery school won't keep her," I tell him. "She's only three, and she's been kicked out of her school."

He frowns. I sense the shift in him as he sees that this problem is not as he thought.

"Goodness," he says. "My poor darling." I hear all the warmth in his voice. I would like to wrap it around me, like a blanket. "That sounds so tough for you."

"Yes, it is," I say.

"If it's really that bad, you need to get help," he tells me. "Find someone who can sort this out. You mustn't just hope for the best, not if things are really that difficult."

"We did see someone," I tell him. "We went to see this child psychiatrist at the Arbours Clinic."

"That sounds more like it. Were they helpful?" he says.

I spoon the froth from my coffee.

"That was why I wanted to see you. There was something he said that I wanted to ask you about. He asked if there was any illness in Sylvie's father's family—you know, some kind of genetic thing—that might explain it. Anyone with odd symptoms. And of course I didn't know. I don't know anything about your family . . ."

It's such an awkward thing to ask. But Dominic bursts out laughing. As though he's hugely relieved now that he knows this is all that I want.

"Well, Ma was away with the fairies before she died, poor old thing," he tells me. "But apart from that, we're a pretty boring crew. No one of any interest whatever. No interesting quirks or perversions, not so much as a foot fetish."

He smiles at me, his sudden smile of startling candor: Sylvie's smile.

"I hope you don't mind me asking," I say.

He shakes his head a little.

"For goodness sake, Grace. I'm just sorry I can't be more help. You know— come up with some feckless ancestor who gambled away all the family silver or something . . ."

"I thought it was worth just mentioning," I tell him.

He frowns. "Maybe this Arbours Clinic guy isn't right for you," he says.

I realize I am obsessively lining things up on the table between us, like when you're a child and you rearrange things or take care to step over the cracks. Seeking to avert disaster.

"He wasn't any help, really," I say. "He wouldn't take Sylvie on as a patient. He said she didn't need it . . ."

"Then you need to go to someone else. Darling, you need to get this sorted. You have to find the right person."

For a moment I don't say anything. I sip my coffee and lick the chocolate powder from my lips. Outside the wind is rising, flinging raindrops against the window like a fistful of stones.

"There *is* someone else I wondered about," I tell him. I'm eager to demonstrate that I've done everything I can. I hate for Dominic to think that I am an irresponsible mother. "There's this man I read an article about. He works at the university in the psychology faculty. He's rather unorthodox, though . . ."

He drinks his coffee, his eyes on me.

"Well, if you think it might help, you should go and hunt him out, your unorthodox psychologist. Why not? Unorthodox can be good," he says.

I take a bite of cake, but it sticks to the roof of my mouth. I swallow hard.

"This man—he's called Adam Winters— he works at a place called the Psychic

Institute. He investigates the paranormal. He says that children like Sylvie could be remembering something—something from a past life."

Dominic's eyes widen. "Okay, I take it all back," he says briskly. "The guy's a complete flake. Obviously."

I think that myself too, much of the time, but now I find myself wanting to rush to Adam Winters's defense.

"But it's kind of scientific," I say.

"Grace, you need to be careful." He reaches out again. He rests his hand on my wrist, slides one warm finger a little way under my sleeve. "You're so very ten-derhearted," he says. "You always believe the best of people. You've got to remem-ber there are lots of weirdos out there. I wouldn't like to think of you being taken advantage of."

"He's a proper psychologist," I say. "He does experiments. It's all quite rigor-ous . . ."

But he's shaking his head as I speak, as though he can't believe I'm saying this.

"Look, I know you think this is all really strange, and mostly I think that too," I tell him. Wanting so much to reach him, to make him understand. "But Sylvie does say such odd things. She's obsessed with this village in Ireland. I found it, it's called Coldharbour."

"Grace, she's just a little kid. She's probably seen it on a TV program. Balamory or something. Or is that in Scotland?" he says.

I push my *pain au chocolat* aside. The chocolate is scented, bittersweet, just on the point of melting, but I can't face it. I've so longed to come into this café, lusting after the cakes in the window, and now that I'm here, I can't eat.

"There was something else I wanted to ask. If you—you know, your family—have any connection with Ireland? Maybe some Irish relatives?"

"We did go to a wake in Ireland once," he tells me. "In Dublin. One of Claudia's many alarming aunts had snuffed it. Well, the Irish know how to do these things, of course. Some very serious drinking went on. But that's it, really—no other connection at all."

He's studying me, but his look is paternal

and skeptical, the way a father might look at a mildly errant child. It's not how I want him to look at me.

"So I can't help you there. Sorry, Grace."

I wish I hadn't raised this.

For a moment we don't say anything.

"So how's the job going?" he says then, in an easy, conversational tone. "Are you still working for that woman who looks like she just came from Woodstock?"

"For now. But I'm probably going to lose my job," I tell him. "Because of Sylvie losing her nursery place."

"Poor Grace," he says. "It all sounds terribly difficult."

"Yes."

He shifts in his chair. There's an awkwardness about him.

"I wish I could help out more," he says. "But we're pretty hard-pressed at the moment, to be honest. The school fees are eye-watering . . ."

I stare at him, but there's no irony in him when he says this.

He takes an envelope out of his pocket.

"This is the best I can do," he says.

I see him quickly glance around to see

if anyone is watching; then he pushes the envelope over the table to me. I can see the bunch of notes inside it. He presses the envelope into my hand, closes my fingers down over it.

I suddenly feel anger, a huge, all-encompassing rage—with him, with everything that has put me in this situation. I long to push the envelope back across the table, to tell him I won't take it, but I could really use the money.

"Thank you," I say. I put it away in my bag.

The money has made an awkwardness between us. I feel such shame, and perhaps he feels a shame of his own. I'm desperate to move on from here.

"And you're all okay, are you?" I ask him. "You know, Charlie and Maud?"

He nods, smiles. He's relaxed at once, talking about his other children.

"Maud's having harpsichord lessons. They say she's got quite a gift, which of course we're all very excited about . . ."

"That's great," I say politely.

He finishes his coffee.

"If that's all, darling," he says, "I guess I should be going."

"Yes, that's all," I tell him.

He calls the waitress over and pays the bill.

"Right, then," he says.

He stands, comes around to my side of the table. He puts one finger under my chin, tilts my face toward him. I feel the warmth of his breath on my face. Desire engulfs me.

"So, Grace, you and me," he says. His eyes looking deep into mine. "We had our good times, didn't we?"

He's the only man I've ever loved, the father of my child. It's not the way I'd have put it.

I watch him walk away from me, out the door and down the street, where the rain is coming on heavily now. Walking briskly, as though he's glad to be gone. The rain that dribbles down the window blurs and smudges the shape of him, the way things blur when your eyes are wet with tears.

## 18

All day I have a sense of loss that I can't precisely explain, as though Dominic has taken something precious from me. I consider ringing Karen, but I know that she'd be horrified. I can hear her voice in my head. *No, Grace. Please don't tell me you've gone and seen the Rat again . . .* She'd say I was crazy to do this, to open myself to this hurt. And of course she'd be right, but I don't want to hear it from her. Sometime I'll tell her—not yet.

We don't have many customers. The rain beats down all afternoon, deterring all but the most determined shoppers. I keep myself occupied tidying up, sorting the shelves where we display our gifts and garden accessories—wildflower seeds in brown paper packets, bottles of lavender linen water, candles that have a scent of figs or licorice. I have a lump in my throat, like when you're trying not to cry.

Once or twice I see Lavinia looking thoughtfully at me. She's about to go out for her smoke when she comes and puts her hand on my arm.

"Are you okay, Gracie?" she says.

"Sort of. Well, I did a stupid thing. It seemed like a good idea at the time, but it was really stupid."

"D'you want to talk about it?"

"Not really. Sorry. I don't think I can." My face is hot. The shame I felt in the café hangs about me. "I was trying to help Sylvie—well, that was what I told myself. But perhaps it was just an excuse."

Her quiet gray eyes are on me. She has a knowing look, and I feel that she's guessed what I did. But she doesn't pursue it, and I'm grateful.

She gives me a quick, warm hug.

"Sometimes life's a bitch," she says.

I cling to her for a moment. I know I should tell her that we've lost the nursery place, but I can't face it, not today.

When I go to my car at the end of the day, I look inside the envelope, count the money. He's given me two hundred pounds.

On the way to pick up Sylvie, I turn off for Tiger Tiger. I shall buy her the dollhouse she wants, that I'd thought I couldn't afford anymore, now that our future is so uncertain. This will be a good use for the money—this indulgent, extravagant gesture.

The shop assistant, a stylish young woman in glossy dominatrix boots, packs the house up in a box with lots of whispery tissue paper. I wonder again why this one is Sylvie's favorite, this simple whitewashed cottage, when it's so much less elaborate than all the other designs.

I choose a Barbie for Lennie, whose birthday it is on Sunday, just two days before Sylvie's, and I find some figures and furniture for the dollhouse. I take them to the counter. The marionettes still hang from the ceiling, the princess in her wisp of silk, the witch with hair like cobwebs. They twist and seem to shiver in a little movement of air.

The woman smiles. "This dollhouse is gorgeous," she says. "This is going to make somebody very happy."

The shadows of the marionettes move over her hands as she closes the box.

"It's for my daughter," I tell her. "She's wanted it for ages."

"Well, she's going to love it," says the woman. She gives a small, nostalgic sigh. "I *adored* my dollhouse when I was a kid. It was my best thing, really. You get hours of play from a dollhouse . . ."

In spite of myself, I feel a flicker of pleasure thinking how excited Sylvie will be.

After supper, when Sylvie goes to play in her bedroom, I unpack the dollhouse and put it out on the floor.

"Sylvie! I've got something for you."

She comes back into the living room. She looks at the house and gives a small, pleased smile. Then she turns to me, a little perplexed. "But it's not my birthday," she says. "It's not my birthday till Tuesday."

"It's an early birthday present," I say.

"Why, Grace?"

"Just because. Because you've always wanted it. Because you wanted it so much."

"Thank you," she says rather formally.

I kneel to hug her.

She waits till I take my arms from her, then goes to examine the house. She runs one finger along the the roof, touching it so delicately, as though it's made from eggshell.

"It's my house, isn't it, Grace?" she says. But she's a little hesitant now— somehow less certain than when she saw it in the window at Tiger Tiger.

"Yes. It's the one you wanted. Isn't it lovely?"

"Yes," she says.

But there's something puzzled in her expression.

I put out the little doll figures and furniture I bought for her. She plays with the house all evening, walking the dolls through the rooms. She seems happy enough, but it's not how I imagined it. There's something a little reserved in her play. I have a sense that the house is not quite satisfactory for her, as though it hasn't delivered what it promised. The front of it was always closed in the window at Tiger Tiger, and perhaps it seemed more real to her when she couldn't see inside. Perhaps it's not as she'd envisaged—these neat, empty rooms, the plywood partitions, the scraps of polka-dot wallpaper on the walls.

I have a sad, incomplete feeling. I'd been looking forward so much to this moment, looking forward for months. But now I feel a faint regret that my gesture hasn't worked out, that I spent all that money on it when I should have been saving it up. It enters my mind that perhaps I bought the house for the wrong person— for myself as much as for Sylvie—wanting her pleasure in it to assuage all the unhappiness I feel.

# 19

Next day I drive home in my lunch hour. I eat my baguette as I go. I tell Lavinia I'm going shopping.

My flat has a hollow feel without Sylvie. Mostly she's such a quiet child, but I can always sense that she's there, as though the atmosphere in the place is subtly changed by her presence. It's so odd to be here without her—as though I am a trespasser.

I sit at my living-room table and look up nurseries in the phone book. The list is reasssuringly long, and I narrow it down to ten of them that I could easily reach. If I find a suitable place today, I won't ever need to tell Lavinia what happened at Little Acorns.

I ring the first one on my list.

"I was wondering if you had any places. It's just for a year, until my daughter starts school."

"I'm afraid all our places are taken," says the receptionist briskly. "Bumps-a-Daisy is a very popular nursery. We could put her on our waiting list, but really I don't see her name coming up before she goes to school . . ."

I work through the rest of my list. They all say the same thing: nobody can take her.

The receptionist at the Leapfrog Nursery tries to empathize.

"You're new to the area, then?"

"Well, not exactly."

"Round here you have to get the child's name down really early," she says. She has a sibilant, sensible voice. She spells it out a little. "We have parents who do it at birth. Or even earlier, some of them, as soon as they've had the ultrasound. It's very competitive, really. You need to plan in advance."

"But sometimes you can't plan like that. Sometimes things happen that weren't meant to happen," I say.

"Well, that's *exactly* why you have to think ahead." Her voice has a note of triumph, as though I have vindicated her.

The last nursery on my list is called the Mulberry Bush. I look out at my rainy garden, at my twisted mulberry tree and the tiny, tight knots of its new dark buds. I tell myself this name is a good omen.

The receptionist sounds effusively friendly. "I'm sure we've got places," she says.

My heart lifts.

"Just let me check. Yes, here we are . . ." She's pleased, like someone proffering a gift. "We could take your little girl for Tuesday and Thursday afternoons."

"No, I'm sorry," I say. "No, that's not really what I'm looking for."

I sit there for a moment longer, staring out at the garden. It's all bare twigs, all dull and dormant, the rosebushes ragged and straggling, a few leaves scattered, sodden, dark as leather, on the lawn. My snowdrops are nearly over, and some primulas I planted have been ravaged by the frost, their leaves all withered and blackened. As I watch, a fox sidles over the grass. It's limping, it must have hurt its leg. Everything seems broken.

I don't know what to do now. Perhaps I could find a babysitter, but how long would that last when she found out what Sylvie was like? Perhaps I could choose a nursery that involved a lot more traveling, but why would they have a place when all these others are full? And how soon would they give up on her? My mind is full of little tracks that don't lead anywhere.

I flick on through the phone book. I realize I am looking for the university number, looking quite casually, just to see if it's there. It's simple to find, and I feel a faint, stupid surprise that this is so easily done, that anyone can ring it.

Watching myself, a little detached, I dial. I don't know the extension I want, and I have to hold for the operator. Vivaldi's *Four Seasons* is playing, the same chunk of it over and over. I can't believe I'm doing this. Sometimes a woman's voice assures me that my call is important. I rehearse what I would ask in my head: *I'd like to speak to Adam Winters. He works in the Psychic*

*Institute* . . . But if I spoke to him, what on earth would I say? I can't imagine it.

The music loops around again, bland, bright, impersonal. "Your call is very important to us." I tell myself this is crazy. I put down the phone.

# 20

It's Lennie's birthday party. The children sit at the kitchen table, assiduously eating, under a sparkly banner that says MANY HAPPY RETURNS, while the mothers stand around and chat with glasses of pinot grigio. The room looks gorgeously festive, all color and shine and glitter, and I think, as I so often do, how fortunate Karen is to live in this beautiful house, with the space to be hospitable. I wonder if Sylvie minds that I don't give a party for her, but when we talk about it, she never seems very concerned.

Sylvie looks happy today. She's sitting next to Lennie, and they're blowing bubbles into their grape juice through curly straws and giggling. It makes an alarming slurping sound, and I briefly wonder whether I ought to tell Sylvie to stop, whether Karen would expect that, but I love to see Sylvie playing about, just like a normal child.

Michaela comes to talk to me. She's wearing a leopard-print cardigan, with half the buttons undone. You can see the deep crack between her breasts.

"Grace, I'd been meaning to tell you, we got the place at Little Acorns. We're so thrilled."

"That's great," I tell her. "I'm sure you'll be happy with it."

"Sylvie still loves it there?" she says.

"Yes, absolutely," I say.

I can't tell her that Sylvie's been asked to leave, can't face it: imagining her expression, shocked, concerned, perhaps a little distanced. Not wanting to talk to me quite so much.

"That garden room is gorgeous," she says. "And Mrs. Pace-Barden seems to have such a lovely touch with the children."

"Yes, doesn't she just?"

I'm worried what else she will ask me, but Fiona is holding the floor, telling the story of how their cat ate their hamster. They thought that the cat had a sock in its mouth, then they heard this terrible sound of crunching, and all that was left was a sad little bit of brown fluff. The children weren't too bothered, but Fiona needed counseling . . . Everyone listens raptly, and I'm glad of this distraction.

I glance at Sylvie and Lennie. They've moved their chairs together so they can drink from the same paper cup. As they suck on their straws, their heads are almost touching. Then Karen brings out homemade biscuits decorated with sweets, and Sylvie feeds Lennie some of the Smarties from her biscuit. I smile as I watch them playing. Sylvie has the solicitous air of a mother feeding her child.

When tea is over, Karen produces the cake. She's made it herself, a Barbie castle with lots of extravagant sugar turrets and towers. She carries it into the living room, places it on the coffee table. The children and mothers follow. Sylvie comes to find me and slips her hand in mine.

"Are you having a good time, sweetheart?" I ask her.

"Yes, Grace. We blew big bubbles."

Her breath has a scent of chocolate, and her lips are stained red from the grape juice. I kiss the top of her head.

We watch as Karen lights the candles. Then Leo turns out the lamps, so only the cake is illumined. We sing the birthday song for Lennie. I always love this moment—the tiny, shimmery flames, the sense of ceremony.

There's a tense, expectant silence as Lennie draws breath to blow her candles out.

Sylvie tugs on my hand and pulls me down toward her. She cups her hand against my head to whisper in my ear, a loud stage whisper, every syllable weighted, bell clear in the stillness.

"They shouldn't sing that, Grace," she says.

"Shh," I say. "Shh."

"They shouldn't, though. She isn't Lennie, Grace." A little impatient with me for not understanding this. "She's not the *real* Lennie," she says.

The silence is a hollowness around us; her words land in the hollowness like a handful of stones. Everyone is looking at us. Lennie frowns at her cake with a look of great concentration. I'm praying she's preoccupied, that she didn't really hear. My face is hot.

"Sylvie, just stop it," I hiss in her ear.

She turns her face away from me. "You're spitting, Grace," she tells me.

Lennie blows, and we all applaud. The room fills up with noise again, and I let it wash over me, grateful. The children crowd together, and Sylvie slips away. Karen takes the cake to the kitchen to cut it into slices.

Leo refills our glasses. He has his genial party smile, and he's wearing a flashing bow tie. He gives me an inquiring look, and I'm worried he's going to make some comment about what Sylvie said.

"So, Grace. I've been meaning to speak to you. Did you find the name of that place that you were looking for the other day? That marvelous stretch of coastline?"

I'm relieved that this is all he wants to say.

"Yes, I think so," I tell him. "I think it's a village in Ireland."

**"And?"**

"A fishing village. It's just a place that Sylvie liked the look of," I say.

The flashing bow tie is disconcerting.

"Oh, come on, Grace, there must be more to it than that." He touches my bare arm teasingly. "Don't leave me in the lurch like this. I'd had such high hopes of you, Gracie. Don't disappoint me now."

"But you know how children can be— when they get an idea into their heads . . ."

Leo frowns slightly. "So why the air of mystery? I mean, I was quite convinced that you and Karen were up to something. You both had a very conspiratorial look. But she wouldn't tell me." He studies my face for a moment. "And you're not going to tell me either, are you?"

I smile at him. I don't know what to say.

He brushes my arm again with one warm finger.

"I'll have to keep working on Karen," he says. "Maybe try the thumbscrews."

He moves on, fills Fiona's glass.

Michaela is talking about her house

renovations. She's making the blinds for her dining room from Hungarian linen cart covers, and her builder is an ex-marine and has the most beautiful abs. "Really. Kind of *architectural*. To die for . . ."

I'm only half listening to her. I feel a vague unease. I glance around the room, and see that Lennie is calling for her mother. Her face flares red, her eyes are bright with tears. Sylvie is beside her, looking quiet and demure. Maybe too quiet. I edge toward them through the crowd of children.

**"Mum!"**

Lennie is shouting, insistent. But Karen is in the kitchen slicing up the cake.

Lennie's voice sharpens.

"*Mum!* She said that thing again. She said it again. *Mum!*"

I rush toward them, but it all happens so quickly. Sylvie says something to Lennie, but I can't make out the words. Lennie spins around and punches her hard in the chest. For a moment Sylvie doesn't react, doesn't cry, nothing. I wait for a scream that doesn't come. Then she bends down, sinks her teeth in Lennie's arm.

I reach Sylvie, pull her away. Lennie

looks in outrage at the exact red mark on her skin. There's an instant of silence as Lennie draws breath, and then she starts to cry—at once appalled and furious. Karen comes in and goes to her.

I hear Karen trying to comfort her. Her voice is rather loud.

"She shouldn't have said that. Sylvie's like that, darling, you know that. She does say horrid things. No, of course she shouldn't have said it . . ."

I pull Sylvie out into the hall. I press her face between my hands, forcing her to look at me. Her skin is so cold against mine.

"Sylvie, you must *never, ever* bite people. Only *babies* bite . . ."

Her face is still and closed. My words feel vacuous, meaningless, as though they just slide off her. I'm doing this for me, really, because the other mothers expect it—bringing her out here, telling her off. I know it won't change anything. I know I can't reach her.

"She hit me, so I bit her," she says. Very calm, a simple statement of fact.

"She hit you because you *upset* her," I say. "If you hadn't done that, then none of this would have happened."

Sylvie doesn't say anything. She squeezes her eyes tight shut so she can't see my face.

"Why did you do it? Why do you say all these things? Why did you upset her like that? And it's her *birthday*, Sylvie."

"She shouldn't have hit me," she says.

I take her back into the living room.

"I'm so sorry," I mouth at Karen. But she isn't really looking in my direction, and perhaps she doesn't notice. She has her arm around Lennie, who is still yelling vigorously while looking with a kind of pride at her very visible wound. You can see the tooth marks. I know Karen must be angry—with me, with Sylvie. Anybody would be.

Fiona comes to speak to me, her face composed in a look of careful empathy.

"Poor you," she says. "It's awful when they do that." She shakes her head a little. Her earrings have a hard, metallic shine. "You feel so awful, don't you? It's so hard to know how to handle it."

I nod, take a mouthful of wine. I tell myself she's just being pleasant, but somehow I feel accused.

"My Alex was a biter," she says. "When

he was smaller, of course—you know, quite a lot younger than Sylvie is now. He once got into this total scrap with a load of other boys—it was like a rugger scrum, really, and he just piled into the melee and chose a nearby hand and bit it. I'll always remember the look on his face when he realized it was his own . . . He was only two then, of course."

"She's never done it before," I say.

Fiona has a skeptical look. I can tell she doesn't believe me.

"I know it probably sounds a bit old-fashioned," she says, "but I always think there's nothing like a really good sharp smack. There are times when nothing else gets through. It can be the only language that they really understand . . ."

I murmur something, move away, go to the kitchen to top up my glass.

I stand for a moment by the window, looking out into the garden. It's almost completely dark now, except in the sky toward the west, where there are still a few tatters of apricot light. The glass reflects the party room, the balloons and brightness and laughing people, but the shapes seem frail, ephemeral, against the gathering dark—as though only the dark has substance.

Karen comes over. I'm so happy to see her, wanting someone to pull me out of this rather mournful mood.

"Grace, I wanted a word," she tells me.

There's a seriousness about her, and this makes me uneasy.

I wait for her. I can tell she's angry. Her lips are thin and hard.

"Grace, look, I don't know how to say this, but to be honest, I don't think this is working really, do you?"

I stare at her. I can't speak. I can't believe she's saying this.

"Sylvie and Lennie," she says. "Their friendship." A crimson flush spreads over her face. She wraps a strand of hair behind her ear. "I'm just not sure that we should carry on. I'm not sure it's any good for them. For either of them, really . . ."

It's like being hit.

"But—they're so fond of each other." My voice is high and shaky and seems to come from somewhere else. "I mean, Sylvie *adores* Lennie. And most of the time they play together so well."

She shakes her head slightly. "I thought

perhaps we should give it a rest," she tells me. "Just have a break for a bit."

I feel a thread of panic.

"So—won't I ever see you?"

There's a little pause, as though this is something she wasn't quite prepared for.

"Maybe you and I could go out for a drink together?" she says.

"But—you know I can't. I don't have a babysitter."

"Yes, I'm being stupid. Don't worry, I'm sure we can work it out," she says, and leaves me.

# 21

We're busy at the flower shop. We're selling tulips and daffodils and baskets of
flimsy narcissi that have an elusive, polleny fragrance—the sort of flowers that
people buy on impulse, especially on a
day like today, with a soft, bright sky and
birdsong and a breeze that smells of growing things. It's good to be so busy, to dis-
tract me from my sense of hurt.

I see Lavinia look at me, her glance
intent, bright, curious—a look that's like a
question. When the shop is briefly empty,
I tell her about Karen.

"Oh, Grace, poor you. How difficult,"

she says. "But friendships between mothers do have their ups and downs. Children can drive a wedge between you."

"Yes. I guess so."

I can't tell her how I really feel, this sense I have that the life I've known—the festivals and birthdays with the other mothers and children, and the coffees in Karen's kitchen, and all the safe, involving rituals of life with a little child—that all this is slipping away from me.

"But I'm sure you two will work it out," says Lavinia. "I mean, you've been friends for ages. You must have a solid connection there."

I feel comforted for a moment. I remind myself it wasn't me that Karen was rejecting, it was all because of Sylvie. But then I remember her face when she said, *I'm just not sure that we should carry on*. That hard, closed look.

In the afternoon I have my dental appointment. My tooth is hurting again, and I know it will need to come out. I leave for the dentist at half past two. The early brightness has clouded over, and now the sky has a smeared look, like a dirty windowpane. There isn't much traffic, and I get there early. I sit beside the fish tank in the antiseptic smell and riffle through the magazines, looking for the *Twickenham Post* that had the article. It isn't there, of course. They wouldn't keep out-of-date newspapers. I feel a relief that's tinged with disappointment.

The dentist gives me a lot of anesthetic, and chats to me as it starts to take effect. He has a litany of complaints—the state of public transport, the rubbish in the streets. Everything is deteriorating. His voice is mournful, but his eyes shine. He relishes this kind of conversation. I reply with increasing difficulty.

Then he takes an implement that looks like a pair of pliers and starts to tug at my tooth. I have to open my mouth very wide—the tooth is right at the back. I feel he's going to split me, that my mouth won't stretch so far. He pulls hard. I can hear his strenuous breathing. Nothing happens.

He shakes his head.

"Your tooth doesn't want to leave you," he says.

He takes a different implement. I don't feel anything, I'm totally anesthetized, but I hear a sound of splintering and cracking

in my mouth. He pulls out a bit of my
tooth—I can see it in his pliers, a bloody,
mangled thing—and then another and
another. He puts them in a paper dish. I
think briefly how, in places where magic
is practiced, people can put a spell on
you if they have a piece of your body—a
hair, a nail, a piece of broken tooth. My
mouth is full of blood, which has a harsh
taste, like iron.

"So what are your plans for the rest of
the day, Ms. Reynolds?"

I rinse with the green antiseptic, blood-
ying the swirl of water in the small white
sink.

"Just going back to work," I say.

"You really ought to take some time off,
put your feet up," he says.

"I'll be all right," I tell him.

"Well, don't overdo it, okay? An extraction can be quite a shock to the system."

I assure him I won't overdo it, and I go
to pay.

"And how's your little one?" asks the
receptionist.

I have a startling, random impulse to
burst into tears all over her and tell her all
my troubles. I push the urge away.

"Oh, Sylvie's fine," I tell her, as I always do.

When I get to my car, I realize that just as the dentist predicted, I have a shaken feeling. The jab is wearing off already, leaving an ache in my jaw, a presaging of pain. I glance at myself in the rearview mirror. I look appalling. My lips have a lining of vampirish blood red, and the anesthetic has changed the shape of my face. My lips at the left of my mouth don't quite meet, and one of my eyelids is sagging. It's how I will look when I'm old.

I don't feel able to drive yet. I turn on the radio, waiting to feel stronger. I sit and listen to Dido and watch the pavements and all the people who pass. A woman with her hair scraped back who's pushing a child in a buggy: she has violet smudges of tiredness under her eyes. A young man talking on his cell phone. I have the window open an inch, I hear him as he passes, hear the threat in his voice. "However you want to look at it, however you want to see it from your point of view, that's fine by me. All right? *All right?*" An elderly woman with toothless gums and lots of lavish lipstick, and two sallow boys in hoodies who have a hungry, restless air and nothing much to do.

And then I see them walking briskly along the opposite pavement: Claudia, Charlie, Maud. *Shit*. I slither down in my seat so I'm completely hidden.

The children are in school uniform, their crisp gray blazers edged with dark green braid. I remember that their school is just around the corner. Claudia's BMW is parked almost level with me on the other side of the road. As I watch, they come to their car, and she opens the trunk and they dump their things inside—the satchels, sports bags, lacrosse stick. Maud gives Charlie a playful punch, and he trips and grabs at her blazer; their faces fizz with laughter. I'm close enough to see them clearly, their gestures and expressions. There's so much of Dominic in them. Maud has his easy assurance and his coloring; Charlie, like Sylvie, has his candid smile. Claudia turns to face them both. She's scolding them, annoyance pulsing over her face. She has a tight, sleek calf-length skirt and high-heeled reptile-skin shoes.

I stare at her over the steering wheel, feeling the complicated emotions she always stirs up in me. I think how, when I was with him, I'd sometimes smell her perfume on him—a woman's scent, distinct from his cologne, a spring smell, fresh as bluebells, a scent I might have chosen. Sometimes I wonder if maybe we're rather similar, for once she was in love with him, and maybe she loved him for the things I do—his certainty, the solid feel of his body. All the old envy surges through me, envy of that whole silken texture of her life, and of all the things she can give her children that Sylvie will never have—the expensive schools with harpsichord lessons and velvet playing fields. I would like to be her, to have all these things, and to lie every night with Dominic beside me.

They get in the car, and Claudia drives away. I sit up in my seat again, I fold my arms on the steering wheel and rest my head on my arms. I wish I hadn't seen her. It feels unlucky, today of all days, with my whole life unraveling. I feel that I've been cursed, as though this is deliberate, planned, and someone has stolen my broken tooth and is weaving a dark enchantment to entrap me. My jealousy sears through me, threatens to overwhelm me.

I don't know how long I sit there held in its hot, unrelenting grip. It might be just a few moments, it might be a very long time. I don't know.

It's the smallest thing that moves me on—the sun coming out from behind a cloud and shining through the windshield, its warmth falling full on my face. I'm grateful for the sudden heat: I raise my face to the sun. And the words that form inside me seem to come from nowhere—or not from within me, anyway. They whisper themselves through me, like a prayer. *Help me.* I murmur the words to myself, then speak them aloud in the quiet of my car, as though I am speaking to someone. Knowing I can't stay here in this bitter, comfortless place, always looking behind me, longing for what I can't have, for what I have no right to, wanting the past given back to me. *Please please help me.*

Perhaps it's just a need to take action, any action, to imprint my will on the hostile pattern of things. But almost without thinking, I find myself scrabbling in my bag for my phone.

"Lavinia. I'm feeling ghastly. I think I'll have to go to bed. I'm so sorry."

"Of course, Grace. Was it awful?"

"Pretty much."

"You take care of yourself, now. You just hunker down and watch some mindless television. Dentists are *evil*. Don't get me on the subject . . ."

I start up the car, do a three-point turn in the road, crashing the gears and holding up the traffic. A lorry driver rages that I am a stupid fucking cow. I ignore him. There's a small, sane, tentative voice inside me that murmurs that I'm behaving oddly and really not myself at all, that I'm disinhibited after the shock of the extraction and perhaps I shouldn't go rushing into anything. I pay the voice no attention. I drive fast, up the hill, away from home.

# 22

There isn't anywhere to park. Whenever I think I've found a space, it seems to be reserved for some important person—a head of faculty or vice-chancellor or some-body. There are warnings that cars illicitly parked will be booted and taken away. Eventually I find a corner behind some dustbins that seems to have been forgot-ten.

I cross a lawn where there are cherry trees, white with a froth of blossom, and go in through a side door. A notice says that all visitors must report to reception. I ignore it. I come to a foyer where there are signs to Psychology, and follow the signs down an echoey long corridor that has a sharp, sore-throat smell of Dettol. There are bulletin boards crammed with notices: the pieces of paper flap in the drafts like waving hands, demanding your attention. Students pass in casual groups—men in leather jackets, languorous girls in denim who keep flicking back their hair. No one even glances in my direction. Through the glass in a door I can see a class in progress—just like school, with rows of desks and a whiteboard, except that all the students listen with absolute attention and the tutor has a piercing in her nose.

The corridor ends at a T intersection with no signpost. I turn left and keep going, but I know I'm lost now. I must have missed an arrow. There are no more signs to Psychology. I feel as though I'm trespassing, stalking along this labyrinth of corridors. A woman walks toward me. She's a little too old for a student, perhaps she is a lecturer. She has sprayed-on jeans and dirty-blond hair in casual, rumpled curls. She gives me a questioning look, and I'm worried that she will ask me what I'm doing. I avoid her gaze. I just keep moving on.

Then, when I've given up hope, I come to glass swing doors, and over them it says DEPARTMENT OF PSYCHOLOGY. I go through.

There's a receptionist at a desk. She's Mediterranean-looking, with smudgy dark kohl around her eyes, and she's talking on the telephone with an air of great animation. Beside her there's a line of chairs against a wall, some filing cabinets, and a washbasin with a paper towel dispenser.

I look around. I'm wondering where to go now. Then, just to my right, I see a door with Adam Winters's name. I go to the door and knock, not thinking about it, just doing it. Nobody answers.

"Excuse me?" The receptionist's voice is shrill. "Can I help you?"

I turn to her.

"I need to see Adam Winters."

My mouth is stiff from the anesthetic. I have to force out the words.

"Okay." She shuffles through the papers on her desk. "When's your appointment for?"

"I don't have an appointment. I just thought I'd drop in."

As I talk, I cover my face with my hand. I know I must look strange.

"I'm afraid you can't see Dr. Winters without an appointment," she says.

"Well, perhaps he could give me an appointment when I see him."

"No, it doesn't work like that."

The room lurches. I'm worried I'll faint. I sit on one of the chairs.

She has large, moist eyes that give her the look of a troubled, solemn child.

"I need to see him," I say again. "I want to ask him about my daughter. I mean, I won't know if I need an appointment till we've talked."

She purses her lips. "I need to see your security badge," she says.

"I'm sorry. I don't have one. They didn't give me one."

"Then you really shouldn't be here," she says. "Everyone has to wear one. They're very strict about it. I'm afraid I'm going to have to ask you to leave."

"Don't worry," I say. "I can just wait here. I promise I won't be a nuisance."

But she turns, speaks into her phone.

Almost immediately, two security men come marching through the doors. They have gray uniforms and severe expressions and are very broad and solid. They stand to either side of me, and one of them places a heavy hand on my arm.

"Madam, we want you to come with us," he tells me.

There's nothing I can do. I get up.

There are voices from the corridor—two men talking urgently. I think they're disagreeing, but I can't make out the words. Then the swing doors burst apart as the first man backs into the foyer, using his shoulder to push them, with a polystyrene cup of coffee in either hand. You can tell at once this isn't going to work. He stops abruptly, seeing the security men and me, and the door swings shut and catches his wrist. The coffee spills all over his arm and his sleeve.

**"Fuck."**

It's odd to see him in color. He's scruffier than he looked in the photo, his shirtsleeves rolled, his shirt hanging out, a shadowing of stubble on his chin. He puts both coffees down on a filing cabinet, pulls some paper towels out of the dispenser. The other man hooks the door back. He's wearing a sharply cut blazer, and he looks with distaste at the mess.

I turn to the first man.

"Dr. Winters?" I say.

He turns toward me, rapidly taking me in, looking from me to the security guards and back again. His eyes widen.

"I want to see you about my daughter," I tell him.

He's mechanically wiping his wrist with the towel, his eyes never leaving my face. There's an extravagant smell of spilt coffee.

"You want to see *me*?" he says.

"Yes."

"Goodness." He has a bemused look.

The man in the blazer raises one eyebrow slightly. "It's all right for some," he says. "Perhaps I should change my specialty." He goes into one of the offices.

Adam Winters turns to the security guards. "It's okay," he says. "She's with me."

They just stand there.

"You go. Really. Trust me," he tells them. "Everything's okay."

They leave reluctantly, glancing over their shoulders as though I am some wild thing.

He chucks the paper towel vaguely in

the direction of the wastebin, then puts down one of the coffees on the receptionist's desk.

"Carla, there you go," he says. "I'll be in my office with Ms.—"

He turns to me, raises a questioning eyebrow.

"Reynolds," I tell him. "Grace Reynolds."

"I'll be with Ms. Reynolds," he says. "If I press the panic button, come right in."

She frowns. "But you don't have a panic button."

"True." He has a sudden, crooked grin. "Well, fingers crossed, then."

He makes a little gesture with his head, beckoning me to follow him.

I can see why the *Twickenham Post* reporter called his office prosaic. It's exuberantly untidy, with papers scattered everywhere, and box files with unreadable labels scrawled along their spines. He clears some books from a chair for me. I sit and instantly cover the side of my face with my hand.

"You look terrible," he says. "The dentist?"

I nod.

"It's my intuitive powers," he says. "That and the massive swelling. Bloody hell. What on earth did they do to you?"

"I had an extraction," I say.

"Poor thing," he says.

He stands behind his desk, sipping his coffee, his eyes on me. I notice his long, slender fingers curved around the cup.

"You need a drink," he says. "But nothing hot, I imagine."

He opens a drawer of his desk, pulls out a bottle of Coke. There's a restlessness in the way he moves and his sudden, rather awkward gestures. I wonder whether he runs, whether he's one of those men who need to be constantly active, to still some inner demon. There are mugs on his windowsill. He chooses a mug, peers into it with a doubtful frown, then fills it.

"Thank you, Dr. Winters," I say.

"Call me Adam," he says.

I drink gratefully. The sugar kick helps, I don't feel quite so strange.

I look around at his office. There's so little to make it personal—no potted plants or posters. The only picture is a single photo on his desk. It looks like him, but much younger—a boy in grubby overalls who's working on a car. Through the window I can see the lawns and cherry trees.

He watches me, pushes his hand through his brown, disorganized hair. It makes his hair stick up, gives him a startled look.

"Why did you want to see me?" he says.

"I have a little girl. Sylvie. She's difficult. She sometimes says weird things . . . I read that article about you."

He nods, but doesn't say anything, waiting for me to go on.

"And my daughter is rather like the child in the article. And I thought—could she be remembering something? I mean, d'you think that's possible? I'd never really heard of it before. And I wanted to ask you about her . . ."

He pulls the chair from behind his desk and sits. He moves his hands apart in a little gesture of acceptance or encouragement. Where his sleeves are rolled up, I can see the fine dark hairs on his arms.

"Okay. So talk to me."

I tell him. About Sylvie's bad nights, and her fear of water, and always drawing the same picture, and saying Lennie isn't really Lennie, and the place she seems to recognize. It all pours out. I must have been rehearsing it even as I was coming here, talking to him in my head although we hadn't yet met.

He interrupts just once.

"The place in the picture," he says. "D'you have any idea where it is?"

"Yes. I found it. It's in Ireland. It's called Coldharbour."

He nods. He looks excited. His eyes are suddenly wide.

"Well done. That's great. That's really useful," he says.

I feel pleased with myself for finding it.

I pause for a moment, sipping my drink. The anesthetic is fading. My mouth hurts with a blunt, dulled pain.

"Grace, are you on your own?" he says then. "You haven't mentioned a partner."

"Yes, I'm a single parent."

"It must be hard for you, having to handle all of this on your own."

So I tell him about Mrs. Pace-Barden and losing the nursery place and my panic about our future—which wasn't rehearsed, which I hadn't intended to say. He leans toward me, his elbows on his

knees. He has an intent look. All the time
I'm talking, he doesn't touch his drink.

When I've finished, he sits there looking at me and pushing his hand through
his hair.

"So what do you think?" I ask him.
"Could you help us?"

He takes a sip of his coffee then, his
long, thin fingers wrapped around the cup.
You can hear the squeak of polystyrene.

"What we try to do here," he tells me,
"is to investigate the things that can't be
explained. To examine the paranormal
scientifically."

"But how could you do that?" I ask him.
"With the things that Sylvie says?"

"You'd investigate the story," he says.
"You'd want to be very objective. You'd
be checking for evidence of contamination. Could she have got her story from
any other source? Is it something she's
seen in a book or watched on television?"

"It isn't," I tell him.

"It isn't anything she's seen?"

"No. Well, it isn't a place that she's
been, for a start. She's never been away
from me. And I've never been to Ireland."

"What about a book, perhaps?"

"I don't see how," I tell him. "Certainly not at home. And they've only got kids' books at the nursery. TV I'm not so sure about. To be honest, I don't always check what she's watching. I just sit her down in front of it if I've got a lot to do."

"Okay. So television's possible, but it seems unlikely."

"So what would you do, then?" I say. "If there's no contamination?"

He's quiet for a moment.

I'm full of hope—that there's some therapy he can offer, helping her let go of all these weird obsessions she has. Or maybe he uses hypnosis, like I read about in that article. I wonder how I'd feel about that—decide I'd be willing to try it, that really I'd let him try anything that might make her a happier child.

He puts his coffee cup down, leans a little toward me.

"If it seemed convincing," he tells me, "you might want to take the child there."

I stare at him. Everything shifts around me. I feel a chill on my skin.

"You mean, *actually* take them *back* to the place they seem to remember?"

I can't believe this. I feel a sense of shock, of outrage even.

"Yes," he says.

I think of the way Sylvie looks at her picture, of all the yearning in her face, of how she'll sometimes sleep with it hidden under her pillow.

"But wouldn't that just make the whole thing worse? It would, I'm sure it would."

"I can see that's how it might seem. But it often helps these children. As though when they've gone back there, they can start to let go and forget. Which it seems is what we're meant to do—to forget . . ."

"I just don't get it," I tell him. I can hear all the protest in my voice. "How could that possibly help if you want them to let go of it? Making it so real to them?"

"The evidence is that it works," he says. "There are documented cases where it's really helped the child."

I find I am shaking my head.

I can't do this, I think. It would be so wrong for Sylvie. If water play at nursery is more than she can handle, how would she cope with such a thing? I feel myself withdrawing from him. He doesn't understand. He doesn't know how bad it is.

How could he? I don't know why I came here. I don't belong in this place, with this clever, overeager man with all his unnerving theories. It's too strange for me.

"I just don't think that approach would be right for Sylvie," I say. "I can't imagine it."

"No, I can see that," he says.

There are little sharp lines between his brows, and I feel I've disappointed him. Maybe I've been too emphatic. There's a fragile feeling between us, as though something has been broken.

"Well, then." I button up my coat.

He looks across at me, frowning slightly. He rubs his hand over his face.

"Look—I could offer her some sessions here. If you think that might be helpful."

Earlier I'd have said yes at once, but now I'm not so sure.

"What would you do if we came?"

"I'd want to start by checking out her general cognitive functioning."

"You mean, see if she's normal?"

He smiles. "Yes. More or less. Then I'd talk to her about what she remembers—about the things she tells you. These children usually have quite fragmentary memories. They might talk about certain places, maybe certain people. You're in luck if they remember a name, but mostly you find they don't. So I'd want to see what she says, perhaps ask her to do a drawing . . ."

"I don't know," I say.

"You could just come in for a couple of sessions—see how you both felt," he says.

I don't say anything.

"And you wouldn't have to pay, of course," he tells me. "We never charge for seeing people here."

He's trying to sound casual, but I hear the urgency in his voice. I can tell how much he wants to do this.

"She can be very reserved," I tell him. "She might not say a thing."

"That's okay," he tells me. "Really."

He's leaning toward me, his eyes on my face. His intensity makes me unsure. I feel myself pull back from him.

I sit there for a moment, not knowing what I should do. I think of Lennie's party, of how I stood alone by the window, looking out into the darkness. I remember the things that Karen said, and how distanced I felt from the other mothers, that sense I had of the life I knew slipping away.

"I guess we could come in for just a couple of sessions," I say slowly.

"That's fantastic," he says.

He asks for my contact details. I give him both numbers, my cell phone and my work.

"Jonah and the Whale," he says, rolling the name around his mouth as though it tastes good.

"It's just a flower shop," I tell him.

He has this way of looking at me for just a little too long.

"I like that—you working in a flower shop."

I feel my face go hot. I'm trying to decide whether this is a compliment.

Our conversation is over. I pick up my bag. But there's something I'm longing to ask him.

"Adam." My voice is tentative, uncertain. "What do you think? Do you think it could be true? That she could be remembering a previous life?"

He puts down his pen. His face is hard to read.

"I once read that in ancient Greece a skeptic was someone who kept all possibilities open. Who absolutely refused to come to a conclusion. That appealed to me. So let's say I'm a skeptic . . ."

It seems a pat answer. People have asked him this too many times before.

"But you must have an opinion, surely."

"I can tell you what I think about a particular case," he tells me. "What the evidence points to. But even if every case you investigate seems to be a fraud, you can't close off the possibility that some future case could convince you—"

"So—if you're not sure you believe in these things, why do you do what you do?"

He smiles his crooked smile and thinks about this for a moment. He smiles a lot, but I feel there's something about him, a kind of sadness, as though he hurts too easily.

"Good question," he says. "There could be lots of reasons. There's a woman I'm in touch with in a faculty in Scotland. She had an out-of-body experience after taking magic mushrooms. She wanted to understand it . . ."

We both know he's evaded my question. I'm curious, but I don't press it.

He's riffling through his papers. "So when can you come in?"

"I work all week. I'm off on Saturdays," I tell him.

"We'll make it a Saturday, then."

"Really, is that okay?"

"My girlfriend's quite long-suffering," he says.

I know he's telling me this for a reason, wanting to make it clear. Stupidly, I feel a flicker of disappointment.

"Does she work here too?" I say.

He nods. "She's a biophysicist," he tells me.

I imagine her—tight jeans and artfully casual hair, like the woman I saw in the corridor: clever, privileged, doing work that's rigorous and valued. I think of my own life, of the only things I'm good at— potting up lobelias, making patchwork angels out of scraps of silk.

He's hunting in his in-box.

"How does this happen? I have all these degrees, and I still keep losing my diary . . ."

But he finds it, and the Saturday after next will suit him. He writes the date on a card for me and adds his cell phone number.

I pick up my bag. I'm about to leave.

His eyes are on me. His face is dark with thought.

"It's tough, isn't it, Grace?" he says.

There's such warmth in his voice, and I find I have started to cry.

He doesn't seem embarrassed. He gives me some tissues and sits there waiting for me.

I scrub at my eyes. Mascara comes off on the tissue, and a slick of bright blood from my mouth. I can't imagine how I must look, my smudged, distorted face.

"I'm sorry," I tell him.

He's leaning toward me in that intent way he has.

"Grace, what's making you cry?"

"It's like—she's slipping away from me." I can't express it. I'm struggling toward the words. "Sometimes when she looks at me, it's like she doesn't see me, doesn't recognize me. She has this closed look . . . She's my daughter—I mean, I gave birth to her, for God's sake—but in some weird way I feel she isn't really my child." I blow my nose. "Shit. I'm sorry."

"And you don't know what to believe."

"No."

"Grace. I can't guarantee I'll solve that one for you—well, for either of us. In fact, I can't guarantee anything. I wish I could, but I can't."

"Of course not. I know that."

I get up. I suddenly feel so embarrassed that I cried like that.

"I'll see you out," he says.

He grins at Carla as we pass her desk.

"Still in one piece," he tells her.

He stops at the swing doors to say goodbye, and reaches out and puts his hand on my sleeve, lightly, just for a second or two.

I walk off through the labyrinth of corridors, thinking about him, this urgent, messy, eager man with the strange preoccupations and the sadness under his smile. Oh my God, what have I done?

# 23

On Saturday evening Karen comes around to my flat with a bottle of cabernet sauvignon.

I'm so happy to see her. But it feels a little awkward between us. There's something new about her, something remote, reserved, as though she's still angry with me.

I tell her everything that's happened—about seeing Dominic, which appalls her, as I knew it would; about losing the place at the nursery.

"Jesus, Grace," she says. "How on earth will you manage?"

"I don't know," I tell her.

She smooths her hair back. She looks somehow out of place on my sofa, in her sleek black cashmere clothes, with her handbag of rich dark leather with all its elaborate pockets and zips. When Karen comes here, I always notice how tatty everything is—my flimsy furniture, my chipped paintwork. I have my gas fire turned up full, but these walls hold a chill that never seems to thaw, and I worry that it's too cold for her.

"You've got to get this sorted, Grace," she tells me. "You've *got* to."

But her voice sounds rather weary. She doesn't think I will.

"I'm trying," I tell her. "We're going to see a new person, Sylvie and me."

I keep my voice quite low. I worry Sylvie could hear our conversation—the walls of our flat are so thin. But maybe Sylvie is fast asleep. There's no sound at all from her room.

"You've found a better psychiatrist?" says Karen hopefully. "I was going to say you should do that—you have a right to a second opinion, of course. You obviously didn't like that doctor you saw . . ."

"It's not another doctor." I take a gulp of wine. I know I'm drinking too fast. "It's someone at the university, in the psychology faculty." I breathe in deeply, not knowing quite how to go on. "I mean, I'm not sure about it, but I thought it was worth a shot."

"Okay," she says warily. There's a question in her gaze.

"It's that guy I read about—the one who investigates the paranormal—"

"*No*, Grace." Her voice has a sharp edge.

"It's not like you think—really. It's all aboveboard. You know, kind of academic. I'm not sure he really believes it all—he just does the research."

Karen stares at me. "Grace. How can some weird ghost-busting creep possibly be *aboveboard*? How can this possibly help Sylvie?"

"He wants to try and understand her—to understand what's going on."

"And how does he propose to do that, exactly?"

"Well, you know. Talk to her, do some tests. Sometimes with these cases—I mean, I don't know what I think about this—but they'd want to take the child back there, to the place they seem to remember."

Her mouth thins. "I think that's a simply appalling idea," she tells me briskly. "He's using you, Grace. He just wants you for his research. Academics are like that."

"Well, some of them, maybe," I say.

"No, trust me, Grace. It's not what Sylvie needs. What Sylvie needs is a therapist. Someone to help her let go of that stuff, not just get deeper in."

"But nothing can make her let go of it. I've tried to ignore it, not pay attention. Nothing makes any difference. I thought I could give this a go—perhaps just for a couple of sessions. Maybe there's something in it. I mean, how much do we really know—about life and death and everything?" I can feel myself becoming expansive because of the cabernet sauvignon. "We don't really understand how the world works, do we? Not really. How could we? Our minds are just so limited . . ."

Karen leans toward me, fixing me with her anxious, troubled gaze.

"Grace." Her voice is gentle. "She said she had a *dragon*."

Afterward, I walk her out to her car. I'm so used to living here now, but I know that these streets must seem threatening to her. There's a nail-paring moon, and a thin glaze of ice on the puddles. The prostitutes are standing on the corner, smoking and talking softly. One of them cups her hands together to light her cigarette, and the burning tip flares briefly like a red and winking eye. An elderly woman who's sleeping rough has settled down for the night in the alley next to Kwik Save, with all her bulging shopping bags beside her. She's wrapped in a filthy pink eiderdown, and I feel so sorry for her, to think how cold she will be. I wonder what Karen makes of all this.

"It was good to see you," I tell her. "We must do this again soon."

"Yes, we must," she says. "Of course."

She drives off a little too rapidly.

I open the door of Sylvie's room, moving very slowly, trying not to click the latch, wanting to check that she's still sleeping.

But she isn't asleep. She's sitting up in her bed, and she's taken the picture down from the wardrobe and has it in her hand. She looks up at me as I come in.

"Where's Lennie, Grace?" she says.

Her face is puzzled, perplexed. The dim light of her bedside lamp seems to emphasize all shadows. There are patches dark as bruises underneath her eyes.

She must have heard Karen's voice. She must have wondered why Lennie didn't come too. I don't want to tell her the truth, don't want her knowing what Karen said—not now, not ever.

"I'm sure that Lennie's fast asleep," I tell her brightly. "And so should you be."

I go to tuck her in.

She holds the picture out toward me. "It's beautiful, isn't it, Grace?"

"Yes, it's a beautiful place."

"Coldharbour," she says. Setting the word so carefully down between us, like some precious thing.

"Yes. Coldharbour. Shall I stick it back on your wardrobe?"

"No," she tells me.

She slips the picture under her pillow and slides down into her bed.

"I had a little white house when I lived in Coldharbour, Grace."

Her voice is calm and measured.

It's so chilly in her bedroom. I pull my cardigan close around me.

"What was it like, your house?" I say.

"It was nicer than this house," she says.

I'm blurred and vague from the wine. It dulls the hurt a little.

"Can you tell me more about it?"

"You could see the sea from my house." Her voice has a yawn behind it, she's on the edge of sleep now.

"Anything else you can tell me, sweetheart? I mean, I've never been there, I don't know anything about it . . ."

"Don't you?" she says.

She pulls her duvet up to her chin. Her face smudges and softens with sleep.

"No, sweetheart."

She yawns widely.

"There were fishing boats on the sea," she says.

I think of the picture and know what Karen would say. *For God's sake, Grace, the boats are there in the photograph . . .*

"I liked to look at the boats," she says. "Before."

She falls asleep abruptly, like a door closing.

## 24

Lavinia brings in a pair of pigeons she's picked up in a salvage yard. They're cast in iron, battered but pretty, painted in cream with a speckling of rust showing through. The woman in the travel agent's certainly wouldn't like them. We put them out on the pavement, next to a statue of Ganesh that Lavinia found in Rajasthan and our rickety wrought-iron table that today holds just white flowers—orchids and snowdrops and crocuses. The orchids look like open mouths.

"So, Grace—how's it going with Sylvie?"

I still haven't managed to say that we have lost the nursery place. I decide I will wait until after our session with Adam Winters next Saturday. Then maybe it will all be different.

I tell her about him. She listens intently, bright-eyed.

"Wow, Gracie," she says when I've finished. "How utterly intriguing. Did he tell you how he'd approach her?"

"He said he'd talk to her about it, perhaps get her to do a drawing . . ."

She nods. She picks a dead leaf from a plant. You can see the cinnamon staining on the insides of her fingers.

"I'd been wondering, Grace," she says then. "Have you ever done that yourself— you know, asked her directly about all this?"

"Well, sometimes. Kind of."

"Like—have you ever asked her why she never calls you Mum?"

I feel how damp my gloves are. I peel them off. I shall put them to dry on the hot pipes. The chill from my hands spreads through my body.

"If you ask her why she does things, she can't really tell you," I say.

"I just thought it might be interesting—to see what she would say to that. To hear it from her point of view."

"Yes. Maybe I should try it."

I don't tell her the real reason. That I'm scared of what might happen. Afraid that Sylvie would fix me with her cool blue gaze, a little frown marked on her forehead, and say, *But you* aren't *Mum. Not really.* Very calm and matter-of-fact. *You aren't* my *mum, Grace.* I know I couldn't bear it if she did that.

## 25

There's a guard who is reading the *Sun* at reception, who gives us our security badges. He's one of the men who tried to throw me out before. I'm embarrassed, but he doesn't seem to realize, perhaps because I have Sylvie with me. Snatches of music drift toward us down the corridors—a band, a woman singing. On Saturdays there are music classes here. But mostly the place is empty, and it all has an echoey bleakness.

We knock, but there's no answer, so we sit by Adam's door.

The man I saw before comes out of the

door next to Adam's. He's wearing his blazer again, and he has a precise, clean, organized look. He glances at us, stops and turns.

"You're Adam's clients, aren't you?"

"Yes," I say. "Well, I came to see him before. I'm not sure we're *clients* exactly . . ."

"He told me a bit about it. So everything's going okay?"

"Yes. Thanks."

He flicks some invisible lint from his sleeve.

"He has his own way of doing things, Adam Winters," he says. There's a hint of disapproval in his voice.

"Yes, I can see that," I say.

"Adam can be very—how to put this?— *enthusiastic*," he says. He straightens the cuffs of his shirt. His cuff links glitter. "Don't you find that?"

I don't know quite how to respond to this.

"I guess I know what you mean," I say vaguely.

"You need to be a little wary," he tells me. "Some of the stuff he's into is really very left field. I wouldn't want to think of you getting carried away . . ." His tone is slightly suggestive, or maybe I'm imagining that. "Well, the best of luck with it anyway. I'll see you around, perhaps."

He walks briskly off down the corridor.

Adam comes in through the doors. He's crumpled and smiling and seems so pleased to see us.

He says hello to Sylvie and takes us into his room. Today it's neat and orderly. He's put a low child's table in the middle of the floor, with a box of puzzles laid out on it. The air in the building is thick and hot, and he's opened the window an inch or two. A slight breeze stirs some papers in a wire tray on the sill.

"We met one of your colleagues," I tell him.

"Simon? Guy in a blazer?"

"How did you know?"

"Only Simon works on Saturdays."

"He doesn't share your interests, I gather."

"Simon's an expert on cognition. His big thing's the decay of long-term memory," he tells me.

"Oh."

"I'm guessing he wasn't exactly singing my praises," he says.

"No. Not really."

He has a rueful smile.

"He thinks I've lost it," he says. "And he's my boss, so it's really rather unfortunate." He draws up chairs, a child's chair at the table and one behind for me. "Psychologists are all so sensible, when the world's so *wild*. I mean, live a little, for Chrissake. You can't box everything up."

Sometimes he makes me uneasy. He's so emphatic, leaning forward slightly, like he's listening out for something, his voice rather urgent, running his hand through his hair. As though he could do anything.

He shows Sylvie to the table.

"Now, Sylvie, what we're doing today—I've got some puzzles for you. And Grace, you could sit behind us." He gestures me to my chair.

He sits at the table next to Sylvie, and takes out wooden blocks and builds them into a bridge, and asks her to make a shape that's just the same. She nibbles her lip; she has a little frown of concentration. He makes a note on a check sheet.

Then he takes a book, and she has to name some images—a feather, scissors, a fish. I watch his slender fingers moving over the page and I see that his nails are bitten. The last test is an inset tray with a car, a tree, two children. She has to fit the cutouts into the holes.

"Okay, we've finished the puzzles. Thank you, Sylvie," he says.

He leaves the inset tray where it is. She takes the cutout figures and spreads them out in front of her, and chooses the car and pushes it around on the desk. She's humming softly to herself.

He turns to me. "D'you have the picture?" he says.

I give it to him.

She's playing with the car still, but her eyes are fixed on him. She has a quiet, expectant look.

"Sylvie, there's something I'd really like to talk about," he tells her.

She nods. "My picture," she says.

"Yes. Grace says you keep it by your bed."

"Yes."

"You like this picture, Sylvie?"

"Yes."

He holds it out in front of them.

When she glances at the picture, she has a slight, pleased smile.

"Can you tell me why you like it?" he says.

She looks briefly back at me, as though needing some kind of permission. I nod.

"That's where I lived," she tells him. Her voice is small but matter-of-fact.

I glance at Adam. I wonder if he feels what I feel, the cold spreading over my skin.

"Could you talk to me about it, Sylvie?" There's a thread of eagerness in his voice. "Anything you remember."

I'm acutely aware of the words he uses—the way he says "remember." I don't know if that means that he believes her, or if he's just seeking to put her at ease by entering into her world.

"Anything at all. Whatever you can tell me," he says.

It's still in the room, except for the air that comes through the half-open window and riffles through the papers in the wire tray like a hand. It's so still I can hear my heart thudding.

Her eyes are on him, her cool, clear, wintry gaze.

"I liked it there," she says. "I don't like it here."

There's that little shock of hurt I always feel.

"Who lived there with you, Sylvie?" he says.

I don't breathe.

For a moment she doesn't say anything. It's like she didn't hear. She pushes the car around the table, threading it with precision between the bricks and other cutouts. She isn't looking at him.

"People live with their family," she says then. Her voice is cool, remote, a little accusing. "Haven't you got a family?"

"Yes, I have a family," he says.

There's a catch in his voice. I glance at him. A shadow crosses his face. I see the sadness in him that I noticed when we first met.

"Can you tell me who was in your family, Sylvie?" he asks.

She doesn't say anything.

"Maybe what their names were?" he says.

I feel he's pushing too hard. Her face is blank, as though the question has no meaning for her.

"Perhaps you could draw them for me," he says.

He puts out paper and crayons for her.

"That would be really great, if you could draw them," he says. "Show me and Grace what they looked like . . ."

She picks up a crayon. She starts to draw. I watch, intensely curious. But it's such a routine, perfunctory drawing—the standard stick figures she's learned to do, a mother and a father with two children in between them, hands touching or clasped together. It's the sort of thing that any child might draw. There's nothing partic-ular about the figures, nothing to distin-guish them from any other family. I think, It's just like Karen said. She's envisaging a different life in which she has a father and perhaps a brother or sister: a life in which her family is complete. The thought depresses me.

"Thank you, Sylvie," says Adam. "So this is the family you remember?"

Sylvie doesn't respond. She takes

another crayon, and all around the figures she draws a border of blue.

"I can see two children in your picture," says Adam.

She nods slightly.

"I'm wondering if these children are boys or girls," he says.

She doesn't reply, intent on finishing her border. The end of the line doesn't meet the beginning. She shades across the gap.

"So which is it, Sylvie?" he asks her.

He's pressing her. I wish he wouldn't. There's a hint of urgency in his voice. I know that she'll withdraw from him. Why can't he see that? I think. Why can't he be more sensitive to her?

"Boys or girls or one of each?" he asks her.

She puts her crayon down on the table. It makes an exact little click. It's very still in Adam's room. Distant sounds scrape at the edges of the stillness—the shrill of a siren, a far-off flute, its bright notes broken and scattering. You can feel the empty quiet of the corridors all around.

"Two peas in a pod," she says.

It's an oddly old-fashioned expression. I wonder where she's heard it, perhaps from Mrs. Pace-Barden.

Adam frowns, perplexed.

"They look alike, these two? The children in your drawing?"

"Yes. Two peas in a pod." She's slightly impatient with him.

She gets up, takes the car from the puzzle, and goes to stand by the window. She has her back toward him. She moves the car through the squares of sun that fall across the sill. In the bleached, thin light, her hair is pale as lint. I can see the tension in her—the pursed lips, her fingers white and stiff where they're gripping the car. There's a little troubled frown on her face. She's shut herself away, and now he won't be able to reach her.

I suddenly think, This is all wrong, this isn't what we should be doing, keeping her fixed on her obsessions rather than moving her on. Karen is right—this won't help Sylvie. I feel a rush of guilt that I have let this happen—all this pressure, all these questions. I can't trust Adam not to hurt her. I terribly want him to stop.

"Adam. I think we should leave it there."
My voice is too loud for the quiet room.

He looks up at me, surprised by my insistence.

"Yes, of course. Yes, if you want to." He stands up rapidly. "Thank you, Sylvie, for coming in. You've been extremely helpful. D'you think I could keep the drawing you did?"

She nods.

"Give Adam his car back," I tell her.

She brings the car and slots it into the tray.

"Did I do the puzzles right?" she asks him.

"You did so well," he tells her.

She smiles. The remote look has left her. She's ordinary again.

"We need to fix up another session," he tells me. "I could do next Saturday, if that suits you."

I feel myself flush.

"Adam, I don't know . . ." I want to tell him no, but I don't know how to put it. "I'd like to think about it—you know, where we go from here."

"Of course. If you want to," he says.

"I'm sorry," I say.

"It's okay," he says.

We talk across each other; it's embarrassing.

He has a disappointed look, and I feel I've let him down. I remind myself what Simon said: I tell myself that Simon was right, that I mustn't get carried away.

"I just need to think it through a bit," I tell him.

"Sure," he says. "You've got my number. Ring me anytime."

He takes us out, past Carla's desk. The distant band is playing "Steal Away to Jesus" with too much bass and raucously out of tune. I turn to wave as we walk away. In the bluish harshness of the tubular lighting his face looks bony, almost gaunt.

It's cold outside after the dense, stale heat in his office. We walk back to the car, past the blossoming cherry trees that dazzle in the sunlight, their blackened branches caught in nets of white. Sylvie's hand in mine has a waxy feel from the crayon. I have a sense of incompleteness, as though something hasn't happened that was meant to happen.

# 26

When Sylvie is in bed, I curl up on the sofa, wrapped up in my duvet because the flat is so cold, and flick through the TV channels. On Channel 5 there's one of those house makeover programs. The presenter must have had lots of Botox, her face is far too still. The program features a couple who don't like the feel of their home, and they have a color consultant and a psychic to advise them. The psychic has earrings like chandeliers, and her voice is emphatic and fruity. She says she feels a ghostly presence haunting their utility room, and she will burn some sage leaves to encourage the spirit to leave. I change channels rapidly.

I hear a slight sound from Sylvie's room and go to look through her door. She's lying on top of her covers, and at first I think she's asleep—that sleep came on her abruptly, before she got into her bed. Then she moves her head, and I see that she is awake. She's crying silently. Her wet face shines in the lamplight. She has the picture of Coldharbour pressed against her chest.

I go to hold her. She leans her head against me. Her weeping is quiet, despairing. Her sadness tugs at my heart. I'm so angry that I let myself be taken in by Adam, let him stir all this up in her.

"Sweetheart, what's the matter? Is it something Adam said?"

She shakes her head. "I want them back," she says through her tears.

"Who do you want back, sweetheart?"

"I want my family back," she says.

"But this is your family, Sylvie. Me and you together."

I'm not sure that she can hear me.

"I want my house and my family. I want them, Grace."

There's a little dull ache in my heart, but I'm desperate to comfort her.

"We'll find the answer, sweetheart," I tell her. I rock her gently against me. "Somehow or other, we'll get there. We'll make things better somehow . . ."

She seems so far away from me. She goes on crying silently, and there's so much grief in her face.

Later, once Sylvie has cried herself to sleep, I ring Adam. I know I have to end it once and for all, my brief flirtation with his impossible theory.

He answers straightaway.

"Grace. Hi. Good to hear from you. We were going to fix an appointment . . ."

There's music playing in the background, languorous jazz piano. I wonder about that whole life of his, which I know nothing about. Perhaps he is with his girlfriend, the seductive biophysicist.

"The thing is," I say, "I'm not so sure anymore—not sure it's right for Sylvie. You know, what we've been doing. Not sure it's going to help her . . ."

There's a brief silence.

"You have to do what you think is right," he says.

I know he's disappointed. He's being so carefully reasonable, but I hear the sag in his voice. I think of how he seemed when we left him in the corridor—that gaunt, stretched look he had. I feel uneasy, that I'm being so ungrateful.

"I'm really sorry," I say.

"Don't worry about it," he says a little too hastily. "I have to admit I'd have loved to work with Sylvie. But it was good to meet you both anyway."

"Yes, it was," I say vaguely.

I stare into the dark of my garden through the gap in my curtains, where light from my French windows spills across the lawn and gilds the twigs of the mulberry. I feel stuck. I don't know how to finish this conversation. Hearing his voice, all the warmth in it, my anger seeps away, and it enters my mind that it's too abrupt to just end our connection like this—with this quick, embarrassed phone call—when he's been so kind to us. That really it wouldn't be polite. That I owe him something more than that.

I clear my throat.

"I wonder—could I come and see you? I'd really like to explain. Just me without Sylvie—perhaps in my lunch hour or something?"

It isn't what I'd planned to say.

"Yes, of course," he tells me.

He sounds surprised. I imagine him—how he pushes his hand through his hair so the hair sticks up, gives him that startled look, like everything amazes him.

## 27

Sunday is a gorgeous day, with a wide-open sky and the light so vivid the world seems crowded with things.

I spend the morning out in the garden with Sylvie. The air smells different, and you can see much farther than before. The trees in the Kwik Save car park are fizzing and seething with starlings, a whole flock of them that have settled there. They're dark as wet tree branches, with greenish beaks and heads that flicker and twitch. I cut back the straggling roses and tie up the dying snowdrops with raffia from the flower shop. Sylvie has a miniature rake, and she rakes the leaves from the lawn.

"I like to work in the garden," she says. She's bright-eyed, rather out of breath.

"I know you do. And you've always been such a help. Even when we first came here, when you were only two. You've always helped me."

"Even when I was really small?"

"Yes, even then," I tell her. "Though I had to keep my eye on you. Once, I had my back toward you and suddenly you went quiet, and when I turned round, you were eating a handful of earth."

"Did it taste nice, Grace?"

"I don't know, sweetheart. You seemed to be enjoying it."

"Did I really?"

"Yes, really."

She's pleased by this picture of her younger, more delinquent self.

"I wouldn't do that now," she says.

"No."

"What was I like when I was little?" she says.

"You had the tiniest fingers . . . Like this."

I show her how tiny by touching her wrist with my fingertip, just a feather touch. But I'm wary. I don't know where this conversation might lead—going back in time like this. It always happens so rapidly, between one breath and the next, the most innocuous comment undermining everything, taking her away from here, from me and the life that we share.

The starlings take off in a great swirling mass. They darken the garden as they pass over, as though the sun has gone in. I wait for what Sylvie will say.

But this time she just smiles at me.

"That's *very* tiny, Grace," she says.

We're invited to Lavinia's for an afternoon party. There will be wine and Earl Grey tea and crumpets, and music around the white piano in her living room.

The house is full when we get there. There are smells of claret and cigarette smoke and the lavish scents of candles from the flower shop. Light through the crystals in the windows throws colors all over the floor.

Lavinia brings me wine and beckons to someone's teenage daughter. The girl is wearing denim shorts and massive slouchy boots and extravagant purple lipstick, and she plainly adores small children. She tells me she is Tiffany, and she'd love to take Sylvie upstairs, where she says there is a PlayStation. Sylvie goes happily with her.

I stand by Lavinia's Buddhist altar, sip rather too fast at my wine. A man comes over to talk to me. He has freckles and an engaging smile, and I immediately like him. Then he tells me he is a healer, and I feel my heart sink a little. I have such a longing for ordinariness. I'd like to talk about the local elections or how much everyone misses the London Routemaster bus—anything concrete and solid and indisputably real. But I ask him politely about it, and he tells me to hold out my hand. I wonder if this is some kind of come-on, like when men try to read your palm, but he doesn't touch me. He holds his own hand out, just over mine.

"There. Can't you feel it?" he says.

But I can't feel anything.

"Can't you sense the vibration?" he says. "A bit like pins and needles?"

"No, I'm sorry," I say.

I feel I have disappointed him. Perhaps I should have pretended.

I'm relieved when the musicians start to play. We all crowd into the living room to listen. There are three of them—clarinet, saxophone, and piano. They're gray-haired and rumpled and casually, dazzlingly skilled. The music wraps around you, seems to become part of you.

Sylvie comes downstairs with Tiffany, drawn by the music. She comes to find me, slips her hand in mine.

"Was she okay?" I whisper to Tiffany.

"Of course. She's gorgeous," she says. "She was really chatty—weren't you, angel?" She bends, smooths Sylvie's hair.

I'm so pleased that it all went well, that Sylvie behaved like any normal child.

Tiffany straightens up again.

"But I think she liked your other house better—the place where you lived before," she says. "She told me all about it. She must have a really good memory."

I try to ignore this, pretend it isn't happening.

"I guess she does," I say vaguely.

"It's amazing when she's still so small,

remembering all those things like that. You must be so proud of her," she says.

"Well, thanks for looking after her. You've been so helpful," I say.

The musicians are playing "Summertime." My heartbeat slows as I listen. Sylvie looks up and smiles at me—her face is shining with pleasure. The music throws its bright nets over everything, and I try to live in this moment and think of nothing else. I tell myself this is good, this is all that anyone could ask for—the music all around us and Sylvie's hand in mine.

Mostly, we are happy at Lavinia's.

But in the night she wakes me. She's standing at the side of my bed. When I turn on my lamp, her vast vague shadow is thrown against the wall. She's sobbing, her body shaking.

I put my arms around her. I feel her sobs move through me, as though we are one person. The sobs seem too big for her body.

"Sweetheart, you're here with me," I tell her, as I always do. "You're safe here.

Whatever you saw—it's all over. What you saw was only a dream."

She goes on crying. Her face is marked with the shiny tracks of tears that glimmer in the light of my lamp. I'm seized by a panicky helplessness. I can't reach her, can't comfort her.

She quiets a little, and there are words in her crying.

**"No no no no."**

At first I think she wants to push me away, that she's telling me to let go of her. But she's clinging to me, pressing up against me.

"Sweetheart, you're safe now. You're safe here with me. It wasn't real, what you saw."

**"No no no no."**

I have the strangest sensation—that it's not Sylvie's voice exactly. The intonation sounds somehow off. As though the words aren't precisely hers, as though they're someone else's words. The little hairs stand up on my neck. The room seems tilted, unsafe.

I push back the covers so she can get into my bed. She climbs in. She's sitting up, her back straight, rigid. Her crying is suddenly torn off.

"Grace." Her voice is high, shrill. "I can't breathe. I can't breathe." She clutches at my arm, her thin fingers digging into me. *"Grace."*

Fear surges through me. I don't know how to help her.

I put my hands on her shoulders, looking into her face.

"You're breathing, sweetheart. You're breathing fine. If you can speak, you can breathe . . ."

I try to keep my voice quite level.

"We'll breathe together," I tell her.

We breathe in time. She takes big, noisy gulps of air. The panic leaves her. She moves down under my duvet, and her eyes roll upward and close.

But I lie awake for hours and hours, hearing her crying in my mind. I'm still awake when the first frail light of dawn slides under my curtains. It's such a lonely sight.

## 28

At lunchtime on Monday I have my meeting with Adam Winters.

I'm late because it's such a struggle to find a place to park. It's a raw, hollow day, with an echoey calling of rooks, and the air is thick and gentle with moisture. As I walk across the campus, I can feel the wet on my hair. I tell myself this won't take long. I'll say what I've come to say and thank him, and then it will all be over, and at least I'll have some clarity, at least I'll know where I stand.

He's waiting for me outside the campus

cafeteria. A hot smell of chip grease hangs about its doors.

"Are you sure this is okay?" he says. "Perhaps we could find somewhere quieter . . ."

"No, really, it's fine," I tell him. "I won't be able to stay all that long. I have to get back to the shop."

"Yes, of course," he says.

He pushes open the doors. A wave of sound crashes over us, and I think that perhaps he was right, that we should have found somewhere more peaceful. The place is milling with students, all laughing and flirting together, so shiny and certain and careless. I envy them, as I always do.

We buy tuna baguettes and coffee, and he takes me to a table by the window. It looks out over a courtyard that has a struggling fountain in a shallow concrete pool. There are coffee rings on the table, and the sauce dispenser has a dark, dried crust of ketchup down its side.

His glance is thoughtful, concerned.

"You look exhausted, Grace," he says. "Is everything okay?"

I explain how Sylvie woke in the night. I don't tell him about the words she said and how strange that made me feel. I tell myself I was probably overwrought anyway.

He murmurs something sympathetic. I wish he wouldn't be nice like this. It makes it harder to say what I've come here to say.

I clear my throat.

"The thing is—I thought I should see you—to tell you why we couldn't carry on. It seemed only fair to come and see you."

The words are lumpy, solid things.

But he smiles at me politely.

"That's really good of you," he says.

I start to unwrap my baguette. The squeak of cellophane sets my teeth on edge. My body feels loose and clumsy, like it's a wooden marionette that I don't know how to control. I wish I wasn't here at all.

"I'm worried it's wrong for Sylvie. That it's the wrong direction to go in. That it's wrong to be concentrating like this on all the strange things that she says."

"I understand," he tells me. "I can see why you might have doubts about it."

We're leaning together across the table to hear each other above the noise. His face is a little too close to mine. I can see all the detail in it—the stippling of stubble on his jawline, the smudges of dark in the thin skin under his eyes. The coffee has a burnt taste, but it's strong and I drink gratefully.

"She was upset after the session," I say. I'm forcing myself to be honest, even though it feels so difficult. I feel I owe him that. "I felt you pushed her too hard."

He sips his coffee, his eyes on mine.

"You don't like her being asked things directly, do you? Not the really big questions," he says. "I've noticed that. And you hate it when I press her . . ."

"But if you ask her directly, she mostly can't tell you," I say. My voice a little shrill. Protesting, justifying myself.

"Yes," he says. "But that doesn't mean she doesn't *want* to tell you. She's only a little kid—it's a struggle for her to express it. She's trying to talk about things she has no words for."

"I don't know. Maybe," I say.

He puts his cup down in the saucer—carefully, as though it could easily break.

"It's almost as though you don't quite trust her," he tells me. "Perhaps you need to trust her to decide what's safe to say."

His voice is gentle, but I still don't like him saying this. For a moment I don't say anything.

"I'm always so frightened of hurting her, of making everything worse," I tell him.

"Grace. She's hurt already."

There's nothing I can say to that.

We sit for a while in silence. Then Adam leans toward me across the table. He has his eager, urgent look.

"Look, I know it seems weird, what I do," he says. "I can understand your misgivings. When I first got into the paranormal, my colleagues were appalled. Well, I'm sure you can imagine—"

"Simon, you mean?" I think of the man in the blazer, of the skeptical tone in his voice. *Adam can be very . . . enthusiastic. Don't you find that?*

"Yes. Among others." He makes a little gesture, as though to push something away. "Simon thinks that reality is what we see and hear. No more than that. That the study of the paranormal is a debasement of science. That people's sense of the unseen is just a delusion," he says.

"He did say something about you being very left field," I tell him.

Adam takes up the paper napkin that came with his baguette, starts ripping little strips off it.

"To be honest, I think he'd like me out of his department," he says.

"But what about having an open mind?" I ask. "You know—that thing you said. 'A scientist should never say that anything is impossible . . .'"

"Simon has this favorite line that he always comes out with," he says. "As though it answers everything. 'If you're too open-minded your brains drop out.'"

Something changes in me when he says that. I see his life quite differently. It's always looked so enviable—his prestigious job, his admiring students. I hadn't imagined that he might know some kind of loneliness too.

"So why do you do it?" I ask him. "Why is it so important to you?"

There's a brief silence between us.

I try again. "Why does it matter so much to you?"

I don't really expect that he'll tell me. I expect him to reply with some impassioned abstraction—how psychologists need to be less defensive and think outside the box, how we shouldn't be so frightened of the things we have no words for. I don't think for a moment that he'll really answer truthfully.

He's silent for a moment, as though working out what to say.

"There was this thing that happened," he says.

There's a new, harsher note in his voice. I'm intrigued.

"What thing?" I ask him.

He isn't looking at me.

"My brother died," he tells me.

I stare at him. For a moment I think I misheard.

"Your brother?" I remember the photo on his desk, the boy in oil-stained overalls who looks like Adam but isn't him. I feel a warning tug of sadness. "Is—was that him in the photo in your office?"

Adam nods. "That's Jake," he tells me.

"When did this happen?" I say.

He thinks for a moment, adding up the years.

"Jake was seventeen when he died. He was two years older than me. It's sixteen years ago now. He died in a car crash," he says.

I'm a little afraid. I'm not sure I want to hear this.

"But—how? What happened?" I ask him.

"We used to take cars when we were kids," he tells me.

"Oh." I feel a jolt of surprise, that he's not quite who I thought he was. "That's not at all how I'd imagined your childhood," I say.

I feel my face go hot. This seems to imply that I've thought about him too much.

He's looking at me curiously.

"How did you imagine it, then?" he says.

"I thought you'd maybe had a rather more privileged background than that."

He shrugs slightly.

"I grew up on a council estate in Newcastle," he tells me. "Quite a rough place, really." His voice changes slightly as he talks. I hear the lilt of his childhood accent in it. "That's what you did—you took stuff. We were pretty accomplished car thieves, my brother and me."

I think about where he has come from, and how he must have struggled to achieve the life he has now. I feel a little surge of admiration for him.

He's looking down into his coffee. In the clear light that comes through the window I can see all the lines in his face.

"I was driving, the night it happened," he tells me. "We'd stolen this crappy old Astra, and the engine was really rough."

His voice is very quiet. I lean in closer.

"I was driving too fast. I could hear the police were after us, I could hear the sirens. I lost control. We went off the road, went head-on into a tree."

"God, Adam."

"I got knocked out for a moment." His face is bleak. I see how raw this still is. "When I came to again, there was blood in my mouth, on my face, and I knew it wasn't my blood. Jake died in my arms before the ambulance came."

He pauses just for a heartbeat.

"I felt it was my fault. I felt I'd killed him."

"No," I say, my voice rather high, protesting. "For God's sake, Adam. Of course you didn't kill him. You loved him, you didn't want him to die. It was an accident . . ."

"That wasn't how it felt," he says.

He's quiet for a moment, and the noise of the cafeteria breaks over us. The sadness in his story presses down on me. I feel all the terrible incompleteness of things. There's so much that never gets said, so much that's unfinished and broken.

"Afterward," he tells me, "some rather weird things happened. One night I woke in the darkness in the bedroom that we'd shared, and I had such a sense of his presence."

I feel a quick, surprising pang of envy—that nothing like that happened to me after my mother died. That she left behind her only the wrenching sense of her absence.

"What was that like?" I ask him. "Did you see something? Hear something?"

"That first time, I just felt him," he says. "Like the way you can know that a house isn't empty even as you enter it. But another time I heard his voice—not in my head, but real. Coming from somewhere outside me. He said my name. It comforted me. But after that, nothing."

I hear all the bleakness in his voice. His hands are clasped together on the table. The knuckles are white, the veins are like wire through the skin. Instinctively I reach toward him, put my hand on his wrist. He looks up sharply. I see how my touch startles him. I feel a little jag of arousal, which unnerves me—it seems illicit, out of place. I take my hand away.

"So that's it. That's what happened. You asked me why this stuff mattered to me, and I wanted to tell you," he says. "To answer your question honestly. Sorry to be a bit morbid."

"No, I'm glad you told me . . . Well, not glad exactly. You know what I mean."

He nods slightly.

I have such a sense of strangeness, suddenly learning about this man who's about to walk out of my life. Everything feels off-kilter. Everything's happened the wrong way around.

He starts to gather our cups and plates together. Something shifts between us, as though some thread that joined us together has snapped.

"Well, I guess you'll need to be getting back in a moment," he says.

"Yes. I suppose I should."

He walks me to the entrance hall.

"Look—the best of luck with Sylvie." He has his familiar crooked smile. "I hope it all works out for you both."

"Thank you."

I walk out into the raw gray day and leave him there.

# 29

I drive slowly back to the flower shop, unnerved by what he told me, reliving our conversation, hearing it all in my head. *I felt I'd killed him*. I remember the haggard look in his face and the veins that stood up in his hands. I think of this burden he carries, that he will carry for all of his life, and I feel so sorry for him.

But as I drive away from him, there's also a steelier part of me that feels a kind of relief. As though my decision is vindicated by the story he told. How could he ever be objective when something so devastating drives him? He'd be always trying to reach his brother—wanting some proof, some evidence that he's still alive somewhere, that there's meaning to what happened. I tell myself that I wouldn't want to entrust him with Sylvie. That it's all for the best I decided not to go back.

Lavinia looks up, smiles at me. "Nice lunch, Gracie?" she says.

"Kind of. Well, I don't know . . ."

She's planting out fritillaries in a vintage wooden apple box. The flowers are a smoky purple, their petals with an intricate pattern like the skin of a snake.

"I went to see that psychologist—the one I told you about," I say.

She pushes her hair from her face. She's wearing an old-fashioned riding coat and rigger boots of oiled leather, and she has a silver poppyhead pin in her hair.

"Good for you, Gracie," she says. "So how's all that been going?"

"Not well, really. I don't think it's the answer. I went to see him to tell him that we couldn't carry on."

Concern flickers over her face.

"Oh, Gracie, what a disappointment. I really liked the sound of him," she says.

"Sylvie was crying after the session," I tell her.

"Well, it would be tough for her, of course. Opening up to a stranger like that."

"I don't know. I think it was more than that. And then he told me just now about this thing that happened when he was a boy. It shook me up, to be honest. Though it helped me understand why he does what he does . . ."

I tell her his story. She listens quietly.

"Poor bloke," she says. "How ghastly. Well, he obviously thinks a lot of you, Gracie, to trust you with something like that."

"But he couldn't be dispassionate, could he? Not after going through that. Not if he's always trying to prove there's something else beyond all this—trying to find his brother . . ."

She rubs her hand across her face. There are crescents of earth in her nails.

"Why we do what we do—that's a pretty deep question, Gracie. Is anyone really objective? I mean, we're all human, for God's sake. We all have hidden things that drive us on." She tamps the soil down deftly with the flat of her palm. Her silver hairpin glitters with the movement of her body. "Anyway, I'll shut up now. Only you can know what's right for Sylvie."

"I used to think that," I tell her. "Now I'm just not sure . . ."

"You need to trust yourself," she says.

I turn a little away from her. I've promised myself that today I will tell her about Little Acorns. I know I can't postpone it anymore, that it's not fair to her. And yet I feel such reluctance. It's as though, while she still doesn't know, I can half pretend it's not happening—as though, in telling her, I will make it real.

"Lavinia." My throat is thick suddenly.

She looks up rapidly, hearing the tremor in my voice.

"What is it, Grace? What's happened?"

"We're losing the place at the nursery. They say they can't keep Sylvie any longer."

"*Hell*, Grace."

She stares at me.

"I'm sorry," I say. "I should have told you. I'm sorry."

"You mean—she's been *expelled*?"

"Kind of."

"But—she's only little. How *could* they? I hate them, Gracie," she says.

"I'm trying to find another place," I tell her. "But nurseries have long waiting lists. I know it won't be easy."

"How long have you got?" she says.

"Till the end of the month," I tell her. "I'm sorry it's all so sudden . . ."

She looks bereft.

"Only till then? Oh, Gracie."

She moves her hands apart in a small, despairing gesture.

"I shall miss you horribly," she says. "It's been wonderful having you here. How shall I ever replace you?"

I clear my throat. "I don't suppose you could keep my job open just for another few weeks?" My voice sounds strained and shrill. "Just until I find somewhere? I mean, maybe I'll manage to find a nursery that will take her . . ."

There's a small, awkward silence between us.

"Grace, I'm so sorry," she says then. "I would if I could—believe me. But it's not like it's the summer, when I could get a student, perhaps. I have to have stability. It really isn't possible to run this place on my own."

Suddenly I see it clearly. Hearing her

spell it out like that, I know how it's going to be—that my job here is ended forever. I see it all in devastating detail, this life unfolding before me, this unraveling of everything I've tried to knit together. It's so wearily familiar, the patching up and making do, so like the life my mother had. Living on child support, resentful, our whole life running aground.

She comes and puts her arms around me, holds me close for a moment.

I don't say anything. If I speak, I'll cry.

My last days at Jonah and the Whale pass very quickly. Every lunch hour I ring nurseries, trying places farther and farther afield, but no one can take Sylvie, not at such short notice. I keep thinking something will happen, that someone will bail me out or come rushing to my rescue. But nothing happens, no one comes.

Lavinia finds a young woman to replace me. She's Polish, with a degree in English and impeccably straightened blond hair. She's very charming and eager to learn, and she'll suit Lavinia perfectly. I feel a pang of envy.

On my last day, Lavinia gives me flowers, a lavish bunch of pink lilies.

"You must promise to stay in touch,"
she says. "Let me know what's happening
with Sylvie."

"I shall miss you so much," I tell her.
"You—and working here. I've loved it."

"I know that, Gracie," she says.

She hugs me, and there's such comfort
in the warm solidity of her body. Yet I feel
in this moment of leaving that it will be
hard to stay close, that our friendship may
be more tenuous than I'd always imagined. The thought saddens me.

At Little Acorns, Beth has put all Sylvie's
things together, her hairbrush and towel
and rucksack, in a neat, small pile on the
table by the door. She holds Sylvie tightly
to her.

"Just you look after yourself for me,
okay, sweetheart? Promise me that."

Sylvie reaches up and kisses Beth's
cheek. Beth's eyes are wet and full. I
thank her for all her care of Sylvie.

We walk to the car through the gathering dark and the pools of orange lamplight.

"Why won't I go to nursery anymore,
Grace?" says Sylvie.

"Mrs. Pace-Barden thought you'd be happier staying at home," I tell her. "You weren't very happy at nursery, were you? You didn't like it very much. Not really."

She thinks about this for a moment.

"Sometimes I did and sometimes I didn't," she says.

## 30

It's our first Monday at home together—
the start of our new way of life.

"What are we doing today?" says Sylvie.

I glance around our living room. It all
looks rather blurred and dusty in the
washed spring light.

"I'm going to clean up the flat, and then
we can do something nice," I tell her.

"Are you going to play with me?"

"Yes. Once I've done the tidying up.
We could have a picnic for all your Barbies and Big Ted. Would you like that?"

She's pleased.

"Yes, Grace."

I kneel down and hug her. Her silk hair brushes my face. She hugs me back with a little smile.

I tell myself I will make this work. I will give her my total attention, and maybe she'll be a bit more at peace now that she's home with me all day. Maybe her troubles were all just stress, and now she will be happier. I can make this work, I know I can.

I clean the room assiduously. The spiders have been busy—the cornices are lacy with webs. I sweep away the cobwebs and I dust and vacuum everywhere while Sylvie plays with her dollhouse, rearranging the furniture, walking the little doll figures through the rooms with the polka-dot walls.

When I've finished, I stand back, admiring my work. There's a scent of polish and everything gleams and the edges of things are exact again. I put Lavinia's lilies in the middle of the table. The buds are opening out now—you can see the rust-colored pollen in the throats of the flowers, and the small, pale hairs like animal hairs. The shiny room lifts my spirits. I open the window a little. There's a fresh spring wind from the garden that smells of roots and green things, and the hems of my calico curtains wave and beckon like hands.

"There, that's better, isn't it?" I'm speaking half to myself. "Our room looks really lovely now."

Sylvie glances up. For a moment she doesn't say anything. Her cool gaze flicks around the room.

"I had a house before," she says. "When I had my family. It was nicer than this house, Grace."

Anger surges through me. My mouth is choked with ugly words that I want to shout and scream at her: *I struggle so hard to build a decent life for the two of us, but whatever I do you just push it all back in my face* . . . I clench my teeth.

I kneel, grab her shoulders.

"Sylvie, just stop this, okay? Stop all this nonsense. *This* is your house. This is where you belong. This is your family— just you and me together. You have to know that—you have to accept that. This is all there is, Sylvie, this life we have together here."

She goes quite still. My face is very

close to hers. She has her eyes tight shut
so she can't see.

"You're hurting," she tells me.

I pull away from her, make myself
breathe. I see my hands are trembling.

The long day stretches before me, and
I don't know how to get through—not
feeling like this, with this ugly anger burning away inside me. I tell myself that we
have to get out of the flat, that outside in
the wind and the freshness I'll start to feel
normal again. Even if we just walk down
to Kwik Save.

"Sweetheart, we'll go to the shop. We'll
need some chocolate fingers for our picnic."

She goes obediently to find her coat
and her shoes.

Kwik Save is almost empty, and the customers are different from the people I usually see, on Friday nights when it's
crowded and everyone's rushing and full
of purpose. I pass an old man with a thin,
frail look, as though the slightest knock
would make him fall, and an elderly lady
who has a faint scent of mothballs; she
has three meals-for-one in her basket,

and I wonder if coming to Kwik Save is the highlight of her day. One of the women I sometimes see soliciting on the corner is buying Pampers and baby milk. She's wearing a baggy tracksuit, and her face is creased and drawn. All these sad, tired people, swept to the margins of their lives. Like me, I think, and hate the thought.

There's a mother and a little boy. I notice them at once—there's something odd about them. The mother has scraped-back hair and a vigilant, fierce expression and deep frown lines on her forehead. I think she probably looks much older than her years. The boy is a little younger than Sylvie. He has a still, rather beautiful face, and his movements are random and wild. As I watch, he flutters his hand in a strange way, close in front of his eyes, and I realize he is autistic. I tell myself I am lucky. My difficulties count for so little compared to the problems this woman endures.

They're in the biscuit aisle now, where I'm looking for chocolate fingers. With a movement that comes from nowhere, the boy throws out his arm and sweeps it through the biscuits. Dozens of tins and packets spill all over the floor. The mother swears. She snatches him up and dumps him in the baby seat on the shopping cart and straps him in, though he's really too big for the seat. He fights against the straps. Sylvie watches with fascination.

The woman starts to put the biscuits back. I go to help her.

"Really, you mustn't," she says.

"That's okay," I tell her. "I know what it's like . . ."

A strand of dull hair falls over her face. She pushes it wearily out of her eyes.

"I'm so sorry," she says. "I'm so sorry. You shouldn't have to do this."

She must spend her whole life saying sorry like this and clearing up the chaos left in the wake of her child.

"It's no big deal," I tell her. "Really."

We pile the biscuits up on the shelf. The boy is starting to cry, with a shrill, high sound like a piping bird's that doesn't sound like a human cry. The woman breaks out a can of Coke from the multi-pack in her cart, and hands it to him. He drinks, the crying stops. A dribble of Coke seeps down his chin, and he doesn't wipe it away. Sylvie steps closer, eyes wide, mouth a little pursed. She has a rather self-righteous look.

They're nearly out of chocolate fingers. I reach to the back of the shelf. There's a choice of milk or plain chocolate, and I turn to ask Sylvie which flavor she'd like. I see—too late—that the boy is waving the drink can wildly, almost like it's a rattle, like he doesn't know what it's for. An arc of brown liquid spurts up from the can.

I put out a hand to grab Sylvie. It all seems to happen so slowly, but I can't reach her, can't get there. Brown liquid splashes over her face. She's still for a moment, rigid, her face white, set, a white mask.

"Sweetheart, everything's okay, it's just a drop of Coke. Sylvie . . ."

Her screams drown out my voice.

I hold her, but she fights me, hitting my chest with her fists. It hurts. There's such ferocity in her. Around me, the whole place goes silent, everyone turning, listening. There's nothing in the world but Sylvie's screams.

The manager comes, a young, gangly man with pitted skin and an appalled look.

"Madam, is everything all right?" he asks me.

"No, not really. Look, we'll just go," I tell him.

I leave my basket of shopping, pull Sylvie down the aisle and out onto the pavement. The manager watches us helplessly; everyone is watching us. My body feels thin, brittle, as though I could easily break. Sylvie goes on screaming.

I drag her through the door of the flat and into the living room.

I'm shouting at her.

"Sylvie, stop it, stop it." My voice is high, harsh. I know this is pointless, but I can't help it.

She screams louder.

I want to scream back at her. I feel such rage that I can't get through, can't reach her, that she behaves as though I don't exist. I have to make her notice me. The rage surges through me, blinds me. I hit her hard, in the face. My hand makes a loud sound.

At once she stops screaming. It's like the sound is torn off. The skin is red where I hit her. She puts her hand to the sore place. She turns to me, her pupils like pinpricks. I see such hate in her face. She opens her mouth and screams again.

I go into the kitchen and slam the door behind me.

I sit at the kitchen table. I rub my hand across my face, and my hand is wet and I realize I am weeping. All the rage has left me. I feel weak, tired, bitterly ashamed. I can hear the sound in my head of my hand on her face, and it horrifies me. There are words in my head, over and over. *I can't do this, I can't, I can't do it* . . . The words go around inside me. *I can't do this* . . . I let myself cry for a long time.

Eventually I wipe my face on my sleeve. I feel light-headed, detached now, drained of feeling. I just sit for a while at my table, staring out the window, which looks out over the alley and across to the next block of flats. There are Dumpsters, and a telephone wire that stretches across the alley, and a sliver of sky with white clouds scudding across it. A bird has landed on the wire, a ragged sparrow that clings on tight as the wire swings about in the wind. I watch the bird for a moment. It's so tiny, fragile, all knocked about, buffeted by the gusts of wind, and I feel a little afraid for it, afraid the wind will blow it off, as though just for a moment I'm forgetting it can fly.

In the living room behind me, Sylvie is still screaming. I open the drawer of the dresser and take out Adam Winters's card.

He answers at once.

"Adam Winters." His brisk work voice.

"Adam. It's Grace. You know, Grace Reynolds."

"Grace." He sounds surprised. "How are you? How's it all going?"

I take a deep breath.

"Not good, really. Sylvie's left nursery now. And today she's just screaming and screaming . . ."

"I rather gathered that." The way he says it, dryly, makes me feel that perhaps this isn't the end of the world, a child crying.

"I've changed my mind," I tell him. "I want to make an appointment. I want to see you again."

"Okay." He sounds pleased. "Where are you? Are you at home?"

"Yes."

"I could come round now. Would that suit you?"

"You mean here? To my place?"

"Yes. It's no problem," he says.

It's suddenly all moving so fast. But I have made my decision.

"Okay," I tell him.

"It's Highfields, isn't it? Give me half an hour."

I go back into the living room. Sylvie is still crying, but more quietly. I kneel beside her and hold her. Her body feels loose and floppy now. In spite of all the crying, her skin is cold to the touch.

"I'm sorry I hit you," I say. "I shouldn't have done that."

She doesn't say anything.

I rock her gently and stroke her back and feel her breathing slow.

"You feel so cold," I tell her.

I carry her into the bedroom and tuck her up in bed and give her Big Ted and a picture book that has her favorite rhymes—"Little Bo Peep," and "Hey Diddle Diddle," and "Mother, may I go out to swim? Yes, my darling daughter . . ."

"You can stay here till you feel better," I

say. "You can just stay in bed for a bit and look at some books."

She opens the book mechanically, scarcely glancing at it.

The picture of Coldharbour is stuck to the side of her wardrobe. It has a ragged look where she takes it down to slip it under her pillow. It's hanging crookedly, and the corners are torn. I get more Blu-Tack and stick it up straight. She watches me; her eyes are shadowed and vast.

"I'll bring you some milk," I tell her.

"I'm hungry," she says.

"Okay. I'll bring you a biscuit too."

I stare at the picture for a moment—the bright sea, the fishing boats. It could be the other side of the world, a place unguessably far.

## 31

There's the sound of a car pulling up by the flats. I go to open the door.

"Grace."

He's wearing an ancient leather jacket. He must have been rushing, he's breathing rather hard.

"I hope it was okay, me ringing like that, but I felt completely desperate," I tell him. "I really didn't know what else to do."

His eyes are on my face, and he has his crooked smile.

"I'm not sure that's entirely flattering," he tells me.

I find I am smiling in spite of myself.

I make him coffee. We sit at my dining table; he seems too tall for my chairs. It's strange to see him sitting here, surrounded by my things. It's all so feminine, my flat— the calico curtains, the scent of lilies.

He sips his coffee.

"So tell me what's been happening."

"Sylvie's in bed," I tell him. "She went berserk in Kwik Save, and I hit her. I'm so ashamed of myself."

"Don't be," he says. "There's nothing to be ashamed of. I think you're incredibly patient."

"I've tried so hard, and nothing works," I tell him.

"Yes, I know that," he says.

Out of nowhere, I feel a little rush of happiness—that he's here to share this.

"I'd love to know what you made of her," I tell him. "I've never asked you properly."

He smiles. "I'm a skeptic, remember?"

"You refuse to come to conclusions."

He nods. "But putting it all together— the way she is, the things she says—I'd love to find out more. The question is how best to go about it."

"When she couldn't or wouldn't answer your questions?" I say.

He nods. "With an older child, you might use hypnosis, try to regress them," he says.

"To take them back into the memory?"

"Yes. Though I'm not very keen on that, to be honest. And of course it's never con-clusive. It doesn't really prove anything, whatever they say in the trance."

"It isn't science?"

"Exactly."

He sits there quietly for a moment. His face is so close I can see the bright flecks in his eyes.

"You know what I want to do," he says.

My pulse skitters off. "Yes."

"There's only one way to investigate a case like Sylvie's," he says.

I nod slightly.

He puts out his hand toward me in a brief, truncated gesture. My skin prickles, expecting his touch.

"Grace. Would you and Sylvie come to Ireland with me?"

I don't say anything. My heart pounds.

"It's not a difficult journey," he says. "We could fly from Heathrow to Shannon and hire a car. Coldharbour's quite a small village, but there are bed-and-breakfast places . . ."

"You've looked it up?" I'm unnerved.

"Of course."

"But—how could I possibly do that? I mean, just for starters, I couldn't afford the fare."

He looks immediately hopeful when I say that.

"No problem. I could pay for you both. I have a research grant for investigating cases. I might then ask your permission to write it up in a journal. You'd get to see what I'd written, of course."

"But what about Simon, your boss? Wouldn't he be angry with you? If he thinks that what you do isn't really science at all?"

"Probably. But Simon can stuff it," says Adam.

I'm staring down into my coffee. Doubts worm into my mind. I can hear Karen's voice in my head, all her warnings and admonitions.

"But—what if Sylvie got more upset— you know, more caught up in these things? I couldn't bear that. I'd feel so guilty."

"Yes, there's a risk," he tells me. "So think about it carefully. I'm not denying that it's something I'd love to pursue. But it's up to you—and what you feel is right for Sylvie."

We sit there quietly for a moment. Outside, the wind is rummaging in the alleyway, banging the lids of the Dumpsters. The sound is too loud, as though it's here in the room.

I sip my coffee, feel the kick as it slides into my veins.

"The trouble is," I tell him, "I don't really know where I stand. I mean, *sometimes* I believe it—believe there's something in all this. But I keep coming back to that thing she says—*I had a cave and a dragon* . . . That's fairy-tale stuff. Just something she saw in a book."

"It could be."

"Maybe it's just some game she's playing, some world she's making up." I remember Karen's words. "A kind of wish fulfillment."

"Absolutely," he tells me. "We could get there and find there's nothing. Nothing significant in this place, nothing with any meaning for her. That the whole thing's just a shadow play. It's your call, Grace. Whether you feel it's worth exploring. Only you can decide."

I think of going to Ireland with him. A little bud of excitement opens out inside me. We couldn't—could we?

"Maybe I'll think about it," I say. "I mean, I'm not promising anything . . ."

I expect him to respond to this—animated, surprised, perhaps, pushing his hand through his hair.

He puts his cup down. He's serious suddenly, frowning, his clever dark eyes on my face.

"Grace, I want you to know this." He's so solemn, it's unnerving. "If we did take Sylvie to Coldharbour, we'd be looking for a death—for the story of a death."

There's a chill like a slight cool breath on my skin. Somehow I hadn't put this together.

"You mean—we'd be trying to find the person that my daughter *used to be* . . ." The room seems to shift around me. Something in me recoils from this.

He nods.

"There's more," he says. "According to the studies I've read, the death these children say they've suffered is very often a violent one."

I feel the cold go through me.

"You mean—some terrible accident? Murder even?"

He nods slowly. "Something sudden and shocking."

"Why? Why would that be the kind of death that's remembered? Why not just a peaceful death?" I think of the man whose funeral we went to in the autumn—with the black plumed horses and all the marguerites. "A good death?"

"It's like the death is incomplete, the person can't let go of it. So—a violent, sudden death, with all the wreckage that leaves."

Jake's death is there in the room with us when he says that. I think how it's something he knows so well, too well— that wreckage. I wonder again whether that's what draws him to Sylvie's case. Trying to find a way of living with what happened. Trying to prove that there's something else, that it doesn't just end there, with the death, the wreckage.

"Yes, I understand," I say.

"I want you to think about that for a while," he tells me.

His look disconcerts me, the intensity of it, stirring something up in me. A charge moves through me, a little jolt of sex. I take my eyes from his face.

"If you do decide to come," he says, "I want you to come with open eyes. If Sylvie *is* remembering something, then the story we uncover won't—can't—be a happy one."

"No. I understand that."

He's treating me so delicately. I wonder how he sees me—perhaps as rather fragile, labeled HANDLE WITH CARE.

We sit there for a moment, and neither of us says anything. Wind rattles at my window. There's a sound of shattering from the streets, the shocking sound of breaking glass. I reach out for my coffee and see the tremor in my hand. When I pick up the cup, the liquid shivers all across its surface.

"Think about it," he says.

"Yes."

"And talk about it to Sylvie," he says. "Find out whether she'd like to go.

Because there's no point in any of this if Sylvie isn't sure. She has to want to go there. Will you do that for me?"

When Adam has left, I go to Sylvie's bedroom. There's a faint wash of color back in her face, and she's out of bed and playing quietly with her Barbies.

"Sylvie. That person who just came round—it was Adam, who we went to see. Do you remember Adam?"

"Yes," she says.

I crouch on the floor beside her. I can feel the thud of my heart; it seems to shake my body. I realize that I don't know how to frame the question, that perhaps I should have planned this.

"Adam and me, we were talking about the place you like—you know, the place in your picture."

Sylvie is suddenly still. Her eyes are fixed on my face, her cool blue gaze like a clear winter sky.

"We were wondering if we should go and see it," I say. "You and me and Adam. Go to the place in your picture."

"Coldharbour," she says. Pronouncing

it precisely, every sound exact, as though it's some precious, fragile object she's placing carefully down.

"Yes. To Coldharbour."

"When, Grace? When are we going?"

"Well, we haven't really decided *when* yet—it was just an idea. Adam wanted to know what you thought. If it was something you might like to do."

"Can we see my family? And my house and my fishing boats?"

"We can see whatever there is to see. But I need to be sure what you want, sweetheart. Would you like to go there? Go to Coldharbour?"

"Yes," she tells me.

"Okay, then. Well, I'll need to talk to Adam. I'll tell him what you said to me."

"When are we going?" she says again.

"I don't know, sweetheart," I tell her. "I'll have to talk to Adam about it."

I make a grilled cheese sandwich for her lunch. When I go back to her bedroom to tell her the sandwich is cooked, she has her Shaun the Sheep rucksack out on her bed. It's bulging. I can see Big Ted and her favorite books, and she's taken some clothes from her wardrobe, some T-shirts and her suede laced boots and her daisy dungarees.

"You've packed," I say.

"Yes, Grace. I'm ready." Slightly impatient with me, as though she thinks I'm being rather dilatory. "Aren't *you* ready, Grace?"

## 32

We cross the edge of the land. If I lean over Sylvie, who has the window seat, I can see the Irish Sea below us—the white fringe of surf that follows the line of the shore, that from up here seems to have no movement, to be as still as something drawn or painted. Sylvie, who has loved everything today—the glamour of the airport, the flight attendants' bright green suits and hats, even her chicken-and-salad sandwich, once she'd carefully removed each shred of lettuce—has finally fallen asleep.

The newspaper I bought at the airport lies open, unread, on my lap. I rest back in my seat, very aware of Adam's arm on the elbow rest between us. I have a sense of astonishment that this is actually happening.

Adam isn't reading either.

"Does your girlfriend . . ." I say. "I mean, I don't know her name—"

"Tessa. She's called Tessa."

"Does Tessa mind you going away like this?"

He's puzzled.

"No. Why should she?"

Perhaps it was a stupid thing to say.

"I just wondered."

"It's not that kind of relationship," he says.

I want to ask what he means—what kind of relationship it is.

We're over Ireland now. The land slides away beneath us, purple plowed fields, a tangle of woods so dark they have a burnt look, a twisting silver river. Cloud blows past us like smoke.

"Look," I say.

He leans across me, so close I can sense the warmth that comes off his body.

We watch for a while, till cloud obscures the ground.

Sylvie stirs, opens her eyes. She stares around, she has a confused look. She clutches Big Ted to her.

"Grace," she says. The word is a question.

I smooth back her hair.

"We're on the plane, sweetheart, remember? We're going to visit the place in your picture," I say.

Sylvie smiles.

The engine noise cuts out, so it feels that the plane is still, suspended. The pilot announces that we're starting to descend. White cloud presses in at the window.

Adam finishes his coffee and folds his table away.

"I'll read to Sylvie," he tells me. "So you can get some rest."

I find *The Very Hungry Caterpillar* in my bag. We change places, so Adam is sitting next to Sylvie. I lean back and stretch my legs out into the aisle.

He starts to read. His voice is expressive, and he's utterly unself-conscious, and Sylvie is enchanted. When he gets to the end, she wants it all again. She looks across at the pictures, pressing her fingers into the holes where the caterpillar has eaten through. I close my eyes, drift in and out of consciousness. He's reciting the lovely long list of food that the caterpillar has eaten, and the thread of his voice unspools through my dreams. "'*One* slice of salami, *one* lollipop, *one* piece of cherry pie . . .'"

When we land at Shannon Airport, it's raining heavily. We eat in a restaurant of unforgiving 1960s concrete, looking out across a slow brown river. Sylvie says her cheesy potatoes taste of sweat.

We pick up a rental car from a wet gray car park and load our luggage in.

"I'm happy to drive. But it's up to you," says Adam.

I'm grateful that he asked me, that he didn't just assume.

Sylvie scrambles into the car. There's a silver-plated Saint Christopher hanging from the rearview mirror. She leans across the front seats and touches it, making it shiver and glitter. Then she settles into her seat with Big Ted and a Jaffa Cake.

We drive through a gentle countryside of gray church spires and little farms. It's subtly different from England—the Gaelic words on the signposts, with their baffling clusters of consonants, the palms in people's gardens, even the electrical towers seem different—but it's dreary under the rain.

Sometimes I glance back at Sylvie. She watches out the window, her gaze acute, alert. Her sleep on the plane has revived her. Sometimes she points out what she sees—a donkey shambling through a field, two black birds on a wire—like any child who's traveling through an unfamiliar land.

After Galway the sun comes out for a while. There are small white houses in fields of stones with hills heaped up behind them, and a washed silver light over everything. Then, beyond Oughterard, we come to a different, harsher land— empty, silent, with mountains all around us and still black lakes choked up with grass and reeds. A sudden squall lashes the car. Where it moves across the mountains, you can see the edges of the rain, though far ahead of us, at the coast, the sky is clear and luminous. I'm getting used to this weather now, the way it shifts and changes even as you look at it, and between the squalls of rain, this light that is everywhere like the light over water. For miles we see no other car or house or sign of people—just a shepherd with his tatty flock, and a church in the middle of all the desolation, with a blue benign Virgin who reaches out her arms toward the road.

"Why aren't we there yet?" says Sylvie.

"We soon will be, sweetheart. It isn't much farther," I say.

"I want to be there now," she says. "*Now*, Grace."

At last the road begins to descend, above us that vivid arch of sky we saw before. We pass the crest of a hill. I hear my quick inbreath. The sea is suddenly spread out before us, unimaginably wide and shimmering with silver light. We drive down the hill into Coldharbour. Tall thin houses line a street that winds toward the shore; the houses are painted many colors, like the colors of fruit—apple, lemon, berry red. There's a scream of seagulls.

# 33

Adam pulls up by a red-painted building that looks out over the sea. A sign says ST. VINCENT'S HOTEL.

"This is it," he tells me.

I get out onto the pavement. I stretch out my arms, and the wind lifts my hair from my neck. I have a sense of so much space, so much air, of all the vastness of the place— the sky, the sea. After the confinement of London it seems extraordinary.

Sylvie scrambles out beside me.

"D'you like it here, Grace? D'you like it?" she says.

"Yes, it's beautiful," I say.

The wind blows color into her face. Her eyes are shining.

Adam leads us up the steps of St. Vincent's.

But Sylvie stops on the bottom step, a little frown etched in her forehead.

"Why are we going in here?" she says.

"It's where we're staying, sweetheart."

"But aren't we going to *my* house?" she says.

I crouch down beside her, take her face in my hands.

"Sylvie, where *is* your house, sweetheart?"

She gives me a small, blank look, as though she can't explain, as though she doesn't really understand the question.

"*This* isn't my house," she tells me.

Her frown deepens. I'm worried she will cry and protest, but she lets me take her hand.

A woman is sitting at the reception desk. She's about the same age as Lavinia. She has an exact blond bob, a sunbed tan, a ready, practiced smile.

She tells us she is Brigid. Adam introduces us.

"And aren't you a petal?" she says to

Sylvie. She has a throaty, resonant voice. "She's gorgeous," she tells me. "Look, let me show you round."

To one side of the hall there's a lounge, with a grandfather clock with a juddery tick and sofas that have a fading print of peonies; to the other side there's a break-fast room and a bar with an open fire.

"I have music here on Friday nights," says Brigid. "You mustn't miss that, now."

She takes us up to our bedrooms. The room that Sylvie and I will share has embossed wallpaper and rather battered furniture, and through glass doors a bal-cony, with a parasol and two plastic chairs, looking over the road to the sea.

I go out onto the balcony. The sound of the sea is loud up here, and the clarity of the wide blue air is dazzling; you feel you could see forever. I gaze down at the shoreline—off to my right, the solid stone jetty with fishing boats tied up, then the line of black, encrusted rocks that reach out into the sea, then, down in front of me, a stretch of smooth white sand. I'm staring into Sylvie's picture. I have an unreal, dislocated feeling.

"It's a beautiful beach," I tell Brigid.

She nods. "So it is. But I have to warn you, it's not so good for bathing. There's a riptide. You have to be careful. But I don't imagine you'll be fancying a swim this time of year."

She takes Adam to his room.

I start to unpack. Sylvie chooses her bed and arranges all her things on the bedside table—her books and LEGO and animals. She makes meticulous little movements, quiet as a cat.

When I'm sure she's quite involved in what she's doing, I take my phone and go back onto the balcony, closing the doors behind me.

"Karen. It's me."

I'm working out how to tell her. But she knows at once from my voice.

"Where are you ringing from?" she says warily.

"From Connemara."

"Oh *no*, Grace. *Please* don't tell me you've gone off with that weirdo."

"I can't talk properly. Sylvie and I are unpacking. I just wanted to tell you we're here."

"You *can't* be doing this, Grace. You *can't*."

"But we couldn't just go on the way we were."

"Grace, you could get into serious trouble with this. You know nothing about that creep you're with. For God's sake, please come home."

"I felt I had to do it—I had to try," I tell her.

"Grace. She's just a little kid with a big imagination. I mean, for Chrissake, Grace. You believe she had a *dragon*?"

"No. But I had to do something . . ."

My voice fades. I hear the doubt in it.

I say goodbye and go back into our bedroom. I have a jittery feeling, as though Karen's wariness has infected me.

Adam comes to our door. He has his leather jacket on.

"Okay, this is the plan," he says. "We'll have a walk around the village—see what Sylvie makes of it. And then I thought we could drive around the countryside a bit, see if she recognizes anything. There's a pub in Ballykilleen where we could eat."

I'm glad he's got it all worked out.

We walk out into the cold, blowing street and the scolding cries of the gulls. The shadows are lengthening now. There's a pavement along the seafront, with steps at either end going down to the beach, and a handful of shops that sell crafts and ices and postcards. Some of the shops are shut up, and they have a bleak, out-of-season sadness, their rolled-up awnings banging in the wind, but there's also a bigger store called Barry's that looks like it's open all year.

Sylvie runs on ahead of us, runs out along the jetty, past the little fishing boats. She seems entirely confident there, so high up above the water, with the solid stone wall to one side of her. We follow.

Sylvie turns toward me. Her face is pink, and she has a wide-open smile.

"This is my jetty, see, Grace."

I've never heard her say "jetty" before. I wonder where she's learned the word.

She's flushed and happy and quite unafraid for the moment. She stretches her arms out wide, reaching out in a big embrace, as though to take everything in. The wind blows her hair straight back from her head. You can see all the joy in her face.

I go to look at the boats. They're painted blue or scarlet, and the water makes a

nervous slapping sound around their hulls.
I read their names—the *Ave Maria*, the
*Endurance*.

"You'd better be careful," calls Sylvie.
"Don't go too close to the edge."

I can't help smiling when she says this.
She has the exact intonation of a parent
warning a child.

There are piles of lobster pots and coils
of sodden rope and orange buoys that are
strung up together like a bunch of balloons. Two men in oilskin dungarees are
sorting out their nets, which lie in a nylon
cloud between them, frail-looking, and
green and glistening like the sea. There's
a plastic box full of rotten fish—a chaos of
gray and silver, their heads cut off, their
eyes blank. The pungent, briny smell of
the harbor wraps itself around us.

We pass a sign that says CURRAN
CRUISES, where you can buy a boat trip.

"Sylvie, look—if you like the boats,
one day we could go on a boat trip," I tell
her, blithe, unthinking. "There might be
dolphins . . ."

Her face closes up. I realize what I've
done.

"No, Grace."

"No, of course not." I'm cross with myself for being so clumsy. I think how frightened she'd be—to be that close to the water, to feel the spray on her face. "Not if you don't want to."

We turn back, follow the road that runs along the seafront. At the farther end of the beach it veers to the left and climbs. There are houses here between the road and the sea; they must have fabulous views from their back windows. We pass a long wall of crumbling gray stone, with plaited creepers and ivies draped across it, and come to a formal gateway. There are pillars with falcons on them to either side of the gate. A plaque on one of the pillars says KINVARA HOUSE. Between the pillars a tarmac drive sweeps around and out of sight. There's a garden of lawns and flowering shrubs—rhododendron, azalea—and a casual litter of snowdrops under an old, twisted tree. A little farther along the wall we come to a small, shabby door, its paint corroding from all the salt. When I press my eye to a gap in the door where the wood has rotted away, I glimpse a house through the trees. It's imposing, double-fronted, colonnaded.

Sylvie pulls at my sleeve.

"Where's Lennie, Grace?"

Whenever she asks for Lennie, I feel that little tug of hurt about what happened with Karen.

"Lennie's in London, sweetheart."

She doesn't say anything for a moment. A shadow crosses her face.

"I want Lennie," she tells me.

I swallow down the urge to say, Well, you should have been nicer to her, shouldn't you? I glance down at her. She has a lost, confused look. I think of something I read in a newspaper article: how little children experience any separation as absolute, how they can't believe that people still exist if they can't be seen.

"Hey, don't be sad, sweetheart," I say.

I bend down, hug her. Her hair blows into my mouth. It's salty and lank already from the sea wind. I can taste the salt on my tongue.

She clutches my shoulders tightly; her fingers dig into my skin.

"Find Lennie for me. You've *got* to, Grace."

"Sylvie, who's Lennie?" says Adam.

She turns to him. She has a candid,

open, slightly condescending smile, a smile that says, I can't believe you don't get it.

"She's my Lennie, of course. I told you, Adam," she says.

## 34

The pub that Adam has chosen is half an hour's drive from St. Vincent's.

The other side of the village, we take a road that passes through Coldharbour Bog. It's a desolate place, the land all bleached or tawny, with gilded grasses flattened by the wind and no trees but an occasional stunted thorn tree, its branches furred with lichen. You can see the black lines where peat has been dug, and there are many pools of water that hold the shine of the sky. This brown, wet wilderness seems to stretch forever.

I lower my window a little, breathe in

the scent of roots and rot. The wind has an animal sound.

"It feels so bleak," I say. "If anything happened here . . . I mean, you'd be miles from anyone."

Beyond the bog, the road begins to rise. We pass narrow fields full of rocks, and quiet villages of sparse, hunched cottages. A rumpled pony stares at us across a broken wall.

I glance back at Sylvie. She smiles at me. She still has that flushed, happy look.

"Is there anything here that you've seen before?" I ask her.

"Yes, of course," she says, and turns away, watching out the window.

I feel how she eludes me.

The pub is called Joe Moloney's. We go to order at the bar, where a hollow-faced man in an old, worn coat gets up and kisses my hand. The landlord has quick, knowing eyes. He gives me an appraising look.

"Well, aren't you the lucky one?" he says to Adam. "You've got a lovely lady there. Just you take good care of her."

"I'll do my best," says Adam lightly.

I feel my face go hot.

We choose a table near the fire. White ash sifts down around the grate, and the burning logs have a sappy smell. Adam and I drink Guinness, and we eat steak pie, which comes with three varieties of potato. Sylvie amazes me by clearing her plate.

"It's nice here, isn't it, Grace?" she says.

I love it when she's happy like this.

When we go out to the car again, the wind has dropped and there's a flamboyant pink-and-orange sunset. We set out for Coldharbour. Behind us, there are mountains heaped up, deeply purple as damsons. There's nobody about except an occasional quiet animal—a slow horse the color of rust moving through a field of reeds, a clumsy sheep that lumbers over the road.

I look back at Sylvie. She's scarcely blinking. Soon she'll be asleep. Minute by minute the countryside smudges and darkens around us.

We come to a rambling farmhouse with a noisy dog chained up. Adam is frowning.

"Does this look familiar?" he says.

"Not really," I tell him.

"Oh. That's not what I hoped you'd say."

He stops and peers out at a signpost. "Ballykilleen? Why the hell are we heading for Ballykilleen? Isn't that where we're meant to be coming from?"

"I guess we could just drive on till we reach the next intersection," I say.

Adam grunts. "A fat lot of good that'll do us. I swear that that last signpost had been turned the wrong way round."

But he does drive on and turns down a side road that doesn't have a signpost, that seems to be going in roughly the right direction. The road climbs. We come to the top of the mountain that rises behind Coldharbour. The view opens out in front of us like a gift unwrapped. Way down below us, the sea is shimmering in the sunset, a track of pink light across it like a bale of bright silk flung out. To the left of the road, there's a hedge of sheltering firs, a birch tree. A couple of small pale cottages are set back from the road.

"Grace! Grace! Look!"

There's a shrill excitement in Sylvie's voice.

"Look, Grace, look, it's *my* house!"

Adam glances quickly over his shoulder at her. He slows, pulls into the shoulder of the road.

Sylvie points to the first of the cottages. "There it is, Grace!"

Her face is radiant.

Adam is leaning across me to look, but I can't see his expression. He's quiet, attentive, his irritation forgotten. Between us the Saint Christopher is gently turning and glittering; it goes on moving long after the car is still.

I stare at the house. It has a run-down look, with no lights on and boards across most of the windows. Its whitewashed walls glimmer faintly in the evening, and one solitary unboarded window catches the sun in a dazzle of saffron and pink. In the dim light, you can't see what color the door is painted. There's a little lawn in front of it, and the shadow of the mountain falls across the lawn. It's clear that nobody lives here. It has the bleak look of all abandoned houses.

I stare, can't move my eyes away, take in the rough white walls, the squat, symmetrical shape of it, the slate gray tiles that are streaked with moss and lichen. There's a feeling in the back of my neck, as though a small cold hand is fingering my spine.

"It's a good house, isn't it, Grace?"

When she turns to me, all the brightness of the sky is in her eyes.

"Yes, it's a very good house. It's just like the house we got from Tiger Tiger."

"I told you," she says.

Adam is tense, alert. I can hear his light, quick breath.

I wind my window down. I can smell mint and a green, fresh scent of pollen. The garden is raggedy and neglected, but some flowers and herbs must still grow here. The grass is mostly rough. Someone has mown a strip across the width of the house, but the rest is very long, and there are daffodils in it, their paleness floating in a sea of black. The gate is open and hanging on one hinge. A nameplate says FLAG COTTAGE. A little breeze shivers the leaves of the birch tree.

I try desperately to remember the sequence of what just happened. When did Sylvie call out? Before or after she saw the house? Is she excited because it reminds her of the dollhouse? Or did she start to get excited *before* she saw the house? I try to untangle it all in my mind, but I can't—I can't be certain. I'm angry with myself for not paying more attention.

"D'you like it, Grace?" she says.

"Yes. I really like it."

Her face is luminous, but I sense such fragility in her. I feel I have to move with the greatest care.

"Aren't we going to see it?" she says.

I don't know what to say.

"*Please*, Grace. I really want to."

She undoes her seat belt and leans across the back of my seat toward me. I feel her moth breath on my face. Her eyes are full of the colored lights from the sky.

I don't know how to handle this. I glance at Adam for guidance.

"Sylvie, it's nearly dark," he says. "What we'll do is, we'll come back tomorrow, first thing in the morning. So we can see everything properly."

She's anxious. "But what if we can't find it?"

"We'll find it, sweetheart," I tell her.

"Adam will mark it on the map. Look, we'll mark it now. It isn't going anywhere. We'll come and find it tomorrow."

*"Promise,"* she says.

"I promise," I say.

This seems to satisfy her.

She sits back, buckles up her belt. As we drive away, she twists in her seat, staring out the window, holding the house with her eyes until it's swallowed up by the night.

Sylvie settles quickly. But it takes me ages to get to sleep, even though I'm exhausted. I lie in bed and stare into the dark.

I hear Adam in the next room, talking on his cell phone. I can hear the tone of his voice through the wall, but I can't make out the words. I wonder if he's ringing Tessa. There are lots of silences his end—she seems to do most of the talking—and he's on the phone for what seems like a very long time. Then I hear his shower running, hear him unpacking, opening cupboards, shifting things around in the room. It's a very old building, everything creaks. It's unnerving, living so close to him, this man

I scarcely know at all, and it feels too intimate—hearing all his movements. Eventually the creaking stops.

I lie awake and listen to the silence. There's no noise at all but the sea, just the faintest pulse as the waves break, a sound that's more felt than heard, as though it's part of your body. I think of why we've come here, remembering what Adam said: *A violent, sudden death, with all the wreckage that leaves*. I realize I'm shivering, pull my duvet close against me. I try to reassure myself with thoughts of London things—our street, our flat, the mulberry in our garden—but already our life there seems remote, the images so small and distant. Like pictures on a page, not something real.

## 35

It's a soft gray day, full of the cries of hidden birds, with rags of mist in the hollows under the hills. We drive out of Coldharbour and join the road we found last night that leads to Ballykilleen. Sylvie leans forward, straining against her seat belt, her gaze fixed on the passing fields and hills.

The house looks messier by daylight. You can see how derelict it is. There's a Dumpster in the front garden, heaped with bits of broken wood and torn-off lumps of rock wool.

We walk in through the open gate.

I feel uneasy.

"Isn't this trespassing?" I say to Adam.

He smiles his sudden, crooked smile.

"Well, technically, yes. If you want to be pedantic."

I go to the unboarded window and peer in, cupping my face with my hands to shield my gaze from the light. Adam comes with me.

The room through the window is empty except for a mirror left hanging on the opposite wall, its glass brown and speckled with age. Our images caught on its pitted surface seem distorted and blurred—we could be anyone. There's patterned wallpaper peeling off, and a ghetto blaster on the floor that looks quite new and shiny, left there by workmen, perhaps. Litter has gathered in the corners, scraps of paper and dust balls, and leaves, some worn to a net of veins, like the rubbish that drifts and masses in the quietest reaches of a river. A slight breeze moves a single russet leaf across the floor.

I turn to Sylvie, but she isn't there.

Immediately I hear her shout from around the back of the house.

"Grace! Come and see!" Her voice is full of triumph.

We go around the side, past a sprawling hedge of ragged yellow roses, with last year's delicate dead flowers still clinging to the stems.

At the back there's a lawn that slopes steeply up the hillside. The grass is uncut and shaggy, and on this misty morning it has a gray shimmer of dew. A plum tree grows at the side of the lawn, and the fruit from last year has been left to lie around it, all rotten now, seeping luscious brown flesh. There's a stone birdbath that holds a pool of rainwater, green with scum—an emerald color, too vivid, unwholesome-looking—and an apple tree that is just beginning to blossom, its flowers palest pink with a scribble of black. I smell the blossom as I pass, its whisper of polleny scent. The air is still, and the birds are astonishingly loud.

In the middle of the garden, where the slope is steepest, three shallow stone steps are set into the lawn. As I watch, Sylvie runs up the steps, turns around on the top one, and then jumps down all three of them, landing in the grass.

"Look, Grace! I'm an *acrobat!*"

She says the word with relish, rolling it around her mouth.

"Yes, you are," I tell her.

She does it again and again. Three steps and turn and jump. She chants to herself half under her breath as she does it—"One-two-three and *jump*." She's breathing hard, I can hear all the breath in her voice.

"Be careful, Sylvie. Those steps look slippery. Don't you go breaking a leg . . ."

She pays no attention. One-two-three and *jump*. It's as though she's settled into a rhythm that feels comfortable to her. Her sneakers and the hems of her jeans are soaked with dew, and the exertion has brought a flush to her face. She looks entirely happy.

There's a click of a back door opening in the house next door to us, the urgent bark of a dog, footsteps coming out into the garden.

"Can I help you?"

A man leans over the wall. He has a creased, pallid face, narrowed eyes, no smile. His dog barks roughly and leaps against the wall, its open mouth red and vivid. I feel a little nervous, thinking how we are trespassing.

Adam goes to speak to the man.

"We were just looking round," he tells him. "The gate was open, and it was just too tempting. It's such a beautiful spot. It seems such a waste that it's empty."

The man's face mellows. He nods. I notice how different his garden is from this one. It's orderly and rather geometric, with cloches and beanpoles and seedlings in neat, measured rows.

"This was Gordon and Alice's place," he says. "Gordon and Alice Murphy."

He leaves a significant pause. It's like he expects some response from us—surprise, or recognition. I feel all the quiet of the gray, wet garden. A pigeon flies out of the plum tree with a sound like something torn.

"Okay," says Adam, vague and noncommittal.

"You'll have heard that Gordon is putting it back on the market?"

"No, we didn't know that," says Adam.

"He's having it all done up," says the man. "Well, you can see for yourselves."

He waves one hand toward the house.

From here we can see through a glass door into the kitchen. The walls are stripped back to the plaster, and the pipes have been exposed.

"Weird, really," he goes on. "When they moved in, Gordon and Alice, all that time ago—well, they ripped out all the old stuff, put posh new units in, laminate flooring, the lot. And a very nice job they made of it."

"I'm sure they did," says Adam.

"But what people want today—they want it to be traditional. So he's changing it all back again. The old flag floors and one of those butler sinks—you know the kind of thing?"

"I think so," says Adam.

"Great massive contraption. My wife can't see the point of it. Still, there you go," he says. "What goes around comes around. Isn't that what they say?"

"Well, fashions change," says Adam.

"He couldn't sell it, of course, before." The man lowers his voice a little. "Well, no surprises there. We had our doubts, me and Maureen, we reckoned the timing was wrong. Folks are wary. I can understand that."

Adam nods, and waits.

The man runs a pensive finger down the side of his face.

"He's been renting it out in the summertime, but he'd really like to sell. He just couldn't find a buyer. Well, I tell a lie. One time there was somebody—not anyone local, of course—a woman from Dublin with a Porsche, she wanted a weekend cottage. But then it all fell through."

"It's a very frustrating business, selling houses," says Adam.

"Thing is, Flag Cottage needs to be lived in again. It's crying out to be lived in. Like you say, it's a beautiful spot. Well, maybe he'll have better luck this time."

"Maybe he will," says Adam.

The man leans toward us, resting his elbows on the top of his wall. He has a thoughtful, solemn look.

"In the end," he tells us, "folks put the past behind them. And that's how it has to be. People move on. That's what we all have to do, isn't it? To forget if we can and put the past behind us . . . well, good to meet you, Mr.—?"

"I'm Adam, and this is Grace."

"Good to meet you, Adam and Grace."

He reaches over the wall and shakes our hands. "I'll let Gordon know you're interested, he's going to be pleased . . ."

Sylvie is still playing on the steps. As we watch, she jumps and loses her balance and tumbles into the grass. I worry she's hurt, but she's laughing.

"Did you see that, Grace? I did a different jump. That was a *jellyfish* jump."

"Yes, I saw it," I tell her.

The man smiles with a sudden, surprising warmth. "That does my heart good," he says earnestly, "to see a little one play in that garden again . . ."

He waves, goes back toward his kitchen door, his dog careering ahead of him.

I feel we shouldn't stay here, now that he's gone.

"Sylvie, we have to leave now," I tell her.

"*I'm* not going," she says, speaking with absolute certainty.

She runs to the top of the steps again.

"Sylvie, really, we have to go. I mean it."

She turns her back deliberately toward me. She covers her ears with her hands, pretending not to hear.

I don't know how to manage this. I glance at Adam.

"Bribery, maybe?" he says quietly.

So I tell her we'll go to Barry's and I will buy her a KitKat.

She pauses on the steps, torn, then comes, but with reluctance. There's a slight pink flush in her face, and she's breathing hard and her jeans are dark with wet.

"See. That was fun, wasn't it, Grace?"

We go around to the front of the house again and get back into the car. I can see the man from the next-door house watching us intently from his living-room window.

Sylvie leans toward me across the back of my seat.

"Did you like it?" she says.

"Yes, I liked it," I tell her. "I liked the house and the plum tree and the three little steps."

"Yes." She has a satisfied look. "We always played on the three little steps."

The past tense chills me.

Adam turns sharply toward her. "Sylvie—who's *we*?" he asks her.

"Me and my family, Adam, of course." That condescending smile again, the smile that says, You just don't get it.

"Sweetheart, could you tell us about the games you played?" I ask.

Sylvie shrugs. "I'm an acrobat, Grace. You saw," she tells me.

I feel how elusive she is, how she seems to slip through your hands.

She turns to the rear window and watches till the road twists around and the house is lost to view.

# 36

Barry's General Store is rather drab and cluttered, selling a few dusty sand toys and a small selection of groceries. There's a glass case holding a birthday cake with complicated icing, and a handwritten notice announces "Erin's Celebration Cakes!!" A convection heater gives off a hot, scorched smell.

Sylvie chooses her KitKat, then wanders off to the back of the shop to look at some plastic windmills. Adam is by the counter, choosing a packet of potato chips.

I flick through the postcards. I want to write to Karen: the memory of the phone call still upsets me. I can hear her voice in my head, all the outrage in it. *You can't be doing this, Grace, you can't. I mean, for Chrissake, Grace . . .*

The woman who runs the shop is leaning on the counter. She has a mug of coffee, and a magazine open at the horoscope page. She's a wiry, angular woman with lipstick pink as cotton candy, and her gaze through her thick glasses is glittery and intent.

"You're on holiday here, then?" says the woman to Adam.

Adam nods. "We're staying at St. Vincent's."

"And very nice too," says the woman. "I hope that Brigid is pulling out all the stops for you."

She sips her drink. There are little stains of coffee around her mouth.

"She certainly is. She does a brilliant breakfast," says Adam.

"And you're getting a chance to explore our wonderful countryside?"

Her eyes are bright and curious.

"We drove over toward Ballykilleen this morning," Adam tells her. "By the longer route, round the coast. The views from that road are amazing."

"So they are," says the woman.

She pauses for a moment, her gaze flicking over our faces, as though there's something that she expects us to say.

Adam smiles vaguely, selects his packet of potato chips.

"I heard you were having a little look at Flag Cottage," says the woman then.

I turn sharply toward her.

But Adam nods and just moves smoothly on.

"It's got such a great situation, that house." He's unperturbed, as though this is perfectly normal. As though you'd expect a total stranger to know your every movement. "We were wondering why it was empty."

"Gordon's decided to put it on the market," says the woman.

There's satisfaction in her voice, in sharing this inside knowledge.

Adam nods. "His neighbor told us," he says.

The woman lowers her voice a little.

"Well, obviously, he wouldn't want to live there anymore."

She watches him, her lips pressed tight together. Her lipstick seems too vivid for the pallor of her face.

"Gordon isn't too keen on village life, then?" says Adam.

She licks the coffee from her mouth.

"Who was it you spoke to?" she says. "Was it Paddy O'Hanlon, next door? Thickset guy with a Border collie?"

"That sounds like him," says Adam.

"Paddy didn't tell you, then? Didn't tell you what happened?"

Adam shakes his head with a slight, apologetic smile.

The woman's voice is hushed. "Time flies, it seems like yesterday. But it must be years ago now . . ."

She's counting on her fingers. Adam waits for her.

She shakes her head. "You know, it must be seven years since Alice disappeared. That's Alice Murphy—Gordon's wife," she says.

"Since Alice disappeared? They're divorced, then, Gordon and Alice?" says Adam carefully.

The woman doesn't say anything. Her pupils through the thick glasses are like tiny, glossy beads.

"The neighbor we spoke to—Paddy," Adam goes on. "I did notice that he never mentioned Alice, and I thought they might be separated."

"I wish," says the woman. "No, nothing so straightforward . . . I mean, don't get me wrong. The ending of a marriage is a terrible thing, of course, don't think that I'm belittling it. But Alice Murphy—it wasn't like that. She simply vanished—off the face of the earth. And her little daughter with her."

A thrill of cold goes through me. I glance at Sylvie. She's still looking at the windmills. She doesn't seem to have heard.

"Alice walked out, then?" says Adam, keeping his voice quite level. "Just packed her bags and took her child and left?"

"We don't know. Nobody knows."

"But what about the gardai? Why didn't anyone find them? It's not that easy to vanish."

"It wasn't for want of trying," says the woman. "We had detectives from Dublin here. They talked to all of us, really combed through everything. I had to go to the garda station in Ballykilleen to give my statement. He was very insistent, the sergeant I saw—went over it all again and again. So you see why Gordon wouldn't want to live there anymore."

"Absolutely," says Adam.

"It was a bad time," says the woman. "A bad time for all of us." She closes up her magazine. "When something like that happens, you feel how fragile everything is."

We leave the car outside the shop and walk along the seafront, Sylvie clutching her KitKat. There's a slight wind blowing up that carries the smells of the harbor— diesel fumes and rotten fish and the chill salt scent of the sea. The water is moving very gently, like some great scaly animal that stretches and stirs in its sleep. There's hardly anyone about.

We sit at the top of the steps that lead to the beach. There's a white splash of birdshit on the concrete.

"Sylvie, can you tell me who lived in your house?" Adam asks her. "Who lived in Flag Cottage?"

"Me, Adam. I told you."

"D'you know what the people were called?" he says.

Sylvie frowns.

"People live with their family, Adam," she says.

I know he won't ask her directly about Alice Murphy, remembering what happened when I first talked to her about Coldharbour: once you've suggested something, you never really know.

"Can you remember anyone's name?" he asks her. "Anyone who lived there?"

"Me and Lennie, of course," she says.

"Anyone else at all, Sylvie?"

"They were my family, Adam. My family lived in my house. I *told* you."

"What happened to your family, Sylvie?" he says.

Her face glazes over. She turns a little away.

"Can you remember anything that happened, Sylvie?" he says, his voice too eager.

But there's a small dead bird she's noticed on the pavement, pale feathers scattered, a wing bone torn and straggling, the bones of its legs so delicate you feel you could see through.

"The bird died, Grace," she says.

"Yes, sweetheart."

"Try and think, Sylvie," says Adam.

She's peering at the blue, translucent bones. Her face is shuttered.

Then she turns to me, pulls at my sleeve. "I want to go off now. I want to look at the boats."

She's impatient. I know that now she won't say anything more.

"Okay, sweetheart."

She runs off to the jetty with rapid, confident steps. The salt wind tangles her hair.

I turn to Adam. "Is that the death we're looking for? Could it be Alice Murphy or her daughter?"

"I don't know. Maybe."

"It's scary," I say.

"Grace, there are lots of ifs about it. We don't know for sure if Alice and the little girl died. We don't even know if Sylvie really recognized Flag Cottage, or just liked it because it reminded her of her dollhouse . . ."

He's reticent in what he says, but he has that look, his eyes wide-open, like everything amazes him.

"It gives us a place to start from, though?"

"Absolutely," he says. "And that woman at Barry's said there's a garda station in Ballykilleen. I think we should go and talk to them."

"But if we go to the gardai—what on earth shall we say?"

He grins. "We'll be devious."

We sit there quietly for a moment. The sun is coming out through the cloud, and the sea holds every color you can think of—turquoise in the shallows, giving back the sky color, and farther out a richer cobalt shade. There's a line of deeper blue where the sea meets the sky. A sense of the strangeness of what we are doing here surges through me.

"When I was a kid," I tell him, "I used to wonder about the horizon. It bothered me. You know—what happens there? What happens over the edge? Did you ever think that?"

He grins. "I guess you were deeper than me, Grace. I was far too busy worrying about my stick of rock. How they'd managed to write 'Whitley Bay' inside it."

I smile. I like to think of him as a child.

When everything was ordinary, before the wreck, before it broke apart. I have an image of him in my mind—lanky, vivid, a little unpredictable.

"I used to try and work it out," I tell him. "What happened at the horizon. And I couldn't get my mind round it. That there's this edge, this limit to your sight, but if you got there, there wouldn't be an ending, there'd just be still more sea . . . There are places where your mind stops."

"Yes, there are," he says.

"And when you get older, you don't think things like that so much. But it's not that you've understood them now, it's just that you've given up trying . . ."

I have a sudden sense of loneliness, of our separateness from one another—here in this place among strangers, at what feels like the rim of the world. I glance at Adam, wanting someone to pull me out of this sadness, but I can't tell him, can't express it.

## 37

I go into St. Vincent's with Sylvie. It's lunchtime now, and the bar is filling up. Noise spills out through the half-open door—laughter and talk, a saxophone on the sound system.

We're just at the foot of the stairs when the door swings wide behind us. A man is leaving the bar. I turn, intensely aware of him. There's something about his self-assurance, his rather patrician manner, that brings Dominic instantly back to me. I can tell he's not a visitor; he moves as though he belongs here. He's tall, broad-shouldered, his hair touched with gray, his face just starting to age. He's wearing a jacket that looks like it's made from the softest cashmere, his linen shirt is the color of wheat, and he has a scarf of dark velvet that he wraps around his neck as he steps out into the cold. No one else in the village dresses so expensively.

He catches my eye, and his face relaxes into a slight, charming smile. I feel the blood hit my face.

"I hope you're enjoying your stay here," he says. His voice is cultured and deep.

"Very much, thank you," I say.

Sylvie pulls away from me. She runs toward the staircase. I hear the rapid drumbeat of her footsteps on the stairs. I'm surprised she didn't wait for me.

The man walks out through the doorway and turns to go up the hill. I realize I have turned, that I'm following him with my gaze.

There are footsteps behind me. Brigid has come to her desk. I give her a small, tight smile, feeling I've been caught out doing something illicit.

"You've met Marcus, then?" she says.

"Well, not *met* exactly . . ."

"I'll introduce you properly sometime. He's Marcus—Marcus Paul."

It's as though she expects me to recognize his name.

"Oh," I say.

"You'll have seen Kinvara House on the beach road?" she asks me.

"The house with the beautiful garden? The garden with all the flowers?"

She nods.

"That's Marcus's place," she tells me. "Though he's often away in Dublin. He has his businesses to run."

"His businesses?" I'm intrigued by this.

"He has a gallery there," she says. "Though, to be honest, some of the artists he shows are really too cutting-edge for my taste. And then there's his designer boutique. He sells the loveliest things, though of course it's all on the pricey side . . . Look, I've got a picture."

It's a page she's cut out of *Vogue*. The article is about Dublin as a mecca for the fashion conscious.

"There you are. That's Marcus's shop," she tells me.

The shop is called Papillon. It has scalloped blinds the color of vanilla ice cream, and bay trees flank the doorway. There are mannequins in the window, all clad in elegant black.

"There," she says. "What a shame I got here too late to introduce you."

When I go up to the landing, at first I can't see Sylvie. I feel a flicker of panic. Then I find her in the farthest corner, sitting on the carpet with her back to the wall. She's hunched, arms wrapped around her knees.

She looks up at me, and her face is pale and accusing.

"Where were you, Grace?" she asks me.

There's an edge of outrage in her voice.

"Just talking to Brigid," I say.

I unlock the door of our room, we go in. Her eyes are huge in her white face. It's as though I have failed her in some terrible, total way.

"I hate it when you talk to people. You should have stayed with me, Grace."

I wonder if the real reason she's cross is because I spoke to Marcus. I remember what happened with Matt and feel a flicker of irritation at how possessive she is, how she always tries to stop me from doing anything independent.

"Honestly, Sylvie. I can't *not* talk to people."

"I don't like people," she tells me. "I don't like people one bit."

I feel an urge to shout at her. I try to swallow it down.

There are stains of chocolate around her mouth from the KitKat. I find a tissue and wipe her face. She must have got chilled on the seafront; her skin is very cold.

## 38

Next day we drive to Ballykilleen.

"Aren't we going to my house, Grace?" says Sylvie as we turn down into the village.

"Not this morning, sweetheart. We're going to talk to the gardai. We'll ask them about the house, about Flag Cottage."

"Are you going to find my family? Are you going to?"

She's leaning forward toward me, pushing against her seat belt. Her face is full of light.

"We'll try to, sweetheart. We'll ask them. But I don't know what will happen."

Her expression clouds over. "But what if they can't find them? What if they can't find my family?"

"Let's wait and see what they say. Policemen often know things . . ."

The garda station is just down the hill from Joe Moloney's, past a trailer park that's all shut up for the winter and a lonely little cemetery where the flowers heaped on the graves are covered with netting to stop them from blowing away. We park, go in. There's a foyer with chairs and a desk with a sliding window, and through the window an office, where a man in uniform is talking on the phone.

Adam rings the bell. The man looks up. He's forty-something, tall and thin, with a long, narrow nose and a thatch of graying hair. In profile he has the look of a melancholy bird. He nods at us and finishes his conversation. He unfolds himself from his chair and comes to the window and pushes up the glass, studying us with interest.

"We're sorry to bother you," says Adam.

"That's what I'm here for, to be bothered," says the man. He's leaning on his elbows, so his face is level with ours.

"There was something we wanted to ask you," says Adam.

"Ask away," says the man.

"It's about a house in Coldharbour that's coming up for sale."

The man nods.

It's my turn to take over. We've decided on our story, but it makes me so uneasy, lying, pretending we're a couple. And I'm very aware of Sylvie hearing everything we say.

"Somebody told us—the woman at Barry's . . ."

My voice seems to come from somewhere else.

"Erin, you mean?" He pushes one hand through his mop of thick pale hair.

I nod. "She hinted that there was a story about it, that something bad had happened there. The thing is, I'm quite superstitious, and I don't want to live in a house where anything really bad happened." I attempt a shy, apologetic smile, yet I know I'm no good at subterfuge.

But he seems to take me at my word.

"That's perfectly understandable. Myself, I don't believe in all that. I don't think things that happen can leave any trace behind. But of course if you do, then it's going to worry you, isn't it?"

I nod gratefully.

"I'll see what I can tell you," he says. "You know the address of the house?"

"It's off the road north out of Coldharbour. It's called Flag Cottage," I say.

To my surprise, the man nods slightly. "I wondered if you'd say that. You'd better come through."

He lifts up a section of the desk. "I'm Detective Sergeant Brian Ennis. You can call me Brian," he says.

We tell him our names. He smiles at Sylvie.

"Could Sylvie stay out here with her books, where we can see her?" I ask.

"Sure," he says.

I have a comic and felt-tips in my handbag. Sylvie sits on one of the chairs in the foyer. I find her a picture to color in.

She reaches up and whispers in my ear. "Ask him about my family, Grace."

"Yes, sweetheart."

She presses up against me, and I feel the fizz of her heart.

"*Promise* you won't forget. *Promise*."

She's radiant with hope, and I'm so frightened for her.

Brian ushers Adam and me into his office, pulls out chairs.

I glance around the room. There's a photo of two girls on his desk: they're in their teens, in vest tops bright as fruit gums, and the older girl has exactly Brian's smile—self-mocking, a little laconic. Through the window there's a car park, with a line of dustbins and a palm with jagged leaves that clash together in the wind. You can hear their rattling through the glass.

Brian sits.

"So. Flag Cottage," he says.

"We heard that something happened there," says Adam.

"Something happened, too right," says Brian. He leans toward us, his elbows on his knees. "It was seven years ago now," he says. There's a solemn, portentous tone to his voice as he starts to tell his story. "Their names were Alice and Jessica Murphy. They vanished without a trace, just simply disappeared. It happened on a Tuesday. They must have left

Flag Cottage about half past six in the evening. Erin at Barry's in Coldharbour saw Alice driving down the street with Jessica beside her."

"How old was she—the little girl?" I ask him.

"Jessica Mary was nine years old," he tells me. His face darkens. "Just the same age as my Amy was then." He gestures toward the photograph. "Anyway, no one reported them missing till the Wednesday afternoon."

He pauses to let us digest this.

I look around to check on Sylvie. She's sitting quietly, drawing, a slice of sun from the window falling across her. The bright light seems to take all her color away.

"But somebody must have realized, surely," I say.

"Nobody knew," he tells us. "Alice's husband was off on the road. He's a computer salesman. I got the call at three. It was one of Alice's friends. They'd been due to meet for lunch at Foley's—that's the seafood bar in Coldharbour. When Alice didn't turn up, the friend went round to the house. She got no answer. So she called us."

He has a mug of coffee on the desk in front of him. He stirs it with a Biro, staring into the mug.

"Sometimes you get a case," he says, "and it's like there's just no way through. No body, no evidence. What can you do?" He gives his head a little shake. "It wasn't for want of trying, believe me. We had the big guys down from Dublin, picking over everything. But there simply wasn't anything to go on."

"But what about Alice's car?" says Adam. "Didn't they ever find it? Wouldn't there be some clue in that?"

"The car was found burnt out, a few miles south of Coldharbour," says Brian. "So any forensic evidence was destroyed."

"Maybe somebody killed them," I say, "and then set fire to the car. So there wouldn't be any evidence left."

He shrugs. "Or maybe Alice set fire to it—before she did whatever she did. Or it could have been kids just playing about. Say they found the car abandoned there and torched it for a laugh. Kids from the Hazeldene Estate in Barrowmore, most likely," he says. "There's a load of budding arsonists up there."

"You said . . . before Alice did whatever she did," says Adam.

Brian nods. "Alice Murphy wasn't a happy woman," he says. "She'd had a lot of treatment for depression. In fact, she'd been an inpatient up at St. Matthew's in Barrowmore—that's the psychiatric clinic."

"Suicide, then?" says Adam.

"That was one of the theories," says Brian.

"But you never found them?" I say.

"We looked. But you know how it is round here. There's so much empty country—places where a body might lie hidden for years." He gives a small, defeated sigh. "Well, as I say, we don't know, but that was always the theory I favored. That Alice took her own life, and took the little one with her."

I glance around at Sylvie, feel crazily afraid for her, as though she might be snatched away. Everything suddenly feels unsafe.

"You think that Alice killed Jessica?" Instinctively I lower my voice.

"Could be," says Brian. "Could be she

took her off up the mountain and gave her some ground-up pills to drink in a bottle of Pepsi. There have been cases like that."

I think about this, how it would be to kill your child—her pulse slowing, her eyes glazing over because of what you'd done. My mind shies from the horror of it.

My thought must show in my face.

"I'm sorry, Grace," says Brian. "I didn't mean to upset you. To be honest, we all found it hard. We had a psychiatrist in to help us. He said—what happens in these cases—the mother gets too identified with the child, she sees the child as part of her, so if she tries to kill herself, she will also kill the child. It's still sick, if you ask me. Beyond forgiveness, really."

For a moment nobody speaks. I listen to the quiet of the office. The wind in the palm outside the window has a cold, harsh sound. I feel slightly nauseous.

"And the other theory?" says Adam.

Brian shrugs. "Perhaps it wasn't as bad as that. Perhaps she just walked off into the sunset. There could have been a lover that we didn't know about. People do sometimes just walk out of their lives.

Some of us favored that notion. But I couldn't see it myself, and Alice did have depression, and it maybe wasn't the happiest marriage in the world. So I'm sticking with my first theory . . . Well, I hope I've answered your question."

"Yes. Thank you so much." I pick up my bag. "We're very grateful," I say.

Brian gives me his card. "If there's any other way that I can be of help, just ring." He has a slight knowing smile. "I'm sorry if I've put you off Flag Cottage."

"It's as well to know," I say vaguely.

He goes to open the lift-up flap in the desk. His eyes are on our faces. He gives us a sudden penetrating look.

"And maybe sometime you'll come and tell me what this is really about . . ."

We go back into the foyer. Sylvie jumps up and tugs at my sleeve.

"Did you find them?" she says. "Did you find my family?"

There are feverish pink patches in her face.

I glance back at Brian, wondering what he will make of this. But he's gone into his office. I collect the comic and felt-tips.

"We'll get in the car, and I'll tell you about it," I say.

In the car she doesn't immediately fasten her belt. She leans forward over our seats. There's a blue bruised smudge on her lip, where she's been sucking an inky finger. Her warm breath brushes my face.

"Did you find my family, Grace?"

I glance at Adam. I don't know if I should leave this to him, whether he'd handle it better, but he nods slightly.

"I'm not sure, sweetheart," I tell her. "We asked about the house—about Flag Cottage."

"Yes. Where my family lived," she says.

"He told us something happened. To the people who lived there."

"Yes, Grace."

She's watching me intently. Her eyes are fixed on mine.

"Can you tell me what happened?" I ask.

"A bad thing happened," she says.

I feel a thrill of fear. Then I remember what I said to Brian: *I don't want to live in a house where anything really bad happened.* Maybe she's just repeating that. I feel again how elusive she is, how she seems to slip through your hands.

"The man we talked to—Brian, the policeman," Adam says to her. "He told us about the people who lived in that house. He said the people disappeared. He said they may have died . . ."

Sylvie nods slightly. "Yes, Adam. People died." Her face is quiet and composed.

"Can you tell us about them, the people who died?" I ask her. My voice is thick in my throat. I feel uneasy speaking like this to a child, talking about death like this. I still feel the shock of what Brian said.

"Who were they, sweetheart?" I say.

Her eyes are on mine. She's rather cool and remote.

"I died, Grace. I died in the water," she says. Her voice so calm and matter-of-fact. I feel the lurch of my heart.

"Can you tell us what happened?" I ask her.

But it's hard to speak, my breath has been snatched away.

"The water was red," she tells me. "I saw the bubbles go up from my mouth."

She fastens her seat belt. She turns

away from us, looking out the window. She has her closed face.

"Can you tell us more about it?" Adam's voice is urgent, eager. I can hear his rapid breathing.

"I told you, Adam," she says.

"Can you remember anything else?" he asks her.

But she can't, or doesn't want to. I know that she's withdrawing from us, she won't say anything more.

I realize I am shivering. There's goose-flesh all along my arms.

I glance at Adam. His eyes are wide and amazed.

He drives us back by a different route that to start with follows the coast. It's a narrow, twisting road, the bright sea to one side of us, to the other side fields of rocks and black cattle and reeds, and shallow blue pools full of waving grasses turned to gold by the sunlight. In the distance, the mountains have cloud shadows skimming across them. I watch the many colors of the mountains, always changing and shifting, gray, then tawny, then purplish blue like damsons. I feel fragile, insubstantial, as though the slightest breath could blow me away.

"I want my family, Grace," says Sylvie suddenly, her voice very clear and definite. "I want my family back. I want them."

"I know you do, sweetheart," I say.

It hurts, as it always does.

The road turns inland. We come to a place where it forks, where you can turn left for Barrowmore or right to go south toward Coldharbour. There's a big old oak that leans across the road, and a broken barbed-wire fence with gorse and bramble bushes behind it, and a few bent, battered conifers twisted away from the sea. Up here, they must take the full force of the wind.

"Grace."

Sylvie's voice is small and panicky.

I turn quickly, see her face. Her skin is white as wax.

"Stop the car," I tell Adam. *"Now."*

He hears the urgency in my voice, pulls rapidly off the road.

I jump out, open her door, pull her out. I hold back her hair as she vomits onto the side of the road.

"You poor old thing," I say when it's over.

I stroke her hair. She has a greenish pallor, and she's trembling.

Adam brings me a box of tissues. I wipe Sylvie's face and her hands. I feel guilty—that we wanted too much of her, asked too many questions.

"We'll just stay here for a moment," I tell her. "We'll take some deep breaths. You'll be better out of the car."

The sun is fully out now, but there's no warmth in the sunlight. Above us, gulls flap emptily through the blue wide air.

"No," she says. "I want to get back in the car, Grace. I want to go back to St. Vincent's."

"You need some fresh air, sweetheart. That'll help you feel better."

A bird calls with a sound like a pot being scraped, and the leaves of the bramble bushes sigh and whisper together. There's a coconut smell from the flowering gorse.

*"No,"* she says.

She clambers back into her seat, sits there, waiting, expectant.

"I really think we should wait for a moment," I tell her. "I'm worried you might be sick again."

**"I want to go, Grace."**

She's implacable. Her mouth is set and tight.

I know there's no point in insisting.

"Well, all right. But you must promise you'll keep looking out of the window. That helps you not to feel sick."

"Yes," she says.

She folds her hands precisely in her lap. She turns to look through the window, rather pointedly, like I told her to. We drive away from the fork in the road, through the yellow glare of the flowering gorse.

"Is she often carsick?" says Adam softly to me.

"No, not carsick. But if she's been crying a lot, she can sometimes make herself sick." I remember the evening with Matt; it seems an age away.

"So it could be because she's upset? Something could be troubling her?"

"Yes."

I think, It was our fault, we pushed her too hard. But I don't say anything.

We drive down the hill into Coldharbour. The tension has left her face now. She's pale, almost translucent, but she doesn't have that panicked look. Her fingers are carefully folded together, as though she's frightened of breaking something, as though there's some precious, delicate thing she's holding in her hands.

# 39

It's Brigid's music night. Once Sylvie is settled, I go to knock at Adam's door.

Brigid has found him a folding table for his laptop. He's moved the table in front of the window, he's put a lamp on the table, he's sitting there in a circle of amber light. He's been pushing his hand through his hair, so it's ruffled and disorderly, and the sleeves of his Guernsey sweater are raggedly rolled up, and he has two half-empty coffee cups beside him on the table. He's chewing the end of a pencil.

I think, This is how he looks when he's

working—disheveled, messy, preoccupied. I like knowing this.

"Did you used to smoke?" I ask him.

He gives a slight, puzzled smile. "Yes. Why?"

"The way you're chewing that pencil . . ."

"I gave up last summer," he tells me. "Heroic feat of willpower. Horrible for everyone around me. They hid when they saw me coming."

I go to the table, stand beside him, looking at the screen. I can see my name and Sylvie's there. This jolts me, though I know I shouldn't be surprised. I understand that our quest here has a different purpose for him, that he hasn't come just to help us. That he's come here looking for something, an answer, a hint of meaning, wanting to find a way of living with his brother's death. I wonder if he will find that.

"Do you make notes on us?" I say.

"Yes. D'you want to read them?"

"No, it's okay. I trust you to be nice about us. Are you?"

He looks up at me for a moment. He's so intent, so serious.

"How could I not be?" he says.

A wave of heat moves through me.

He holds my gaze for a moment more. Then he turns from me and closes down his laptop.

"Grace! Adam! Let me buy you a drink," says Brigid.

We sit at a table near the fire. The four musicians are setting up—two violins and a flutist, and a heavy man in a crumpled shirt who has a bodhran, an Irish goatskin drum.

Brigid comes over to us with a tray of whiskeys.

"I hope you don't mind if I join you," she says.

"That would be great," I tell her.

She sits and sips her whiskey.

"Now, tell me, how do you all like Cold-harbour?" she says.

"It's a beautiful place," I tell her.

"It is that," she says. Her gaze rests on me a moment. Her thickly powdered face looks floury in the firelight. "And I gather you have an interest in our history round here?"

I nod.

She leaves a little pause. The flutist plays a brief bright flurry of notes.

"They tell me that you've been asking about Alice. About her disappearance. That you went to see Flag Cottage and you were asking about her."

"Yes," I tell her.

"Alice Murphy. Well, that's been our one big story, of course. And such a mystery."

It's an invitation to confide. I glance at Adam. He nods slightly.

"We went to talk to the gardai in Ballykilleen," I tell her.

"Brian Ennis?" she says.

"Yes."

Her mouth is set and tight, as though she doesn't quite approve of Brian Ennis.

"Brian thinks Alice killed herself," she says.

"Yes, he told us. Did you know Alice?" I say.

"Yes. I knew Alice."

"And what did you think? Did you think it was suicide?"

She sits there for a moment, not saying anything.

The musicians start to play. It's a vigorous hornpipe, rather repetitious, the kind of thing you could probably hear in any Irish bar. The drummer in the crumpled shirt beats out an insistent rhythm.

"Let me tell you about Alice," says Brigid then. The flickering red of the fire is in her eyes. "Alice was gorgeous. A bit like one of the Corr sisters, that dark-haired Celtic look. Clever, too—brilliant with figures. That was why Marcus took her on—because she had such a good brain on her."

"Marcus?" I remember the man I saw in the hotel lobby. I'm startled. "You mean, Marcus Paul? Alice worked for him?"

She's amused by my surprise. "She worked as his assistant when he was staying at Kinvara House. Did his accounts and everything."

I'm baffled by what we're hearing— this image of Alice, this pretty, competent woman.

"But Brian told us she'd been depressed," I say. "That she'd been in hospital."

"Yes, sure, she had, poor woman. But I bet he didn't tell you *why* she was depressed."

"No. Not really. Though he hinted it wasn't the happiest marriage."

Brigid nods slightly. "Sometimes you'll look at a couple, and you'll think, Now, how did that happen? Those two don't belong together. You know what I mean?"

"Yes, I think so," I say.

"They'd come in here for a drink sometimes. He'd be telling one of his long, rambling jokes, and there'd be this look on her face—her eyebrows raised, mouth tight, like she despised him. And sometimes there'd be such an edge in his voice when he spoke to her," she tells us. "Kind of threatening."

The music changes. The man in the crumpled shirt is singing in Gaelic. His voice is rough, untutored, midway between speech and music, and there's a dark silk thread of sadness stitched into the song.

"I did wonder, to be honest, if he hit her," she goes on in a hushed voice. "Gordon has quite a temper on him. There was one time when he stormed right out of the bar. She was talking to one of his friends and getting a little too cozy, and that kind of thing could set him off. And at times she'd wear her sunglasses even though it was dull, and I'd wonder what she was hiding. It worried me, but of course you don't like to ask . . . So when it happened, well, I did wonder if Gordon had found out something—" She hesitates. Her voice has a flicker of excitement running through it. "If Gordon had discovered there was something going on . . ."

We wait. My heart pounds.

"Sexual jealousy is a terrible thing," says Brigid then. "And it can drive people to terrible, desperate deeds."

For a moment, no one says anything.

"You think that Alice was having an affair?" Adam says carefully then.

"To be honest, I wouldn't have blamed her if she was," says Brigid. "She was a beautiful woman who married a bit beneath her. And Marcus, of course, he's a very attractive man. Well, you've seen him, Grace—wouldn't you say he was attractive?"

"Yes, I can see that. You know, that women might think that . . ."

Adam looks at me curiously. I'm cross to feel myself flush.

"I thought you liked the look of him." She has a fat, satisfied smile. "I can tell, you see, I can always tell." She takes her glass and drains it. Her exactly manicured nails gleam palely in the firelight. "So there you have it—that's what I've wondered. And so did a lot of people. Whether it was Gordon's doing—"

"But Brian said Gordon wasn't at home."

"True enough," says Brigid. "Gordon was off in Limerick. But let's face it, there are ways and means, if you're willing to pay. That's the way the world works. If there's something you want doing, you'll find a person to do it."

"And Jessica?" I ask her. "Why was Jessica killed—if she was?"

"Maybe it didn't work out as they'd planned," says Brigid. "Jessica maybe wasn't supposed to be there . . . So that's what we thought—what we all thought. Look, your glasses are empty, and I didn't even notice. I'm so sorry."

She goes to get more whiskey.

I must be drunk already. I have a hot, blurred feeling. The bar is filling up now, and faces loom toward me—somehow too big, their gaze too blatant and intrusive. The violins are playing together; the music is full of yearning and just a little off-key.

Brigid comes back with the drinks, settles herself at our table again.

"You know, I still don't get it," she says slowly. "You two intrigue me. And all this interest in Alice Murphy. I mean, you're not here just to have a good time, are you? I don't think that's what brought you . . ."

I feel a warm rush of gratitude toward her for being so open with us. I wonder what else she can tell us, if only we're honest with her. The whiskey loosens me, gives me a hot, rash urge to confide.

"It's because of Sylvie we're here," I say.

Adam is staring at me. I can see the concern in his face. I take no notice.

"There's something about that child," says Brigid. "Something so thoughtful. She seems too old for her years."

"It's funny you should say that," I say. I see Adam reach out toward me in a little restraining gesture. I know he wants to stop me. I ignore him. "You see, sometimes we wonder if she's remembering something. If she's remembering a past life . . ."

Brigid's eyes widen. She has a flushed, excited look. "Goodness. You mean *reincarnation*?" she says.

Immediately I wish I hadn't said it. But the words hang there between us, and I can't take them back.

I nod slightly.

"Well, why shouldn't it be so?" she says. "Why shouldn't Sylvie be an old soul? There's a whole great spirit realm around us—that I'm sure of." Her keen eyes glitter in the firelight. The violins soar and waver. "Maybe it's Alice Murphy come back to settle a score." There's a thrill in her voice. "Maybe Alice's soul wants vengeance."

"I don't know," I say. "I don't know."

A wave of nausea surges through me. I hate this. I wish I hadn't confided in her.

"If there's any way I can help you," she says.

"That's very kind," I tell her.

Adam puts his hand on my arm, as though to stop me saying more.

"I guess it's time we turned in," he says to Brigid.

I finish my glass. We say good night and go upstairs to our rooms.

I don't immediately go into my bedroom.

"Could we talk for a bit?" I say. "I don't want to be on my own."

I'm not quite looking at him. There's a sudden awkwardness between us.

"Okay," he says. But he doesn't move, just stands there, an uncertain look on his face.

"We could go out on my balcony," I tell him.

"Yes," he says.

We walk quietly into the bedroom. Sylvie has kicked off half her covers; her body is sprawled on the bed, arms and legs stretched out as though she'd been flung from a great height. I worry that she had a nightmare and I wasn't here. Perhaps I shouldn't have left her.

I pull the duvet up over her. Her face has a wholesome glow in the apricot light of the lamp, and her eyes are moving under her tight-closed eyelids. I hope this dream is a happy one.

I open the balcony doors, then pull

them shut behind us. The doors make an emphatic click, but Sylvie doesn't stir.

I sit on one of the plastic chairs. The cold silk touch of the air is welcome after the thick, beery warmth in the bar. The lamps along the jetty cast light across the water that's broken up into sparkly shards by the ripple and shift of the waves, and the sky is vast and deep, with a moon nearly full and a lavish sprinkling of stars.

Adam is leaning on the railing, looking out at the sea. It's so quiet, I can hear the creak of his shoes when he moves.

"You never see stars like this in London," he says. "Here there's real darkness, the real thing."

"Yes," I say. "I guess so."

Something in my voice makes him turn to me.

"You're cold," he says. "You're shivering."

To my surprise he takes off his sweater and wraps it around my shoulders. The wool is still warm from his body. I pull it close against me.

"I hated that." My voice is a little slurred, I can hear the whiskey in it. "I wish I hadn't told her—you know, about Sylvie. About the past life thing."

"Yes. Well, I did think you were taking a bit of a risk with that," he says.

"I hated those things she said," I tell him.

"Brigid's a bit of a drama queen," he tells me. He's got his back to the railing now, he's looking down at me. "She was loving every minute of it. She just wanted to tell a good story. She could have made half of it up."

"But that thing about vengeance," I say. "About wanting to settle a score. It was horrible. It was a horrible thought."

"Yes. But you shouldn't pay too much attention to her."

We are silent for a while. I stare out at the sea and sky, the glittery vista of cold stars, all that dizzying indigo emptiness.

"Sometimes I think—who is my daughter, really?" My voice sounds strange to me, and I'm not looking at him. "Sometimes I'm so afraid."

"Don't be," he says. "Don't be frightened."

He comes toward me, he's standing beside me, he puts his hand on my shoulder. I rest my head against him. It seems the most natural thing, to do this, to lean into him.

He pulls me up to stand in front of him. He reaches out one hand and touches the side of my face. His eyes are on me, but it's so dark, I can't read his expression. I want him terribly.

"You're so cold," he says again.

He kisses me with extraordinary direct-ness. My body is fluid, gentle, eager. I press myself into him. We kiss for a long time.

He draws away from me a little, easing his hand across my face, learning my face like somebody blind. Then he pulls me back toward him, kisses me again. Searching, oblivious, like a blind man. I want to stay here forever, in this moment.

Then at last we move apart, and I don't know what will happen now and I feel all the distance between us open up again.

"I'd better get some sleep," I say.

"Yes," he says. "Yes, of course."

"You'll need your sweater," I tell him.

I give it back to him, but with reluc-tance, feeling the cold brush my skin as I slip it off my shoulders.

I open the balcony doors very quietly. Sylvie has pushed the duvet down, but her eyes are shut and her face is calm in the apricot warmth of the lamp. There's a slight graze on my skin from the stubble on his jawline, where he hasn't shaved since this morning.

"I'll see you tomorrow," he says.

He opens the door to the corridor and leaves me.

## 40

Next morning I put on my tightest jeans and my boots with the spindliest heels. I'm shivery with anticipation, longing to see him again.

I go down to breakfast with Sylvie. He's there already.

"Did you sleep okay?" he says.

"Yes, fine, thank you. Sylvie didn't wake."

He smiles at us, but he's just the same as always. I feel briefly as though what happened last night was something I made up. I wonder what I mean to him—whether his kiss meant anything or whether I'm just a pleasant diversion for him while he's away from Tessa. His hands are clasped together around his cup. I look at his slender wrists, his long, thin, clever fingers. I would like to touch him, but I don't feel that I can.

I sip my coffee gratefully. Sylvie eats her buttered toast. Her mouth and the tips of her fingers are smeared and shiny with grease.

"Are we going to my house, Grace?"

"No, not today," I tell her. "We're going to drive through some different places. To see if you recognize anything. Maybe from before . . ."

It sounds so strange to say that.

On the table there's a vase of tulips, their petals red and frilly, like the skin inside a mouth. Sylvie reaches out and touches a petal with her fingertip.

"But I want to go to my house."

"Sweetheart, I don't know if we can go there again," I tell her.

"Yes, we can. When are we going?"

There's such insistence in her voice.

"I don't know."

She frowns at me, as though she thinks

there's something that I'm willfully over-looking.

"But I need to see it *properly*. I need to go *inside*."

"I don't see how we can do that, Sylvie," I tell her. "We can't just go barging in. The house belongs to other people."

"I want to. I want to see my bedroom and my family." She gets up out of her chair, comes around to stand beside me at the table. She reaches out and cups my face in her hands. It's how I hold her sometimes to try to make her listen. Her hands have a warm smell of butter and press hard into my skin. "*Please*, Grace."

Adam leans toward us across the table.

"You know, it's just possible, Sylvie, that we could make it happen. If we could get hold of the man who owns it."

"Yes, Adam. When can we do it?"

"Maybe in a day or two. I'll start by talking to Brigid."

"Yes. Talk to her, Adam," she says.

We drive north through empty country, beyond Ballykilleen and Barrowmore. It's a heavy gray day, and the tops of the

mountains are dulled and blurred by
cloud. Sylvie doesn't say anything, just
sits there quietly, looking out the window.
We stop for lunch at an abbey that's open
to the public, and eat sandwiches in a
bland café with country music playing.
Sylvie chooses some lurid yellow cheesecake. She draws a smiley face in the topping with her fork, but doesn't eat the
cheesecake.

We loop back through the mountains
and then down into Ballykilleen and along
the road toward Coldharbour that to start
with follows the coast. The bulging clouds
are darkening to the color of a bruise. We
talk about the weather, and how soon the
storm will begin.

I glance back at Sylvie. Her eyelids are
heavy, perhaps she's half asleep.

"Sylvie, don't forget to say if there's
anything you recognize . . ."

She doesn't reply.

If she falls asleep, I shall talk to Adam
about what happened last night. I shall
say, *That was a lovely evening, thank
you* . . . Keeping it light and casual, but
letting him know how I feel. I watch him as
he turns the wheel, and think of his hand

caressing me, moving over my skin. Heat surges through me.

Eventually our road turns inland. We come to the place where it forks, the left turn going southward toward Coldharbour—the place with the oak tree that reaches out over the road.

"Grace."

Her voice is tiny and full of panic. I know what that voice means.

"Oh, God," I say. "Stop, Adam. *Now*."

He brakes sharply.

I pull her out of the car. She vomits onto the side of the road; her whole body shakes with it. I hold her shoulders until the sickness has passed.

"Better now?"

She doesn't say anything.

"You'll soon feel better," I tell her.

Adam brings me a box of tissues. He's looking at Sylvie intently. I know he's thinking the same as me.

"Adam," I tell him quietly. "It's just the same place. It's where it happened before."

He nods.

"There must be a reason," I say.

"There *might* be a reason," he tells me.

I watch the thoughts that chase one

another like cloud shadows over his face—doubt and excitement and doubt again. "Grace, d'you think you could hang on here for a moment? I'll see what I can find out."

"Of course," I tell him.

There's a rough gravel track that leads off around the corner. He disappears briskly around the bend in the track.

I kneel beside Sylvie on the verge, smooth the hair back from her face. Her breath has a sour smell.

"I don't like it here, Grace," she says.

"We'll be going soon," I tell her.

A little breeze shivers the leaves of the bramble bushes, and the world has that echoey, hollow feel that comes before it rains. She scrambles into the car, and I sit in the back beside her.

"Where's Adam?" she says.

"He's just gone to look round the corner," I tell her. "To see if there's anything here."

She doesn't say anything for a moment. She pulls Big Ted from my bag and presses him against her, so her face is completely hidden.

A small cold rain is falling now, spattering on the windshield, hissing on the gravel path.

"There isn't," she says after a while. Her voice is muffled.

"Isn't what?"

"Anything here," she says. "There's nothing. Tell him to come back," she says.

"He'll be back in a minute," I tell her.

"I want to go now," she says. "I want to go back to Coldharbour."

She squeezes my wrist, presses so hard it hurts me.

I put my arm around her. There's a clammy chill on her skin. Being sick has chilled her.

"Hey. You're so cold."

I take off my sweater and wrap it around her.

*"Now,"* she says.

"He really won't be long. I'll read you a story," I say.

I look through the books in my bag, find *Where the Wild Things Are*. I open it on my lap, expecting the usual magic, that it will enchant her as it always does. She peels my fingers from the page, closes the book, pushes it back in my bag.

**"I want to go, Grace."**

Her eyes are narrow as she looks at me, the pupils like black pinpricks. I know this look. It's the face she has before she starts to scream.

I ring him, thinking briefly of what Karen would say, how much she'd disapprove of me giving in to Sylvie, but ringing him anyway.

I hear his ring tone from his jacket, on the backseat. He's left his phone in his pocket.

"I'll go and find him," I tell her.

"You can't leave me."

"Sweetheart, you can stay in the car. I'll just go to the corner, see if I can spot him. You'll still be able to see me."

"No," she says. "No." She starts to open her door.

"But it's raining, you'd only get wet," I tell her.

"Grace. You can't leave me here. You *can't*."

There's no point making an issue of it. I get out, help Sylvie into her raincoat. The keys are in the ignition. I find myself locking the car, although we're miles from anywhere.

We head off down the track. There's a stretch of barbed-wire fencing to the right of the track, and to either side a thicket of hazels and nettles, and one or two stunted fir trees, and a yellow-flowered scraggle of weed. We pass a derelict concrete shed scrawled over with graffiti. People have dumped rubbish in the bushes—a rusting baby buggy, a takeaway wrapper that looks from a distance like some extravagant flower.

"It's not a nice place," says Sylvie. She clutches my hand.

"I know what you mean," I tell her. "It does feel kind of creepy."

Behind us there's a far, open view across country. It's empty, no sign of people, just grassland and rocks and the coiled white strand of the road. The tangled vegetation presses in around us; the gorse flowers are yellow as sulfur. It's very quiet.

We come to a place where you can see through the bushes, the view on our right hand suddenly opening out. It was obviously once a quarry, though I can't tell what they quarried here. There are steep rocky walls that fall away, all overgrown with spiky plants, the brambles and gorses that flourish in poor soil, with last year's withered blackberries still clinging to the bramble stems. The berries have a scorched look, as though fire had passed over them. Down below us, there's a wide, still pool. The water is dark, opaque, it must be thick with mud and sediment, and it has a transient glitter as a little wind grazes its surface. A couple of seagulls are floating about on the pool.

Sylvie stops quite suddenly when we come in sight of the water. She stands there gripping my hand. The raindrops thicken and spit on the gravel path in front of us.

I pull at her. "Come on, Sylvie, we've got to find Adam. Then we'll go back to St. Vincent's."

She's shivering as though from a chill, like the chill you get with a fever. I kneel down, hold her. She's gasping as though she can't breathe. She retches again, spits out a little bile.

"Sweetheart, let's go a bit farther. Just see if we can find Adam."

But she doesn't react. It's like she can't hear me at all.

To my intense relief, I hear Adam shouting. He's way down below us at the edge of the pool; he must have climbed down the side of the quarry. Down there, at the water margin, there's a strip of muddy ground where people have left rubbish that they've dragged or pushed down the side—old tires, a fridge, some oil drums.

He waves at us. He's poking around in the rubbish, using a stick to upend a sheet of corrugated iron. He lets it fall, and an echoey clattering rips the silence apart. It's shocking, too loud for this silent place.

"Adam, we need to go," I shout.

"Okay, I'm coming," he calls.

He starts to climb a narrow path that snakes up the side of the quarry, half hidden between bramble bushes. A thick, pale smoke of sand and soil comes up from his feet as he climbs. I wish he'd hurry.

I put my arm around Sylvie.

"There. We've found him, sweetheart. We can go back to the car."

She doesn't move, just stands there clinging to me, shivering.

Adam reaches the top of the path. There's a slight sheen of sweat on his forehead, and his hair is slick with wet.

He stops abruptly as he joins us, stares at Sylvie.

"Grace. What's going on?" His voice is full of breath.

"Nothing. Nothing's going on. Sylvie's just really upset."

He stares at her, his fierce, urgent look.

"For God's sake, let's just go," I say. "We need to get Sylvie away from here."

I half pull, half carry her back to the car. She's difficult to carry. Her body is rigid, her wet plastic raincoat keeps sliding away from my hands. I put her in her seat, pull her wet raincoat off her, wrap my sweater around her. She's still shivering violently.

I'm about to close her door, but Adam stops me. He crouches down on the ground outside the car.

"Sylvie—what happened?" he asks her. "Did something happen to you here?"

She's staring straight ahead of her with fixed, unseeing eyes.

"*No no no no.*" She has a little gasping voice we can only just make out.

Adam is insistent.

"Sylvie, what are you seeing? Can you tell me what you're seeing? Something happened here, didn't it?"

Her eyes are huge, all the color is wiped from her face.

"Did someone hurt you, Sylvie?" he says.

It's as though she doesn't hear.

*"No no no no,"* she says again in her small, choking voice.

I see all the fear in her face. Cold creeps through me.

"Is that the water you told us about— the water where you died?" he says.

It's shocking when he says that.

*"No no."* Her voice fades, like she has no breath.

Adam glances toward me, perhaps wanting me to question her too.

But I'm desperate to get her away from this place—from whatever she's imagining or reliving, from whatever it is that haunts her.

"Adam, we need to go, we need to get away from here."

"Who said that?" says Adam to Sylvie. "Who said these things? Who said, 'No no no no'?"

Sylvie starts screaming, a thin, high-pitched scream, the scream of a panicked animal. She doesn't sound like a child.

"Adam, *for God's sake.*"

"Okay, we'll go," he tells me.

But I know he's reluctant. He has that overeager, fanatical look on his face.

He gets in the car and we drive away. Sylvie goes on screaming. I feel so angry with him for putting her through this. I daren't say anything. I know if I speak I will shout at him. The harsh rain lashes the windows, blotting out the view around us. There's nothing but the storm and Sylvie's screams.

But as we drive down into Coldharbour, her crying stops abruptly. I turn, and she is asleep. Perhaps the rhythm of the windshield wipers has soothed her.

Some of my anger seeps away now that she's quiet. I feel like I've been holding my breath. I let myself breathe deeply.

"We need to speak to Brian," says Adam. "Find out about that place. Find out if anything's happened there."

I glance across at him. His knuckles are white where he's grasping the steering wheel. I feel a flicker of some different, gentler emotion, some empathy or compassion. I sense how he suffers, how driven he is. But I still feel he shouldn't have done it.

"I wish you hadn't pushed her like that," I tell him.

"Grace, it's what we came for. We have to understand it."

"She was so upset," I tell him. "I always feel as though you'll *break* her when you do that . . ."

"You can't protect her, Grace. Whatever happened, has happened. You can't undo it, you can't protect her from it. We have to help her face it."

I glance back at Sylvie. She's still very pale, but the strain has left her face now. She's slumped down in her seat so the seat belt catches her throat. I reach back and push it away from her neck. It's left a red mark like a scar or a cut on her skin. She shifts and murmurs something, but I can't hear what she's saying.

## 41

Sylvie plays on her bed with her LEGO. She still seems white and subdued. I go to stand on the balcony, staring out at the sea. I keep seeing all the fear in her face at the quarry.

I think, Karen was right, we should never have come. It's happening just as she predicted: Sylvie seems even more desperate now, just getting deeper in. We're putting her through all this pain, but to what end? There's nothing certain, nothing clear, nothing but hints and guesses. Most likely we will never reach the heart of the mystery.

The rain is easing off now. There are glints of light in the sky. I turn to watch her through the glass, my small pale child, with her quiet, decorous movements and the silk hair that shadows her face, and it suddenly seems so clear, so obvious, to me. So simple.

I go back into the bedroom, kneel beside her.

"Sylvie, I've been thinking, sweetheart. I guess we shouldn't have come here— that it was stupid to come. It's time to go back home again."

She turns to me with a puzzled frown, as though she can't make sense of this.

"*What*, Grace?"

"Sweetheart, this isn't working, is it? It isn't helping you, really. It's only making you miserable. I'm going to take you back home."

Her mouth is a thin, tight line.

"I'll talk to Adam," I tell her. "See if we can get a flight to London tomorrow." I smile at her lightly, encouragingly. "Sylvie, let's go home."

Her eyes are on me, cool and clear.

"I'm not going back to London," she tells me. "You can't make me."

"But sweetheart, if you're unhappy here . . ."

"I don't like London," she tells me. "I don't want to go back to London." She stares at me. She's tiny and fragile and utterly implacable. "London isn't home."

I hate it when she says that.

## 42

We go back to Ballykilleen to speak to Brian.

We leave Sylvie waiting in the car with picture books and a packet of potato chips. I stand where I can see the car. I wave, but all I can see is the top of her head.

Brian doesn't seem at all surprised to see us.

"You two again? Well, that was quick," he says.

"Brian." I swallow hard. "We didn't quite tell you the truth, the time we came before. As you suspected."

He nods, waits for me to go on.

"Why we came to see you—why we came here at all—it's because of my daughter," I tell him. "Because of Sylvie. There's something wrong, and we don't know what. She sometimes gets very upset." I clear my throat. The words are hard to form. "And we think, well, that it's possible—that she could be remembering a previous life."

He raises one skeptical eyebrow. "Well, that's a new one on me, Grace."

I feel the heat in my face.

"It's why we asked about Flag Cottage. She seemed to get so excited when she saw it, she keeps saying she lived there before . . . Adam's a researcher, he works at a university." I hope that saying this will give us a more respectable air.

To my relief, he doesn't laugh or immediately dismiss what I've said. He muses on this for a moment.

"To be honest, I'm not the kind of man who goes in for that kind of thing. You die and there's an end of it, that's how I see it," he says. "But the fact is, in this line of work you need an open mind." He leans a little toward us. His elbows are resting on the desk, his long hands wedged in his thatch of thick pale hair. "Some forces use psychics, of course. When they can't get a lead on a case. It's done a lot more often than the public might suppose. Well, you'll know about that from your researches, Adam . . ."

Adam nods.

"So let's push the boat out," says Brian. "Let's imagine that your little girl is really onto something. Talk me through that."

"There's a place we've driven past," I tell him. "Driving to Coldharbour from here, where the road turns away from the coast. There's a big oak tree and a track that leads off the road. It looks like there's an old quarry there."

"That's Gaviston Pits," says Brian. "They've quarried there for centuries. Dreary spot, I always think."

"Sylvie keeps being sick when we pass it. It's happened twice now. Always at just the same place."

"Poor little kid," says Brian with ready empathy.

"And we wondered if something had happened there—maybe a crime or something?"

He shakes his head. "The only major

crime round here has been Alice's disappearance. If it *was* a crime, that is. And her
car was found ten miles away, on the road
going south out of Coldharbour. There's
nothing at all to link Alice with Gaviston
Pits."

I don't say anything. I feel a little drag of
disappointment.

"So I guess we've got ourselves a mystery here," he tells us. "Kids can get frightened of anything, of course. When my
Amy was little, she had a thing about
feathers. Oh, and those hot-air dryers you
get in public lavatories. Absolutely terrified."

"But there's water at Gaviston Pits," I
say. "And she told us this thing . . ." My
voice sounds thin and hollow. "She said
she died in water." Something unreadable
moves over Brian's face when I say this.
"She couldn't tell us where it was. But we
saw the water at Gaviston Pits. You could
drown—or hide a body."

"You're thinking, if it was suicide, that
maybe Alice drowned herself and Jessica
there?"

"We wondered."

He shakes his head.

"She'd never have managed to get from the road to the water. The sides are too steep, she'd never have found a way down."

"There's a path down the side," says Adam. "It isn't all that difficult."

Brian is surprised. "You've been there?"

"Yes," says Adam.

Brian doesn't say anything.

I glance toward Sylvie. The car is steaming up; she's drawing faces on the window. She's restless. Soon she'll come and get us. I'm trying to remember all the things we need to say.

"We talked about it with Brigid—you know, at St. Vincent's," I say.

"Yes, I know Brigid," he says.

"And Brigid was hinting that people suspected Gordon. That Gordon used to beat Alice up."

Brian's mouth is tight. "People can suspect all they like. But Gordon was out of the frame. He was on the road in Limerick when Alice disappeared. We saw the hotel register."

"And what about Marcus Paul?" I say. "I mean, Alice worked for Marcus. And Brigid said they were close . . ."

Brian is shaking his head even before I've finished.

"His alibi checked out," he says. "Marcus was in Galway on the day it happened, with Brigid, at the races. In the VIP tent, most likely, guzzling lots of champagne. Lucky beggars. You'll have met Marcus, of course?"

"Sort of. Well no, not really," I say, then think how stupid this sounds. I see Adam glance at me, startled.

"Marcus—well, he's one of those men— how to put it? Marcus knows how the world works." I can hear the respect in Brian's voice. "It all looks so easy for Marcus, he wears his life like it's tailored just for him." I think of the man I saw in the bar—his patrician air, his rather proprietorial gaze. This seems an apt description. "You've probably seen his house from the road. Kinvara House. Finest house in the county, that."

Sylvie is beckoning through the car window. She thinks we're taking too long.

"This quarry—Gaviston Pits," says Adam. "Did you search it after Alice and Jessica disappeared?"

"Well, not as such," says Brian. "There really wasn't a reason to."

"Could you search it now?" I ask him. "Would you consider doing that?"

He smiles indulgently at me. "Sorry, Grace. The case is closed. It's cost us hundreds of thousands already, with nothing to show for it—no result, nothing."

"But, if they might be under there . . ."

He shakes his head. "It isn't that easy," he says.

Adam looks rather deliberately toward Brian's desk and the photos of his children.

"Jessica Murphy was just the same age as your daughter Amy, you said."

He's trying to speak so casually, but I see the urgency in his face, the little lines between his brows, as sharp as though cut with a blade.

Brian nods. "There are cases that really get to you," he tells us. "And this one got to me. I remember how it happened. It was when the family gave me a list of the things that Jessica had on. I remember the items even now. Trainers with air bubbles in the soles, and those bits of jewelry they go for—lockets and bracelets and so on—and an *NSYNC sweatshirt. Exactly like the things my Amy wore."

"It must really bring it home to you," says Adam.

Brian nods. "Yes, it does that . . . Look, I might just take myself off and have a snoop around Gaviston Pits. Considering what you told me . . ."

## 43

Sylvie doesn't want breakfast. She says she will stay in the bedroom and play.

I hesitate. I don't like to have her out of my sight. But I tell myself I mustn't be overprotective. Nothing could happen to her—it's such a small hotel, and we won't be far away.

"Okay, sweetheart. If you need me, just come down to the dining room," I tell her.

"Yes, Grace."

Adam is at our table already when I get there.

"No Sylvie?"

"She wasn't hungry," I say.

He has a rather triumphant smile.

"I got hold of Gordon," he tells me. "I got his number from Brigid."

This amazes me.

"But—how did you explain it? What did you say?"

"I was pretty straight with him, really. I said that we'd driven past Flag Cottage. That Sylvie seemed to have some kind of psychic connection with it, and that she'd begged to see inside it. He's working there this morning, and he'd be happy to show us inside."

I eat my breakfast quickly. I'm longing to tell her.

Outside the door of our bedroom I feel a flicker of panic—I can't hear any sound from the room. But then I go in and she's there, of course, rearranging her animals.

"Sylvie. We're going to do what you wanted. We're going back to Flag Cottage, and we're going to see inside it. Adam's fixed it," I tell her.

Her face is luminous.

She's already dressed for the day, but she insists on changing. She wants to put on her favorite clothes, her suede laced boots and her daisy dungarees.

"Do I look nice, Grace?" she says when she's ready. "Will they still like me?"

"You look lovely," I tell her, and hold her for a moment.

She's so happy, I'm frightened for her.

The man who opens the door is very tall and broad-shouldered, with dandruff-flecked black hair that falls forward over his face. He's wearing paint-stained clothes, and there's a blur of wood dust on him. He must have been working hard. His forehead glistens, a smell of sweat hangs about him.

"I'm Gordon Murphy," he tells us.

He brushes his palms on his trousers and reaches out to shake hands.

I glance at Sylvie. She has a happy, expectant smile.

I'm rather nervous of him, remembering what Brigid said, how there were people who thought he'd murdered Alice. But he's not what I'd expected. There's something hunched and cowed about him, that look tall people sometimes have, as though he's never quite grown accustomed to using up so much space.

We introduce ourselves.

"And this is Sylvie," I tell him.

"*Honestly*, Grace." She smiles benignly at me, as though I amuse her with all my mistakes. "*Honestly*. Of course he knows who I am."

She pushes past him into the hall. I'm startled. It's so unlike her to move ahead so boldly. Gordon stands aside, and we follow her in.

The hall has no furniture. Paintpots are piled in the corner. There's a resinous scent of wood dust and the headachy smell of new paint. There's a chill in the place, as though it hasn't been heated for ages, and it has that sad, transitional feel of all uninhabited houses.

"Sorry it's all such a mess," he says. "I've been doing a bit of sanding."

The kitchen and the living room lead off from the hall. Their doors are open. Sylvie darts into the kitchen. It looks much as it looked from the garden, the walls stripped back to the plaster, lumps of insulation hanging loose. Sylvie spins around rapidly, her bright glance flicking across the room. There's such intensity to her.

There's a cupboard door beside the sink, as tall as a door to a room. Sylvie pulls it open. Inside is an old-fashioned walk-in pantry with floor-to-ceiling shelves.

I'm embarrassed.

"Sylvie. You mustn't do that. You can't just go opening doors in other people's houses."

But it's as if she hasn't heard me.

"Don't worry," says Gordon. "It's okay by me. She can have a good poke around if she wants."

The pantry is almost empty—there's just a pack of Marlboros and a tin of instant coffee powder. Whatever she's looking for isn't here. Her shoulders seem to sag a little. She closes the door, goes back into the hall. Gordon follows.

She pushes into the living room, the room we looked into before. The tarnished mirror still hangs on the wall, holding the white of the sky and the budding green of the garden, but Gordon has swept the rubbish away and he's started sanding the floor. A mist of wood dust hangs in the air; it catches the back of your throat.

"It's a lovely room," I say to Gordon.

"I'm planning to open the fireplace up," he tells me. "But the old boiler's still behind there, so it's quite a lot of work . . ."

"You're selling up, your neighbor told us," says Adam.

Gordon nods. "It's a while now since I lived here. We had our troubles, back then." It's as though the air in the place is subtly changed when he says that. "Well, maybe you've heard a bit about that."

"Yes. Just the outline," says Adam. "I'm so sorry."

"I could never live here again," says Gordon.

He's standing in a pool of light that falls through the wide window. In the unforgiving sunlight, you can see how lined his face is.

"No. Of course not," says Adam. "Of course you wouldn't want to."

There are questions we need to ask him, about the disappearance, about his family. But I can't ask these things—not now that I've met him and seen the grief in his face—can't say, *Sylvie might be remembering a past life here with you. She could have been your daughter or your wife . . .* It seems too bizarre, too intrusive, to say that. Adam too is quiet. Perhaps he feels the same.

Sylvie glances around briefly, but whatever it is she wants so urgently doesn't seem to be here. She opens a door to the side of the hearth. There are steep stairs behind it. She clambers up the stairs.

"Sylvie, be careful," I call, not wanting to let her out of my sight.

"She'll be okay," Gordon tells me. "There aren't any holes in the floor or anything."

Our footsteps seem too loud on the uncarpeted stairs.

We follow Sylvie into the bedroom that runs along the front of the house. It's a big room stretching the width of the place, with a steeply sloping ceiling. It must have been a child's room. There's a rickety dressing table with cartoon cutouts stuck to it, and Tom and Jerry wallpaper that someone has started to strip in a rather random way.

Sylvie walks around the edge of the room, trailing her fingers across the things she passes—the glass top of the dressing table, the mantelpiece, the walls—with quick little darting gestures.

Gordon watches her, smiles. "I guess you like this room the best. Well, no surprises there."

"It's my room, isn't it?" she says to Gordon.

"This is the one you'd choose, then, is it?" he asks her. "If you lived at Flag Cottage?"

She frowns slightly. She turns to me.

"It's beautiful, isn't it, Grace? It's the *best* room."

"This was always a favorite room," says Gordon. "It's got a great view of the sea."

He gestures toward the window.

"I was wondering whose bedroom this was?" Adam's voice is tentative, careful. "When you were all living here in the house?"

"It was my daughter's room," says Gordon. A shadow crosses his face.

There's a low built-in cupboard beside the fireplace. Sylvie opens the cupboard door, gets down on her knees, half disappears inside. But there's nothing much in the cupboard, just an empty cardboard box and some scrunched-up sheets of newspaper. She crawls back out again. Her hands are dark with dust, and there's a lost, troubled look on her face.

I go to look through the window. When we came here at sunset, with the sky all colored, it seemed such a wonderful place, but today the view seems bleak to me, these lonely fields of gorse and stones, and beyond them the endless shivering gray of the sea. The sadness of the house presses down—a feeling of incompleteness, of something torn or broken.

There's another bedroom along the back of the house, looking out over the garden—the shaggy lawn and blossoming apple tree—and next to it a bathroom. Sylvie leads us through the rooms. In the bathroom the shower curtain is pulled across the bath. Sylvie pushes it back and checks behind it. But now there's something saddened and disconsolate about her. Every room we enter, she seems less happy, less sure, her brightness clouding over.

"Well, that's it. Now you've seen the whole place," says Gordon.

"Yes. Thank you," I say.

At the top of the stairs, as Sylvie is just about to go down, she waits for Gordon, and reaches out and puts her hand in his. He seems at once touched and unnerved. He glances back at me anxiously, not knowing what I'll make of this.

"Your little one's right," he tells me. "You need to take care on these stairs. We wouldn't want to go flying, would we?" Trying to smooth it over.

They walk down the stairs together. Adam watches everything.

She stops three steps from the bottom, lets go of Gordon's hand.

"I want to be jumped down," she says.

I go to swing her down the steps.

"Not you, Grace," she tells me. *"Him."*

But I do it anyway.

Gordon turns to face us. "Well, that's the grand tour," he tells us. "Now, anything else I can help you folks with at all?"

"No, I think we've got the picture," says Adam. "You've been extremely helpful."

"Yes, thank you," I say. "You've been so kind. Sorry we bothered you like this . . ."

I'm about to walk to the door.

Sylvie goes up to Gordon, presses herself against him, lifts her face toward him as though expecting a kiss. A hot embarrassment washes through me.

Gordon blushes. He doesn't know how to handle this. He takes a step away from her, ruffles her hair with a small, uneasy laugh.

"Sylvie. We need to go now," I tell her. "Let Gordon get on with his work."

She doesn't move. There's a little frown of perplexity in her face. I feel a flicker of panic. For a moment I think that she isn't going to come—that I'll have to drag her away from him, that she'll start screaming.

"You need to say goodbye now, Sylvie," I tell her.

I go to take her hand. To my intense relief she lets me pull her away from him. Her hand is cold and limp in mine, as though some vital energy has sunk in her.

We thank him again and go out onto the path. Gordon shuts the door behind us. Dust from the house has clung to us. You can feel its dryness on the tips of your fingers, and there's a yellowish bloom like pollen on our clothes.

Sylvie is frowning. "He didn't give me a kiss," she says as we go to open the car. "Is he cross with me, Grace?"

"No, of course he's not cross with you, sweetheart. He doesn't really know you. People don't kiss other people that they don't really know."

"He *does*. He *does* know me. Grace, he *does*."

We climb into the car, and Adam drives away. Sylvie twists around as she always does, staring out of the rear window until we turn the corner and the house is lost to view.

I turn to face her. "What were you looking for, sweetheart?" I say. "Why did you open the cupboards?"

"Lennie wasn't there," she says.

Whenever she talks about Lennie, I feel a surge of hurt about Karen and what happened.

"Lennie's in London," I tell her, as I always do.

She ignores this. It's as though I hadn't spoken. She speaks over me.

"I couldn't find Lennie. Where's Lennie hiding?" she says.

Adam pulls the car over, stops abruptly on the shoulder of the road. He twists around to face Sylvie.

"Sylvie, who's Lennie?" he says. "Who *is* she?"

"She's like me, Adam. She looks like me. Two peas in a pod. I *told* you."

It must be as Karen suggested. It's that complete and perfect family that Sylvie has invented, and a perfect imaginary friend—someone a bit like Lennie but who will always do what she wants, like another part of her.

But Adam doesn't think this.

"Did you and Lennie play hide-and-seek?" he says.

"Yes, of course, Adam," says Sylvie. "Me and Lennie."

She sounds quite matter-of-fact, but she looks so fragile and pale. Her mouth quivers.

"D'you think you could tell us who Lennie is?" says Adam.

Sylvie begins to cry, quietly, bleakly. Her tears spill over her face, and she doesn't brush them away.

"Leave it, Adam," I tell him. "Just leave it, okay?"

He shrugs slightly. I know he disagrees with me, but he starts up the engine again.

I take a tissue, reach back to wipe Sylvie's face.

"Don't cry, sweetheart."

She pushes the tissue away. "I can always find Lennie," she says through her tears. Her voice is fierce with protest.

"She's really good at hiding. But in the end I always find her. Where's Lennie gone to?" she says.

"I don't know, sweetheart. I don't really know who Lennie is."

Her tears go on falling, and I can't stop them.

"You've got to find her for me, Grace," she says.

# 44

The next day, Sylvie seems happier. She comes with me to breakfast and eats a lot of toast.

"Can I go and look at the boats?" she asks when she's finished. "I like to look at the boats."

I tell her yes. We walk to the seafront with Adam.

It's a blue and glimmery day, the tide far out, the beach a perfect white crescent, so pure and clean it's like it's just been made. Way down by the sea, the sand has a sheen where it's been smoothed out by the water, with no mark of a human footprint, just the exact webbed print of a bird. I'd love to walk there.

"Sylvie, why don't we go down on the beach? It looks so lovely," I say. "We wouldn't have to go anywhere near the sea."

"No." Her closed face. "I don't want to."

There's someone new on the seafront today: a woman has set up her stall in front of a shop that sells Irish crafts and bodhrans with your name on them. She's hoping maybe for tourists or for day-trippers from Galway, though it seems a little optimistic so early in the year. The woman is young, she looks about nine-teen, and I wonder if she's an art student; she has earrings made of feathers, and tattoos. She sells Celtic crosses on leather thongs, and woven belts and bracelets, and there's a sign with photographs, to show she will braid your hair. We say hello as we pass, and Sylvie stops by the photographs.

"I want a hair braid," she tells me.

"Okay. If you'd like one."

We pay our five euros. The woman smiles at Sylvie.

"Shall we choose your colors?" she says.

She has her threads laid out on a tray. She looks at Sylvie with an artist's appraising eye.

"You're a real little Nordic blonde. You're so lucky to have that coloring." She turns to me. "Isn't she lucky?"

"Yes, I guess so," I say.

"Nothing too obvious, I think. We don't want to overwhelm her."

She pulls out sherbet colors, strawberry, lemon, pistachio.

"D'you like them, darling?" she says to Sylvie.

Sylvie nods.

She sits on the stool in front of the woman. The woman starts to weave. She has deft, clever hands with bitten nails. The cuffs fall back from her wrists as she works; you can see the tattoos on her forearms, the intricate serpents and arabesques, and the serpents seem to slither around as her muscles tense and ease.

Adam and I sit on the seawall and watch. I think about Flag Cottage.

"D'you think we'll ever make sense of it all?" I ask him.

I hear how tired my voice sounds.

Maybe Adam hears it too. He takes my hand between his hands. Desire moves through me at the touch of his skin. I hear my breathing quicken.

"Grace, don't despair," he tells me. "We just need to keep on asking—give Sylvie a chance to tell us."

We sit for a while in silence. I look around at the white, blowy beach. The salt breeze fingers my face. Way out, there's a lobster boat, with a smoke of seagulls behind it. The silence spills over between us and scares me.

He moves his hand to cradle my head, pulls me toward him, just brushes my mouth with his mouth. It's the lightest kiss, but I feel it right through me. I feel undone by his touch.

Sylvie comes running back to us, and we edge away from each other. When I blink, there's a dazzle against my darkened eyelids, as though all the light from the water has got into my eyes.

Sylvie spins so her braid flies out.

"It's pretty, isn't it, Grace?"

Adam photographs her on his cell phone. The image is bright and blurry with her movement. He shows her the picture, and she's pink and flushed with pleasure.

I'm thinking about what Adam said. *We just need to keep on asking.* I decide I will seize this moment—when she's so relaxed and pleased.

I crouch down, put my hands on her shoulders, holding her there in front of me.

"Sweetheart, there's something I need to ask you," I say.

She's smiling, looking into my face.

"Yes, Grace."

My mouth is thick, like blotting paper. I wish now I hadn't started on this. I'm scared I will make her unhappy.

"It's about Flag Cottage. About the people who disappeared . . ."

"Yes," she says.

"And what you told us about before . . ."

My throat seizes up. I can't quite say it out loud.

"When I died, Grace?"

"Yes. Then."

Her face is quiet and serious.

"Can you tell me what happened?" I ask her.

"I told you," she says. "The water was red."

"Is there anything else you remember?"

"The water was cold and red. It hurt me, Grace. It hurt me *here*," she says.

She touches her chest with one finger.

I shiver when she says that.

"What hurt you, sweetheart? Was it a person who hurt you? Can you tell me?"

Her expression is blank, as though she doesn't understand the question.

"It hurt, and I saw the bubbles," she says. "Lots of bubbles went up from my mouth."

I move my hands to her face. I feel how chilly her skin is.

"Sylvie. Can you tell us what happened before? Before the water?"

She doesn't say anything. Maybe she doesn't know, can't answer.

"Sweetheart. Before the water. Who was there?"

Her face is shuttered. I feel her slipping away from me.

I try again.

"The water where this happened, sweetheart. Where was it? Can you remember?"

She doesn't say anything.

"Is it a place that we've seen?" I ask.

But she slides from my hands, goes running along the seafront. She stops by the window of Barry's and studies her reflection in the pane.

## 45

That night, we eat again at Joe Moloney's in Ballykilleen. Sylvie plays with her hair braid, wrapping it around her hand.

"D'you like it?" she says. "It's really pretty, isn't it?"

"Yes, it's pretty," I tell her.

It's utterly dark when we leave, all around us the great still scented quiet of the Irish night. Adam drives slowly. A dazed sheep runs in front of the car, then lurches off into the blackness.

We come to the right turn that leads across Coldharbour Bog. There's a sign that says YIELD, and usually Adam stops here. He brakes, but the car glides forward, over the line.

"Shit," he says.

My pulse races off.

"What's wrong?" I ask him.

"I think it's the brakes. They feel kind of spongy," he says.

He drives on very slowly to a place where the road is wider, pulls over, turns off the ignition. It's so quiet in the car without the engine noise.

I can see the black of the sky and the denser dark of the mountains, and the lights of Coldharbour far off, like a handful of bright beads flung down.

"But can't we just drive on—you know, really slowly?" I say.

"No, we can't," he tells me.

I feel the dark edge closer.

"*Please*, Adam." There's a shred of panic in my voice. "I don't want to stop here."

"No. There's no way I'd risk it. Not with Sylvie in the car."

"But if we just drive very slowly?"

"*No*, Grace."

There's something hard in his voice—I sense he could get angry with me. I glance at him. He looks shaken. I think about Jake, of the fear he must have that something like that could happen again. I feel a surge of protectiveness, wanting to reach out and put my hand on his arm.

"I'm sorry," I say. "I'll shut up now."

"I'll ring the AA. We'll just have to wait," he tells me.

He turns on the map light, starts flicking through the information folder. With the light on, there's a deeper darkness to the night outside. We're so exposed now, people miles away could see us.

"Adam. If it's the brakes, could someone have done something to them?"

Yet even as I say it, it seems a wild idea.

"Grace. Calm down," he tells me. "I'm sure nobody's tampered with anything."

But I see his frown, the sharp little lines between his brows.

I wind my window down. Cool air touches my cheek, carrying the smell of the peat bog, that heavy scent of roots and rot and wet. The countryside smells stronger at night. In the frail gleam from the map light, the cotton grass has a bleached look. You can hear the strange, scraping croak of some hidden frog or bird, and a hissing in the grasses, the incessant seethe of the wind.

Adam is making his call.

"Can't you be any quicker? We've got a young child in the car."

I hear the anger in his voice. He's more worried than he's admitting to me.

"They'll be an hour," he tells me.

I feel afraid, but I don't know what I'm afraid of.

I turn to Sylvie. "We're going to have a bit of a wait," I tell her.

She undoes her seat belt, leans across the seats between us. She's looking at the Saint Christopher that hangs in the front of the car. She taps it with one finger, and it sends out sparkles of light.

"You could read your comic," I tell her.

I hand her Big Ted and the comic and a felt-tip.

"I'm hungry," she tells me.

I have emergency supplies that I bought at Barry's this afternoon—a Twix, a packet of potato chips. I give her the Twix; she pushes down the paper, takes a bite. She sits back in her seat, but she can't seem to get comfortable, and I take off my sweater to make a pillow for her head. She opens her comic and works on one of the puzzles, using her felt-tip to trace a path through a maze. Now and then she picks up the Twix and takes a little bite. There's a sepia trace of chocolate around her mouth. Whatever scares me about this place doesn't seem to frighten her.

We sit there in the quiet. My breathing seems too loud. I hear the click as Adam clears his throat. The Saint Christopher goes on moving long after Sylvie has touched it, as though it's stirred by some secret movement of air.

And then the moon rises, moving above the mountains—a full moon, bright and sudden, like a light switched on. You can see the patterning on it, the penciling in of cold, vast craters and seas. Everything is washed in its cool whiteness. I realize I am shivering without my sweater.

When I first hear the car, it's a very long way off. Sound travels for miles across this empty land.

My heart pounds. I turn slightly toward Adam. He's tense, alert. I know he's heard it too.

The sound grows slightly louder. The car is coming down from the mountains, coming the way we came. Sometimes it's louder, sometimes it fades where a wall or hillock blocks the sound, but always drawing closer. It stops for a moment, and I know it's reached the intersection at the edge of the bog, the road we came by. I will it to turn left, to follow the road that leads off toward Barrowmore, willing it with all my strength—as though with the force of my mind I could actually make it change course. But it starts up again, and the noise draws nearer, coming straight toward us, its approach quite steady across the flat, straight road through the bog. The sound is so clear and distinct, you can tell when the driver changes gear.

I glance at Adam again. He's drumming his fingers rapidly on the steering wheel.

I'm watching in the wing mirror. I can see it now—the thin, long thread from its headlights, bright where it falls on water or gilds the blowing grass. Then the road turns a little, and the light shines straight in the mirror, so I'm briefly dazzled. I hear the engine slow. The car pulls to a stop behind us. I hear the thud of my heart.

The driver turns off the headlights. A door swings open, a man gets out, straightens, comes toward us. He's a big man, but I can't see him clearly in the darkness. Then he moves through the square of flimsy light that falls from the side of our car.

"Thank God," I say. With a quick, warm rush of relief, I recognize Marcus Paul. "It's Marcus. It's okay, Adam, it's okay. I know who it is."

I open my door. Marcus Paul comes to my side of the car. He has a tentative half smile. I'm so happy to see him.

"Now, I think it's Grace, isn't that right?" he says. "We met at St. Vincent's, didn't we? Brigid told me who you were."

"We've broken down," I tell him.

"I kind of worked that out." His smile is a little ironic.

"This is Adam," I tell him.

"Delighted to meet you, Adam," says Marcus. He bends and reaches across me so he can shake hands with Adam. He's wearing some cologne that has a spicy, opulent scent. I feel a flicker of inchoate desire, briefly reminded of Dominic.

"And this is Sylvie," I say.

I turn toward her.

Sylvie is intent on her maze. She doesn't even look up at him.

"Sylvie. Delighted," says Marcus.

He smiles at her, but she's staring at her comic. He reaches to shake her hand, he's being charming, treating her like a grown-up, but she won't put her hand out, so instead he pats her arm.

"I like Twixes too," he says.

I feel a flicker of irritation that she won't even smile at him when he's so polite to her.

"I can give you folks a lift back to the village," he tells us.

"We'd be so grateful," says Adam.

"What I suggest—you could leave the car here till the morning and see Jimmy Flynn at the garage. He's got a tow truck."

"I will," says Adam. "Thank you."

"And when we get back to the village," says Marcus, "I'd be delighted if you'd all come to my house for a drink."

I'm so happy at the prospect of seeing inside Kinvara House.

Adam rings the AA to tell them not to come.

"What are we doing?" says Sylvie.

"We're having a drink at Kinvara House. We'll go in Marcus's car."

"*No.* I'm not going to."

I feel a brief, hot rage.

"Well, sweetheart, that's what we're doing," I tell her briskly.

"I don't want to, Grace."

This time I won't give in. I'm longing to see inside the house and to get to know Marcus a little better. I'm not going to pass up my chance of that.

"Sylvie, it'll be fine. It's that great big house, the one with the falcons and the gorgeous garden. You'll love it . . ."

I hunt for a tissue to wipe the chocolate from her mouth. She has muddy legs and an ice-cream stain on her fleece. I wish she looked a bit cleaner. I want Marcus to think I am a good mother.

I wipe her mouth. She twists away from my hand.

"You're hurting, Grace."

We climb into Marcus's car, which has a rich male scent of leather. Sylvie stares out the window. I have a weak, shamed feeling—as you do when you've been afraid, yet your fear has proved utterly groundless.

It doesn't take long to reach Coldharbour. It's good to leave the bog behind and all its chilly emptiness, to drive through lighted streets, past the petrol pumps and the cheerful windows of Barry's General Store.

Marcus turns in at Kinvara House, between the tall stone pillars. The drive is narrow: azalea bushes drag against the car windows, the touch of their flowers and foliage as soft as the touch of a hand. The color is leached from the flowers by the headlights, so they all look palest amber. I glimpse the garden through the gaps between the bushes—everything beautifully tended, but just a little casual around the edges—wide, sleek lawns and drifted narcissi that glimmer in the moonlight. The drive sweeps around and we see the facade of the house, its elegant windows and colonnade and the stone steps up to the door.

Sylvie has her face pressed to the car window, with both hands cupped around her eyes, as you do when you're in a lighted place and you're looking out into the dark.

When I open the car door, the scent of

azalea brushes against us, a clingy, voluptuous scent, so different from the thick,
earthy smells of the untended countryside.

Sylvie has Big Ted with her. But as we
reach the threshold and Marcus puts his
key in the lock, she grabs at my handbag
and forces Big Ted inside. Perhaps she's
worried that it's babyish to have a cuddly
toy. She pushes hard, keeps pushing at
him, then wrenches the zipper shut, so
my bag is bulging but he's completely hidden.

The door swings open; inside, the lights
are on already. The hall is spacious and
lovely, all decorated in tranquil colors,
white and palest gray. The stair has an
elegant curve and is made of some pale
mottled stone, with a banister of black
metal. On a side table there are white
orchids, their complex blooms like gaping
mouths. An imposing gun is mounted on
the wall, beneath a pair of oars, perhaps
from his university rowing team. There are
alcoves along one side of the room, illuminated with amber light, displaying an ivory
chess set, a jade Tang horse, a dancer
sculpted in bronze.

Sylvie stops on the threshold.

"Sweetheart, what's the matter?"

She has one hand in mine and the other hand over her eyes.

"I don't like guns," she says.

"No, of course not, sweetheart. But no one's using that one. It's just for decoration, that's why it's up on the wall."

She presses against me. "Bad people have guns," she says.

It's what I've always taught her, but I wish she wouldn't say it now.

"But it's only meant to be looked at," I tell her. "There's nothing to be frightened of."

I feel the conflict in her—that she doesn't want to come inside, yet she won't let go of my hand. I pull at her, follow Marcus.

The room he ushers us into is wonderfully proportioned—high-ceilinged, with tall arched windows looking out over the sea. There are floor-length curtains of some sheer white fabric, pulled back so you can see out into the night; I glimpse the black water, the track of the moon, the lamps along the seafront. In the center of the pale oak floor there's an antique

Turkish carpet that has an intricate pattern of tangled leaves and flowers. The fireplace is made of white marble, and logs are blazing in the grate.

"It's beautiful," I tell him.

"Yes," he says simply, accepting this. "I'm very lucky to live here. I fell in love with the place—it's twenty years ago now. I drove past and I knew I had to have it. I've made a few changes, of course. I put in a new staircase and built a music room on the side. But I hope I've respected the feel of the place."

I sit with Sylvie on the sofa, which is covered in soft white woolen fabric. She has a smell of chocolate, and her hair is greasy and limp. She presses up against me and grabs my arm and wraps it all around her. Adam takes one of the chairs. He sits back and stretches out his legs, and the frown lines ease from his face. I wonder if he was more alarmed when the brakes failed than I realized.

"There's quite a view from these windows," says Marcus. "You must come in the daytime sometime so you can see it properly. It's quite spectacular."

I like the way he assumes that we'll be friends.

There are bottles of spirits on a side table, and tumblers of Waterford glass. He pours us Irish whiskey. He offers Sylvie lemonade. She doesn't look at him, but she nods. He gives her the lemonade in one of his opulent glasses. She cradles the glass very carefully in her hands, but as she wriggles back in her seat, a little lemonade slops on the immaculate sofa.

I'm intensely embarrassed.

"Oh no. I'm so sorry." I reach in my bag for a tissue.

"Really—don't give it a thought," says Marcus. "Houses are meant to be lived in."

I like him so much for saying that.

"I'm afraid Sylvie's rather tired," I tell him. "We've had a tiring day."

"Sea air can take you like that," he says.

He gives me my glass, and his hand brushes mine, so I feel the cool touch of his skin. The whiskey has a rich color, like a peaty stream. I drink, and the whiskey slides into me, warming me through.

"Brigid told me a bit about you," says Marcus then.

He's leaning on the mantelpiece, gazing benignly down at us. He's tall, imposing; next to him, Adam looks somehow insubstantial. I remember what Brian said. *Marcus knows how the world works— he wears his life like it's tailored just for him* . . . I think how we're so young still, me and Adam.

"She tells me you're researching family history," he says. "That you've got a family connection to this place?"

"Yes. Kind of," I say.

"So which one of you is it?" he says.

He's looking with interest from me to Adam and back again.

I tell him that it's me. I wonder if he can read the discomfort in my face.

"You must let me know if I can be of any help," he says. "Though of course I'm just a newcomer here. Well, relatively speaking. So—let's drink to your quest."

We raise our glasses and drink. I feel a shiver of unease. I think how crazy our purpose is, how irrational. In this exquisitely ordered room, I feel distanced, detached from it all—from the things I half believed in. I think how Marcus might react if he knew, how he'd give a disbelieving smile or maybe raise one eyebrow in a charmingly quizzical way.

I look around me, wanting to move the conversation onward, and my eye is drawn to a painting hanging on the wall. It's a portrait of a woman, done with photographic precision. She's thin but lovely, unsmiling, all blue shadows and beautiful bones, staring coolly out of the picture.

"I love the painting," I tell him.

He smiles. "The artist is a good friend of mine. Geoffrey Falke. He's a portrait painter in Dublin."

"He's a wonderful artist," I say.

"He's particular about his subjects," says Marcus. "The women he paints all have to have some special quality about them." His eyes rest on me a moment, and I feel the warmth in his gaze. "If he met you, Grace, I know he'd want to paint you."

"Well," I say, shrugging, at once flattered and self-conscious. "I doubt it."

He shakes his head a little. "You're so self-deprecating." He turns to Adam. "Isn't she?"

Adam murmurs something.

I flush. I glance at Adam and try to smile,

but the smile comes out wrong. I feel Marcus noticing this moment of awkwardness between us, perhaps seeing now that we aren't a couple and sensing my embarrassment. I'm grateful when he moves the conversation on.

"So tell me what you think of our beautiful village," he says. "As long as it's complimentary, of course."

"It's such a peaceful place," I say.

He nods. "Nothing much happens here, and I have to say I like that. It makes a real break from the city—that dog-eat-dog kind of world."

I lean back on the sofa. I hear the luxurious soft shuffle of the wood fire, and feel a surge of pleasure. I can't believe our luck, in meeting Marcus, in coming here.

He takes a casual sip of whiskey.

"Though we've had our share of tragedies even here," he says. "You'll probably have heard about Alice and Jessica Murphy?"

I feel his warm gaze on me. I don't know what to say.

"Yes," says Adam. His voice sounds sharper. I can tell he's suddenly alert. "Brigid told us."

"It was a terrible thing," says Marcus. "Alice worked for me, of course. Did Brigid tell you that?"

"Yes, she told us," I say.

"I blame myself for not seeing how depressed she was. I knew she'd been ill, but I really thought she was recovering. Sometimes we can't see what's right in front of our eyes . . . Well, you're a psychologist, Adam, I know. You'd have some thoughts on that . . ."

"It can be hard, certainly," says Adam. "Depression is often covert."

"The thing is, Alice was a very private person." Marcus's face is pensive, concerned. "And maybe no one could have seen it. But of course I blame myself . . . At least we know that the gardai did everything they could. The investigation was really quite meticulous. And now I guess that everyone just wants to let it lie. It's good to let the past go, to put it behind you. Wouldn't you say so?"

He's waiting for some response from us.

"I know what you mean," I say vaguely.

"Well, there you go," says Marcus. "Sadly, I guess these things happen everywhere. Now, tell me, have you been to Foley's? We always say they serve the very best oysters in Ireland."

"Yes, I'd heard they have quite a reputation," says Adam.

They talk about Irish seafood.

I notice an antique desk that's pulled up to one of the windows. It has an inlay of gilt and looks very light and feminine, like something you might find in a French château. I wonder if this was where Alice worked. I think what it must have been like for her—living at Flag Cottage with a husband who sometimes hit her, then coming here to see Marcus, to work in this beautiful high-ceilinged room, at this desk with its view of the sea. It must have seemed like Paradise. How could she not have fallen in love?

I need to go to the loo, and Marcus directs me to an upstairs bathroom. Sylvie insists on coming; she clings to my hand. We cross the hall, keeping well away from the gun.

I'm about to go upstairs when Sylvie tugs at me.

"It's that way, Grace," she says.

To our left, where she's pointing, there's

a narrow passageway. At the end, you can see a downstairs cloakroom through an open door. I think, How did she know that? Did it seem familiar to her? Or did she just happen to spot it? But I can't answer these questions.

We go in. There's a washbasin, a toilet, a Chinese vase with a crack in it. It's where they've left the forgotten things, the things that don't belong. On a shelf is a bust of Beethoven; someone has put a trilby hat on his head. The window is open at the top because the catch is broken. Cool air that's sweet with azalea comes in. Outside, the pane is almost entirely covered by creeper. I peer out, hoping for another enticing glimpse of the garden, but the creeper is dense and tangled, and I can't see through. The branches creak as they rub against the window, as though something is moving the creeper, although the air is almost still.

"I want to go," says Sylvie. "I want to go back to St. Vincent's."

There are smudges of blue in the frail skin under her eyes. I feel bad about keeping her up so late.

We go back to the drawing room.

"I guess we should head off," I say. "It's long past Sylvie's bedtime."

"Yes, of course," says Marcus.

He sees us to the door.

"Thanks so much for rescuing us," I tell him.

"A pleasure." He shakes my hand. His musky scent is all around me. "I hope you'll come and have a drink with me again. And the very best of luck with your researches. You must absolutely let me know if I can help at all."

He says goodbye to Sylvie. She puts her hand over her eyes.

I'm about to apologize to him, but he preempts me, as though he knows what I feel.

"Don't worry," he says. "It can all be a bit much, can't it, when you're four? Being away from home and so on . . ."

I'm grateful to him for being so understanding.

We walk along the seafront to St. Vincent's. You can just make out the phosphorescence where the waves break, so faint you think you're imagining it, like the frail blue-white dazzle a sparkler leaves on the dark.

"What did you think of Marcus? Did you like him?" I say.

"Well, I certainly liked his single malt," says Adam.

But I sense a slight reserve in him. I wonder if he's jealous of the attention Marcus paid me, and there's a greedy, yearning part of me that's glad.

We say good night outside my room.

"I'll go to the garage first thing," says Adam. "You two could have a lie-in."

I take Sylvie into our bedroom. It seemed so pleasant before, but it looks a little drab now, with its embossed wallpaper and battered chest of drawers, after all the glamour of Kinvara House.

## 46

We're already up when Adam leaves, and Sylvie says she will go with him. She wants to ride in the tow truck.

I walk down to Barry's to buy a post-card for Lavinia, and linger for a moment by the window admiring one of Erin's cakes that has just been put on display. It's covered in glossy dark chocolate, with a border of marzipan trumpets. A scrawl of scarlet piping says MANY HAPPY RETURNS.

Erin is there, with her copy of *Galway Now* spread out on the counter in front of her.

"That's a fabulous cake," I tell her.

"Well, what a coincidence," she says. "You know how you asked about Alice? That cake is for Alice's daughter."

I stare at her. Her words hang there between us, but they don't seem to make any sense.

"Alice's daughter? Alice Murphy, you mean?"

Erin nods. Her dark eyes glitter through the lenses of her glasses.

"She's seventeen on Sunday. She's a genius on her clarinet—so I thought a musical theme."

Everything shifts around me.

"Well, it's beautiful. She'll love it," I say lamely.

Brigid is in the entrance hall at St. Vincent's, arranging pots of hyacinths along the windowsill. Their smell spills everywhere.

"Brigid. I want to ask you something."

"Of course, Grace."

"I was talking to Erin at Barry's. And there was this cake that she said she'd made for Alice Murphy's daughter . . ."

Brigid nods. "Of course, it'll be her birthday. She's quite a little woman now."

"But—I thought that Alice's daughter *disappeared* . . ."

"Didn't anyone tell you? Didn't Brian explain?"

I stare at her blankly.

"Jessica was a twin," she says. "She had a twin sister, Gemma."

"Nobody said . . ."

"Well, Brian should have told you," she says in a reproving voice. "They were close as anything, those girls, you couldn't prize them apart. Well, Alice did try, of course. She wanted to put them in different things, but they always wanted the same. They were sweet together, Jessica and Gemma."

"I didn't know," I tell her.

"They were often down here in the village," Brigid tells me. "I used to see them playing at Kinvara House when Alice was working there and the girls were off school. She used to take them with her. Marcus was easy like that. As long as she got the work done, he didn't mind what she did."

"They used to play at Kinvara House?"

"That garden is heaven for children," she says.

"Yes, it would be."

I remember the garden glimpsed from the windows of Marcus's car—the velvet lawns, the glimmering drifts of narcissi.

"Alice said it was magic for them," Brigid tells me. "I could sometimes hear them laughing, when the sea was still. If you walked past the house, you could hear their shouting and laughter . . . Of course, after her mother and sister went—to be honest, I don't think Gemma ever laughed like that anymore."

The sadness of this tugs at me. The hyacinth scent is all around me, clingy and drenching and a little claustrophobic. I'm never sure if I like the smell of hyacinths.

"So where was Gemma?" I ask her. "On the day it happened?"

"She had a clarinet lesson."

This shocks me—it seems so random, and somehow so banal. Gemma didn't die, because she had a *clarinet lesson*.

I remember something Brian told us.

"But—nobody seems to have raised the alarm till the Wednesday afternoon. Why didn't Gemma ring the gardai?"

"She didn't go home that day," says

Brigid. "I had this from Polly O'Connor—she was Alice's closest friend. After the clarinet lesson, Gemma went to a sleep-over party at a friend's house. You know the kind of thing—they'd paint each other's nails and stay up sharing secrets. Alice hated sleepovers, I remember. She said the girls never slept and came home horribly grouchy. She said her heart always sank when they got invited to a sleepover."

"Just Gemma? Why not the two of them?"

"Jessica had a cold; her mother wouldn't let her go."

It's that terrible randomness again—that it could so easily have been different. The hyacinth scent is so thick it's hard to breathe.

"And afterwards?" I ask her. "What happened to Gemma?"

"She lives in Barrowmore now. Gordon travels a lot, and he couldn't always be there for her, and Deirdre Walker said she'd give her a home. Deirdre is Gordon's sister." She lowers her voice; she has a conspiratorial look. "To be honest,

Gemma's probably better off with that arrangement. You remember what I told you about Gordon?"

"Yes, I remember." I don't say that we've met him, though maybe she knows already.

"She's a good-hearted woman, Deirdre Walker," says Brigid. "A bit of a worrier, but I guess that's not surprising, after everything that's happened."

My pulse skitters off.

"D'you have her address? D'you think she'd see us?" I say.

Brigid nods. "I'm sure she would. Like I say, she's got a good heart. I'll find her number for you."

I ring Adam. He's still at the garage with Sylvie. I tell him about Deirdre and about Jessica having a twin.

"Full marks, Grace." There's a thrill in his voice. "That's a huge step forward."

I like him praising me like that.

He says we should try to see Deirdre at once. The car should be ready by lunchtime.

"What was wrong?" I ask him.

"Some problem with the brake fluid. They've topped it up and replaced a damaged pipe."

"Did they say how it could have happened?"

"Well, you know what people are like round here. Someone could have siphoned it off, but then again, maybe they didn't." He puts on an extravagant Irish accent. "I'm ruling nothing out and I'm ruling nothing in . . ."

I feel a vague unease when he says that.

I ring Deirdre from our bedroom.

"Deirdre Walker speaking." A formal, rather cautious voice.

"My name's Grace Reynolds," I tell her.

There's a whole careful speech worked out in my head. But she responds before I can begin.

"Oh yes. Grace Reynolds. I thought you'd be in touch."

This startles me.

"You've heard about us?"

"Of course I've heard about you. Gordon told me. That you've got a little girl who's psychic, who seems to remember this place."

Her voice is measured and pleasant, but I can hear the anxiety in it.

"She's four," I tell her. "She's called Sylvie. She seemed to recognize Flag Cottage."

"Yes, Gordon told me that," says Deirdre.

I breathe in deeply.

"Deirdre. I wondered if we could possibly come and see you?"

There's a long, tense silence. I hear the thud of my heart.

"I've been thinking about this," she says then. "What I should do if you called. I've given it quite a lot of thought, to be frank with you. And this is what I've decided. I don't mind seeing you as long as Gemma isn't here. You could come this afternoon when she'll be at college." She clears her throat, as though it's hard to say this. "But Grace, you mustn't bring Sylvie. I absolutely don't want Sylvie to come."

## 47

I leave Adam and Sylvie watching television in the lounge at St. Vincent's.

The house is on the coast road that climbs up out of Barrowmore. It's a bland modern house with a view out over the sea. She opens the door as I arrive; she must have been watching out for me. She's wearing a woolen jacket that has a woven pattern of fruit. The colors are too bright for her. Her face looks tired and faded.

"Thank you so much for seeing me," I say.

"That's quite okay," says Deirdre, but she doesn't smile.

She takes me into her living room. There's a floral three-piece suite, a piano with lots of framed photographs on it, the chemical sweetness of air freshener. On the mantelpiece is a picture of the Virgin, with a halo of sugar-pink roses and eyes that seem to follow you around the room. Outside, in the back garden, gulls are fighting over scraps.

She brings in tea and angel cake.

"Your little girl's four, you said, Grace?"

"Yes," I tell her.

Her face softens. "I always say four's a perfect age." There's a touch of yearning in her voice. "I have three of my own, you know. Well, they're all grown up now. But then Gemma came, of course."

"Yes," I say.

We drink our tea. The shadows of seagulls move over the room, the glide and weave of their wings, and their screaming is loud in the stillness. I bite into my angel cake, but my mouth is dry, I find it hard to swallow. Now that I'm here, I don't know how to begin.

"You want to talk about Gemma," she says then.

"Yes. About Gemma and Jessica. I know it must seem strange . . ."

"Gemma and Jessica," she repeats. She's picking some fluff from her sleeve. "They were very close, those two. They weren't identical—I'll show you a picture later, you'll be able to see for yourself. But they were incredibly close. Alice wanted them put in different classes at school. You know, to help them establish their own identities. But they were so unhappy, and in the end they were put back together again."

She pauses for a moment, and I sense the conflict in her—that there are things she's never said, because they feel too dangerous, and yet she longs to share them.

"They lived in a world of their own," she says. "They even had words they'd made up together, and secret places where they used to go. Sometimes I've thought—perhaps they provided a haven for each other, a kind of safety. Because Alice couldn't always give them what they needed. You know, because of her illness. They were rather left to fend for themselves. I remember once they went off together and no one could find them for hours . . ."

She takes a slow sip of her tea.

"They were everything to each other," she says quietly.

"I know that can happen, with twins," I say.

She puts down her cup precisely in its saucer.

"When it . . . happened—I think Gemma felt the loss of her sister still more than the loss of her mother. As though it was, I don't know, an amputation. Does that make any sense to you?"

"Yes, it does," I tell her.

Deirdre's mouth is working. "As though she felt a part of her had gone."

She gets up, takes a photograph from the piano. "Look, here's Gemma," she says.

It's a school photograph. The girl in the picture is twelve or so, just on the cusp of womanhood, with the almost luminous loveliness girls sometimes have at that age. She has long dark curls that fall loosely over her shoulders, milky skin, an open smile.

"She's gorgeous," I say.

"Well, this was four years ago," says Deirdre. "She's really blossoming now. There's that rather magical moment—they have their braces off and they seem to leave childhood behind. Though of course in lots of ways they're really no more than children."

She puts the photo back on the piano, turns to face me directly. Her eyes are raw in her white face.

"I know it wasn't Alice's fault—that she was ill, that depression is an illness. I know that. But I can't help feeling so angry that she chose to take Jessica with her." Her voice cracks. "That's so selfish, so cruel. I didn't think she had it in her, to be as cruel as that."

She turns a little away. The seagulls weave their shadow pattern across her.

"I used to hear Gemma crying at night, and I'd go in to her, of course I would, but what could I do to help her?"

I murmur something banal about how hard it must be.

"You feel so helpless," she tells me. She moves her hands slowly together as though she is trying to warm them. "Look, there's something upstairs I know you'll want to see."

I follow her.

The room has a view out over the beach—she's given Gemma her best bedroom. This touches me. It's blowy out there, you can see the white tops of the waves. The room has that mix of the grown-up and childlike that I remember from my own teenage bedroom. There are gingham curtains trimmed with braid, and heaps of Beanie Babies, and other, more teenage things—jewelry, pop posters, a wind chime made from delicate pieces of shell. The window is open—the wind chime shakes in the rough salt wind from the sea, with a sound like many tiny bells, at once delicate and discordant.

Deirdre shows me a framed photograph hanging on the wall.

"This is her old family." Again, there's that crack in her voice. "This was the last photo they had taken—before it happened."

It's so strange to see them, these people I have imagined. Gordon I recognize of course, though here he looks quite different, younger and unburdened. Alice has high cheekbones, and glossy dark hair pulled back, and the sleek, assured smile of the woman who knows she is beautiful. The girls may not be identical, but they still look very similar, with the same unruly brown curls and creamy skin. I don't know how to tell them apart.

"This was Jessica," says Deirdre, pointing, reading my thought.

The poignant past tense tugs at my heart.

I stare at the gap-toothed smile, the confiding hazel gaze. I stare and stare. I tell myself, This is Jessica, this is her face, this is who she was. I realize that, ridiculously, I'd thought she might look like Sylvie, expecting her appearance to offer some answer, some clue. But she could be anyone.

I glance around the room, trying to take it all in, wanting to remember it so I can tell Adam about it. On the wall by the photo there are holiday postcards, an Arctic Monkeys poster, and certificates from Gemma's music exams. My eye skims briefly across these things, my gaze moving hungrily onward, searching for anything I can learn about her; then I find myself drawn back to the certificates again. They have Gemma's full name on them. "This certificate is awarded to Gemma Eleanor Murphy for Grade 5 Clarinet. Highly commended."

Eleanor. I hear the name in my head, like someone has just spoken it. I think of all the things that Sylvie has said. *You aren't my Lennie. They shouldn't sing that, she isn't Lennie, Grace. Where's Lennie hiding? I need to find Lennie.*

I feel a rush of cold, like the room is flooding with icy air.

I turn to face Deirdre. There's goose-flesh all over my body.

"Did they have special names for one another? Pet names, perhaps, like sisters sometimes do?"

"I couldn't answer that," says Deirdre. "If Gemma talks about her sister—and she hardly ever mentions her—she always calls her Jessica, like it's safer to be more formal. Like she wants to distance her, not bring her too close."

The wind chime is juddering wildly now, and I think how fragile they are, those spheres and crescents of seashell, as thin as paper and pale and brittle as bone. If the wind blows any harder, they will surely shatter.

"Gemma's a very private person," says Deirdre then, and I remember how Marcus said exactly this of Alice. "She buries everything and keeps it hidden. You know, I don't think that's such a bad thing. What would talking do for her? It wouldn't bring them back." She's leaning on the windowsill, looking out at the sea. "Sometimes I think that's how people cope—that maybe it's better to bottle it up. I know they say it's good to talk. But some things—if you let them out, well, maybe they couldn't be borne..."

I want so much to comfort her, but I don't know what to say.

"Coming here to Gemma's room, you can tell it's a happy room," I say. "You can feel she's happy here."

This sounds so glib. I wish that Adam were with me.

A rainbow silk scarf is draped across the foot of the bed. I notice because it's the kind of scarf Lavinia might wear. It's the loveliest thing, made of silk that is almost transparent, its lavish colors washing together as though they are melting and wet. I run my fingers lightly across the fabric. The silk is so fine, I feel it could snag on my skin.

"She has such pretty things," I say.

"That's from Marcus, from his dress shop in Dublin," says Deirdre.

I turn to her sharply.

She makes a little throwaway gesture, as though to say, What can I do?

"He's very fond of Gemma. Well, she's got her mother's looks . . ."

I wonder what she's telling me— whether she's hinting they have a sexual relationship. Her face is flushed. Perhaps she thinks I'll be shocked, that I'll feel she should have stopped it.

"I know it must seem odd," she says. "I mean, with the age gap and everything. But he's very charming, of course."

I try to reassure her. "Older men can be very attractive, especially to a teenager," I tell her. "Sylvie's father . . . he was a lot older than me."

She's grateful for this. She gives me a tentative smile.

"The thing is," she says, "I've never felt I can be really strict with Gemma. She's not my own daughter, not really mine. If she was my own child—well, I might put my foot down. But she was nine when she came to me. She was quite her own person by then."

"I guess they have to find their own way," I tell her.

She takes me downstairs. The noise of the wind chime follows us, that sound of something forever on the point of breaking. In the hall, she stands by the door, but she doesn't immediately open it.

"I don't know if that's been any use," she says.

"It's been very helpful," I tell her. "I'm so grateful."

"There's something I want to ask you," she says. "The thing is, you might see Gemma when she goes to Coldharbour, when she's visiting Marcus."

"Yes."

"You must absolutely promise me you won't say anything to her. And especially that you won't let Sylvie talk to her."

I feel a judder of disappointment.

"I know you'll think that's harsh of me," she says. "But she has a new life now. I hate the idea of dredging up the past. She's a very resilient girl. But what happened to her was devastating. I don't want everything to come unstitched again . . ."

"No, of course not."

She takes my hand in hers. Her fingers are tense and urgent.

"Promise me, Grace," she says.

She's standing very close to me, and she's searching my face with her gaze. I can't refuse her.

"I promise," I tell her.

"Thank you," she says. "Look, I'm not going to tell her you came. Though she'll probably find out, of course. People do talk around here."

She opens the door. It's cold on the doorstep, and she wraps her woolen jacket close around her. Her eyes are on me, tired and troubled and kind.

"Grace. Do you really believe them— these things that Sylvie says?"

I want to be truthful with her, but I don't know what the truth is.

"I do and don't at the same time. Both things together," I say. "Sorry. That sounds so stupid . . ."

"No, it doesn't." Her gaze on my face. "Now, don't forget what you promised me, Grace."

At the gate I turn to wave, but Deirdre has gone.

# 48

I wake to hear Adam's voice through the wall. He's talking on his phone. His voice is intense, hard-edged, though I can't quite hear what he's saying. I wonder what can have happened to upset him.

I leave Sylvie in our bedroom, playing with her LEGO. He's at our table already. He has a troubled look.

"Are you okay?" I ask him.

He smiles his rueful smile. "You heard, then," he says.

"Not really. Not what you were saying. But you didn't sound very pleased."

He says nothing for a moment, just sips

slowly at his coffee. It's pleasant in the dining room. Sunlight falls across us, and there's a vase of narcissi that have a thin, peppery scent.

"You were right about Tessa," he says then.

I'm puzzled.

"I don't remember what I said," I tell him.

"You wondered what she thought about me coming here with you. Whether she'd be okay with it."

"Oh."

"It appears she isn't," he says. "She isn't okay." He's looking down at his hands, not looking at me. Again, that slight crooked smile. "Could be I've been talking about you a little too much."

I know my face is flaring red.

He looks up then, looks right into my eyes. My stomach tightens, flips over.

Like Sylvie, I'm not hungry; I just eat a bit of toast, but I keep refilling my coffee cup. I would like this meal to last for hours, to sit here close beside him in the sunlight and the flower scent.

We talk about what Deirdre said, go through it all again.

"It seems to make sense of so much that's happened," says Adam. He's animated, his eyes gleam. "Like that thing that Sylvie said about the children in her drawing."

"Two peas in a pod."

"Yes, exactly," he says.

"I wish Deirdre hadn't made me promise to keep the girls apart."

"She didn't really give you a choice. And I guess it's utterly comprehensible from her point of view—after all that Gemma's been through." He shakes his head a little. "But God, it's just so tantalizing," he says.

I think that he might have handled her better, not agreed so readily.

"Perhaps I gave in too easily. I'm really sorry," I say.

"Don't be," he tells me.

He puts his hand on my wrist—lightly, just for a second or two. Warmth floods me.

I'm talking to Sylvie already as I open our bedroom door. "Time to get going, sweetheart. You need to put on your shoes . . ."

My words fall into silence.

"Sylvie?"

I knock on the door to the bathroom. No

answer. I open the door. The tap has been left running, but the room is empty. I curse myself for my self-indulgence, for spending all that time with Adam, not coming straight back here.

I go out into the corridor.

"Adam!"

I'm calling for him before I get to his room.

He comes to the door. He's pulling on a sweater.

"It's Sylvie. She's gone."

*"What?"* His eyes widen.

"Adam, has someone taken her? D'you think she could have been snatched?"

"She's almost certainly still in the building," he tells me.

But there's a shred of anxiety in his voice.

We hunt through the lounge, the bar, the garden. Sylvie isn't anywhere. I'm calling for her; my voice sounds thin and shrill. I'm full of a jittery energy. I need to run, but I don't know where to run to. Panic floods me.

Adam puts his hand on my arm. "We should go back up to your bedroom—see if anything's gone."

He runs upstairs ahead of me. On the landing, he glances through the window that faces over the sea.

"Grace. *Look*."

Far off on the beach, between the road and the water, there's a little running figure, tiny against that wide white stretch of sand. I know at once that it's Sylvie. There's something about her purposefulness, the urgency of her movement.

"Thank God."

I feel a rush of relief—that she's there, that she's alive still. Then a different panic grabs at me—that she's crossed the road on her own and she's running straight to the sea. I can't imagine why she's out there on the beach, in the place where she didn't dare step before. I'm so afraid for her.

I race downstairs and straight out through the foyer. Adam is behind me, but I'm moving faster than him.

I run out into the street. The salt wind slams into me. I'm already stepping into the road when Adam grabs at my arm, wrenching me out of the path of a truck that I simply didn't see. I feel the rush of hot, scorched air from its engines as it passes. The driver swears at me. My breath is coming in shuddery gasps.

Adam keeps hold of my arm, steers me across the road once it's clear. Then I slip from his grasp and run down the steps to the beach, lurching at the bottom, clutching the handrail to save myself.

She's a long long way in front of us. She seems to be running straight toward the sea. Fear has its claws in me. I think how quickly the tide comes in; I think what Brigid told us about the treacherous currents. A child can drown so quickly.

It's hard to run on the beach. My feet sink in, the wet sand sucks at my shoes.

She veers off left past a line of rocks that stretches toward the sea. I start to gain on her, and now I can see ahead of her. And then I understand—I see who Sylvie's running to. The girl is way out ahead of Sylvie. She has her back toward us, and I can see her narrow shoulders and the long, loose fall of her hair. She's wearing a short denim skirt and her legs are bare and white as milk, and she's taken off her sandals and is holding them in her hand. There's something about the way she's walking, rather slow and languid, as though she likes the sensuousness of damp sand on her skin. The scarf at her neck is caught by the breeze, the ends of it curling and spiraling, and you can see all the colors in it that wash into one another as though they are melting and wet.

Sylvie is shouting something. I can only just hear what she's saying, as the wind plays around with her words.

"Lennie! It's *me*! Lennie!"

The girl walks on—perhaps she didn't hear. She comes to the second set of steps. Her scarf swirls out behind her; it has the rainbow shimmer of spilt oil. She pauses for a moment, drops her shoes. They fall on their sides, and she kicks at them to straighten them.

"Lennie! Wait for me! It's *me*! I'm coming!"

The girl turns. I can see her face and I recognize beyond doubt the girl in Deirdre's photograph. She stares for a moment at Sylvie. I realize I've stopped running. I'm waiting, everything's waiting. The wind dies down and the beach feels huge and hollow, so empty under the vast, shiny arc of the sky. I can hear the sounds of the seafront—the swish of passing cars, a dog that barks at a seagull. The sounds are clear yet seem unguessably far.

The girl's dark hair has blown over her mouth and she pushes it back with her hand. In the clarity of the light off the sea I can read her closed expression, all the blank incomprehension in her face. Then she shrugs a little, turns, goes up the steps to the road.

Sylvie stops, quite suddenly. From where I am, she looks like she's been shot—she seems to crumple, her body folding in on itself. She's kneeling, clutching herself with her hands, her arms wrapped tight around her. The wind brings the sound of her sobbing to me. It catches at my heart.

The girl with the long dark hair pays no attention. She climbs to the top of the steps, walking more briskly now that she's got her shoes on. She turns toward Kinvara House, walks off along the road.

At last I reach Sylvie. I kneel beside her and wrap my arms around her. I can feel her juddering heartbeat passing into my body. I press my mouth into her hair. Anger sears through me. I'm angry with everyone, everything—with everyone in my world but Sylvie. Angry with Adam for bringing us here and opening Sylvie up to all this anguish. Angry with myself for agreeing to come, and with Deirdre for her caution and the promise she made me make. Angry most of all with this cool, remote girl who just walked on, who wouldn't give anything.

At last Sylvie quiets down. I'm aware of the world around us again, and of Adam's hand on my arm. The knees of my jeans are wet and stiff with sand.

"Shall we go back now?" I ask her.

Sylvie doesn't say anything.

I help her to her feet. I have her hand in my hand. Her skin is very cold. She's crying quietly now. We start to walk back up the beach. The tide has turned and is coming in, and our footprints fill with water that holds the blue of the sky.

Adam glances across at me.

"Are you okay?" he says quietly.

"No. Not really," I tell him.

At the foot of the steps by St. Vincent's, we sit and take off our shoes and tip out some of the sand. One of Sylvie's sneakers has come undone and she reties the laces, doing it slowly, methodically. Her face is streaked with tears. She climbs a few steps above us and sits there, drawing with her finger in the thin crust of sand on the step. The sea is blue and innocent, and far, far out, on the rim of the visible world, you can see that darker immaculate line, the water meeting the sky.

We stay there for a moment. I'm not quite able to move. The adrenaline has seeped away, and I'm left with a crushing tiredness.

Adam turns toward me. "That's the girl you saw the photo of at Deirdre's? That's Gemma?"

"Yes."

"And Sylvie has really never seen a picture of her?"

"No," I tell him.

He shakes his head very slowly. His eyes are startled and wide.

Sylvie hears us.

"She's my Lennie, Grace."

"Yes, sweetheart."

I have a sudden keen sense of the tenuousness of everything, as though this life, this world is flimsy, thin—like soap film or a fine stretched cloth of patterned silky fabric, a fragile, provisional, rainbow-colored thing.

Sylvie climbs down the steps to sit beside me. Her eyelashes are clotted from her crying.

"Why wouldn't she talk to me?" she says. "Why wouldn't she stay with me? She just went off and she wouldn't wait for me, Grace."

I don't know what to say to her.

## 49

Brigid knocks at our bedroom door.

"Deirdre Walker to see you!" she says brightly.

I feel a quick surge of gratitude. This is a gift, a stroke of good fortune. Now I can persuade her to let Sylvie and Gemma meet.

I call for Adam, and Sylvie comes downstairs with us. I'm determined not to let her out of my sight. Deirdre is waiting in the lounge. I settle Sylvie in front of cartoons on the television, then go to say hello to Deirdre and introduce her to Adam.

But Deirdre doesn't smile or greet me. Her face is white and frayed.

"I wanted to tell you how angry I am. After what you promised." Her voice is harsh with accusation. "You spoke to her, didn't you, Grace? You went and spoke to Gemma. After everything I told you."

She has the air of a woman who isn't used to confrontation, who has steeled herself to do this.

"But we didn't speak to Gemma. You have to believe me," I tell her.

"I know you did," she says.

We stand there for a moment. Her brittle anger seems all wrong in this homely, decorous place, with its faded peony cushions and the juddery tick of the clock.

"This is what happened," I tell her. "We did see Gemma, we saw her on the sand. Sylvie had run after her, she must have seen her from the window. I was chasing after Sylvie, for a while I couldn't catch up, but Sylvie didn't reach Gemma. Sylvie called out, but Gemma didn't answer. I certainly didn't approach her. I promised you I wouldn't, and I didn't."

She's studying my face.

"That's really true, what you just said?"

"Yes. I promise," I say.

She sits quite suddenly then, collapsing on one of the chairs, as though without her anger she has nothing to sustain her.

"I'm sorry I blamed you," she says.

She sits there, crumpled, defeated. She rubs her hand over her face.

Adam sits beside her.

"We could have some coffee," he tells her.

"Yes. Thank you."

Brigid brings a tray of coffee. Deirdre takes a cup, clasps it so tight in her fingers you can see the pale bones through the skin.

"There's something I didn't tell you when you came to see me, Grace. Gemma's been quite unhappy—just for the last week or two. She told me she's been having dreams about her mother and sister." She puts down her cup without taking a sip. "Then last night she had a nightmare. She was so upset when she woke, she was crying at breakfast this morning. That's why I was sure you'd spoken to her."

"Have you told her about us?" says Adam.

"I haven't said a thing," she says. "But maybe she's heard about you. People could have been talking—the kids at her college, perhaps."

"If it's our fault she's unhappy, I'm really sorry," I say.

She inclines her head, accepting this.

"There's this thought she keeps going back to," she says then. "This memory she has. Well, I don't know if it's a memory. Something that's just resurfacing."

There's a quick moth flutter of feeling in the corner of my mind, a thrill of apprehension.

"It's about the afternoon before they disappeared," she tells us. "Gemma remembers her mother going to answer the phone. She thinks she said, *Okay, I'll be there for seven*. She says her mother sounded happy. Like she was meeting someone she knew, not going off to die . . . She can remember her mother in the hallway, looking in the mirror, putting her lipstick on. Pressing her lips together to spread the lipstick evenly. She says her mother was humming to herself."

I glance at Adam. He has a vigilant, intent look.

"Has she ever told anyone this? The gardai—Brian Ennis?" he says.

"Not at the time," says Deirdre. "She was only nine when it happened. She was in a state of shock—she was almost mute for a while. She'd only talk to me or her dad. So no, she didn't mention it then. She was so confused, I think it was all a blur to her."

"But since then?" says Adam.

"No, I don't think so," says Deirdre. "It's only in the last couple of weeks that it's really begun to obsess her. She certainly hasn't been to see the gardai. The thing is, half the time she doesn't believe it herself. She says, 'Deirdre, what do you think? D'you think I'm making it up? Can you *invent* memories?'"

"Is that what you think?" asks Adam. "That she's inventing it?"

"I'm really not sure." She gives a slight self-deprecating shrug, as though she's not used to being asked for her opinion. "But I do know this—that Gemma would give anything for proof it wasn't suicide. That's the thing she can't bear, even now—that her mother chose to abandon her and took her sister with her."

She's silent for a moment. The clock ticks, and we wait for her.

"I read this thing about suicide once," she says then. "Something in a magazine. That losing someone to suicide is more than a bereavement . . . It's the most terrible way for someone to die—for those who are left behind."

"Yes," I say.

"I try to tell her—your mother didn't leave *you*, she left *life*. But she still feels so abandoned. She so desperately wants there to be some other explanation."

"Yes," I say. "Of course she would."

"I'd better go, then." She pulls her cardigan close around her, as though it could protect her. "I shouldn't have blamed you," she says.

We say goodbye at the door.

I turn to Adam. "She seemed to be saying she thought that Gemma was making it up. That memory of her mother."

"Yes," he says.

"So what do you think?"

"She could be right. You can see why Gemma might do that, how it might fulfill a need for her. Believe me, I can understand that. Wanting to find a different story, a different explanation—something that doesn't hurt quite as much."

I know that Jake is in his mind: there's such a raw look on his face. I would like to put my arms around him.

"So, yes," he goes on, "it makes total psychological sense . . . But that doesn't mean it didn't happen," he says.

We sit for a while in silence.

"You know Brigid's hit-man theory?" I say then. "That Gordon found out about Alice and Marcus and paid a hit man to kill her? What Gemma said could fit with that."

"Yes, it could," he says.

"Perhaps we should tell the gardai?"

"We could. But it wouldn't have much value as evidence after all this time. Not when she didn't talk about it when it happened—"

The sudden ring of his phone makes me flinch. I have a tense, brittle feeling.

"Brian," he mouths at me.

I'm expecting him to tell Brian about the things that Deirdre said, but he just listens. I can't work out what Brian is saying.

"Absolutely," says Adam then. "Well, that's brilliant news." He ends the call and

turns to me. His eyes are shiny with triumph."They're going to search the
quarry," he says.

I have a sense of shock. That this is
happening. That we have made it happen.

"Brian went to look at it. He found that
path I found. I'm impressed he took Sylvie
so seriously," says Adam.

There's a sudden click of stilettoes—
Brigid coming to fetch our tray. She fixes
us with her glinting, curious gaze.

"Good news, I imagine?"

"Yes, excellent, thank you," says Adam.

I wonder how much of our conversation
she heard.

She reaches out to take the tray and
catches the milk jug with the side of her
hand. It wobbles and spills.

"So stupid of me."

Her lips are tight, she's cross with herself, though the milk is all caught in the tray.

"It really doesn't matter," I tell her.

"It matters to me, Grace. I hate being
clumsy," she says.

That night, I can't sleep. I hear the familiar
sounds from Adam's bedroom—the surge
of the shower, and then his voice on the

phone, talking to Tessa presumably. The phone call ends, there's the click of the switch on his bedside lamp, then silence. I wish he was moving about still. I feel safer hearing him there.

In the end, I pull my coat on over the T-shirt I sleep in and take a bottle of Jameson's from the minibar—it's just a miniature bottle, I don't bother to find a glass—and I go out onto the balcony.

I sit there, the village stilled around me, above me the sky with its pale seed of stars, spread out before me the glimmering black of the sea. The only human illumination comes from the lamps on the jetty, which rim the little lapping waves with lines of orange light. There's a faint cold track of moonlight over the water. I see that the moon has waned since the night we broke down in the bog, when it was so bright and round, rising over the mountain—its waning a reminder that our time here has almost gone. I count it off on my fingers. In two days we'll be flying home. I'm ambushed by a sudden longing for London, for its streets and buses and smells of smoke; for the London night, which is always lit and busy, not dense and hidden and full of secrets like the Irish dark.

A shiver of wind from the sea stirs the fringe on the parasol. I wonder what they will find in the quarry, and feel again that surge of emotion, the mix of excitement and dread. I notice my teeth are chattering, that the cold has got into my clothes. I wrap my coat tight around me. Out of nowhere, I think of something Lavinia once said to me—the thing the old priest had told her. *It's not the dead we should be afraid of, but the living* . . . Her voice is in my head, nicotine-stained, nostalgic, as though she were here beside me.

**It's the living we should fear.**

## 50

We drive north along the coast road. There's a light morning mist and a whisper of wind off the sea.

We come to an intersection I recognize, where a right turn onto a minor road will take you past Gaviston Pits, rejoining the road to Barrowmore farther up the hill.

I glance at Adam. "Shall we? You know, just drive past, find out if anything's happening . . ."

"They may not even have started yet," says Adam.

But he takes the road to the right. The sky is bright and pale as tin, the sun shining whitely through the mist, the distant mountains blue as ash. The road twists out of sight of the sea.

As we near the track to the quarry, we see a flash of rotating lights.

"Something's started," I tell him. "Something must be happening."

Adam slows. We round the corner under the oak tree that reaches out over the road. Four garda cars are parked by the entrance to the quarry, their insistent lights raking across us, and behind them there's an ambulance and a big white van marked TECHNICAL BUREAU, which I guess must have the forensic gear inside. The sight is imposing—all this equipment, all these official vehicles. I think how we have made this happen. Suddenly I wish we hadn't: it feels too big a thing.

We have to stop quite a distance beyond the quarry entrance because of all the vehicles.

"There's an ambulance," I say.

"Yes," says Adam.

"What does that mean, that there's an ambulance?"

"I don't know. It may not mean anything. Maybe they always bring one just so it's there if it's needed. I mean, if they do find something . . ."

I glance at Sylvie. She has *The Very Hungry Caterpillar* open on her lap. She's pressing her finger into the holes where the caterpillar has eaten through. She seems unaware of everything that's going on around her. We're parked much farther down the road than usual. I hope we're far enough away from the place where she always gets sick.

A fevered curiosity has me in its grip.

"I need to see what's going on," I tell him.

"Yes, you go." Though I know he's curious too, that really he'd want to come with me. "I'll stay here with Sylvie."

I get out. Sylvie clambers into my seat and thrusts her book into his hands.

I walk along the path. It's mistier here than it was on the coast. The world is breathing out moisture, I can feel the wet on my hair. The brambles snatch at the legs of my jeans, and the air around the flowering gorse is thick with coconut scent.

I come to the track that Adam found,

that snakes down the side of the quarry. Someone has cut back the bushes, and I have to stop, there's tape across the path. Down at the bottom of the track, at the muddy margins of the pool, there's a group of gardai standing. Most of them are in uniform, and they're quietly talking together, and it all seems very calm and unrushed, but I notice that nobody smiles. I see a diver surface: in his rubber wet suit he's sleek as a seal, and silver ripples move out from him. He pushes up his face mask and shouts to the waiting people, and his voice has the echoey, lonely sound of voices heard across water, as though he's calling from very far away. Then he pulls his mask down and glides back under the surface of the pool.

Brian is there, talking with a lean blond woman. She has a hard, polished look and an authoritative air. I think she must be senior to him.

"Brian!"

He hears, looks up and sees me: he doesn't seem surprised. He raises his hand in greeting.

"You can come through," he calls.

He has such a solemn air. I wish he weren't so serious.

I duck below the tape and scramble down the path. Insects buzz around me. They seem too loud, and ominous, like the crackling of a kettle boiling dry.

When I come to the water margin, Brian turns to me and puts his hand on my arm.

"Grace, this is Inspector Maria Grenville," he says. "Maria, this is Grace Reynolds, who I told you about."

She has cool gray eyes and an efficient handshake.

There's a little silence. The woman's gray gaze is on me. She tucks a strand of hair behind her ear. I realize that Brian must have told her all about us.

"Grace," says Brian then. "What I'm going to tell you now is in the strictest confidence."

I nod, not quite understanding.

"It's not how we'd normally do it. But the situation is really very unusual," he says. "And we've sent officers round already to speak to Deirdre and Gordon . . ."

My pulse is skittering off. I feel the beginnings of fear.

Brian clears his throat. "It looks like you've been proved right—you and Sylvie," he says.

I'm not so sure now that I want to be right.

"We've found something," he tells me.

For a moment he doesn't say anything more, and I realize I am holding my breath.

"They were on the floor of the quarry," he says then.

"They?"

"The divers found two bodies—an adult and a child."

My heart lurches.

"Oh God."

"Obviously we don't know for sure, not till we get the forensic reports."

"They're Alice and Jessica."

"Yes, probably, Grace," he tells me. He's anxious, a little defensive. "Hindsight's a wonderful thing, of course . . . But we should have searched more thoroughly before."

"Do they show—? I mean, can anyone tell—how they died?" I say.

He turns to the woman.

"There were stones found by the bodies and caught up in their clothing," she says. "We can't be sure, but they don't look like stones you'd find in the quarry."

"You mean—someone weighted them down?" I say. "Alice, before she killed herself? Alice put stones in their pockets—her own and her daughter's—so that they'd drown?"

"That would be one theory," says the woman. "That this was all Alice's doing."

But there's something distanced about the way she says this. I know she doesn't think it.

"And the other theory?" I ask her. "What would the other theory be?"

"It all needs to go to forensics, of course," says Brian.

"Yes, I know," I tell him.

"But we think there's the mark of a gunshot on the child's rib. We think that the child was shot before her body was put in the water. It may not have been that that killed her, but it does look as though she was shot."

"Alice?" I say. "Could Alice have shot her?"

He shakes his head. "No one who knew her believed that Alice had ever handled firearms, and no one reported a stolen gun. It's as hard to get hold of a gun here as it would be in England," he says. "So that does seem highly unlikely."

"You think someone else killed them?" I say.

"There are lots of ifs and buts," he says. "But that's our thinking at the moment. That they were shot by some other person. And the stones were put in their clothes to make sure the bodies stayed down, to hide the evidence. The drowned resurface in four or five days—they fill with gas and come up again. People sometimes forget that. Your murderer isn't always the brightest spoon in the drawer. This guy, though—you feel it was all quite organized. He knew what he was doing . . ."

"Now, let's not get ahead of ourselves," says the woman.

"Sorry, ma'am." He turns to me. "But basically, yes, that's our thinking. That our theory about what happened may have been totally wrong."

"D'you have any suspects?" I say, thinking of Gordon and what Brigid told us about him. But even as I think this, I don't want it to be true, remembering the bashful man who showed us around Flag Cottage.

The woman gives me a severe look. "Obviously we have to wait for the forensic surgeon's report. We need to take it a step at a time."

"Yes, of course," I say.

"I'll ring you, Grace," says Brian. "As soon as there's anything else."

"Can I tell Adam?" I say.

"Certainly," he says.

"You've been very helpful," says the woman. She shakes hands again, rather formally. "We'll keep in touch," she tells me.

"Thank you," I say.

I climb back up the stony path, slipping a bit as loosened pebbles skid away from my feet. At the top I duck under the cordon tape. Ahead of me at the quarry entrance, the ambulance is pulling out. I suppose it will be going to Barrowmore Hospital, to the mortuary there. I think of those hushed, bleak rooms that you sometimes see on television, with steel pull-out drawers for the bodies. The ambulance moves slowly. It has its flashing lights on, but it isn't using its siren. It seems unnervingly quiet, like something seen in a dream.

I'm nearly back at the car. I can see Adam reading to Sylvie. They're laughing together. I guess they're chanting the list of food that the caterpillar has eaten: "*one* piece of chocolate cake, *one* ice-cream cone . . ." They haven't seen me yet.

I turn, run back along the path. There's something else I've suddenly thought of, something I have to find out. I dive below the cordon tape and scramble down the track.

Brian is still there with the blond inspector, looking out over the water.

"Brian." I'm gasping for breath, my voice is husky and thin.

I clutch his wrist. The woman looks sharply at me.

"Brian," I say again. "When you said the bodies were probably Alice and Jessica, was there anything about them that made you think that?"

He hesitates, looks to the woman as though for permission. She nods.

"They found a bracelet," he tells me. "On the floor of the quarry by Jessica's body. It must have fallen off her wrist as she—well, bodies decompose, of course. It isn't very pleasant . . ."

"A bracelet?"

He nods.

"This little charm bracelet she had. It was on the list of her things when she went missing. I noticed because my daughter had a bracelet exactly the same."

I don't say anything. I'm staring at him.

He thinks I haven't understood.

"They were quite a fad with girls in those days," he tells me. "They got them from Claire's Accessories in Galway. These little bracelets. You know the kind of thing?"

"I can imagine," I tell him.

"My Amy simply had to have one," he says. "They used to collect the charms and swap them. They thought the charms would bring them luck." He's chewing his lip; his mouth is puckered, as though he has a bitter taste. "Well, maybe it worked for some of them. But not for Jessie," he says.

My heart is pounding so hard, I wonder if he can see it, if it's making my body shake.

"Could you show me?"

Brian hesitates.

"I mean, I know there must be rules about this," I tell him. "But it could be important—you know, for Sylvie."

He glances at the woman.

She nods slightly. "I'm fine with that," she says. "In the circumstances."

He puts his hand on my arm.

"Okay, I'll show you," he says.

He climbs the track ahead of me. He seems to walk so slowly, taking each step with such deliberation. Something inside me is screaming at him. I'm seized by a desperate urgency—I could run all the way up the path.

When we reach the road, he takes me across to one of the garda cars. A muscular young sergeant is sitting in the driving seat. He smells of some rather astringent cologne and he's drinking coffee from a flask. He turns and half smiles at Brian—not a proper smile. He too has a touch of solemnity.

Brian opens the side door.

On the seat there's a box that holds evidence bags of clear plastic. Brian riffles through the bags, touching them so delicately. He finds the one he's looking for and holds it out to me.

The sun is coming out now, and it shines on the plastic and turns it opaque for a moment—or maybe there's something inside me that refuses to see. The world is stilled around me. There's a splash as the sergeant tips the dregs of his coffee out the window, the snap of a twig as Brian shifts his weight, and both these sounds seem far too loud. I realize that I'm shivering. Then Brian lowers his hand, so the light doesn't fall directly on the plastic, and I can see them clearly now, the bracelet and the charms.

The bracelet part and the charms are made from different metals. The bracelet part is some sort of alloy, all stained with a black-brown tarnish, but the charms must be plated with silver, because they haven't corroded—even under all that water, after all those years. I stare at the bright shapes of them. A pair of ballet shoes, a heart, an intricate *J* for *Jessica*. A tiny, glittery dragon, catching the light of the sun.

# 51

"Adam."

I mouth at him through the car window, beckon to him. My body feels strange, like it's not quite under control.

He speaks to Sylvie, gets out of the car, closes the door behind him. His expression changes once he's there in front of me—he has a somber, expectant look, no smile. I wonder what he's responding to, what he can see in my face.

I stand there for a moment, not knowing how to begin. I feel I can't quite trust myself, that I might do something out of place—burst into tears or collapse in mirthless laughter.

"Adam," I say quietly. "They've found them."

"My God," he says.

I see the shock in his face, now that it's really happened.

I glance toward the car. Sylvie doesn't look up—she seems immersed in her book.

"They think it was murder," I tell him. "I mean, they don't know, but that's what they think. There was a bullet wound."

My voice is shaking.

He puts his arm around my shoulders, wrapping me in his warmth. I lean against him. I want to hide in him.

"There's something else, isn't there?" he says.

I nod. My mouth is like blotting paper.

"There was a bracelet. By the remains of the child." The words are solid things in my mouth. "It must have fallen off her wrist when—well, you know . . . Adam, there was a dragon charm."

He takes his hand from my shoulders, turns to face me. His eyes are wide. For a

long, long moment he doesn't say anything. The air between us feels shimmery
and thin.

"Sylvie's dragon," he says.

"Yes."

He's staring at me with that look of wide
amazement.

"I need to ring Deirdre," I tell him. "I
want to make sure she knows everything.
It doesn't seem right—that we're here and
she isn't."

"No, I can see that," he says.

I scrabble in my bag for my phone.

"Shit."

I stare at the display: it's out of charge.

"You can borrow mine," he tells me.

I have Deirdre's number in my bag. I
ring on Adam's phone.

She answers immediately.

"Deirdre Walker."

Her voice is too high-pitched. I wouldn't
have known it was her.

"It's Grace," I tell her.

"Grace? That's weird," she says.

She sounds distracted. Perhaps I've
confused her by ringing from Adam's
phone.

"Has somebody come to see you from the gardai?" I say.

"About the quarry?" she says.

"Yes."

"He said they think they've found Alice and Jessica," she says.

I wonder if she's in shock. She sounds remote, like she's not really taking it in.

"I'm so sorry," I say. "I just wanted to check that you knew everything."

"Thank you so much, Grace. That's very thoughtful," she says.

"I knew that you'd want to think about what it might mean for Gemma. I don't know if they told you, but they found a bracelet with the child's body. I guess they might ask Gemma to say if it's Jessica's bracelet . . ."

"They might ask Gemma," she repeats, her voice still tight and high. "Well, here's the thing—why I said it was weird that you called. I was just going to ring you about it."

"Oh."

"I can't find her. I can't find Gemma," she says.

"You can't find her?"

A cold dread moves through me—that this is all our fault, it's all because of me and Adam and Sylvie; that we have made this happen. I realize I expected something like this, feared it.

"She told me she was going to spend the night at Kirsty's house," says Deirdre. "Kirsty's her closest friend. Last night, this was. I rang Gemma just now, but her phone's switched off. And then I rang Kirsty, and Kirsty told me that Gemma had never shown up. She'd texted Kirsty to tell her there was something she needed to do."

I'm hunting in my mind for some banal explanation.

"You don't think perhaps she was doing something and didn't want you to know? Maybe staying the night with Marcus? You know how teenagers are."

"That's the first thing I thought of," says Deirdre.

"You've rung him?"

"The phone at his house is on voice mail. I don't understand it. There's usually somebody there . . . Why I was going to ring you—I wondered if she'd heard about Sylvie, if she'd gone looking for you."

"It can't be that. We haven't seen her," I say.

"Oh."

"You must speak to Brian," I tell her.

"Yes. I will. But I need to search for her myself, I need to be out there looking. I know all the houses she visits. I'm going to look up all her friends, go to the places she goes." I can hear the tremor in her voice. "Look, I know she's probably fine. But after . . . everything—you can't tell yourself you're stupid to worry. You know that the worst can happen."

There's such fear in her.

"You don't have to do it alone," I tell her. "We'll come with you."

"You can't do that," she says.

"No. Really. We will. We'd like to help."

"Would you?" She sounds so grateful.

"You could meet us here," I tell her. "You could speak to Brian, and then we'll help you look for her."

"I'll come straight over," she tells me. "I'll be there in fifteen minutes."

I give Adam back his phone.

"She can't find Gemma," I say.

"Yes, I gathered that."

"I said we'd help to search for her."

He's looking into my face with a frown, like he's troubled by something he sees in me.

"Grace." His voice is soothing. He reaches out and pushes back my hair. "You mustn't worry too much. She's almost certainly fine. Kids do run off sometimes."

"I know," I tell him. "But Deirdre was frantic."

I glance toward the car. Sylvie's face is pressed against the window. She's white and still and watching us intently. I feel guilty suddenly. For a moment, listening to Deirdre, I'd almost forgotten her.

I open the door, and she scrambles out.

"When are we going?" she says.

"Soon, Sylvie."

"I don't like it here."

"No, sweetheart."

I crouch down, put my arms around her. She lets herself be held.

"Sylvie, was this the place where it happened?" I say. "The place where—what you said . . ."

I can't quite form the words.

But this time she won't tell me anything.

"I don't like it here. I don't want to stay here," she says.

I glance over her shoulder—at the garda cars, the cordon tape, the man in a baggy forensic suit who is walking along the path, moving so slowly, as though the things he has seen are weighing heavily on him. I think of the horror of what they found beneath the water—just letting my mind touch lightly on this, then pulling abruptly away, as though the very thought could hurt me. Suddenly all I want is to take her away from this place.

I look up at Adam. "Could you stay and wait for Deirdre, if we go now?"

"Yes, of course," he tells me.

I press my face against Sylvie's. Her skin is very cold.

"Let's go off somewhere happier," I say.

"Yes, Grace."

"Why don't we go back to Coldharbour? We'll do something nice. I could buy you an ice cream from Barry's."

She scrambles back into the car.

# 52

I drive carefully back toward Coldharbour. I haven't driven this car very much, and I keep on grinding the gears. I glance at Sylvie in the rearview mirror. She still has her book on her lap, but she's staring out the window. She's quiet, but she doesn't look upset.

I clear my throat.

"Sylvie. I need to tell you something sad," I say. "You know there were all those garda cars at the quarry? They found two bodies there. The people who they were . . ." I take a deep breath. It's a struggle to find the right words. "They were

called Alice and Jessica—a mother and a
little girl. They used to live at Flag Cottage.
Somebody killed them a long time ago. A
bad person killed them."

I keep looking back at her, wanting to
gauge her reaction. She's looking at her
book now.

"Yes, Grace," she tells me. "Alice and
Jessica died." Saying the names so precisely. It's like the way she says Coldharbour—slowly and exactly, as though she
wants to hold on to the words.

"Who killed them, sweetheart?"

She presses her fingers through the
holes in the page.

"The water was red," she tells me.

"Sweetheart. Can you remember anything else about it?"

She shakes her head.

"I want my ice cream, Grace."

"Sure, sweetheart. Maybe we can talk
about it later."

I drive slowly on, past reedy fields
where heaps of peat are drying out. We
pass a rusted tractor and the black, broken hull of a rowing boat that's held in
place by stones.

I'm thinking over what Deirdre said. I

remember her voice—high-pitched, and sharp with panic. *You know that the worst can happen*. I feel her fear as though it is my own. I wish that I could help her.

We drive down the hill into Coldharbour. The sun is coming out through the mist, shining and veiled, like a pearl. We come to the wall of Kinvara House. Everything has a gray morning shimmer, and the plaited creepers and ivies are drenched and gleaming with dew. Nothing could be easier than to go and knock on the door, to ask if Gemma is there. As soon as I've thought this, it seems so right and obvious. Because really this seems the most likely explanation—that she spent the night with Marcus here. And if she isn't here, at least Marcus might know where she is.

I turn in between the stone falcons.

"Grace. My ice cream," says Sylvie.

"You'll have your ice cream soon," I tell her. "We'll only be a moment."

The garden stretches to either side, the white spilt pools of narcissi, the velvet, voluptuous rhododendron flowers. I haven't been here in daylight before. It's good to see all the colors of the flower beds, the salmon-pink azaleas, the Gothic reds and purples of the rhododendrons. It's such a relief to be somewhere so peaceful and tended after the horror of the quarry.

"What are we doing?" says Sylvie.

"I want to ask Marcus something," I tell her. "It'll only take a moment."

I draw up in front of the house. I turn to face her.

"Sweetheart, I want you to wait in the car for a moment. Just while I go to the door."

She has her book pressed tight against her chest.

"Grace, you can't leave me here. You *can't*." She's imperious.

"You'll be able to see me," I tell her. "Look, that's where I'm going—just up those steps to the door. Not any farther than that. You'll always be able to see me."

"No. I'm coming with you."

I get out, open her door. It's not worth making a fuss about.

We climb the steps. The scents of the garden brush caressingly against us, the languid sweetness of azalea, the subtle sherbet smells of the little spring flowers.

I ring. The bell has an old-fashioned jangle—you can hear it echoing through the house. I think of the hall and its elegant stair, of all those imposing, immaculate spaces on the other side of the door. But we can't see through the frosted glass.

Nobody comes. I ring again. Still nothing, just the hollow sound of the bell. It seems to be as Deirdre said—that nobody is here. Yet this seems surprising. You'd expect there to be somebody—a cleaner, or someone who does the accounts and typing, just like Alice used to. His house seems so perfect, so orderly; he must have people to run it.

We go back down the steps. The blinds are drawn in the ground-floor windows on either side of the door, presumably to protect his expensive fabrics from fading. The house has the look of a blank face with closed eyes.

I feel frustrated. I'm reluctant to give up so quickly—there must be somebody here. Perhaps we could look around the back. There might be someone working in the garden.

I lead Sylvie off to the right of the

house. There's a sprawling herbaceous border and a twisted old magnolia with flowers like cupped, veined hands. A horse chestnut tree is just coming out, the new leaves hanging down like bits of crumpled linen.

"Where are we going?" she says.

"We're going to walk right round the house. I need to find Marcus. We might find someone to ask. A gardener or someone."

She clutches at my hand, pushing her fingers between my fingers.

We turn a corner of the house, and the view opens out before us, that whole wide windswept loveliness of the bay. The sea has a pewter glimmer in the faltering sunlight, and its sound is suddenly louder here, its heavy surge on the shore. To our left are the high arched windows of the drawing room where Marcus entertained us. The curtains are drawn back here, and there are paving stones under the windows so you can go right up to the glass.

The light off the water reflects in the window and makes it hard to see through.

I press my face to the pane, shielding my eyes with my hands. It takes a while for my sight to adjust.

I'm hoping to see some sign of Gemma or Marcus. But the room is empty, and untidy. Two drawers have been pulled out of the desk, and papers are strewn around carelessly, as though someone was riffling through them and didn't have time to put them back. One of the whiskey tumblers has broken, and no one has bothered to sweep up the glass. The fragments glitter harshly in the light that falls on the floor. The sight of the broken glass unnerves me.

A sudden cold dread fills me. What if Gemma was here, what if she got caught up in something—a kidnapping, a robbery? Then I tell myself these are wild, crazy thoughts. I'm shocked, upset because of the discovery at the quarry. There must be some simple explanation: it's probably just that his cleaner hasn't come in.

"What is it, Grace?"

"I don't know, sweetheart. It just looks rather messy. It's probably nothing," I say.

We walk on around the house. There's a place, a darkened corner, where the building forms an L-shape, and creeper stems the color of rust reach out across the wall. A little chill wind from the sea lisps in the leaves of the creeper. Here, there's a side door into the house; the paint is peeling from the salt. The door is slightly ajar. I push it, and it opens. Inside I can see the passageway that leads to the entrance hall, past the door of the downstairs cloakroom.

"Marcus?" I say into the dark of the passage. My voice sounds hollow.

There's no answer.

If only I could find Marcus, I think. He'd know what to do, he'd know what has happened to Gemma. If only I could speak to him.

A sudden impulse seizes me. I bend to Sylvie.

"Sweetheart, listen. There's something we have to do now. The girl you saw on the beach . . ."

"Lennie," she says.

"Yes. Lennie." It feels so strange to call her that. "We don't know where she's got to. And so we're going to look for her. We're going to slip in here and have a quick look round. We'll see if we can find her, or if someone can say where she is."

"Yes, Grace," she says, accepting this.

I lead Sylvie down the passage past the cloakroom door. We walk silently, like sleepwalkers.

I call out.

"Marcus! Gemma!"

The sound of my own voice unnerves me. It's too urgent, too loud for this quiet place.

Sylvie must feel this too. She presses a finger to her lips.

There's a noise behind us. I spin around. But it's just the door moving against its frame; it makes a sound like knocking, as though someone wants to get in. It makes me nervous. I go back and shut it properly. It shuts off the sound of the sea, it shuts off everything. The silence of the house envelops us.

We walk along the passage, emerge into the airiness and gleaming space of the hall. But here too there's disorder. An overcoat has been flung down in the middle of the floor. On a side table I notice a shredder that must have been recently used, the bin beneath it overflowing with flimsy ribbons of paper. I look around for a telephone, but there doesn't seem to be one. We pass the Tang horse and the orchids. I notice with a thrill of fear that the gun has gone from the wall.

Sylvie must hear the catch in my breath.

"What's wrong, Grace?"

"Don't worry, sweetheart," I tell her. "But I think we ought to go now."

I keep my voice very calm, I'm trying not to frighten her.

"Is Lennie here?" says Sylvie.

"I don't know, sweetheart," I tell her. "But it's really time to leave."

"We've got to find Lennie," she says.

I reach for her hand. She slips past me. She runs ahead of me, up the pale curving stair.

"*No*, Sylvie."

She pays me no attention. I run after her. My chest is tight; it hurts to breathe.

She reaches the top of the stair. On the landing there's a window that has lavish velvet curtains, and in front of us is a bedroom with a wide-open door. She goes through the door. I follow.

This must be the main bedroom. You can see it's a beautiful room. The bed has a red satin coverlet, the curtains have an intricate pattern of Chinese flowers and birds. But the wardrobe door is pulled open, and opulent men's suits and shirts are all tossed on the bed, on the floor.

"It's untidy, isn't it, Grace?" says Sylvie rather severely.

I move a jacket with my foot. Underneath, there's a glint of color, something that doesn't belong amid all this masculine clothing. I kneel to look. It's the rainbow scarf that Gemma wore. The silk is crushed and torn.

I think of something Deirdre said: *Gemma remembers her mother going to answer the phone . . . She thinks she said, Okay, I'll be there for seven . . . She says her mother sounded happy . . .* I think how she may have told Marcus—will certainly have told Marcus. And where that memory might lead now, all the questions it might answer—with the finding of the bodies, the bullet wound, the stones.

I grab Sylvie's hand. My palms are suddenly wet, and Sylvie's skin slides against me.

"We have to go, Sylvie." My voice is

shrill and rapid and doesn't sound like my voice. "We shouldn't be here, really. We'll go and get that ice cream . . ."

There's the softest footfall behind me.

I turn, my heart in my throat.

# 53

Marcus is standing in the doorway, perfectly groomed and unhurried, despite the disorder in his house. He's smiling at me pleasantly. I remember that smile from the night when we were stranded in Coldharbour Bog, when he rescued us and welcomed us in for a whiskey at his fireside. I remind myself how kind he was then, and I push away the thoughts I was starting to think. With him actually standing there, my suspicions seem like crazy fabrications. There's something about his presence—his easy smile, the scent of his cologne—that immediately makes me feel calmer. I've been overwrought, emotional—I know that.

"Marcus. I'm so glad we've found you."

I know it will all be all right now. Marcus will take over—he'll know where to look for Gemma. Marcus, who knows how the world works, who wears his life like it's tailored just for him.

He inclines his head a little.

"Grace," he says. "And Sylvie. Well. It's nice, as ever, to see you. Though you could have come in by a rather more orthodox route."

I feel my face go red.

"I did ring the bell, but nobody answered," I tell him. "The thing is—Deirdre phoned this morning, and Gemma's disappeared. I came here looking for her. I was wondering if she was here or whether you'd maybe seen her?"

I'm aware of Sylvie pressing against me, as though she wants to melt into my body.

Marcus doesn't answer my question.

"Technically, it's trespass, of course," he says. His smile is amused, flirtatious. "But I'll overlook that—as it's you."

Hs eyes are on me, taking me in.

"I'm so sorry about that," I tell him. "But I didn't know what else to do. We were looking for Gemma. I thought that she might be here, or that I could find you and ask you . . ." I know I'm babbling on—I'm nervous, embarrassed. "And here you are," I say lightly. Trying to sound at ease, like him.

"Yes. Here I am," he says.

"I'm sorry about the trespassing thing," I say again. Though I'm rather unnerved that he seems to mind. "You know how it is, in the heat of the moment. It happens so quickly, you do things you shouldn't have done."

He still has that slightly flirtatious smile.

"You certainly do. In the heat of the moment," he says.

Sylvie seems to be messing about, trying to get my attention, deliberately shaking my hand. Then I look down and see that she's trembling, her entire body quivering. I wish she wouldn't.

"What I thought—if Gemma isn't here—you might know places she goes to, places where we might find her," I say. "D'you know what might have happened?"

"So you've come here to ask about Gemma," he says.

It's rather odd, the way he puts it—pushing my question away. There's a sudden little movement at the edges of my mind, a scurry of alarm, or fear. But I tell myself that nothing bad can have happened, that all must be as it should be. He's so relaxed, so unconcerned.

"Deirdre's out of her mind with worry," I tell him.

"Well, yes, she would be. Deirdre does worry," he says.

I wish he'd answer my question.

"I was wondering when you last saw Gemma," I say. I hear the shrill note in my voice. I know I sound too emphatic. "Deirdre did mention—I mean, I know that Gemma comes here sometimes . . ."

His eyes are still on my face.

"And, well—her scarf's here," I tell him. "We saw it, it's here on the floor . . ." I'm bending to pick it up. "Look . . ."

He raises one hand in a slight, controlled gesture that stops me in my tracks and chills me.

"Yes," he says. "Her scarf's here."

"I don't understand," I tell him.

He raises his eyebrows a little. "No, you don't understand, do you, Grace?"

There's a cold edge to his voice now. My heart lurches off. I hold Sylvie close against me.

With a small, cool part of my mind, I'm working out how to push past him—whether he would let us go. His body fills the doorway. He looks quite relaxed, but he's a fit man, and he's so much bigger than me.

"Your coming here like this was unfortunate, really," he says. "You can see that now, can't you? For you, certainly. Maybe for me . . . Still, I guess the jury's out on that."

I take a step toward him, holding Sylvie tightly.

"I think we ought to go," I tell him.

Again, he raises his hand in that little chilling movement.

"I'm sorry the way it's all turned out," he tells me. There's a tinge of regret in his voice. "Believe me, I've nothing against you. Not as people. You seem perfectly pleasant, both of you." He shrugs. "But there we are." He laughs briefly, like something has just occurred to him, something he finds amusing. "We'll blame it on the heat of the moment," he says.

He turns, pulls out the key that was in the lock of the door. He steps briskly out onto the landing. He slams the door shut, and I hear the click as he locks the door behind him.

## 54

I listen at the door, hear his step move off along the landing. Each step, I think, He's nearly gone. I let myself breathe out. It's something to be so grateful for—that he's no longer standing there looking down at us with that mocking, chill expression. I tell myself they'll come looking—Adam, Brian, Deirdre—that they will certainly find us. I see it clearly in my head—the gardai breaking down the door, the relief in everyone's eyes. They'll come to Kinvara House to hunt for Gemma and they'll rescue us.

But then I hear footsteps drawing nearer

again. My heart thuds so hard it hurts me. I wonder if he is coming to kill us; I wonder if he has his gun. I grab Sylvie, push her behind me.

But the footsteps seem to pass our door, and I don't understand this—why he should come back like this and then just leave us alone.

Then I smell the hot, sharp scent of petrol from the landing.

"Oh God," I say. "Oh God."

Panic wipes my mind clean.

I sink down on the bed, I cover my face in my hands. Despair floods through me. Nobody knows we're here. Perhaps they'll come looking for Gemma, but not soon enough to save us. There's no time now.

It slams into me then, the reality of it, like a physical blow. The absolute wrongness of everything—all my decisions, all the choices I've made. I'd wanted to help Sylvie, to try to make her happier. She had only me to look after her, and I've led her into danger, let us be drawn to our deaths.

I feel Sylvie's cool touch on my skin. She puts her hands over my hands.

"You're hiding. Don't hide, Grace. Don't hide away," she says.

She peels my hands from my face. She isn't trembling anymore. Now she seems much calmer than me.

"Sorry, sweetheart."

I think how much I love her. I take her hands in mine.

There's a smell of smoke now, and a sense of movement out there on the landing, a sense of an alien presence, something alive yet not alive. I think, What kills you in a fire? I've heard it's the smoke that gets you, not the flame, that you choke before the fire can reach you, the thick smoke blotting up your breath. There's a scream of protest in my head. *Not now. Not like this. Please God. Don't let it happen like this*.

"I don't like it here," says Sylvie.

"No, sweetheart."

You can hear its sounds quite distinctly now, the crackle and hiss of it, moving close to our door. The sour smoke catches in my throat.

Sylvie's forehead is creased in a frown, as though something puzzles her.

"So why don't we go, Grace?"

My eyes fill up at her innocence, at her child's view of the world, the way it seems so simple to her.

"Let's go," she says again.

Helplessness washes through me, an overwhelming despair.

"I can't get out. I don't know how. I can't get out," I tell her.

"Can't you, Grace?"

Still that little troubled frown.

"No, sweetheart. The door's locked."

I get up, go to it—going through the motions—rattle the handle. It doesn't budge. The fire is raging so near to us now, I can feel the heat that sears through the gap between the door and the frame. It's so hot I pull my hand away. The paint on the wood is blistering.

I go to the windows. There are window locks. Well, of course there would be. He's thorough, he thinks of everything, the house would be secure. I look in all the locks, but there's no sign of the key to them. But even if I could open the window, it wouldn't do us any good. There's a long drop onto paving stones.

Sylvie comes to stand beside me at the window.

"We could get out onto the sill," she says. "And onto the roof of the music room."

"The music room?"

"It's just round the corner," she says.

I kneel down, put my hands on her shoulders. I shall humor her and play along, wanting to keep her mind occupied. Anything to protect her from the fear I feel.

"How would we get off the music-room roof?" I ask her.

"We could climb down the creeper," she tells me. Her voice is calm and matter-of-fact. "You'd have to jump at the bottom. You don't mind jumping, do you, Grace?"

She reaches out and cups my face in her hands. It's what I do when I'm trying to make her listen; it's an adult gesture, somehow, as though she is the woman and I am the child. Her eyes are very close to mine. I see how blue they are, that remote, pale, perfect color of a frosty winter sky.

My heart tilts. The scene at the quarry seems to unscroll again in front of me, the bracelet in the evidence bag, the dragon charm that glittered in the sun. I think how

I have doubted her. Never really trusted her, never asked for her help. Never let her change me.

"No, sweetheart. I don't mind jumping," I tell her. "But, Sylvie, look—you'll have to be the leader. You're going to have to tell me what to do."

We look out the window together. I notice a narrow brick ledge about eighteen inches below the sill. It runs on past the window and around the corner of the house. It looks like it's just for decoration—it's scarcely as wide as one of my feet, and the brickwork has a crumbly look.

"You'll have to be very careful," she tells me. "You'll have to hold on tight. But it's not very far to the corner."

"I'll have to smash the window," I tell her.

I look around the room, hunting for something heavy. There's a lamp with a solid ceramic base. I rip the plug from the wall.

I don't know whether to hit or to throw. I grab one of Marcus's shirts and wrap it around my hand.

"Sylvie. Stay right on the other side of the room. You must keep your back to the window and cover your eyes with your hands. Can you do that for me?"

"Yes, Grace."

She's covering her eyes, but she can't resist turning her head and looking out through her fingers.

"*Really* cover them," I tell her.

You can hear all the sounds of the fire now—its roar and crackle and seethe. There's a sudden rush: it must have caught some fabric on the landing, perhaps the velvet curtains. I didn't know before how noisy fire could be. Pale curls of smoke sneak in through the hinge of the door.

I turn my head away, close my eyes. I punch at the glass with the lamp base.

The sound of breaking is shockingly loud. It echoes, it seems to go on forever, the fractured fragments splintering on the floor.

Wherever he is, he must have heard. I listen, but there are no footsteps. Perhaps he couldn't reach us now; perhaps the fire is burning too fiercely on the landing. Then I hear the sound of car tires screeching away down the drive.

I pick out the bits of broken glass that

stick up from the base of the window, making a gap we can climb through. My arm is cut, thick drops of bright blood dripping on the floor. It looks dramatic, but it doesn't hurt me.

"Sylvie, you'll have to help me. I don't know how to do this."

"No worries, Grace." She smiles; she's pleased with this rather grown-up phrase. I think of the magician at Karen's Halloween party, when he flourished his cloak and the rabbit appeared in Sylvie's lap. *No worries*.

I start to climb out through the gap in the glass.

"No, I'll be first," she says. "I'll show you."

I bite back the urge to stop her.

She takes a chair, climbs up on it, clambers out onto the ledge. She slides along with tiny steps, leaning her body into the wall, always keeping the same foot in front. She finds handholds in the window frame and where a drainpipe comes down.

"See, Grace? I'm an *acrobat* . . ."

She edges her way along as far as the corner.

"Now," she calls over her shoulder to me.

I climb out. There's a shrill, sharp sound in my ears, a mosquito whine of vertigo. I'm acutely aware of the void beneath me, all that vast space of white air. There's some ornamental brickwork just above my head. I cling to it with my fingers. My chest hurts because I am holding my breath.

"Don't look down, Grace," she tells me.

She disappears around the corner.

I creep along the ledge, shuffling along with my right foot always in front of my left. I don't dare to take a proper step. I reach for the drainpipe as Sylvie did. I can feel how flimsy it is. I press my body into the wall. I make myself breathe. I count my breaths.

Around the corner, the flat asphalt roof of the music room is just below the level of the ledge. Creeper grows over the edge of it. With a rush of relief I step down onto the roof. The tips of my fingers are grazed and stinging where they clung to the brickwork.

The roof is about three yards across. There's grass below us; here, the lawn comes right up to the wall. Sylvie goes to the edge of the roof, then turns and slides over it on her stomach, holding on to the branches of the creeper with her hands.

"You do it like this," she tells me.

I go to join her, slither over the edge as she did. I watch her scramble down the creeper. A little way down, where there's just one stem and no branches, she jumps and lands on the lawn.

I find a foothold in the creeper, ease my weight onto my foot. But I'm heavier than Sylvie, and there's a high-pitched creak like a voice crying out. I shift my weight to my other foot, and the creeper starts to tear. I feel it shear away beneath me. I grab at another branch, but that too comes away in my hand. I fall on the grass with some of the creeper on top of me, and a dust of cement and crumbled brick that the creeper has ripped from the wall.

"Are you all right, Grace?"

"Yes, I'm fine," I tell her.

She comes to me, and I hold her close.

"There. We did it," I say.

Blood from the cut in my arm drips on her.

"Your poor arm," she says.

"It's okay," I tell her. Though now it's

really hurting me—as if, now that we're almost in safety, I can allow myself the distraction of it, can let myself feel the pain. And with the pain the fear returns— my fear for Gemma, and all the desperate questions about what Marcus has done.

I sit there for a moment. I breathe in deeply, drawing in great gulps of air.

"Sweetheart. We have to find her . . . We have to find Lennie."

It still unnerves me, calling her that.

"Yes. Where is she, Grace?"

"I don't know, sweetheart."

The blood from my arm drips on the grass. I watch the vivid pool of red that soaks through the soil so quickly. How rapidly—casually, almost—your blood can seep away.

"What shall we do, then?" she says.

"Sylvie, listen. When you talked to me about Coldharbour—you sometimes said, 'I had a cave and a dragon.' D'you remember?"

"Yes, Grace."

"Sweetheart, can you tell me about the cave?"

Anxiety clouds her face.

"We weren't meant to go there, we weren't allowed to go. We got scolded, we were naughty girls for going there."

There's some other person's inflection in her voice. It troubles me—it's like a stranger speaking through my child. I push away the sense of disquiet I feel.

"No one will scold you now. You can tell me about it," I say.

She doesn't say anything.

A panic like nausea surges through me.

"*Please*, Sylvie. It might be important."

But her face is blank and closed.

"Sylvie, just try for me." Fear has its claws in me, but I keep my voice quite ordinary so as not to alarm her. "Try and think about the cave . . . It's for Lennie, to help her," I say.

She closes her eyes; screws up her face, as though she's struggling to conjure some scene in her mind.

"Sylvie. The cave. Anything you remember. Please tell me . . ."

A shadow crosses her face.

"It's cold, Grace." Her voice is quiet and serious. "It's very dark and secret."

I shudder when she says this—it sounds

like a tomb. I'm so afraid for Gemma, I'm sure that Gemma is dead.

"Can you show me where it is?" I ask her.

She turns and leads off, walking vaguely over the lawn. I follow just behind her.

I glance back. There's a red, unnatural glare at the first-floor windows: the fire is spreading. There's a sound like a small explosion, one of the windowpanes shattering. Yellowish wisps of smoke coil upward, and scraps of paper, charred and sooty, hover like little black birds.

She moves across the grass, past the skimmed-milk pools of narcissi. She hesitates. A pigeon flies off through the horse chestnut tree and she pauses, watching its flight. She seems uncertain, distracted. It's clear that she doesn't know where to go, that she has no memory to guide her. I've done the wrong thing again. I shouldn't have wasted time asking her. I'm just about to catch up with her and grab her and run to get help.

But suddenly her step quickens. Past a great weeping willow she turns to her right, where there's a tangled shrubbery of rhododendron bushes. She moves with a sudden certainty. She pushes in under the rhododendrons. I follow. Some of them are such huge old things, with the lowest branches growing out high on the stem, she can almost walk beneath them without bending. Then we come to younger, denser bushes. She crawls on hands and knees. I crawl behind her. Some of the branches are broken, the red blooms spilt and scattered. The torn-off petals still have their color—it must have happened recently. Someone has pushed through here before us.

Abruptly, we come to a clearing: a mound of earth, a door. It looks like some old storage place or icehouse.

"It's here, Grace."

The door has no lock; it's held in place with wire wrapped around the latch. My heart pounds. I untwist the wire.

Inside, it's completely dark. A cold, damp smell of trapped air fills my mouth, my nose. Instinctively I take a step back.

"Sylvie—I want you to stay out here, okay? Just stay out here and wait for me."

It's like she doesn't hear.

She pushes past me.

I follow her. Inside there are stairs going down.

We've taken only a few steps down when the door swings shut with a soft, dull thud behind us. With no light from the doorway, the blackness is impenetrable. There's a close, sour, heavy smell of earth. The walls, the dark, press in on us. It's like being buried alive.

I edge my way back to the door, feeling the steps with my foot. I'm half afraid that I won't be able to open it from inside, but I manage to make it move a bit, and I prop it ajar with a stone.

"Sylvie, wait for me."

But she's gone on down into the dark.

"Grace!"

Her voice sounds high and distant, a thin little thread that's swallowed up by the silence.

I feel my way carefully down the steps as my eyes adjust to the dark. I come to a tiny shadowed room, airless, low-ceilinged. The walls are shiny with slow drops of oozing water.

"Oh God."

I stare at the body in the corner. Just for an instant I think it's a heap of clothes flung down. Her dress has a sheeny glimmer in the thin, faint light that filters down the stairway. I can make out the shape of her body. She's sprawled out awkwardly, as though her limbs are fixed at the wrong angles. She's lying on her side, and I can't see her face, just the back of her head and her long dark fall of hair.

I don't know what he's done to her. For a moment I recoil from knowing. I think of the utter callousness with which he's killed before.

But Sylvie doesn't hesitate. She runs to her, kneels beside her, cradling Gemma's head in her arms.

I go to them. I roll Gemma onto her back. Her body is resistant, and heavy as something drenched. There's an inky fingerprinting of bruises all across her face. Her eyes stay shut. She's silent.

"Grace." There's fear in Sylvie's voice. "Is she all right, Grace?"

I bend my face to Gemma's, hold my ear to her mouth.

"I don't know, sweetheart. But I think she's breathing . . ."

Sylvie nods a little.

For both of us it's the sweetest sound, that fragile, faltering breath.

# 55

The hospital is in Barrowmore, just up the hill from Deirdre's house. We walk down a bland gray corridor, through harsh smells of disinfectant. The morning sun throws exact white squares on the floor.

"I hate hospitals," I tell Adam.

"Me too," he says. "They make me think of being six and having my tonsils taken out. I ate quite implausible quantities of raspberry ripple ice cream. But I still hated it."

The corridor passes the children's ward. There's a rain forest mural, a box of well-worn toys. Sylvie walks close to the wall, trailing her finger across the painted animals.

"Adam! Grace!"

Brian is hurrying down the passage toward us. We'd hoped to meet him earlier, but we're later than we'd planned, as breakfast was slow this morning, with no sign of Brigid.

Brian's smile lights up his face.

"You're okay, Grace? You've recovered, you and Sylvie?"

"Yes, we're fine," I tell him.

"I've just been to talk to Gemma," he says, "to bring her up to date. She's got a bit of a bruised look, but they're really pleased with her progress."

I grasp his wrist.

"And you've got Marcus? Please, please, tell us you've caught him."

"I'm sorry, Grace." He screws up his mouth, as though he has a bitter taste. "Marcus seems to have got away. We warned the airports, of course, but we think he's left the country."

*"No."* I can't bear the injustice of this.

Sylvie tugs at my hand. "Grace. Can we go now?"

"Very soon, sweetheart. Perhaps you could play for a bit?"

She goes to look in the toy box, but reluctantly.

"So tell us," I say to Brian. "Tell us what you've found out."

A woman is wheeled toward us on a stretcher. She's on a drip, and her face is stretched and gray. Brian waits for her to pass. Curiosity gnaws at me.

Brian turns toward us. "No answers yet," he tells us. "But we're working on it. The forensic accountants are coming down from Dublin. They'll be trying to trace the movement of money between his accounts."

"Oh," I say.

It's not what I was expecting, this talk of banks and accountants.

"We won't know the full story for quite some time," says Brian. "But there was plainly a lot that Marcus wanted to hide."

"How can you tell that?" I ask him.

"He left before he'd destroyed all his paperwork," Brian tells me. "I guess you interrupted him—he probably thought that someone might come looking for you. We found some documents at the house. There's a lot of stuff to work through, but we do know already that Marcus has several offshore accounts and there's far too much money in them."

I think of Marcus's perfect manners, his patrician air. It's still so hard to make sense of.

"It seems likely that the gallery and the shop were just a front—that he used them for money laundering," says Brian.

I picture the stylish shop with the vanilla scalloped blinds. Nothing is as I'd thought it was.

"Alice was a clever woman. Good with figures," he says. "Perhaps she'd asked a question that concerned him. Maybe something she said in all innocence. But perhaps he thought that in time she might start to suspect him. That could have been why he killed her."

"And Jessica happened to be there, and that wasn't part of the plan?" I say.

"Could be. That poor, poor kid," he says.

All the "if only's" whisper in the air around us. If only she hadn't had a cold, if only she'd gone to the sleepover. It's always so troubling, this randomness of what happens: how devastation can creep up on you in such a casual way.

"With Gemma," he says, "it was nearly another dreadful case of bad timing. We've been going through her movements. On Monday she went to see Marcus. She told him she'd decided to come and see us, to tell us about her memory of the night her mother died. Just at the point that he found that we were going to search the quarry—"

He stops as Sylvie comes over. She pulls at my sleeve.

"*Now*, Grace."

She's purposeful, frowning. Her mouth has a tight, set look.

But I'm desperate to hear Brian out.

"Sweetheart, we'll only be a minute."

I lead her back to the toys. Outside, the scream of an ambulance siren rips the morning apart.

"Gemma doesn't remember what happened yesterday morning," says Brian. "There were traces of Rohypnol in her system. It seems that Marcus drugged her to give himself time to get out."

"But why?" I say. "Why didn't Marcus

kill Gemma? It's not like he has any scruples about murder. So why did he just drug her and leave her like that?"

Brian's face darkens.

"We've interviewed people again—the original people we talked to. There's someone in the village—Polly O'Connor. Polly was Alice's best friend. And yesterday Polly told me things that she hadn't told me before. She said the rumor was true—that Marcus and Alice were lovers."

I can hear the outrage in his voice, and I wonder why he finds this shocking—something as familiar, as banal, as an affair.

"Now, Gordon was off on the road a lot. And Alice and Gordon—well, to be frank, they didn't have much of a sex life. I'm only telling you what Polly O'Connor told me . . ."

I suddenly see where this is going, and everything in me recoils.

Brian's throat moves as he swallows. "And Alice believed that Marcus was the father of the twins."

Nobody moves.

"You see, maybe Marcus knew," says Brian. "Maybe Alice had told him. He'd already killed one of his daughters. Maybe even Marcus couldn't stomach killing his other child."

"But—for God's sake," I say, "he had a *relationship* with Gemma . . ."

Brian shrugs.

"Gemma was always a risk," he says, "a bit of a loose cannon. There was always the possibility that she might remember something and incriminate him. Maybe seducing her was his way of keeping control . . ."

"There's something I don't understand in all this," says Adam then. "How come he knew it was over? That you were searching the quarry?"

"Tell me," says Brian, "where were you when I rang you to tell you about the search?"

"Just in the lounge at St. Vincent's," I tell him.

"Was Brigid anywhere near?"

I remember Brigid coming to fetch our tray. How she knocked the milk jug over, how she seemed annoyed by her clumsiness.

"Yes, she was, as it happens."

"Brigid's left the country too. It was Brigid

who gave him his alibi the day of the murders," he says.

I think of our conversations with her, of the way that she'd encouraged us to confide, of how she'd hinted that Gordon was the murderer. I feel a surge of nausea.

Brian shakes his head a little. "I really admired him, you know? I thought he was so impressive." There's something troubled and inchoate in his voice.

"That's how it looked," I tell him.

"To be honest, he seemed to be everything that I'd have liked to be. The house, the business—everything I'd have aspired toward, if only life had been different . . ." He moves one long hand pensively over his face. "Well, that's the latest installment. I'll see you folks around, no doubt."

I put my hand on his arm. "You won't be seeing us, Brian. We fly back to London today."

"Well, look, I've got your numbers. I'll let you know what happens."

He shakes hands with Adam. To my surprise, he hugs me.

"The best of luck with the little one," he says.

He waves in Sylvie's direction and goes off down the corridor.

I go to kneel by Sylvie, take her face in my hands.

"Sylvie, there's something I need to tell you. The police are looking for Marcus, but they haven't been able to find him yet. He's gone to another country. He's a long, long way from here . . ."

Her face is white and strained. Perhaps she's scared that he could come and find her.

"They'll catch him and put him in prison," I tell her, trying to reassure her. "I know they will—that in the end they'll catch him."

But I've misread the cause of her anxiety. She stands up, grabs my hand.

"I want to go now. I want to go and see her. Can we go now, Grace?"

## 56

"Gemma Murphy? Sure. She's in a room of her own." The nurse has emerald eye shadow and a crisp black bob. "Today's her birthday, of course. They're having a little party . . ."

She takes us to a side room. Deirdre is there, and Gordon. Gemma is sitting up in bed, though her face is horribly bruised where she was knocked against the branches as he took her to the icehouse. There are lots of flowers and greeting cards.

Deirdre smiles warmly at us.

"Gemma, this is Grace and Sylvie and Adam."

Gemma grins. "I'm sorry I look so crap," she says. She touches her face with a careful, tentative fingertip. "They showed me my reflection this morning. I mean, I look completely putrid."

"Gemma . . ." says Deirdre, prompting her.

A flush spreads over Gemma's face.

"There was this speech I was going to make—to thank you for saving my life. Deirdre got me to practice, but really it's too embarrassing." She smiles her wide-open smile. "But thanks anyway. I'm just so glad you were there."

There's a bag of jelly sweets on her locker, and a Dizzee Rascal CD, and she's wearing a T-shirt that says JUST WAIT TILL I'M FAMOUS. She's not what I'd expected, this vivid, emphatic teenager—not at all the fey and wistful creature I'd imagined.

"I'm so glad we could help," I tell her.

"She's coming home tomorrow," Deirdre tells us. "They just want to keep her in for one more night—just to keep an eye on her."

"That's fantastic," I say.

Sylvie doesn't say anything. She'd been so impatient to come, but now she has a lost look. Her hand in mine feels very small and cold.

"Now, I think you've met Gordon," says Deirdre.

He comes toward us, shakes our hands.

"We're so grateful to you," he tells us. "For what you did for Gemma. And for laying this to rest." His eyes are moist and full. Deirdre puts a hand on his arm. "It means so much—to all of us—to know what really happened. To know that Alice didn't choose to leave us . . ."

There's a choke in his voice, and I don't know what to say.

The birthday cake that I saw in Barry's is on a table by the bed, with seventeen candles stuck in it. Under the tubular lighting, the chocolate has a dull and muted shine.

Deirdre follows my gaze.

"You must join us in some cake," she says. "I'm just going to light the candles."

But it's a family party, and we are strangers to them. I worry we are intruding.

"Really, we should be going," I tell her.

"We just came to check that Gemma was okay . . ."

"You can't go yet," says Deirdre. "Honestly, I won't let you. Not till you've had a slice of Gemma's cake."

She starts to light the candles. The clinical little room has a smell of celebration, of warm marzipan and melting wax.

"No singing, okay?" says Gemma. "Or I'll freak."

"Okay. No singing," says Deirdre. She shakes out a match and lights another, smiles ruefully at Gemma. I have a sense of her relationship with her willful foster child—at once wary and indulgent. I admire her.

"There," she says. The candles are all lit now, and flickering extravagantly. "Maybe Sylvie here could help you blow them out."

Sylvie edges toward the bed. Gemma takes her hand and leans toward the birthday cake: the yellow flames are dancing in the darkness of her eyes. She blows the candles out, and wisps of blue smoke blur her face. Sylvie doesn't join in, just stands there staring at Gemma.

"There. We did it. You really helped," says Gemma, smiling at her.

Deirdre has brought paper plates. We stand around eating the cake. It's scented and rich, but my mouth feels dry and I find it hard to swallow. The things that aren't being said seem to hang in the air between us.

Maybe Deirdre senses this.

"Gordon and I are going to grab a coffee," she tells us. "We'll leave you four to have a bit of a chat."

They leave, and the room is silent.

Sylvie just stands there with that lost look on her face, and I don't know what to say or do, or how to make it easier.

"Your braid's all coming undone," says Gemma.

Sylvie puts a hand to her braid, where it's messy and ragged from yesterday, from crawling through the bushes. I'd offered to take it out for her, but she wanted to keep it in.

"Did Siobhan do it for you?" says Gemma. "That girl with all the snake tattoos? The girl who sells the belts and stuff?"

Sylvie nods. Her eyes are large in her white face.

"I know how she does it," says Gemma. "I got her to give me a lesson." She gestures to the bed beside her. "You could sit yourself up here," she says, "and let me put it right."

Sylvie climbs on the bed, sits with her side to Gemma.

Gemma takes her hairbrush and brushes Sylvie's hair.

"You're the blondest girl I ever saw," she says.

She cuts the knot and unpicks what's left of the braid. She lays the threads out on her blanket, all the sherbet colors. Then she takes the threads and knots them in Sylvie's hair and starts to weave, wrapping them over and over. Their heads are close together. They're sitting under the window and white sunlight spills across them, and the room is full of the festive scents of chocolate and candle wax. I watch the movement of Gemma's hands, their fluid, intricate patterning.

She ties off the end of the braid. All the snagged, unraveled pieces are woven together again.

"There," she says.

She has a mirror on her locker. She

holds it up for Sylvie. Sylvie, a little self-conscious, smiles at her reflection.

"You're ready for anything now," says Gemma.

She puts the mirror down again, placing it well to the side of her so she can't see her own reflection.

"I try not to look at myself," she tells us. "I hate it, with all these bruises."

Sylvie reaches out and touches Gemma's face. It's the lightest touch, as though she is touching something unguessably precious. Gemma puts her arm around her.

"I saw you before," says Gemma to Sylvie. She's speaking quietly, I can only just hear. "I saw you on the beach that day. I didn't know who you were." She has a slight puzzled frown. "Well, to be honest, I still don't really—"

Sylvie doesn't say anything. She rests her head against Gemma. She seems entranced or hypnotized, all the tension eased out of her face. It's as though she's oblivious to me, as though this is where she should be.

My heart sucks at my ribs. In everything that's happened—the fire, the cave, the danger—there's been nothing that has made me so afraid.

I feel Adam put his hand on my arm—to comfort me, or maybe to restrain me. Perhaps he's afraid I might go and snatch her away. I'm glad he's here with me.

They sit there for what seems like an age.

At last I take a deep breath. I steel myself to speak to them.

"Sylvie. Maybe—in a moment—we'd better say goodbye . . ."

My voice has a shake in it.

Sylvie starts at the sound of my voice. She stretches, slides off the bed.

"Look, Sylvie," says Gemma, a little embarrassed and uncertain. "If you want, you could come over, once I'm out of hospital. You know, if you'd like that . . ."

Sylvie just stands there for a moment, staring at Gemma, drinking her in, her eyes unblinking and huge. I'm clasping my hands together, the palms are damp with sweat.

Then Sylvie shakes her head. It's a very slight movement, so slight you could easily miss it.

"We can't come and see you," she

says, and her thin, small, definite voice is
bell clear in the quiet. "We've got a plane
to catch from Shannon Airport." She's
rather self-important, relishing the grown-
up phrase. "We're going back to London.
Me and my mum have got to go back
home."

There's a little pause—just a heartbeat.

"Sure," says Gemma then. "Well, that's
for the best really, isn't it, now?" She rests
her hand for a moment on top of Sylvie's
head. "I tell you what, they're going to
really like your hair, in London . . . I'm glad
I put it right for you. I told you that I would."

## 57

We walk to the shore for the last time. There's a fast, fresh wind off the sea, and the water far out is a flat, bright sheet of silver.

"Sylvie—look—we could go to Barry's, get you that ice cream I promised you."

But to my surprise she shakes her head.

"I want a boat trip, Grace," she tells me.

"A boat trip? Sweetheart, are you sure?"

She nods.

I can't believe this.

She grabs my hand. "I really want to," she says.

I glance at Adam. He gives me a knowing smile, as though he's pleased with himself. In fact, he's looked rather pleased all day, like a man who's discovered something. Not an answer or anything certain, but perhaps a thread of comfort or a bit more hope than he had.

"Is there time?" I ask him.

"Absolutely," he tells me. "We're all packed up and everything."

Sylvie leads us along the jetty, through the smells of salt and fish, past the boats called *Ave Maria* and *Endurance*, and the lobster pots and the nylon nets and the coils of sodden green rope. By the sign that says CURRAN CRUISES there's a small blue dinghy, the *Venturer*, tied up. It has an engine at the stern, and room for perhaps twelve people.

The skipper has a face as wrinkled and brown as a walnut, and his eyes are acute as a bird's. Yes, he can take us around the bay. He will do it just for the three of us, and we can leave now if we want. The trip will take us half an hour.

Adam pays. The dinghy tips as I step in; my heels, as usual, are far too high. The skipper helps me to a seat. Sylvie climbs down deftly and goes to sit in the prow. Adam sits beside me.

The skipper starts the engine, and the boat moves gently forward, breaking up the water into scattered fragments of light. As we edge out beyond the shelter of the jetty, the wind slams into our faces.

I look briefly behind us. Coldharbour is receding from us, so tiny already it looks like something remembered or imagined. I can see the whiteness of the beach and the shops along the seafront and the soft spring apricots and purples of all the budding trees. The burned upper floors of Kinvara House are stark against the blurry pastels, the black roof rafters sticking up like bones.

Sylvie is leaning forward at the prow of the *Venturer*. She holds her hand over the side, so the white spray dampens her skin. The wind blows color into her face and pushes her hair straight back. She's laughing.

"Look," I say to Adam.

**What if we just don't get it? What if our dying isn't at all as we've always believed it to be?**

Adam smiles.

"How did this happen?" I say.

"Maybe she can let go of it now," he tells me. "She made a choice back there. The only one she could make, but perhaps it still had to be made."

"I'm so grateful," I tell him.

He gives a slight self-deprecating shrug.

"It may not be easy," he tells me. "When you're home again. It may not be over yet, with Sylvie. It may not be all straightforward. But I think it will be better."

"Yes. I know that," I tell him.

There's silence between us for a moment, full of the yearning cries of gulls.

"Grace." There's a hesitancy about him, and he isn't looking at me. "When we get back to London, I'd like to fix—you know, a time that we could meet . . ." He looks up at me then. We're sitting close together; I can see the bright flecks in his eyes. "I mean, if you'd like that . . ."

"For your research?" I ask him. "So you can finish your article about Sylvie?"

For a moment he doesn't say anything.

"For that too," he says then.

His hand is resting on the bench between us. I put my hand on his. I love it when he looks startled like that. For now this is enough, this tentative shining moment.

Then, just a few yards to the side of us, the sea takes form and leaps. A dolphin. It's radiant, pristine, dazzling: we watch the immaculate arc of its leaping, and then again and again.

"Will you look at that?" says the skipper. He lets the engine idle. He has an expression of pride, as though the dolphin is his. "Well, looks like it's your lucky day. She doesn't show herself that often. And what a beauty she is."

We wait for a while, but the dolphin has gone. But my eyes are still full of its vividness, so when I close my eyelids its dazzle is there in my mind.

"Yes," I say. "She was beautiful."

The skipper starts up the engine again.

We're a long way out from the shore now. Quite suddenly the sea gets choppy; we're moving beyond the sheltering arms of the bay. The little boat lurches alarmingly. Sylvie is leaning over the side, and I panic that she could fall in. I reach out and grab the hem of her fleece.

The skipper, so at ease on the sea, is amused by my protectiveness.

"She'll be okay, ma'am," he tells me. "You mustn't worry yourself."

Sylvie feels my tug and looks over her shoulder toward me. Her face is luminous. Then she turns to look forward again, to face the way we're sailing, with the depth of unknowable darkness below her, and before her the blue far horizon where your mind stops, and all around, the acres of shining sea.

# Acknowledgments

My thanks are due to the following people: Sarah Crichton, my brilliant and inspirational editor; Cailey Hall, for being unfailingly helpful; Kathleen Anderson, my marvelous agent, for all her hard work on behalf of my writing; Catherine Burke, my U.K. editor, for her wonderful commitment to the book; all the team at Mira; and my U.K. agent, Laura Longrigg, who has supported me in so many ways, both intellectual and emotional. I am deeply grateful to all of you.

Thanks also to Vicki Tippet and

Madeleine Fullerton, for sharing stories and book recommendations, and to Lucy Floyd, for her wise comments on an early draft of the book.

Of the books I read while writing *Yes, My Darling Daughter*, two were particularly fascinating: *Children Who Have Lived Before*, by Carol Bowman, and *Old Souls*, by Tom Shroder. Thanks as well to Lynne McTaggart and the "Living the Field" course.

Finally, thanks to Mick, Becky, and Izzie, for all their love and encouragement, and because they loved Connemara as much as I did.